Praise for *Glowfly Dance*

'An extraordinary tale of migration, love, abuse and loss … Jade Gibson has created a prose that is poetic, well observed and crisp for the voice of her witness, who bears testament to a past that is cruel, but para-doxically rendered … beautiful, moving and healing for the reader.' – Lawrence Scott, author of *Light Falling on Bamboo*

'This book glitters with sunlight and the trust of a child as Jade Gibson leads you in soothing, circular rhythm through beautiful blessings into cold, damp fascinating places that only the dark side of the soul should ever dare to enter. When you can't bear the terror, Jade's almighty courage and her searing writing gift burn a path to freedom, leaving you forever changed.' – Tracey Farren, author of *Whiplash*

'A magical yet danger-filled story web that is slowly but tightly spun. It is a dense and brilliantly crafted body of work … Saying that you couldn't put the book down sounds like a cliché, but it was literally my experience. Jade writes with a visceral intimacy and immediacy that transports you into the room, into the drama, into the heart. Through Mai's beautiful eyes we travel from place to place, enter intimate and terrifying spaces, meet vivid and authentic characters … This is a story that will stay with you.' – Malika Ndlovu, author of *Born in Africa But*

'This work is shocking, harrowing and at the same time beautiful … Incidents where memory is distilled with a searing clarity are balanced by a lyrical embrace of the peopled landscapes the narrator encounters on the cross-continental journey she is caught up in. A brave book by a writer of unmistakable talent.' – Miki Flockemann, University of the Western Cape

'Inspired flights of language radiate outwards and upwards from the harrowing social and cultural realities, through the spell-binding beauties of nature and landscape ... to a deeply felt sense of glorious participation in the cosmos and in a secret life.' – Kenneth Ramchand, University of the West Indies and Colgate University

'Told in prose of luminous intensity ... In *Glowfly Dance* a girl of indomitable spirit comes of age in a world made desolate by cruelty. In moments of deepest beauty, in the harshest and hardest of times, Mai is always present, always able to record. She has to tell her story, for if it is left untold, like the light of glowflies it will fade into darkness forever.' – Máire Fisher, author of *Birdseye*

'Jade Gibson tells this story of an abusive, inescapable affair as beautifully as such a story can be told ... places are as alive and vivid on the page as the human characters.' – Marian Palaia, author of *The Given World*

'The author holds the reader by the hand and with the beguiling innocence, insistence and compulsion of a child, she accompanies one on an unforgettable journey ... Gibson's book is a near-breathless roller-coaster chronicle, filled with poetic and lyrical potency.' – Wanjiku Muiruri-Mwagiru, author of 'The Plough'

'Wow ... am left with tears in my eyes and an ache in my heart. *Glowfly Dance* draws the reader in like a glowfly toward the light with its first lyrical promise of freedom.' – Kristie McLean, writer, photographer and activist

Glowfly Dance

JADE GIBSON

Jade Gibson 2015

To Toria,
*   To travels and*
*   growth*
*   19 Jan 2016*

UMUZI

Published in 2015 by Umuzi
an imprint of Penguin Random House South Africa (Pty) Ltd
Company Reg No 1953/000441/07
Estuaries No 4, Oxbow Crescent, Century Avenue,
Century City, 7441, South Africa
PO Box 1144, Cape Town, 8000, South Africa
umuzi@randomstruik.co.za
www.randomstruik.co.za

© 2015 Jade Gibson

First edition, first printing 2015
1 3 5 7 9 8 6 4 2

ISBN 978-1-4152-0751-2 (Print)
ISBN 978-1-4152-0654-6 (ePub)
ISBN 978-1-4152-0655-3 (PDF)

Cover design by Jacques Kaiser
Cover photography © Michelle, 'Heart Shaped Box',
Flickr.com, modified from the original
Text design by Monique Cleghorn
Set in 11.5 pt on 15.5 pt Minion

Printed and bound in India by Replika Press Pvt. Ltd.

This book is printed on FSC®-certified paper.
FSC (Forest Stewardship Council®) is an independent, international,
non-governmental organization. Its aim is to support environmentally
sustainable, socially and economically responsible global forest management.

1

Glowing

When glowflies emerge, they fly out of the bushes, the leaves, the grass, the trees, the dark earth, spinning in circles through the air, leaving trails of light, a secret calligraphy of letters that appear, then disappear, fading slowly into darkness. I am flying. I look out of the window, and the aeroplane wings flash with light, on and off, on and off. Soon we will land, and I am wondering where stories end and where they begin. People think that when you are fourteen you know nothing, but I have seen so much, I have a thousand stories, burning and shining and rising within me, and all I can do is try to catch them, one by one, because I only have the moments, fading in and out, when everything else is gone.

I see him.
I see her.
They are making love.
It is Mexico.
It is hot.
It is sunset.

He holds her tight, his eyes slanted like the wings of gulls flying in the sky. His skin smooth and dark like olive oil slipping around her limbs.

Hold me tighter, she says.

Forever, he says, the sky red like blood oranges, clouds teased into streaks, the sun smouldering on the horizon of the sea. Waves roll. Outside, glowflies dance, gulls' wings sail through an invisible architecture of spaces shaped by the wind.

Forever, she says, fingers sliding across skin, his fingers swimming through her long brown hair. They are salty, salty with sea and the scent of oranges. Their shadows dance by the light of a solitary lamp, weave patterns in and out across the wall, leaving no traces.

The glowflies catch the word *forever*, write it against a darkening sky, passing it between them until, copied so many times, its echoes become meaningless. The red of the sky turns to inky black, reflections of stars dance on pounding waves. The moon comes, slices through sky like a silver blade, silver moon dancing on fingertips, cobwebbing her hair, glinting in the pointed corners of his eyes. Glowflies reflect on the sea's surface, and you can't tell their reflections and the sky and the stars apart. On the beach, waves wash away their footsteps, first the toes, then the heels, and then even those are gone.

Forever, they say.

But forever is never for ever.

The scent of oranges pierces the night, fills it with wet earth.

A woman, flying. She flies over sea, over clouds spread like cotton fleece, over mountains, rivers stretched like veins across land, fingers of land pointing to sea. Underneath her, the world turns, teeming with life. She flies, thoughts within her, dreams within her, as Mexican orange groves shake in the breeze, and birds sail unfettered in a blue sky.

She lands, steps out into the sound of engines, the smell of oil and fumes in the airport. London is buried in the harshness of winter. She stands on the airport ramp, breathes in air as cold as ice, and shivers, draws her coat closer. She looks around her. Blank buildings stare back, heavy clouds under low sky. Slowly clutching her hand luggage, she walks down the ramp. Without the sun, the sky feels barren. She steps onto tarmac, hard and slippery with ice. Again she shivers, pulls her coat tighter. As she steps forwards, grey puddles seep around her shoes. She remembers clouds puffed high with sun, her bare feet on warm sand smooth and soft as velvet, the rolling waves, the colours of fish. As she walks, she feels the heat of Mexico gently slip away, until only the soft rocking of waves deep inside her is left. She walks forwards, under a grey flat English sky, and it begins to rain.

It was my first journey across the world.

She never spoke much about it, says my granddad. She went travelling round the world, then came back and had you. He was from Puerto Rico. I think.

Your father was Filipino, says my mother. We met and travelled and lived together for a while in Mexico. You were nearly born in the snow, the taxi got stuck on the way to the hospital. They wouldn't believe you were coming so fast, not for a first child, they said, but when I arrived they had to rush me in, you were in such a hurry to get out into the world, and you were born almost immediately.

You were born in the East End of London, says my granddad, within the sound of Bow Bells, and, och, that makes you a true Cockney, and he laughs, and I laugh back.

I never see my father. My father never sees me. But I see with the eyes he gave me. Slanted like the wings of gulls flying in the sky. And, when my mother speaks of Mexico, her eyes mist up with the lights of memory. Mexico was beautiful, she says, the sights, the sounds, the sea. At night, you could smell the scent of oranges from far away, travelling for miles, down from the orange groves, drifting like perfume through the warm night air. The oranges in Mexico were delicious, especially the blood oranges, so sweet, and red inside, bright, bright red, just like blood, and when you opened them the juice ran out down across your hands and stained them, sticky.

They call me Mai.

Some people are made to be stories and some stories are lived to be told. In the lights of glowflies there are memories, traces of paths where we have been, and if we don't see them, they fade, invisible, into night air, and if we never record them, how are we to know they ever existed? I began before I was born, travelling through the air like the scent of oranges, in the story of my father making love to my mother, the closest I ever got to him – and on my birth certificate there is a straight dotted line where a father's name should be, like the horizon he sailed back across. Some things you don't have to know, because that's the way it is. And if I don't tell the story of what follows after, of why I am flying again now, and of how everything in life goes around in circles, but when you come back again it has all changed and is never the same again, then that story, too, will shine brightly, then disappear like the lights of glowflies and fade away into darkness.

So now, I'll start ...

One two three, one two three ... I am three years old. I swirl on a thousand footsteps, feeling the soft pressure of Granddad's shoes on the bare soles of my feet and the pull of his arms on mine – hold tight, Mai, hold tight – you are dancing ... one two ... one two, and I feel the sweep of the floor under my feet, fast, fast, and the music is swinging, swinging around and Granddad does his steps, like being on a merry-go-round, where the horses go up, up in the air and down again. The music is beating, beating, like my breaths and laughter, like the tick tock in my chest, that's your heart, says granddad, it goes boom boom and makes your blood go round and round, and I feel the warmth of its pulse in my granddad's fingers and in my granddad's hands too, over and over across the floor.

You're a good girl today, come and dance, Mai, says Granddad. I don't know how to, I say. Come here, says Granddad. Hold my hands. Put one foot on my foot and one on the other. Take your shoes off first, or you'll damage mine. Whoops, hold tight. Okay, take your socks off then, so you don't slip. And now the leather on Granddad's big brown shiny shoes is cold and tickly under my bare feet, but I don't slip off. Then Granddad lifts up his foot and mine lifts up too. Then he lifts up the other, and my other lifts up as well. See, now you can dance, says Granddad.

I can dance, I can dance. Dancing is when your feet move and the world spins around you. Dancing is when the music goes poom poom, and if I hold tight to Granddad's hands and try hard not to slip off Granddad's shoes, I can keep dancing all the steps Granddad shows me. One two, one two … Swing … says Granddad, and my feet follow. Tango … one two three four … Waltz … Cha-Cha … Lindy … Foxtrot … but now my feet slip off, and he laughs. Okay, how about rock 'n' roll?

We spin around and around Granddad's sitting room, past Granddad's huge new wooden music player with big tapes that go around and around on top, and records that go around and around inside, past the multicoloured fish in the fish tank, around Granddad's brand-new orange armchair and sofa, and across Granddad's brand-new orange spiky sitting-room carpet. The orange chairs and carpet are all made out of the new plastic stuff you get in the shops now, says Mummy, that's Granddad being fashionable, but the carpet's not at all practical. What do you mean? says Granddad. What's wrong with my carpet? It's the Height of Fashion, you have to keep up with the times, you know.

Just look at all the holes in it, says Mummy.

Granddad's brand-new orange spiky carpet is full of holes like the craters in the moon. Man danced on the moon, says Granddad, these days you can fly anywhere that you want to. The holes are burnt black on the edges and are grey in the centre where the floor shows through. They are big enough to put the end of my finger in as I count them, one two, one two. That's the cigarette holes, says Granddad. I put ashtrays everywhere, what more can I do? You could tell them to use the ashtrays, says Mummy. I do, says Granddad, but they drink and forget, do you want me to follow them around with an ashtray and catch the ash as it falls? You shouldn't have so many parties, says Mummy. Och, if friends come to my door, I can't turn them away like the English do, says Granddad, I have to be sociable. I don't call them friends, says Mummy, what kinds of friends burn holes in your carpet, they only come for all the free drinks you give them. What do you mean? says Granddad, they bring their own drinks too. They only bring beers, says Mummy, not the best Scotch whisky like you provide them with. I'm not going to give them that rubbish stuff, says Granddad. A Scotsman never gives bad Scotch.

What are parties, Granddad? I say. Granddad's parties are where people come and talk and drink, and then they play music and dance, and burn holes in Granddad's carpet, says Mummy. Can I come to your parties? I ask, thinking of all the people dancing around and around in circles. Not yet, Mai, says Granddad, you will have to learn to dance properly first, and that takes a very long time … you will have to grow up first … and Granddad laughs. One two, one two … Jitterbug … says Granddad … The Twist … how about the Rumba?

I was a very good dancer when I was young, says Granddad, I

used to win all the competitions in Aberdeen. I was short, but I had quick reflexes. My feet used to move so fast you could hardly see them, they were just a blur, no one could keep up with me. Even though I was small, I was very popular with the girls, everyone wanted to go out with me because I was the best dancer. In those days we wore special shoes, called winklepickers, they were the Height of Fashion, but they've gone completely out now. They were called that because they had ends so pointed and sharp, they said you could pick winkles out of their shells with them.

The only pointy shoes I know are the joker's in Granddad's card pack. No, they weren't like that, says Granddad, not red with bells on and curled up at the ends, they went straight out and were black and shiny and very smart – we kept them so polished you could see your face in them. One two, one two ... Mambo ... Lindy ...

Granddad's very proud of his big new wooden music player that he keeps polished and shiny too. That's Granddad showing off again, says Mummy, Granddad likes to show off. What do you mean? says Granddad, I designed it, it's the latest at the company, it's the Height of Fashion, I deserve one of my own. Not out of your own pocket, at the cost of a month's salary, says Mummy, the company should have given you one.

Granddad designs record players, says Mummy, he's very good at his job. I came to London from Aberdeen, says Granddad, and I made my way up the ladder from floor boy to manager of my own design team, and I'm from a Working Class Family in Scotland, and that's why I like my whisky and haggis and mealy pudding and I'm proud of it. I was so clever at school that I was the only one in the whole area to go to grammar school. I was good at everything, an all-rounder, good at maths, at science, at writing, you name it, especially at drawing. Give me a piece of paper, I could draw anything, especially horses, everyone used to want me to draw horses. I grew up at the top of the hill over Aberdeen fish market, and in those days, the fish market was huge, fish of all shapes and sizes, it went on forever, but the oil has taken over now. You could smell the fish all the way from the top of the hill, and the smell got stronger and stronger as you went down. The road down the hill was made of cobblestones – that's big stones they used to put on the road – and was very steep, so you had to be careful, as the women would put lots of water on the fish to keep it fresh, so it was always wet and slippery. I used to cycle through the market on my way to school and my bicycle would shake and rattle on the cobblestones and get faster and faster. I liked to do a no-hands – you know, when you take your hands off the handlebars and keep cycling – to show off to the girls in the market. That's how I lost my front teeth, says Granddad, when I was fourteen. There was a group of girls right down the bottom of the market, so by the time I got to them my bicycle was going very, very fast. I lifted my hands from the handlebars to do a no-hands but, just as I did so, my bicycle hit a huge cobblestone right in the middle of the road. Well, my bicycle stopped, but I didn't – I went sailing head first over the handlebars, landed on the cobblestones face down, and knocked out all my front teeth. That taught me to not show off, says Granddad. Right in front of all the girls, and he laughs. I have false teeth now.

Yes, my family was Working Class, but we weren't stupid, says Granddad. My grandfather built himself a television, piece by piece, and we were the first family in the street to have a TV. I remember when he first turned it on. In those days the TV itself was huge, a big wooden box, but the screen was tiny, and the whole street was crowded into our tiny sitting room, packed so tight we were like sardines, everyone pushing and shoving to see, and if one person moved, all the others had to move too. My grandfather gave a big speech, about how things were changing and how the world would never be the same again. And then he turned the switch, and we all waited to see our first television show ... well, we waited and waited ... but nothing happened. All we could see was a small square of fuzzy dots, and then my grandfather realised he'd forgotten to build the reception. But over time, says Granddad, he built an aerial, and then the whole street could watch TV.

Your family is artistic too, says Granddad, your great-uncle is a stonemason.

The other is a butcher, says Mummy. That's not so artistic.

On your Nana's side, your great-grandfather was a violinist and a bagpipe major, says Granddad, and he travelled Europe in an orchestra and I have his violin and when you are older you will learn how to play it.

I was a good sportsman as well when I was young, says Granddad, I played in the local football team and played tennis for Aberdeen. But I wasn't as good as your mother, she was a natural, especially at tennis. When she was ten years old she could beat grown men, a real slice on her serve, an ace every time. She qualified for Wimbledon without any training, but then she got a trainer and he messed up her serve, and she lost confidence and gave up. If she had carried on she would have been Top. I wouldn't have been Top, says Mummy, I played some of the top women players and they were built like men, over six foot tall, and I'm only five foot two and they hit the ball so hard I couldn't see it. To survive in Wimbledon you have to be the best, and I'd only have been a lower-ranking player. You gave up too early, says Granddad, you just needed proper training, you should have got another trainer. You're too stubborn. You never even bothered to come to my matches, says Mummy, not even my final. I was busy working, says Granddad. I still wouldn't have been Top, says Mummy. See, says Granddad, I told you – stubborn – so you went off to have fun travelling the world instead, and look where that got you?

Then they both look at me and go quiet.

Enough, Dad, says Mummy.

You're clever too, Mai, says Granddad, you take after me. Granddad shows me drawings he keeps locked in the cupboard of his music player, funny people with round tummies and stick arms and legs and MY NAM IS MAI written in big letters. See, you did these when you were only two years old, you're going to be an all-rounder too. Don't make her big-headed, says Mummy. It's the truth, says Granddad, do you want me to lie?

One two three four, social, says Granddad, one two three, waltz, and I imagine my feet climbing the big ladder ... one two ... one two ... like when Granddad came to London and became a record-player designer.

What's Working Class, Granddad? I ask. It's not where your nana is from, says Granddad.

Mummy says Granddad thinks Nana's family looks down on him, because they're not as Working Class as his family. Her parents were snobbish, they had their ideas, they didn't want me to marry your nana, says Granddad, they thought I was beneath her, but I married her anyway, and he laughs. Your nana's family is from Ireland, says Mummy, they came to Scotland when she was young, but really she's Spanish, because lots of people came and settled from Spain a long time ago and married among each other. Love makes the world go round, sings Granddad, one two ... one two ... and we whirl around and around across Granddad's orange spiky carpet.

One two one two, the music stops. Scratch scratch goes the player and Granddad leaps up. Damages the needle, he says, makes it go blunt. He fiddles with his music player and music comes out again. One two, one two … the floor becomes an ocean, an orange ocean, and if I fall, I drown in it. It's important to keep my feet right there, not losing his.

So, what is freedom then, Mai? asks Granddad.

Freedom is when you dance, I say. And when you fly. What do you know about flying? asks Granddad. Have you got an aeroplane? Don't be silly, Granddad, I say, I watch the ladybirds fly. They open their wings and they go up in the sky. Like this? asks Granddad, and he takes me by one leg and one arm, swings me up in circles in the air and I shriek. I open my arms out like wings and I am an aeroplane. See, now you're flying, Mai, says Granddad, we need to get you a red dress with black dots and then you can be a ladybird. You can only be free when you fly or you dance, says Granddad. And when you fall in love, he says, but you wouldn't know about that yet. Love is what makes the world go round, he sings, and Granddad laughs, and he spins me around in the air, and I'm flying and I'm dancing and I'm free.

When I dance, it is like when I swing on the swings with Nana pushing me. One two, one two … Nana is nice because she walks me through the park, holding my hand. I watch her legs and feet go back and forth, brown shoes with laces and little heels, thick wrinkled stockings that poke out from her below-the-knee thick skirt, because that is where my head reaches up to. Up you get, says Nana. I climb up on the swing and Nana pushes me from the front, and I am flying. I watch the sky spinning above me and her legs and feet get bigger and smaller … one two, one two … as I go backwards and forwards, as her hands catch the sides of the swing and push me back again. Down you get, says Nana, and she lifts me down. Then Nana walks me home again, one two, one two … our legs moving backwards and forwards as I hold her hand, and my feet kick the fallen leaves up in the air on the path as we walk. I haven't seen Nana for a while.

Your nana wants to see you, says the lady in the blue dress, come with me. She takes my hand from where I am sitting on the orange spiky carpet reading my *Big Book of Animal Stories* and she walks me down the corridor to the spare room. One two, one two … she opens the door of the room and walks me inside the doorway and lets go of my hand. Stay here, she says, there is more light here, your nana will be able to see you better. She walks to the other side of the room.

Inside is dark. Nana is hidden, wrapped in dim light. She is lying on the big bed in the spare room that I get to stay in when we visit. It is very quiet. There is a strange smell in the room, and the quietness seeps into the floor and the walls of the room and up through my feet. There are lots of people like shadows in the room, I can't see them properly but they are all looking at me. A chair moves, someone coughs. Nana looks like a moonscape of dips and bumps and craters under the bedspread, only her big feet sticking out at the end, wrapped in thick stockings, her toes bent and crooked.

All the time, I hear Nana breathing. When Nana breathes, her feet breathe too, twisting and curling, and the bedclothes become mountains and valleys, and then they go down again. Her breathing is loud, loud, like the wind whistling around rocks, like a grater grating carrots, stopping sometimes, struggling to get through, like when the record stops and makes the scratchy scratchy sound.

Come closer, Mai, says the lady. Your nana can't see you there.

I peer into the darkness, but all I can see properly is Nana's feet. One two, one two, I step forwards, but Nana's feet are stopping me, like the biggest mountains I cannot climb. Why don't Nana's

18

feet dance around the room like Granddad's? Why doesn't somebody open the curtains so I can see Nana properly and Nana can see me?

Come closer, Mai, says the lady.

One two, one two …

You are hardly moving at all, says the lady.

Perhaps she's shy. It's Mummy's voice at the other end of the bed. She's not used to so many people.

Don't be shy, Mai, says the lady.

One two, one two …

Take bigger steps, Mai, says the lady.

The lady leans over the other end of the bed. Take the cushions higher? she says. Like this? Is this better? She moves the cushions, and now I can see Nana like a dim shadow at the other end of the bed.

It's all right … I think … I can see her …

It's Nana's voice, but it's not her voice. It's like a whisper hidden in all the breathing in the room. Her toes scrunch up as she talks and the blankets move too. We have to keep waiting, in the pauses between her breaths, as if she is searching for the words, until she finds them again.

Say hello to your nana, Mai, says the lady.

Hello, I say to Nana's feet.

Is that Mai? … says Nana's voice … She was just … a tiny … wee thing … Has it … really … been so long? They grow … so fast … What … is she wearing? asks Nana.

Her blue-and-white checked dress, says Mummy's voice. And a blue ribbon in her hair.

But even Mummy's voice sounds strange, like it's all thin and stretched out.

Hello, Mai … says Nana … How are you?

I'm fine, thank you, Nana, I say like Nana taught me.

You're a big ... girl ... now ... aren't you? says Nana.

Yes, I say.

How old are you ... now?

I'm three years old, I say. I will be four soon. I stretch up as big and tall as I can. In February.

Someone sniffs, a chair scrapes, a handkerchief lifts, a flash of white in the darkness.

Have ... you been ... a good girl?

I'm worried now. Is that why all these people are here? Did I do something bad? One two, one two, I shuffle from foot to foot. Yes, Nana, I say.

Will you promise ... to stay a good girl ... for your nana?

I'm relieved. She only wants me to stay good.

Yes, Nana. I promise.

I smile. It's still my Nana.

I have been ... away ... in the hospital ... says Nana. Soon ... I will be going ... somewhere ... else ... far ... from here ...

Is it another hospital, Nana?

Something ... like that ... It is ... very beautiful ... Where ... I am going ... no one ... is ever ... sick ... I will be looked after ... very well ... It is ... far away ...

I'm excited now. Palm trees and beaches in Mummy's magazines and the lights of Mexico.

A holiday place?

Yes ... in a way, says Nana. It is ... a very ... special place ... But ... you mustn't worry ... I will be ... very happy ... there.

When are you coming back?

The only ... thing is, says Nana, it is so ... special ... that once ... people stay there ... they cannot ever go ... back again ...

I think hard. Don't worry, Nana, I say. I will come and visit you instead.

It is … too far … from here, says Nana … But if … you stay … a good girl … one day, you will come … and be with me there … We will be … very happy together …

Okay, Nana.

The room is very quiet. I wait for Nana to start talking again, but now her voice seems stuck, like when the record sticks, damages the needle, says Granddad. Everyone is watching and waiting for someone to take the needle off. And then Nana's toes curl up and the bed turns into mountains and Nana coughs. And now I know why Nana's voice sounds funny, because all the time there was a cough waiting right behind it, waiting to get out. Spit it up, says the lady, spit it up, and she and Mummy lean over the far end of the bed, and the lady holds a metal bowl under Nana's head. Nana spits, and spits again, and the coughing stops.

It has been nice … speaking with you … again, Mai … says Nana.

It has been nice speaking with you too, Nana, I say.

Nana tries to say something else, but the coughs start again. The lady says spit, spit, but this time the coughs don't stop. They fall out one by one, and it's a strange noise, it's loud, loud, like it comes from deep within the bed, like branches cracking, like twigs breaking under my feet when Nana walks me through the park. I'm worried about all the coughs.

Perhaps Mai should leave now, says Mummy.

You can take her out, says the lady, I'll manage here.

Mummy pauses. Are you sure? she says. It will be … okay?

There is still time, says the lady. It will be fine.

Your nana is tired now, Mai, says the lady, say goodbye to your nana.

Goodbye, Nana, I say.

Nana tries to speak again, but she can't because of all the coughs, so she lifts her hand and waves, and I wave back.

Mummy walks over and takes my hand and leads me to the door. I turn around before I leave and look at Nana, hidden among the dark shapes in the room. Have a nice holiday, Nana, I say, among all the coughs. Get better soon. Then I am outside and back in the light.

Mummy walks me halfway down the corridor and then she stops. Go back to the sitting room and play quietly, Mai, Mummy says. You must only disturb us if there's an emergency, we might be a very long time, it's important you stay very, very quiet. Mummy is looking at me, but really her eyes are somewhere else, and her voice is all stretched out and her face is pale like it is stretched out too.

Yes, Mummy, I say.

Mummy walks back down the corridor quickly and closes the door behind her, and I walk back to the sitting room and I am a good girl like Nana told me and I play quietly like Mummy said and I don't make any noise.

Mummy says cigarettes ate Nana up. Cigarettes burnt a hole in Nana's lungs, Mummy says, they gave her the lung cancer because she smoked two packets a day, burnt her up from the inside, and the radiation treatment they gave Nana in hospital burnt and blistered her skin, and caused nearly as much pain as the lung cancer, but it didn't work, in the end Nana was spluttering and spattering for breath, and she was only forty-nine.

Forty-nine sounds very old to me, but Mummy says people get much older than that. Forty-nine is seven times seven, says Granddad, when I ask, and he should know because he's good at maths, good at everything. Granddad used to smoke, says Mummy, but he gave it up the day he found out Nana had the lung cancer and he never smoked again, but his friends smoke, who come to Granddad's parties and burn holes in his carpet. Every time we go round to Granddad's now, there are more and more holes in his carpet. They started appearing like stars after Nana went away. Granddad's alone on weekends now and his friends come around to keep him company, says Mummy. I puzzle over the holes. Every hole I put my finger in is an invisible party person dancing around and around who came to Granddad's parties while we were away. If parties are where people have fun, why do they burn holes in Granddad's carpet? I count the holes, one two three … Look, there are more than last time, I say. I know there are holes in my carpet, says Granddad, you don't need to remind me.

You are trying to forget, says Mummy. Why do you have to have so many people around all the time? Because they are my friends, says Granddad.

Everyone likes my Granddad, because he has good parties and he gets on with everyone.

Mummy shows us photographs. They are old, grey, small. She opens Granddad's brown album carefully. Amy sits beside me. Amy is my little sister, and Mummy says I'm a big girl because I used to help bathe her when I was only three.

In a thick rim of rectangular white, Mummy sits beneath a tree in a wide-skirted dress, spread out on the grass. Around her are sitting seven young men, all posing. The men spread around her as if they are spreading out from her dress; it goes in at the waist and has a full skirt that spreads out below her knees and covers most of her legs. Mummy leans back on her hands, her arms reaching behind her so her body slopes backwards, and one ankle crosses over the other. The tree is in the centre of the photograph, but really it is Mummy who is in the centre, and her smile. The young men around her are also smiling. One smokes a cigarette, his hand held deliberately in the air for the photograph.

This is me when I was nineteen, Mummy says. Those boys were all my friends.

Were they your boyfriends? Amy and me ask.

In a way, they could have been, says Mummy. I was a bit of a tomboy, because I was very sporty. They treated me like one of the boys, but if I wanted, I could have gone out with any one of them, I was very popular.

Mummy looks very pretty. Her pale dress is under the pale blossom of the tree and the blossom is lying on the ground all around her. She is younger in the photograph, but she doesn't look very different. She sits like a fairy queen, surrounded by the young men around her. They lounge around on the grass, but their eyes look towards her, their feet point towards her, the inclination of their heads, although they are smiling for the photograph, is towards her.

Why didn't you marry any of them then? Amy and me ask.

That one there, holding the cigarette, she says, the nice-looking one, he was my best friend, Jack. He was very nice, he would have done anything for me. He was really rich, and he wanted to marry me, he kept asking and asking, he was desperate to marry me. But I kept saying no.

Why? Amy and me ask.

I don't know, says Mummy. At the time, I think I was looking for something else, someone a bit more 'special', maybe more exciting. Jack always seemed just like a good friend to me. Now that I look back, says Mummy, I think I would have had a nice life with him. Instead, I married Amy's father. Looking back, maybe I should have married my best friend. Or any of them, for that matter.

I think how me or Amy wouldn't have existed if Mummy had married Jack, on the right, sitting smoking a cigarette. How she would have been rich and would have had a very different life.

If you married him, we wouldn't have been born, I say.

No, says Mummy.

So you're lucky to have us both instead, says Amy.

Yes, says Mummy.

We feel nice. But I wonder about it. Mummy keeps looking at the photograph, as if she is stepping back into it, remembering every moment, everything that was said, as if she's even smelling what it was like to be there. I can't imagine how it must have been, this very youthful, smiling, lively, fit young woman in the photograph. She looks very happy, confident. She looks as if the sun is there just for her, and like she's got it inside her and radiates it outwards again.

You could still marry him, Mummy, I say.

Eventually he got tired of waiting and married someone else, says Mummy. He has his own family now.

In the photographs, I see Nana. Nana is all grey too. I can see past her wrinkled stockings; I can see her plaid skirt and her white blouse, right up to her face – a little white nugget in the photograph – with her hair pulled up in a perm on her head, and her glasses.

Nana had grey eyes, says Mummy. They were very unusual. In the photographs, everyone has grey eyes. Nana is smiling, standing straight like a tree. This is Granddad, standing next to her, says Mummy. The man standing next to Nana is much shorter than she is. He has a dark moustache and a cap on his head. We laugh at the picture of the man. That's not Granddad, says Amy. Yes it is, says Mummy, it's when he was younger. Who, Granddad? we ask. Was he younger once?

He looks funny, I say. He doesn't look like Granddad at all.

One two, one two … We step through photographs, grey faces and grey smiles. Photographs are like little pieces of Mummy we never knew. Mummy smiles a lot and she looks pretty. There's one of her when she's three, the same age as Amy is now, says Mummy, wearing a big dress that is too large for her and she's holding out the edges of the dress and she's smiling with flowers in her hair, like a little princess. That's me dressing up in Nana's dancing dress, says Mummy, like you do in mine. Mummy still has two favourite dancing dresses she keeps locked in the cupboard, one is the yellow and brown one, and the other is satin, red and shiny and smooth, tiny waisted and wide skirted. Amy and I like to dress up and pretend to be princesses in Mummy's dresses, but last time I spun in the red satin dress like a waterfall around me, I trod on the hem and it ripped the stitching at the waist, and now Mummy says I can't play with the dresses all the time.

Then there's another photograph of Mummy when she's a bit older than me and Amy, maybe she's six or eight, and she looks a bit like Judy Garland, with plaits on both sides of her face, and she's smiling, with straight teeth and big eyes. I can't get over how pretty Mummy looks as a little girl, with her big eyes all shining and bright, and I see lots of hope, like she's expecting promises to come true, and her smile has lots of energy, as if it has colour in it even though the photo is black and white, as if it wants to take off and float out of the surface of the photograph.

Then there's a photograph of Uncle Gregory who we never see, he's one and a half years older than Mummy, he's not so pretty, he's missing a tooth and his eyes are kind of starey and he's a bit scrawny and his hair stands up on top of his head. He got a lot better looking when he got older, says Mummy. We used to see a lot of Uncle Gregory and our Aunt Natasha and our two older boy cousins, but Mummy says he and Aunt Natasha split up, and we won't be seeing much of our cousins any more, because Uncle Gregory is now the black sheep of the family. Your Uncle Gregory is very selfish, says Mummy. He only turned up once, a few weeks before your nana died, driving his red sports car, with a big bunch of flowers on the doorstep, and then he was gone. But you know what, your nana loved him. She spoilt Uncle Gregory stupid, and it was enough for him just to bring her flowers, only once, and she was so happy about it. He did nothing else, and I looked after Nana for months, until she died. I think Nana came to visit me once, says Mummy. To say thank you. I was in the park, all alone, and suddenly the air was filled with freesias, Nana's favourite flower, but I couldn't see a freesia anywhere, and I felt like she was with me. I think maybe she came to say goodbye.

Then there's a photograph of Mummy and Uncle Gregory together and they are sitting on a big stone lion, with pigeons circling around them. That's Trafalgar Square, says Mummy. It was after the war, because all the children in London were sent to live somewhere else in the countryside and now we were back with Granddad and Nana and we were very happy.

Granddad is sitting in his orange plastic armchair, watching the football. I was injured in the war, says Granddad. But I was unique, because I got injured before I even went to fight. I was in the Home Guard. We had to run an obstacle course during our training, and, as part of it, I had to climb a fence, but when I climbed it, it collapsed, and I fell and hit my head on my own rifle butt and knocked myself out. I was out of action before I even got to fight, the only injury in the country on home ground, and it was self-inflicted, and he laughs.

Then there's a picture of Mummy a bit older dressed up in a yellow-green dress with leaves and flowers, like autumn. Puppy fat, says Mummy. I was seventeen there. Are you going to a party, Mummy? we ask. Mummy looks at the photograph. Yes, she says, I probably was. Did you dance there? we ask. Yes, she says. Did you go to balls? we ask. I went to one or two, says Mummy, but mostly dances. I think of Mummy spinning around and around, reds, yellows, greens and browns whirling around with her, her feet flying across a big dance floor with all the young men waiting to dance and her best friend Jack begging her to marry him, her skirt swirling out, flying.

Your mother used to dance a lot, says Granddad from his armchair, but she doesn't dance much now, she's very good. I'm not that good, says Mummy. Yes you are, says Granddad, you take after me. I saw your mother dancing once, she was so light on her feet, they barely touched the ground, it was like she was floating all over the floor.

Feet stepping, dress swirling, we swirl our way through photographs, watching Mummy and Uncle Gregory grow older and bigger, and other people we've never met – your relatives in Scotland, says Granddad from his orange armchair. Their grey faces stare out, as if they are trying to look back at us, as if they'd like to talk with us, too.

Then Amy and I climb up on the arms of Granddad's armchair where he is watching TV and we ask him to show us his false teeth, but he doesn't want to, he's shy. He only pushes them forwards just a little bit with the tip of his tongue to please us, and we scream with laughter – Do it again! Do it again! we shout. No, says Granddad, you've seen it once, I'm not going to. Go on, Granddad! we scream. Please! Show us your false teeth! We reach up and try to pull his teeth out of his mouth but then Granddad gets annoyed. Granddad's getting pissed off, we yell, Granddad's pissed off! That's enough, says Granddad, stop it, I'm watching the football, and if you don't stop right now you'll get a slap. Granddad has never slapped us but we stop just in case, and we watch the football men with him, lots of little grey men in baggy shorts and numbers running up and down a grey field. Granddad's a fan of Manchester United and he hates Arsenal. See that,

Number 11, Robbie whoever, says Granddad, he should never have been put on the team – if it were me, I'd have put the other guy in reserve in. Robbie's useless, see the bloke can't pass, see, useless … Oh NO, fudged it, why would they put him on? Goal … GOAL … C'MON … GOAL … NO! HE MISSED IT! … USELESS! Absolutely bloody useless! I told you, you can't focus all on attack – you've got to defend too.

Granddad manages his own football team at work, we went to see them once. Granddad was dressed in a big coat, which made him look even shorter, but he was very excited, because his team might go up a division if they won. You must shout what I shout, he told Amy and me. The man blew the whistle and they started kicking the ball around and Amy and me shouted the same as Granddad, even though we didn't know what we were shouting about. But then the rain started, and all the umbrellas came up like mushrooms and people began to move away from around the field, and then it rained so heavily you couldn't see anyone any more. Then the whistle went and everyone left.

Who won? we said.

The game got rained out, said Granddad, there has to be a rematch, and everyone came up and slapped Granddad on the back and slappped each other and said well played, John, pity about the rain. But Amy and me knew Granddad was proud anyway because we came to see him manage his work football team.

Best mealy pudding comes from Aberdeen, says Granddad, as he pokes the steaming white sausage until it splits open, straight from home … mmm … delicious … made of oats, oatmeal … fresh from your relatives in Scotland. Amy and me like the mealy pudding. And the haggis too, ssays Granddad, stronger flavoured, with spices added.

What's haggis, Granddad? we ask, looking at the round steaming thing Mummy puts on the table. Round Scottish animals, says Granddad. Run around the hills like rabbits and live in burrows. They're hard to catch. See the knobbly bit at the end? That's its tail. But we're not sure. Granddad looks serious, but his eyes are twinkling. Where's its legs then? we ask. Worn down from all the running around, says Granddad. What about its nose? we say. Cut off, says Granddad. Nah, Granddad, we say, it's not true. Why doesn't it have any eyes then? Boiled out in the soup, says Granddad. Don't tease the kids, Dad, says Mummy. Why not? says Granddad. Doesn't do them any harm.

I'm good at cooking too, Granddad says. Give me a tin opener and I'll cook you anything. Granddad's favourite joke. Aw, Granddad, we say, you told us that before. No one finds that funny. I do, Granddad says, I find it funny. And he laughs.

One two three … blossom falls … blossom on my sister Amy. It floats in the air – you're getting married I say – and it lands all over her face and some even gets in her mouth and she spits it out. Blossom falling … catch it, catch it … it creeps across the garden, painting it pink. It is magic when the sun shines and the blossom turns pinker and pinker, and when it falls it is raining pink.

In spring all the blossom on Granddad's big tree in the back garden comes out, floods of petals falling onto the path below, like a huge pink carpet, and Amy and I get married, throwing confetti at each other like at the churches. The tree is so big, Mummy has to lean out of the first-floor window to pick blossom to put in the house.

Don't pick all the blossom, says Granddad, all that blossom is going to turn into big fat juicy cherries. There's plenty of blossom, says Mummy, the house will look nice and you won't miss it. I look up at Mummy, all the blossom floating around her among the green leaves, and she looks like a fairy princess, like she is wearing a crown.

Amy and me don't believe Granddad, but when we come back later, all the cherries are hanging above us. Granddad says, I told you so, come on, try one, and they are big, fat and juicy. Granddad has to get a big ladder to pick all the cherries. There are so many it would take us years to eat them, but Amy and I try anyway. We eat and eat, cherry juice all over our faces, and we spit the pips out at each other. Don't do that, says Granddad. You're making a mess. And don't eat so many cherries, you will get stomach ache. But we don't get stomach ache. I think Granddad is disappointed, because he would have liked to say, I told you so.

You're just lucky, says Granddad, just wait till the pear tree ripens, then you'll get stomach ache.

Large, red and fragile, the poppies in the garden lose their petals, drop them to the ground while the roses still flower. Amy and I watch the green pods turn brown, and when we shake them, they rattle. Don't eat them, says Mummy, they're poisonous. So we're careful, we just pop them open and watch their seeds fall out, like dust.

Crack them over the earth where the poppies grow, says Granddad, then there'll be even more poppies next year, so we do.

The pear tree ripens and Amy and I get stomach ache from eating too many green pears. I told you so, says Granddad, and he laughs. Mummy says next year there will be cherries and poppies and pears again. She says everything goes in circles, but every time you come back, life has changed – but everything always looks the same to me. Mummy gathers up the pears and brings them home in a big sack to wait for them to ripen.

See you later, alligators, says Granddad when he drops us at home. In a while, crocodile, we say. Granddad always says that.

31

One two, one two ... Granddad takes me flying, the carpet is like an ocean, the music rolls like the waves of an ocean, his false teeth click together in the grin under his moustache – hold on, Mai, hold on – and we are turning, spinning like the dancers on music boxes, slowly, slowly, one two, one two ... I feel Granddad's big fingers holding mine, laughing and listening to the music that seems to become part of the orange carpet too, rolling and rolling like the waves. I cross my fingers, hoping it will go on forever ...

The music player goes round and round and Granddad and I dance together, hand in hand, and foot on foot, and more and more cigarette holes appear in the orange carpet every time we visit. And even though Nana is on holiday, everything is still shining and beautiful and fresh, and I am going to discover the world, and freedom and flying, and one day I will know what love is. But sometimes things in life happen, and then everything changes, and nothing is ever the same agian.

2

Flying

Ladybirds fly up and when they are in the sky they drift away. Like little ships, like the red boats in my bathtub, they spin off, only they have black sails. They sit like a drop of blood on my finger, and then they open their red backs and out comes a black lace fan and the wings spread out and they go up, up in the air. They fly up, watching everything grow smaller and smaller beneath them. And then they are gone, travelling the world.

The world is a big place. Up there there's the big space of the sky stretching out. Sometimes the sky is dark and gloomy or wet and windy, but I like the times when it is sunny, like now, when the sun is a big burning ball that bounces off everything and makes everything shine and all the colours dance around me like the colours in my kaleidoscope. It is the hottest summer. It is a summer of outside-ness, never indoors. Spring burst the flowers open and spilled all the blossom from Granddad's cherry tree and the grass went thick and green and the sky a perfect blue. The pavement is so shiny it hurts your eyes when you look at it, specks of light shimmering off its surface as you walk.

Amy and I skip along the pavement, ducking under the branches with sticky wriggling caterpillar threads hanging from them. How many have we got? I ask Amy. One hundred and fourteen, she says, but one just flew away. We can still count those, I say.

We are collecting ladybirds. Amy is pushing the pink plastic pram where Jemima the doll used to sit, which today is full of ladybirds and twigs and branches from the hedges in the street. Yesterday we had eighty-six. If you want to catch a ladybird, you have to be very careful and push it gently from the hedge so it walks onto your finger or it will fly away. Or you can slide the twigs of the hedge between your fingers over the pram so the leaves and ladybirds come off in one go, small green leaves like lots of little green fingernails falling.

This summer there are so many ladybirds. Mummy says it must be a ladybird epidemic, she has never seen so many. There are ladybirds everywhere, on the hedges, the walls, the ground, flying through the air. Ladybirds are lucky, says Mummy, they eat all the greenfly. Amy and I look at the greenfly that cluster like thick slime around the stems of Mummy's roses. If ladybirds are lucky then Amy and I must be very lucky because we've collected hundreds. We have been collecting ladybirds all day, adding them to the branches in the pram for the ladybirds to sit on. Sometimes we find a white ladybird, white with black spots on its back, and that is extra lucky.

Mrs Willows our next-door neighbour peers over her hedge, holding her large shears in her hand. Mrs Willows has white hair in waves on her head and a thin blue wool cardigan that hangs from her shoulders. The skin over her top lip is long and furrowed, and there are silvery grey hairs you can see when the sun shines on them. She sees us pushing the doll's pram, and all the pieces of hedge in it, sticking out like a green hedgehog.

What's that you've got there? she says.

Just ladybirds, we say.

You'd better not be damaging other people's hedges, says Mrs Willows. Some people spend a lot of time trimming theirs.

Amy and I look at each other and make a secret face, the kind you only use your eyes for. We're not, we say, the branches are from all different hedges.

Mrs Willows gives us A Look. H'mph, she says. Looks like you're destroying hedges to me. I'll tell your mother you've been up to no good. Your mother should know better than to let you run around wild like a pair of vagabonds vandalising hedges.

We turn the corner into our gateway, with Mrs Willows still peering over the hedge at us, push the pram as fast as possible down our pathway past the roses to our front door, and then to the right, past the front window with the lavender bushes and foxgloves Mummy also planted, and around the side of the house to the back garden.

Mrs Willows can't see us back here, I say.

She's a nosy parker, says Amy.

Mummy says we're not to call Mrs Willows that, I say.

I know, says Amy, but she is, and we giggle.

We look at the doll's pram outside the back kitchen door and at the ladybirds clambering all around the pieces of hedge. Now what? asks Amy. I have an idea, I say. First, we need some string. I know where some is, says Amy. She goes running inside and comes out again with a reel of white sewing cotton, wrapped in plastic. I got it from Mummy's sewing box, she says.

Watch, I say.

I unwrap the cotton thread and tie one end to the handle of the pram. Then I unroll the thread some more and tie it around the latch on the back kitchen door, and then back around the pram handle again. I wrap it twice around the broom handle leaning on the wall outside the kitchen, keeping the string tight all the time, then back to the pram and out again to the latch on the windowsill. Then I take the string around the back of an old garden chair from the shed, then around the pram, the chair, the door latch, the broom, again and again, in different ways and different places, until there is cotton thread stretched everywhere, between everything.

It looks like a giant spider's web, says Amy. What now?

Now, we put the ladybirds on the string, I say. Amy fetches the branches from the pram, one by one, and we walk the ladybirds onto the strings, sometimes teasing them from our fingers, sometimes from the branches. Finally, all the strings are covered with ladybirds, ladybirds everywhere.

See, I say, the ladybirds are all tightrope walking. It's a ladybird circus.

We watch the ladybirds, the sun shining off their red backs with black dots, their legs like little ballerina legs under their shells, tickly like feathers. Then we have races, starting ladybirds at different ends of the string, laughing when they meet and cross over each other, sometimes walking across each other's backs, sometimes opposite, tickling each other's tummies.

Mummy has finished cooking and she comes to the back door to tell us to eat. But the door can't open because of all the strings tied to it, and it sticks, so she pushes hard. Bam bam bam the strings break and the door flies forwards and the broom falls and the pram nearly falls too.

Mummy looks angry. She stares at all the loose pieces of thread floating in the breeze, some with ladybirds still attached to them. What on earth are you two doing? Mummy shouts.

It's a ladybird circus, Amy and me say. We haven't seen Mummy so angry before. Maybe Mrs Willows said something to her about the hedge. Can't I leave you for one minute without you getting into trouble? shouts Mummy. Is that all my brand-new cotton thread you've used up?

We used a bit, I say, but there's still some left. I hold the cotton reel out to her, but as I do so I realise there is only a tiny layer of thread left. We can put the thread back on, I say.

How do you expect me to use it, now it's all stretched and broken, snaps Mummy. I have to buy a new reel of cotton now, and where is the money supposed to come from? Things are hard enough right now without you two making it even harder.

Mummy has never been so angry with us.

We're sorry, we say, we didn't know, we wanted to make a ladybird circus. Mummy looks at all the cotton wound onto everything and she looks at our faces. Then her face softens. It's okay, Mai and Amy, she says, I'm sorry, I shouldn't have shouted at you. I didn't mean it that way. Things are very difficult for me right now, especially financially, and I've been very stressed. Wind what you can of the cotton back on and then tidy up and come in for dinner. Next time, ask me before you take things from my sewing box, she says.

Amy and I wind as much of the used thread back onto the cotton reel as we can. And we try to put the ladybirds back among the branches in the pram, to sleep for the night, but some of them escape, up into the sky above us, and we try to catch them, running across the garden, but they go up above the rows of council houses, up into the sky, leaving us down on the ground, getting smaller and smaller, and then they are gone, vanishing into sunlight.

Where we live is a council house. All the other houses in our street are council houses. Our house is where the road bends around on the corner. Our garden is shaped like a triangle and smells of hedgerows, leaves and cocoons and dark, dry earth. The edge of the world is at the edge of our garden, because when our ball goes through the hedge the neighbours on the other side confiscate it. We don't see much of the neighbours. Their garden is much bigger than ours and is brown earth in neat lines, like wrinkles, and sometimes there are pieces of string with bits of paper hanging from them. The neighbours are trying to grow vegetables but they are always angry because the birds eat all the seeds, says Mummy. On the other side is Mrs Willows and her daughter who is sixteen and is always grumpy. Mrs Willows is a friend of Mummy's and they chat over the wall and sometimes they go for tea at each other's houses.

On Thursdays Mrs Jolly the social worker comes up the road towards our house on her motorbike phut phut with her helmet on her head, looking like an astronaut. Mrs Jolly is friendly and she always smiles at me and Amy and says hello before she goes to talk with Mummy in the house. When she comes out she smiles again and asks Amy and me, how are you doing? and we say, fine thank you, and then she smiles again and says, now, be good girls and help your mother around the house, things are not easy for her right now, she's having a hard time, she could do with your help. Then Mrs Jolly puts her helmet back on her head and goes off again phut phut like a space lady going to the moon, the engine growling into the distance.

In the back garden is the chicken house made of wood, and with wire fencing Mummy put around it. Amy and I both have chickens, plump, run around, squawk and lay eggs. Henrietta is Amy's chicken and Isabella is mine. They rush out, clucking and cluttering, pecking and scrabbling on the earth, gobbling everything up when we feed them, scraps from the kitchen and special yellow chicken seed we pour over the chicken-wire fence. Mummy collects eggs and cooks them for breakfast. Fresh, like farm eggs, says Mummy.

Amy's chicken has a lump on its foot. The lump gets bigger and bigger, it looks like she's carrying a football on her claw. We argue about whose chicken is prettier. Amy says Henrietta is prettier, but she doesn't like the big lump on her chicken's foot. We stare at it. It looks ugly. It has a chicken disease, says Mummy. Amy gets upset when I talk about the lump on her chicken's foot. We have guinea pigs too, mine is Sherbet and Amy's is Snow White. They live in the small outside shed next to our kitchen. You can't call your guinea pig after a fizzy sweet, says Amy, but I do anyway.

Socks, round fluffy ball of a kitten, comes clambering onto our doorstep. She stays, even though her mother and fellow kitten live doors away down the street. Soon the owners say we might as well keep her because she spends more time at ours than anywhere else and Mummy feeds her anyway when she shows up. Mummy says Socks loves children, that's why she stays around. So we get to keep her from when she is tiny. We call her Socks because she has white feet and black fur.

Socks is my best friend, next to my sister Amy. Socks is Mummy's best friend too. Socks crawls under my blanket at night, her warm body hugging mine.

At the front of the house is the stone coal-bunker with a slanted wooden roof, which the coal man lifts up when he delivers coal to us. There is also a low stone wall we can jump over, not like the hedge all around Mrs Willows our neighbour's on the left. Roses go along the path from our front door to the gate and Mummy dries the lavender she planted under the front window and puts it into little cushions she puts around the house, to make it smell nice, she says. We don't go near the lavender bushes because the bees like them and we are scared of bees. There are foxgloves also under the window, red and pink trumpets that the bees crawl inside and out of again. In Spain rich ladies used to put them inside their eyes to make their eyes grow large, says Mummy. Why? we ask. Because they thought it made them look more attractive.

But you mustn't touch them, they're poisonous. If you eat them you get sick and can even die. So we stay away and instead watch Mummy's roses after she waters them, drops sparkling in the sun on the petals, greenfly thick around the stems we daren't touch.

At the top of the stairs next to my and Amy's room is wallpaper with red roses on. If you take a paintbrush and wet the roses the red comes out and you can draw pictures, so I do, red stick men and women with fat tummies on the corner where Mummy can't see them.

Dandelions grow on the green patch of grass on the pavement opposite where the road bends. We lift them up to our lips when they are white and feathery and blow the parachutes away, into the air. He loves me, he loves me not …

Get off the grass! screams the old lady who lives opposite us, appearing behind the curtains of the first-floor window. Get off the grass! Don't pick the dandelions! Dandelions make you wee-wee! They'll make you wet the bed! No they don't, we shout back. Yes they will, she shouts. They'll make you wee-wee! Her voice is a high-pitched whine. You will wee-wee! Get off the grass, you can't play there! When we pick the dandelions a whitish fluid comes out of the dandelion stalks and sticks to our fingers. It smells a bit like pee. Is that the stuff that does it?

Old Wives' Tales, Mummy says. The old lady lives on her own and has gone a bit strange in the head. Does she have a husband then? we ask. He died a while ago, Mummy says.

Next time we see her at the window, her thin face peering behind curtains brown with age, white hair standing up on her head like the dandelion parachutes, Amy and I say to each other, it's the Old Wife again. She never comes out of her house, she only peeps out from behind her first-floor window and shouts at people. Sometimes she just stares out. Sometimes when you get old it happens like that, Mummy says, it can be very lonely and difficult when you grow old and live on your own.

Amy and me feel sorry for Old Wives like that, stuck in there and can't come out, never go outside.

It is my first day at school. The other children gather around me at break time. They ask me about my eyes.

Why are your eyes funny? they say.

My eyes aren't funny, I reply.

Yes they are.

What do you mean?

They go up at the sides, they say.

How?

Like this. They pull their eyes upwards into slants. Like they're stretched out.

And they laugh.

I don't know, I say. I'll ask my mummy when I get home.

At home, I look in the mirror. My eyes look the same as they always have.

What's wrong with my eyes? I ask Mummy.

What do you mean? says Mummy.

The children at school say my eyes look funny.

Mummy looks at me for a long while.

There's nothing wrong with your eyes, Mai, says Mummy. Your eyes are perfect.

I think about it. Don't read in the dim light, Mummy is always saying when it gets dark and I forget to turn on the light, it will damage your eyes, you will strain them. When I go back to school the next day, I tell the other children, I think my eyes are stretched from reading too much in the dim light. They are strained.

And we all agree it must be the best explanation.

Ching Chong! shouts the biggest brother. He reaches down and picks up a rock from the street, a broken piece of tarmac. He throws it at me.

I see it coming, too late to stop. It hits my forehead, bang, and falls to the ground, just as Mummy opens the front door and pulls us inside. The boys laugh, then run away, fast.

Amy and me were playing outside with the three boys who live in the house next to the Old Wife. Then we started arguing with them and then we started fighting. And they chased us to our house and we leapt over our garden wall and ran up the path to our front door. Then they threw the stone.

Lucky it didn't get your eye, says Mummy as she wipes away the blood dripping from my forehead as I cry, you could have lost your eyesight.

The three boys used to be our friends, but I don't like them any more. Mummy says the boys are coming back to say sorry.

The boys come to the door and say, we have come to apologise because our parents said we had to come and say sorry. Then they look at us and we look at them.

Okay, I say.

I'm sorry I threw a rock at you and called you Ching Chong, the eldest boy says. Our mummy and daddy said we can show you our pet parrot, says the youngest boy.

We go to their house and in the front room is a big dome-shaped cage with a cover. He's sleeping, says the youngest boy. The oldest boy lifts the cover and inside is a large green parrot who opens his eyes and looks at us and says 'hello' like an echo when we say it. We make friends again with the brothers.

But I still don't know what Ching Chong means and I don't ask.

Amy and me are in the garden and Mummy is taking photographs of us playing. Take one of me, Mummy, I say, and I grab the washing line and swing from it, with my feet in the air. The line stops swinging and I put my feet down on the ground again. No, Mummy, you weren't quick enough. Try again.

Don't swing on the washing line, Mai, says Mummy. It will break.

No it won't, I say. Look.

I grab the line again and swing hard. Snap. It breaks. I fly forwards through the air and land on the ground on my stomach. I can't breathe at first. Are you okay? asks Mummy. Yes, I gasp. Does it hurt anywhere? No, I say, still gasping for air. Don't worry, she's only winded herself, says Mummy to Amy. She'll get her breath back, she'll be all right in a minute. I told you not to swing on the line, says Mummy. You didn't listen, and look what happened.

Mai's always naughty, says Amy.

I start to cry. Cry baby, says Amy. She comes over and sits on my back, one leg on each side of me, so I can't get up. You were naughty, Mai. You must stay here. Now you have to have your photograph taken, to show how naughty you were. Come, Mummy, take a photograph, to show how stupid Mai is.

Get off, I say to Amy, but her weight is holding me down. Amy stays put.

No, says Amy. You're a naughty girl and Mummy must take a photograph first.

I bang my fists on the ground. Tell her to get off me!

Mummy's looking at both of us. She's trying not to laugh, but then she starts laughing.

Mummy takes the photograph. In it, I am lying on top of the broken washing line, facing the camera, my mouth wide open, tears running down my face with rage, and Amy sits on my back, one leg on either side of me, in her white summer dress, with her arms folded. Under her floppy white summer hat, Amy has a big grin on her face for the camera, while I scream and pound my fists on the ground in anger.

South Greenstead, where we live, is by the sea. The sea roars, and smells clean and salty. When the tide goes out, the waves go right back, until you can't see them any more. They leave a brown surface, wrinkled like the furrows in our neighbour's garden. Mummy says the sand turns to mud because South Greenstead is where a river joins the sea. Granddad tells us they bring sand to South Greenstead with bulldozers from Southend to make it like the seaside, because otherwise it would be just mud. Granddad likes to joke, says Mummy. It's true, says Granddad.

The mud is in ripples and my feet squish when I walk, a warm feeling that strokes up under my soles and pushes my toes apart. I stand and look out at the sea splashing. The waves are like giant hammers, they keep moving and moving. My toes are so deep in the mud, I feel they go right through the ground. People with buckets dig in the mud. They're digging for worms, says Mummy, for bait. We don't know what bait is but we've checked the buckets and there are worms there. Ugh, we say as they squirm around, pink and muddy.

Sometimes Mummy takes Amy and me for a picnic. At lunchtime, the sea becomes bare legs and bathing suits. There are green changing huts where you can change your clothes but Mummy says people have to pay for the huts, so we always change on the beach, under a towel. We wriggle out so no one can see our bare bums, and giggle. Amy and me make all kinds of things. We build sand-ditches and sandcastles. We dribble the wet sand so it piles up into a tower. We even make our own car out of sand, with a seat for us to sit in and a steering wheel made from a plastic lid we found on the beach. We eat sandwiches that get sand in them. We return, fingers salty from the cold waves and from searching for dried seaweed with swollen sacs to pop and pearly shells and green winkles that cling with the limpets among the green and black slime growing on the wet wooden posts of the wave breakers.

You never know what you will find on the beach. Once I found a small stone with a pattern in it, shell coiled up in the stone. Mummy said, that's a fossil, from a long time ago, you must look after it carefully. What is a long time ago? I ask. It is a time in the past when everything was different, she said.

In winter, dark branches creep around the sea, fallen from the trees. The waves get big and the sea is frightening. Dead branches with fir cones fall from trees onto the sand, and the sand gets dirty and littered with old leaves, dead berries and dirt. It gets colder and colder. I like it when the wind blows hard and no one else is there. That's when I feel close to the sea, when it's a bit strange and smells wild. Then I can walk with Mummy and Amy and collect dried cones from the fallen branches and smell danger in the cold waves that swell unpredictably. Mummy says if you walk long enough you get to Southend.

Once, I was building in the sand, and a huge wave sprang up and caught a little boy about two years old standing close to where I was sitting by the water's edge and threw him to the ground, soaked. He cried, and everyone rushed to get him.

It must have been a freak wave, a grown-up said. So you have to watch out.

The sea's surprising like that.

Mrs Willows tells Mummy she is going to teach me the piano properly because I am always messing around on hers when I visit. I sit on the big square stool with my feet dangling in the air and stare at the open book on the piano in front of me. I'm going to go out of the room for half an hour, says Mrs Willows, and when I come back I want you to know the names of the notes. What are notes? I ask. The dots in the book, she says. You must learn the letters under them. Why? I ask. That's what you need to do to learn to play the piano, Mrs Willows says, and she leaves the room.

I look at the black dots on their black fence with letters A B C written underneath. 'Three Blind Mice' it says at the top of the page. I know the song. I press one of the piano keys in front of me. It feels nice, cold and smooth, and makes a jangly sound. I press my finger on the key next to it. I play about more with the piano and I forget all about the black dots.

Mrs Willows comes back again. What are you doing, messing around on the piano? Have you learnt the names of the notes? she says. I don't need the dots to play, I say. It's quicker this way. Look. I put my forefinger on the first note and then the second, plink plink, all the way through on the keyboard. See, 'Three Blind Mice', I say. I can play a bit of 'Silent Night' too … see … But now the notes go wrong.

Mrs Willows' hairs on her upper lip twitch and her blue eyes narrow. Don't be such a cheeky girl, she says. I asked you to learn the names of the notes, not to play the song.

But I don't need to know the names of the dots, I say.

Learn the notes like I told you, child, or I'll spank you.

I look at Mrs Willows. I don't like her any more. No, I say. The dots are silly.

Mrs Willows slaps my leg, dangling from the piano stool. You're the most difficult child I have ever known, says Mrs Willows, as I burst into tears.

What happened? says Mummy afterwards. Mrs Willows says you are absolutely impossible to teach and has refused to give you any more piano lessons.

She told me to learn the dots to play 'Three Blind Mice' but I didn't know why I had to do it, I say.

Mummy looks disappointed. If you want to learn something, sometimes you have to do what people tell you, even if you don't see why, says Mummy. Like that time I told you not to touch the hot iron and you wanted to know the reason why and you touched it and burnt your finger. Sometimes you don't have to know the reason, you just have to know that's how it is. Now you won't get to learn the piano at all.

So now Mrs Willows doesn't like me and I don't like her. And every time Amy and me pass Mrs Willows in the street cutting her hedge she shakes her head and goes tut tut, she doesn't know how my mother puts up with me, I'm such a handful, look at me, I'm a real vagabond, always messy and I never do what I'm told. She heard I was the only little girl to be spanked on my first day at school because I refused to put my foot up after gym to have my shoelaces tied like the rest of the children and never told the teacher I could do them myself. And she heard I painted little red people all over the wallpaper at the top of the stairs. And several times I was caught trampling the neighbour's vegetables trying to get our tennis ball back, and what kind of example am I to my little sister? And however much my mother brushes my and my sister's hair it gets all messed up again, and she knows who is behind it, I'm always getting the two of us into mischief. And she heard how I forgot to take the letter to my mummy about school photo day and I was the only child in the school photograph with my hair like a scarecrow, she's seen the picture. And she heard when me and Amy had a fight I cut Amy's favourite doll Jemima's hair short, and it was even my idea to sit on the cot mattress and slide down the stairs and that's how we smashed up Mummy's favourite vase. And that when I was smaller I would never go to bed and I would stand at the top of the stairs and scream until I threw up. And it is true, I did do those things, except I don't remember the screaming and throwing up, but I don't care because I know Mummy and Amy love me and I love them and Granddad says I'm just creative and curious, and I'm going to be an all-rounder when I grow up.

We go to town. To collect our Social Security, says Mummy. We walk up the long cobbled street to the top of the hill, the pram with Amy in going bump, bump, me holding onto the side. Mummy goes inside a place and comes out again. Then Mummy takes Amy and me to the library to get books and bring them home to read, and she takes out books too. Then she takes us to the shops, and buys things. Bumpy cobblestones, under my feet, one two, one two …

Butcher's, red meat and sickly blood smell, reeking out of the door.

Sewing shop, materials and white thread in the window.

We pass a doorway that smells funny, all stale and smoky. Mummy says, that's a pub, you can't go in there.

Chocolate-cake shop, lots of creamy things in the window, and Amy and I stare at it as we go past. We never buy any. Mummy says, I'll make you cakes when we go home, and she always does.

What beautiful little girls, says a lady walking by in town. Are these your little sisters?

No, I'm their mother, says Mummy smiling.

Goodness, says the lady, you look so young, I would never have believed it. I thought you were their sister. The lady and Mummy chat and Mummy laughs a lot. Then the lady looks at me and says, what a pretty little girl, is she …?

I hear a word. It sounds like ornamental.

Yes, says Mummy, she is.

When we get home I ask Mummy what ornamental means.

Ornamental? says Mummy. Are you sure that's the word? It's not something else?

Yes, I say.

Mummy looks at me for a while. Well, ornaments are pretty things you put on a shelf for decoration, she says, so I guess ornamental means something you can put on a shelf to look at.

I feel good. I must be so pretty they want to put me on a shelf so everyone can look at me.

At school the girls want to play Mummies and Daddies in the sandpit. We're playing Mummies and Daddies, they say, do you want to play too? But I don't, because I don't understand, so I just watch. The boys want to play in the sandpit too, with their cars, and make roads and stuff, but the girls say, no, we were here first, you have to play Mummies and Daddies instead. Okay, say the boys.

The girls tell the boys to go shopping while they stay at home and make cakes, and the boys drive their cars up and down in the sand. Then the girls pretend to be shopkeepers, and the boys come to buy things from them.

The boys say, we'll race each other to the shop, but then they crash and they have to fix their cars at the garage, and they spend ages getting them fixed, so the girls say, stupid boys, it's no point playing with you, get out of the sandpit. But the boys say, no, please, we want to play Mummies and Daddies, and the mummies say, well, you are taking so long, all the children are getting hungry, how come you are home so late? The boys say, we got held up. And then they say, my daddy goes to the pub, he doesn't have to come home all the time like you want us to.

It all looks strange to me. My mummy doesn't send anyone to

the shop, she goes and gets it herself. She walks or gets the bus and we get to go too, and Mummy paints the walls and fixes the plugs, lots of things the girls ask the boys to do.

Because I don't understand Mummies and Daddies, the other children say I can't play with them in the sandpit.

Amy's birthday is coming. Mummy says she has a big surprise for her and it's also for Christmas and my birthday which is later, a special present for both of us.

Mummy digs a big hole in the back garden beside the wall. Mummy lets us help dig too, with our seaside spades and buckets. Why are you digging up the garden? we ask. She says, it's a secret, you'll see. Then when the hole is big enough for me and Amy to sit in it together Mummy gets thick black sheets of plastic stuff and puts it inside the hole and fixes it down.

In the morning we run downstairs and out into the back, and overnight Mummy has filled the hole full of sand and now we have our own sandpit. Amy and me sit with our knees pulled up and make sandcastles with our buckets and spades. We make sand-pies and pretend we are in the cake shops we pass in the street in the town centre, and I tell Amy it is chocolate cake and I feed her it with a big metal spoon and she eats half, drinking it with water to help it go down. Does it taste nice, Amy? I ask. Yes, she says. When we go in Amy can't eat dinner, she says she's full, she already had lots of chocolate cake in the sandpit, and Mummy looks at me funny, but I say nothing.

I'm really proud that our mummy built us a sandpit while all the other kids fight over the sandpit at school. It doesn't matter how many mummies and daddies they have, few of them have a sandpit, and what use are mummies if they just keep sending daddies to the shop and can't go themselves, and the daddies just go to the pub all the time and crash their cars?

Mummy takes us to dance class. Amy and me stand in the corner of the wooden hall, watching the other children running in circles, little boys and girls flapping their arms up and down. Some of the girls have gymslips with short built-on skirts flapping around their thighs, like their hands. The piano tinkles and feet patter, whirlpooling around the room.

Now you are butterflies, says the teacher. Flap your wings.

Mummy nudges us to join in. Go on, says Mummy.

When is she going to teach them real dancing? I ask. I don't want to be a butterfly. Where is the jitterbug and lindy and fox-trot like Granddad does?

This is real dancing, says Mummy. This is where you have to start. It's a ballet class.

Now be flowers, says the dance teacher.

The children's feet stop and they stand still.

Open your petals, slowly … Petals unfold.

Mummy looks annoyed. I paid good money for this, Mummy says.

A nearby mother smiles at us. Maybe they're shy, says the mother.

We're not shy, I say.

The ballet teacher comes over. She has a sickly sweet love-everybody smile and a sickly sweet love-everybody voice. Sorry we're late, says Mummy, the bus … Don't worry, says the teacher. Do they want to join in?

Amy and me look at her. No, we say. Being flowers is for babies. It's sissy.

Don't worry, it can take a little time, says the teacher to Mummy. Perhaps if they watch a little first, they'll be more comfortable, they can join in the next class …

Now let the wind blow you around the room, she says to the children.

51

Amy and I stand and watch the whirlpool of limbs and feet.

I expect all of this is very new to them, says the smiling lady to Mummy. They must be shy. My little one's not shy, she loves ballet. See, there she is, dancing over there ... isn't she just delightful? She points to a little curly haired blonde girl in a pink tutu.

Have your little ones ever seen a real ballet? the lady asks.

No, says Mummy. But they see it in the picture books.

My dear, you simply *must* take them to one. You can't expect them to like ballet if they've never even seen one. My little one has seen several already, I take her as often as I can. Last week we took her to see *Swan Lake* ... There are often ballets in town, you really must take them.

Where do you live? asks the mother.

South Greenstead, says Mummy.

Oh, that's the council estate ... says the lady, that's very far from here. It's so nice you are giving them some culture, you must really want them to learn to dance. And you have such adorable children, the lady says. Are they *both* yours?

Yes, says Mummy.

Oh, says the lady, looking at me, but this one ... she looks very different ... quite ... exotic?

Yes, says Mummy.

The lady looks like she wants to ask something else, but she doesn't.

Now, fall to the ground and lie there, says the teacher. The children fall down. Feel the sunshine on your face and relax, says the teacher.

Such a pity your two children are so shy, the mother says, as the teacher says it's end of class and the children spring up. Maybe next time they'll join in? Hello, darling, the mother says to the little girl as she runs over, you were wonderful. Now we must go and meet Daddy, he is picking us up. Is your husband going to pick you up too? she says to Mummy.

No, we're getting the bus back, says Mummy.

But it's so far, says the lady, your husband really should come and pick you up.

He's away right now, says Mummy.

Oh, where is he?

He's abroad, Mummy says.

Oh, says the lady, looking all excited, do tell me *where*?

In Africa, says Mummy. The lady gasps.

Oh, *Africa* … such an interesting place … When he gets back, you really both must come around for dinner so he can meet my husband. My husband is an engineer. And such … *exotic* children … I'd love to find out more …

Goodbye, says Mummy. I'm sure I'll see you next week, she says. Mai and Amy, come on.

The next week, we are back again. The children are butterflies like before, then water, rainbows and sunsets, trees blowing in the wind.

Amy and I still stand and watch.

Hello again, says the mother from the week before, have they changed their minds then?

It's still sissy, I say.

Didn't you take them to the ballet? the lady asks Mummy. There was one on the weekend.

I haven't had time, says Mummy.

What a pity. Such lovely children, says the lady, looking at me. This one here … she looks so … *different*?

Mai has a different daddy from me, says Amy.

Go and dance, Amy, says Mummy.

How *interesting*, says the lady. So, is your husband back from Africa yet?

Not yet, says Mummy.

When will he be back?

It's taking longer than expected.

The ballet teacher comes up to us. Would the girls like to join in this time? she asks.

It's boring just watching everyone else going round and round, but I can't be a butterfly with Amy watching because she'll think I'm sissy. No thank you, I say. And you? the teacher asks Amy. Come on, join in for a little bit.

Amy runs off with the children in the room. She is a whirlwind spinning around and around and then she is a teapot, see its spout, tip me up and pour me out, and then the class ends.

Amy returns, smiling. You should have joined in, Mai, she says, it was nice.

I think to myself, maybe next time.

Well it was lovely to see you again, says the lady, hugging her little smiling pink-tutu blonde girl, we really must chat, maybe over coffee, you can tell me everything. And perhaps, when your husband gets back … we can do dinner at my place? The woman pauses. That is, if …?

I'm sorry, we have to go now, says Mummy.

But my dear, wait, says the lady. We haven't—

We really must rush, says Mummy, we'll miss our transport. If we're late for the first bus, we'll miss the second … And Mummy gathers our things and takes our hands and she pulls us both fast, out of the door.

We get to the bus stop, everyone out of breath.

I am wasting my money, says Mummy. If you two just stand there like dummies every class saying it's sissy, and on top of that I have to put up with that awful woman who only asks questions

54

so she can gossip with her friends about me living in the council area and how exotic my children are, and where is my husband, and how wonderful her daughter is who she can afford to take to the ballet all the time, and if you won't dance, there's no point me paying money for you to learn.

Amy danced, I say.

That was for five minutes at the end. And you didn't dance at all, says Mummy.

I want to do real dancing like tango and jive and go to parties like Granddad does, I say.

That's it, says Mummy. I'm not taking you back again.

At home, Amy and me play at being ballet dancers.

We are dancing, flying ballet dancers and we leap from bed to bed flying through the air. We spin around and dive onto the floor. It's fun. We pretend we are real ballet dancers, lifting our legs high up in the air like the picture books, until we fall over. But we are never butterflies.

I have two boyfriends at school. One is called Timothy. He is fair haired and good-looking, and the other one is John, who is a bit slow and tubby with dark hair. They are best friends in class. John is still on the beginner readers and Timothy is on the advanced series. When I grow up I'm going to marry both of them. Timothy is lively and funny and outgoing, so I'm going to go to parties with him, and John is going to stay back and do the cooking and cleaning because he likes to stay at home. They both agree it is the best solution.

Miss Brown is always giving me stars for my work and when we get three stars in our exercise books we get a sweet and there is a star for every page of correct work, so I am always getting sweets. I share my sweets with my boyfriends and they both love me very much because they don't get as many sweets as I do for their work, especially John who doesn't get many at all.

I play kiss-chase with them both at break time. Just them and me.

I am laughing. The sun sparkles on the playground like a dancer tiptoeing across and all the children are like frogs in a lily pond. The laughter, the sun sparkling on the grey of the concrete, the blue sky and the groups of girls turning upside down in the sun, knickers flashing as they stand on their hands – I can see your knickers, I can see your knickers, shout the boys, and we race around screaming and laughing. The playground goes on and on, along the white lines and hopscotch squares, up to the grass, where we climb up to sit in a row along the metal bar of the climbing frame, dangling our legs:

Ten green bottles
Standing on the wall
And if one green bottle
Should accidentally fall …

And then we swing upside down and hang head downwards in upside-down land watching the playground, so that the sky is an ocean and the grass is green sky and everyone is racing around like a whirlwind, the mad rush between lessons where so much energy has built up sitting still that we have to run it out, scream it out, a wild screaming flock of butterflies released into the sun on a crazy dance through the playground, the girls playing hopscotch, groups of boys running, arms outstretched, as aeroplanes, the fresh-smelling grass where we lie and roll.

I open my arms hanging upside down, swinging in the air, and I am flying, free, like a bird.

A bird falls from the sky at home. It has flown into the window, smack bang against the glass, says Mummy, the poor thing is stunned, maybe its neck is broken, she doesn't know. A young bird, a sparrow, says Mummy. She puts it in a shoebox with some warm material, but the bird dies after two days and I see Mummy is sorry for it. I tried to save it, says Mummy, I tried to save it, why did it have to die, why do things have to die, why can't anything work out right? and she wipes the tears away from her eyes, but they keep running down her face, even though she keeps wiping them away.

Mummy takes the bird and we have a funeral for it in the garden under the hedge, buried in the shoebox. And now I know why Nana didn't come back again. Things curl up and die. Death is when something stops moving and being and cannot fly any more. They fly into windows, like birds, and this squeezes the life out of them. They are free and then time ends, and they do not move any more.

3

Shimmering

There are candles, bright lights lighting up the dark, the smell of wax mixed with their brightness so the flame and smell become one. Mummy puts the candles beside the bath. Night lights, Mummy says.

Bloody hell, not another electricity strike, Mummy says, when the darkness comes suddenly. Don't move. Amy and I stand in the dark wrapped in towels until Mummy comes back and the sudden bright ferocious light of the candles dazzles our eyes until we can make out shapes again, and there is Mummy and the bath walls. The light flickers around the bathroom where the steam from the bath reflects the light from the wall surfaces, the strange new world the bathroom has become.

Here, she says, you can see now. Lights for your bath.

The water puddles and pools in the candlelight when we step in. But it's cosy.

Amy and me play shadow pictures with our hands and make birds flying and dogs with sharp teeth, and Amy puts her foot in the air and wiggles her toes.

What we see has a strange, comforting look, like the way things are seen in dreams, and the bath is a large glowing pond, where candle lights dance like fairy ballet dancers on its surface.

Mummy makes a fire. We huddle around the fireplace in our small front room, watching the coal burn, Amy, Mummy and me, watching the sparks drift up with the flames, the cold air around us. Mummy puts chestnuts on the fire. When they cook, their shells go black and they come out of the fire hot, hot, and their skins crack, but you must prick them first or they will explode. Then you must peel the shells off, and the nut inside is yellow and wrinkly and rubbery, like a little brain, Mummy says, but you must be careful and wait a little before you peel them, because you can burn your fingers. The cooked chestnuts smell nice but the nicest part is eating them, because they taste even better than they smell. Sometimes Mummy makes crumpets. We cook them on the end of a long fork until they go brown, and then we put butter on so it drips through to our fingers and we have to lick the butter off.

And then Mummy gets the small chocolate bar she keeps in the fridge, as a special treat, and we have a small piece each, and put the rest back for next time.

After we finish eating, we always start talking. Where's your favourite place, Mummy? we ask. Mexico, she says. We like the story. Mummy tells it staring into the fire. She tells it while we watch the big flames jump and shake and all the little coals tremble when the fire is crackling and it is cold outside.

Mexico was beautiful, Mummy says. The sun was always shining and the sea was crystal clear. The oranges were delicious, so many, they pulled the branches to the ground with their weight, especially the blood oranges, which were red inside, bright bright red, just like blood, and when you broke into them all the juice ran out down across your hands and stained them, sticky. We try to imagine oranges that are bright red inside. Like strawberries. You could smell the scent of oranges from far at night, Mummy says. It travelled for miles down from the orange groves, drifting like perfume through the warm evening air. The glowflies danced to the edge of the sea, and their reflections shone on the water with the reflections of the stars, and you couldn't tell the reflections and the sky and the sea apart.

I see pictures in the fire, dancing up and down. The heat of Mexico, as the flames burn brighter. The sea, crystal clear. I peer into the dark smoke, drifting upwards. I see the glowflies dancing in the sparks the fire makes, the puffed-up clouds in blue sky and then the sunset, in the burning coals among the red.

And the avocados were huge and delicious too, says Mummy. Ripe off the trees, still firm. You could hear the cicadas all night. I would have liked to have stayed in Mexico, says Mummy.

What's an avocado? says Amy, who likes food. It looks like a pear, says Mummy, but you don't eat the skin. It's oily inside. Ugh, says Amy. She only likes sweet things. Was the food you ate in Mexico nice? asks Amy. Yes, it was delicious, says Mummy. Hot – and we watch the flames rise and fall – and spicy.

I want to see a glowfly dance, I say.

What else was there? says Amy.

Well, lots of water, because I stayed in a village by the sea. The sea was so clear you could see right to the bottom. And you could snorkel and watch all the fish. The fish were all different colours, some even looked like rainbows.

BIG FISH?

Yes, those too.

SHARKS?

Only once …

TELL US ABOUT THE SHARK! Amy and me know the story. We shudder with delight.

Well, once, I was diving, and I had wandered off a bit from the group to go look at the coral, says Mummy. And then it went completely dark, because an enormous shadow passed over me.

I looked up, and I saw a giant fish hovering directly above me, it was huge, about nine foot long.

Were you scared?

Of course. I was petrified. I just kept very still and it stayed there looking down at me for a while, then it swam on past me. When I got to the surface the diving instructor said it was a huge barracuda, it must have been curious to see me swimming down there on my own and just wanted a closer look. He didn't want to say anything in case I panicked, and then it might have attacked me. I got such a shock.

Why did you go to Mexico, Mummy? I ask. I worked for a rich family for a year in America as an au pair, says Mummy. And when the work finished I went travelling on my own down to Mexico.

That's where you met my daddy, I say. That's right, says Mummy. He is handsome, isn't he? I ask, thinking of princes in storybooks. Yes, Mummy says, he was. He was very clever. He liked books, he was always reading. He studied English literature but he loved science fiction, he had science fiction books everywhere. His family in the Philippines was very rich, and he was travelling around the world on a year off after studying in university abroad. Did you love each other? I ask. Yes, says Mummy. We did. He was nice, but he had a short temper, he lost it quickly, and then it was over, just as fast. What's his name? I say. Mummy says something and I laugh because it sounds funny. That's not a name, I say, it sounds more like you have hiccups. It's his surname, says Mummy, his name is from another country so it sounds different. His first name was William.

Is my daddy rich and handsome too? asks Amy. He's very good-looking, says Mummy, but he's not generous with his money though. Your father has green eyes and dark hair, Mummy says to Amy. Your great-great-grandfather married an Indian princess when he lived in India, your great-great-grandmother. At least, that's what they say. He likes to read books too, doesn't he? says Amy. Not really, says Mummy. He is clever but he is lazy. He's very irresponsible. And self-centred. Mostly, he likes to go sailing, says Mummy.

At least my daddy married Mummy, says Amy. Mai's daddy didn't.

Mai's daddy did ask me to marry him, says Mummy, but I didn't want to, because I would have had to go and live with his family in the Philippines, says Mummy, and they are very different from me, and it is very far away and hot there and a long way from Granddad and Nana in England. And then I married Amy's father. It doesn't make much difference anyway, says Mummy, neither of them are here now.

Did you love my daddy too? asks Amy. Yes, says Mummy. But your daddy wasn't very nice to me. Mummy pokes the dying embers with the poker to bring them back to life. After we got married, he went to look for work in South Africa when you were still a little baby. We were meant to follow him out there, once he got the legalities sorted out, he said, because Mai is half-Filipino, it would be difficult for her to come. Well, I waited and waited, but he never sent the money to come over and he didn't come back. I think he met someone else instead. He arranged a divorce behind my back over there with a dodgy lawyer, and he did a dirty legal trick and got away with the bare minimum, because he arranged to pay hardly any maintenance. What's that? asks Amy. Money for your upkeep, says Mummy. I took it to the courts, but they said there is nothing I can do, because he lives in Africa. Then Mummy looks angry or sad or something because her cheeks go in a bit and she bites her lip and her eyes change like they are looking somewhere else and you can't see what she is feeling. She pokes the embers again as flames lick higher and higher.

Is my daddy sailing in Africa now? asks Amy.

Most likely, says Mummy.

Don't worry, says Amy. You've got both of us now instead, and we love you and you love us.

Yes, I'm very lucky to have you both, says Mummy, and she hugs us.

Mummy stares into the red of the coals as if she is seeing things in there. I look too, but I don't see much, only flames leaping around like dancers. I think of the fire and how hot it is and I think that must be what it is like in Mexico. I like the embers at the bottom, that glow red hot and then fade to white ash. Sometimes a coal falls out and Mummy puts it back with the tongs. She shows us how to make the fire with newspapers and matches, but we are not allowed to play with them on our own, we're too young, she says. I stare at the fire, all the flames dancing around. A piece of ash lifts up in the air, above the flames and then drifts up the chimney. We watch. The embers burn and we stare into them, me trying to see the Philippines, my sister South Africa. The places don't mean much to us, words that we spin into the air, like the flames that burn themselves out until they don't exist any more. We watch the fire burning and the flames disappearing, and even the tightness in Mummy's face loses itself in the light that flickers, and our thoughts disappear like dreams into the shapes of the firelight, more real than the stories of our fathers.

I don't want to go to the Philippines because it is hot and dusty, I'll stay right here by the fire. But Amy, she's always asking about her daddy. I don't see why Amy should even care, she's not going to see her daddy, he's not coming back. I'm quite happy with things as they are because I love Mummy and Amy and Granddad and they love me. I stare into the fire, and the fire stares back. What is a daddy? There's lots of them in stories, there's a lot of them around, but I've never met one. That's because your daddy is overseas. Oh. Over and seas. I know the sea. It is outside my school, the big waves crash and roll and it gets muddy if you go out too far. I stare out at it, and across the horizon there are people sailing and daddies I never knew. Where is overseas? It is the Philippines. What is the Philippines? I don't know. It is somewhere beyond where glowflies dance, writing messages in the dark, round and round in circles, places where I have never been.

I ask Mrs Willows the next-door neighbour where babies come from. She says that when two people love each other and get married a baby comes along, and Mrs Willows should know because she's very old. In my *Big Book of Animal Stories*, Mr Bear met Mrs Bear and they fell in love and they got married, and One Fine Day in spring, they opened the door and there was Baby Bear on the doorstep. I reckon that's what happened with my mummy and daddy, only when I got there my daddy had already left to go home to the Philippines.

So I tell Mrs Willows, my mummy and daddy must have loved each other so much that they didn't even have to get married, because I came along anyway, so I must be really, really special. And Mrs Willows looks at me and shakes her head, and says, this child, she's absolutely impossible.

Cold, ice, snow. Snowflakes fall. We catch them with our tongues, fast, sticking them out of our mouths for the flakes to land on, pink with cold, breath steaming from our mouths. Snow tastes like ice cream without the sugar, and it makes your tongue go numb.

Cold, ice, snow, and the flakes fall like large white pieces of paper and cover the garden in white, the chicken coop snowed over and the wire netting ridged with icy layers of frosting like a lace blanket and the top of the chicken hut solid white. The snow swallows the hedges where the ladybirds were in summer, the lavender bushes barren and brown.

When the snow comes it looks as if the world has gone to sleep, and we must rush out to wake it up. As if the sky opened up overnight and poured it all down. Cold, ice cold, but we don't feel it. Over breakfast, Amy and me watch the snow falling, noses pressed against the windows, breathing steam onto the glass and drawing patterns with our fingers as the snow gets thicker and thicker, and the garden disappears more and more. I stare out at the garden, wondering why it has grown so large, stretching forever, and whether the snow will spoil if I walk on it. Then Amy and I pull on our coats and gloves and wellington boots and rush outside across its crunchiness, kicking footfalls in the air, the snow so crisp our boots are hardly wet, and we run our hands through the strange pile of frozen sky. You can smell the snow. It smells fresh and washed, like water. The snow comes up to our ankles. It's dry, very dry, and crumbly. All the time, the fresh, watery smell, and then we are playing with the other children in the street, pounding hand-patted snowballs at each other's faces, screaming with snow-filled mouths and ears, and snow-filled minds. We shout and roll and squash and shape the snow into balls, in scooped-up handfuls, until our hands go numb and red and we rush in again for tea, stamping and stomping the snow off, putting our black wellies on the low white shelf Mummy painted inside the kitchen door, hanging our soggy mittens to dry.

The snow is never so thick again for a long time. The chickens jump from foot to foot when we feed them, as if the cold soil is too much to bear, cluttering and clucking. The lump on Henrietta's foot has chewed her leg into a swollen ball making her jump even more frenetically on the frozen earth as she pecks for scraps. It's an infection or growth, says Mummy, and Amy worries about it, trying to will the lump into nothing, and Mummy says there is not much we can do.

The guinea pigs die in the cold, because the shed door blew open and the snow and the cold came in. We come out in the morning and the guinea pigs are frozen. Stiff. Amy is crying. They're dead, they're dead. The snow has iced over the cage, solidified the wire walls that Mummy built. The plastic cover hanging over the sides crackles when we move it. The guinea pigs lie huddled together at the bottom of the cage. They have to be pulled out of the mounds of snow. It was too cold for them, says Mummy. The frost killed them. We should have brought the cage inside. Amy is crying, loud.

I don't cry because I'm Amy's big sister and big sisters don't cry. But I don't quite understand how it happened. How come they die, they curl up in the corner of the cage, and the life goes out of them, so in the morning they are just two sad frozen shapes, half buried in snow? All I know is our guinea pigs no longer run around, and are still and quiet. We bury the guinea pigs in the garden, in the snow and the earth, in two shoeboxes, next to the bird that died a while ago. Amy cries and she says a special prayer for Snow White and Sherbet. I'm sorry, she says, I'm sorry you both died. I hope you have a nice time in heaven. I hope there is a lot of fresh grass and nice things to eat and at least you'll be warm up in heaven where the sun is.

Guinea pigs don't go to heaven, I say.

Guinea pigs have their own heaven, says Mummy.

Amy's still crying. I still don't cry because then Amy will say I'm a sissy and big sisters are not allowed to be sissy, because I have to be big and strong and there's nothing we can do about it anyway, because that's just how things are.

Mrs Willows says we are in for a cold spell. Mummy digs a path from the front door to our gate and it goes slippery with ice. In the road, big machines come and scoop the snow up, and put salty grains from big red boxes on the side of the road that make the road go orange and make slush around our boots on the pavement. But nobody pours salt or orange sand onto our garden. Nobody clears a path through it. Over the week the snow gets thicker and thicker and we wake each morning to see the previous day's footsteps covered over with a smooth fresh layer on top, as if it had never been touched. First we make a snowman. By the end of the week it has drowned in new layers of snow. Amy and me scoop snow up and throw it across the garden at each other, until I get a new idea. Let's make an igloo, I say. A snow house. Like the Eskimos. Then we can live in it.

It's a big task. First we make a huge pile of snow, like a sandcastle, enormous and white, digging and scooping the snow with our spades and buckets into the wheelbarrow to carry it from the back to the front, adding to the huge mountain of snow in the front garden, growing bigger than ourselves. What are you making? ask the people who pass by. They are curious. An igloo, we say. An igloo? They laugh. We don't care. The next day we add even more snow and the mound grows fat and round at the sides. Then we pat the snow down with our seaside spades for ages until its sides are smooth and unwrinkled, making the mound hard and solid. Next, we dig away the inside, making a single doorway, first a mouth, then a cave, then a whole hollow, shifting the snow out in our buckets. It is getting late but Amy and me carry on working and we are still working as the sky greys and the hedge becomes a smudge at the edge of the garden.

Finally, we have a shell of hard, tough snow and a snow home big enough for the two of us to nearly stand inside, grown enormous, perfect. We sit inside, feeling special.

Let's pat the walls down one last time, I say, you do the outside and I'll do the inside.

I hear the pat pat of Amy's spade outside. It goes on and on, the night growing dark behind the smudged hedge, the snow beginning to glow with that strange light it captures when all else turns dim. It is so dark I have to squint to see as I pat at the inside wall. Then I think of a new idea, of making a window, so we can peer out at the sky in the morning when we have breakfast.

It is so dark, I can hardly see what I am doing. I push my spade through the wall and feel it come out the other side, as the snow packed into the thick wall follows, losing strength, and the igloo opens its huge mouth and swallows us up. The walls become sky, and the window the sky, soft packed snow caving in on my head, crumbling onto my arms, pushing me to the ground, enveloping me in sudden cold harshness. And I fall with the snow, under the snow, and the snow under me, snow on my shoulders, on my hair, on my face.

Are you all right? I lift my head up and look at Amy. The igloo lies around us in pieces, a mound of snow again, on my back, arms and legs, and around Amy, sitting with her spade still raised.

It fell down, I say. You look funny, she says, covered in snow. You too, I laugh. She laughs back. Then we sit in the snow, rolling back with laughter, looking at the huge mound of snow around us, after two days' hard work. We laugh in the dark until the wetness of the snow creeps into our clothes and we feel stiff with cold. Then we go in for tea. We can rebuild it tomorrow, I say.

I don't tell Amy I was making a window. But overnight it gets warmer and in the morning there is only a melting pile of snow to play snowballs with, and a memory.

After winter comes spring. Snow melts into snowdrops and into daffodils and young lettuces and tomato plants in the rim of the garden where Mummy grows vegetables. The coal man comes less often. The fire lies dead in the grate, chestnuts forgotten, the room warmed by the sun which appears more and more often, and the neighbours' garden still doesn't have vegetables.

Amy's chicken Henrietta dies from the lump on its foot, Mummy says the disease spread up her leg. Henrietta is buried under the hedge among the young grass and dandelion plants with the guinea pigs and the dead sparrow. Amy says a prayer to ask if the chicken and sparrow and guinea pigs can all go to the same heaven and live together. Amy cries for days, then forgets as the grass grows taller.

I don't remember him arriving. Somehow the memory of him remains like a smell, musty, dark, like a shadow, like a lean shadow. He arrived as a smell does: something difficult to define; something that crept into our lives; slow, insipid, surreptitious. Or else he arrived suddenly – appearing as if from nowhere. I don't remember when he came. I don't remember how he got there.

When we had babysitting, was that when he arrived?

Mummy used to read us stories but now we have a tape recorder. We are allowed to play one chapter every night before we go to sleep. On the tape recorder Mummy recorded Brer Rabbit stories. We have Winnie the Pooh too. And fairy stories. Sometimes we cheat and play an extra chapter but Mummy doesn't seem to notice.

Fee Fi Fo Fum ... I smell the blood ...

Jack had a seed and he planted it and it went up to the sky. When he climbed up, there was a big giant who chased him down again.

Cinderella went to the ball and although she was poor and had ragged clothes she had glass shoes and a fairy godmother and married a prince. Paddington Bear was lost at the station and the message said, Please Look After This Bear. The Wolf pretended he was Granny because he wanted to eat Little Red Riding Hood. Come closer, he said, so I can see you better. The Wicked Witch had a house of sweets and the two children ate from it, but really it was a trick and she was going to eat them up. The Three Little Pigs hid in their house, and the Wolf was outside. I'll huff and I'll puff and I'll blow your house down, the Wolf said.

At night Amy and me leap into bed, taking a run first, then a jump, just in case there's anything underneath the bed that might grab our feet. We're secretly scared that, if we don't jump, then one day there might be something under there that isn't one of us.

Mrs Willows is babysitting us. Joan, her sixteen-year-old daughter, built like my pencil box, square and solid, with short brown hair cut to her shoulders, is babysitting us too. Joan stands with her arms folded and just stares at us, like she is going to sit on us and squash us flat, which is what they might mean by babysitting.

I bet you don't know where your mummy is this evening, says Joan, and she snickers. She's gone out to have a Good Time. And I bet you don't know what that means, and she snickers again.

Quiet, Joan, says Mrs Willows and she gives her A Look and Joan shuts up, but Joan is still grinning.

Mrs Willows' house is different from ours. It has a lot of things in it, like little china animals and a real wooden rocking chair and everything has patterned cloth covers on and the sitting room smells of armchairs. Mrs Willows says Amy and I can't play on the furniture, we must keep ourselves busy and read quietly.

I am swinging on the rocking chair. Stop swinging on that, child, says Mrs Willows, you'll break it. But it's a rocking chair, I say, you're meant to swing on it.

Not standing on the bottom leg, you're not. It will break, child.

No it won't, I reply. See? It's not breaking.

If you don't stop that immediately, you'll get a smack, says Mrs Willows. I stop, but after a while I start swinging again. What's wrong with you, child? says Mrs Willows. Can't you keep still for just one moment? No, I say. I know I'm on the slippery slope downhill, but there's nothing I can do. Mrs Willows hates me and I hate her. I swing so hard I nearly take off.

Why do you keep doing that? asks Mrs Willows. I want to go pee, I say. The toilet is upstairs, says Mrs Willows. No, I want to go to our one at home, I say. Don't be silly, child, says Mrs Willows, your mother is out for the evening and I'm not going all the way next door just so you can use the toilet. Joan will take you upstairs to show you where the toilet is. But I want to go home, I say, and swing on the rocking chair again. Stop that, says Mrs Willows. You will break the rocking chair. If you don't stop, Joan and her boyfriend won't take you to the fair tomorrow. Why can't you be good and sit quietly like your little sister?

Mai, Mummy says we must be good, says Amy, looking up from the floor, where she is reading her book.

Last time I went to the fair I won a china parrot because I got three balls down a hole. But I feel the words coming out of my mouth and I can't stop them. I don't want to go anyway, I say. Not with you.

Mrs Willows' eyes narrow. Right then, we won't take you, you're not going to the fair. I mean it, says Mrs Willows. You're the most impossible child I have ever known, a total vagabond.

If you don't go to the toilet it will turn into rocks inside you, says Mrs Willows.

It's not true, I say. You're an Old Wife and I shouldn't believe you.

Mrs Willows' eyes are so narrow now that I stop rocking the chair immediately. See, Mai, says Amy, you can't come to the fair with me now. Certainly not, says Mrs Willows, that will teach you. Now go straight up to the toilet with Joan before it turns into rocks inside you and we have to take you to hospital. I'll have no more trouble from you.

The next day I stand at the gate with Mrs Willows and watch Amy's head at the back of the car as it drives away. Amy turns her face back at me and stares with her big brown eyes and short dark brown hair that sticks out and goes down to her shoulders. Amy's eyes look sad. We always do everything together. It serves you right, says Mrs Willows.

Me and Mrs Willows wave goodbye, and I watch Amy's head getting smaller and smaller as it goes down the road. Amy's eyes watch me and then she turns her head back and I can only see her sticking-out hair, blurred behind the car's back window, and the car turns the corner and then it is gone.

Amy brings me a stick of rock from the fair. It was nice, she says, I had a good time. Why were you so silly, Mai? Why didn't you stop swinging on Mrs Willows' chair? You could have come with us.

I don't answer Amy because I don't know. I only know that Mrs Willows thinks I'm the worst child she has ever known, and when Joan said I bet you don't know where your mummy is, she was laughing at us and had a funny look in her eyes and I don't like either of them at all.

We are playing in the garden. We hear the tinkling sound and jump up to see. The ice-cream van has come and parked outside the wall of our garden in the street, its bright colours gleaming in the sun. Amy and I run and shout towards the house to ask Mummy for money to be the first in the queue for ice cream. All the other children in the street are running to their homes for money too.

His red car is driving up the street.

He sees us and winds down his front window. He looks angry. Stop that! he shouts out the window. We stop dead in our tracks, still in the garden. He screeches his car to the kerb to park it, behind the ice-cream van, and leaps out over the garden wall and comes towards us. Why are you running and shouting? he shouts angrily. We were just going to ask Mummy for money for ice creams, we say. He glares at us. Stay inside the garden, he says. You are not to run and shout. He goes inside the house, through the front door.

All the other children are lined up to buy ice creams in front of the ice-cream van. They look back at Amy and me staring at them in the queue over the garden wall.

Amy and me wait, and watch, and are very quiet, as one by one the children queue up and leave with their ice creams. The ice-cream van starts its motor again, and then, tinkling, it is gone.

His red car arrives on Fridays.

Red car, red car. When we see it, something goes cold inside us, and we stop living. When we see the car, we stop playing and go very quiet. We hear its engine coming up the road, creeping along almost noiselessly around the corner, sense its redness, freezing us still in the garden, ears perked like dogs. Then it stops outside our house.

When he arrives silence falls.

Silence falls. Silence in the garden, and our playing is quieter, hidden. He's coming, we whisper to each other.

The weekend stays quiet, intimidated. Like a weekend that wants to pass quickly, vanish before it started.

He has pale skin and dark but balding hair, and eyes that look into you. Eyes that are angry, but calm. Eyes that look like they are trying to grip onto something, but we're not sure what.

His name is Rashid, says Mummy. He comes from a very high-up family in Morocco, and he is a chemical engineer, and he is very clever because he went to university when he was very young. He's not religious, because he's been in England most of the time. I met him at a work function at Granddad's company.

Because he works in London he can only come here on weekends, says Mummy. Mummy looks happy. He brings nice chocolates, says Mummy, here, let's have some.

Mummy is out. Rashid tells me off for talking too loud. I call him a pig.

What did you call me? he says.

A pig, I say. This time my voice has shrunk so much I don't recognise it coming out of my throat.

He lifts me high in the air and takes me upstairs and he throws me down on my bed. He's hitting me over and over. I feel it on my legs, my sides, my arms, hands falling and falling, everywhere. It doesn't stop. I am screaming.

You will never call me a pig again, Rashid says.

I look at his eyes and they are pink, little red veins all over them, and the vein in the middle of his head stands out and beads of sweat roll down his forehead. He looks more like a pig than I have ever seen him before.

This is what you will get, he says. And next time, it will be worse.

But I say nothing, because I am just crying while his palms rain down on me.

Now we are mice. Little animals. We play outside, where freedom is. Inside, on weekends, it feels like we are in a cage. Creeping.

I don't think Mummy knows how quiet Rashid makes us.

4

Shadows

Fresh grass, fresh daisies, yellow dandelions and hedgerows green with leaves.

Amy and I go to Granddad's. Mummy isn't with us. Your mother is getting married, says Granddad. Rashid is going to be your stepfather, he says.

Amy and I make a lot of noise, and won't stay in bed. We creep downstairs again and hide behind Granddad's chair. He is watching football, with a glass of beer he takes sips from on the side of the chair. We giggle quietly behind the orange plastic armchair but soon we get bored of sitting still. So we giggle loudly so he can find us. Who's there! cries Granddad, then he realises it's us. Then we run up the stairs, past Granddad's fish tank, giggling again, with Granddad chasing us.

A few days later we go home again. Now Mummy is married to Rashid. She is married but she doesn't look any different.

We have his surname now. Akbar.

We still don't see him much because he still works in London and only comes on weekends.

I am big enough to take Amy to school on my own now. Amy is one year below me. Mummy says I must always hold Amy's hand, especially when we cross the road, and we must do our highway code. We reach the path that takes us to school. On the pavement there is a box of matches. We open it and there are matches inside the box. Go on, says Amy, dare you. Mummy says we mustn't play with fire, I say. Dare you anyway, says Amy.

So I take the match and strike it against the box. The match head flares up on my second attempt. We both gasp when the match bursts into fire and I drop it, frightened, and jump back. Put it out! shrieks Amy, but I don't know how to. The match burns away on the concrete, into a twisted charcoal stick. You can still see a little of the wood at the one end, pale and cut into straight box-edges before it turns into black dust.

Don't play with fire. The words echo in our heads and we leave the rest of the matches behind.

We could have caught the concrete alight, says Amy, and then the whole street would have been up in flames. And everybody would have died and there would be nobody left.

At school they collect cans of tinned food, dried food, strange things, we don't know what they are. Go home and ask for things for Harvest Festival, says the teacher. It's to add to the collection for the old people and the poor. For the needy. The pile of cans grows, like a treasure heap. We go to Mummy and she gives us two cans to take in.

When the Harvest Festival comes, our school takes us to a big church. The church is filled with flowers, dried and fresh, all along the edges. The church is huge, the ceiling so high above us. At the end of the church are our cans all piled up in a big heap. Amy and I try to see the ones we put in, but there are too many. We sing hymns from school assembly, and everyone keeps getting up and sitting down again. Amy and I copy the people praying and getting up and down. There is a man standing at the front who talks a lot and speaks of giving and helping other people. I wonder why we are all here inside this big strange building with all these flowers and tin cans. Then the man at the front says God wants us to spend more time in church. I like singing the songs, but God must be strange, I think. He wants people to stay inside singing songs to him all the time instead of outside helping people. The ladies behind me sing so high they hurt my ears. Amy and me get to take some cans to an old lady near us and she gives us sixpence. Mummy sends us back again to return it. You are meant to be giving things, not taking, says Mummy.

Mummy swells up in her tummy. We have to keep feeling Mummy's stomach and listening for things. We don't really know what we're listening for.

I can hear your dinner going down, says Amy and she laughs.

It is early evening and we are in bed, falling asleep. The light goes on and Mummy comes into our room. Amy and I sit up, wondering what Mummy is doing. Mummy pulls our suitcases out from on top of the wardrobe, then places them on the end of Amy's bed and sits on the end of Amy's bed with them.

Mummy is crying.

She opens the drawer and takes out some of our clothes and folds them. Then she puts some of them in a suitcase. She keeps taking clothes from the drawer and folding them away into our suitcases, still crying. The room is so quiet. Only the sound of Mummy crying, and the clothes being folded.

We stare at her.

Why are you crying, Mummy? we ask.

Mummy keeps sorting slowly through the drawers, tears running down her cheeks. She keeps packing. Then she stops and sits still on the bed, her hands still clutching at some of our clothes, the tears rolling down her cheeks even more. We want to catch them with our hands and put them back again.

What's wrong, Mummy? we ask. But she just keeps crying.

Is it us, Mummy? I ask. Did we do something wrong?

Mummy shakes her head. We're glad it's not us. But something's wrong. We can't believe she is crying. Mummy never cries.

The bedroom door opens and Mummy jumps suddenly and so do we.

He is there. Rashid. He stares at us, little eyes looking at us. Looking evil into us. As if he's suspicious. He looks around the room, at us, then at Mummy, then at the suitcases on Amy's bed. His eyes rest on the suitcases.

What are you doing? he asks Mummy. His voice is sharp, like a razor. It cuts into us with its sharpness. Where are you going?

Nothing, Mummy says. I'm just packing away some of the children's summer clothes. Her face is still full of tears but she looks away.

Are you trying to leave?

No, you can see, Rashid, says Mummy in a quiet voice, I'm just packing some of the children's clothes away.

Rashid looks at us. The silence is thick and cold, like snow, only thicker and colder.

I hate you, says Amy. You made my mummy cry.

The silence lasts for a very long second. Then Rashid steps forwards and raises his arm sideways. He hits Amy hard, so she falls sideways on the bed. Mummy jumps.

Amy's crying now. She cries loud, not quiet like Mummy was.

Please, Rashid, says Mummy. Please, not them too. She's only a little girl. She saw I was upset and is just trying to protect me, she doesn't know what she's saying. Please leave her alone. She doesn't know any better.

Rashid points his finger at Mummy. His finger looks frightening. Menacing. A big pointing finger hovering over us. Shut up, woman, he says. Or you're next.

He points his finger at Amy. You won't insult me again, he says. Then he walks out of the room and closes the door behind him and now it is very quiet.

Amy is quiet because she's too frightened to cry. I think Mummy is too frightened to cry as well.

Mummy hugs Amy. I'm very sorry, Amy, says Mummy. I'm so sorry you got hurt. I couldn't stop him, because if I had tried he might have hurt you more.

Amy leans forwards on her bed.

Don't worry, Mummy, says Amy, Rashid's a pig. We'll look after you. I don't care if he hits me anyway, we won't let him hurt you.

Yes, Mummy, don't worry, I say. We'll protect you.

We don't really know what to do. We haven't seen Mummy cry like this before, quiet, like she's scared. Why was she crying?

Mummy keeps packing the suitcases for a while, but I can see her hands are shaking. Amy falls asleep in her bed. Mummy locks the cases and then puts them back on top of the wardrobe. I am lying in bed drifting off to sleep when she quietly puts out the light and closes the door.

From now on, Rashid is always a pig. But Amy and I only whisper the word. In case he hears us. And now all the noises in the corridor at night become his footsteps. And all the cars we hear in the road are red until we see them. And the house when he comes on weekends is more and more like a cage.

The first time I noticed something was wrong, Mummy says, was when he was working in the garden and I brought him a bowl of hot soup. He said it was too hot. And he threw it at me. He missed, and the bowl hit the garden path and smashed, and soup went everywhere, all over the garden.

81

Why, Mummy?

Because he's like that. Because he said it was too hot. I should have realised, says Mummy. I could have got out then. But I didn't realise, I thought he was just in a bad mood. It was shortly before we were married.

Our favourite conversation in bed at night is three wishes.

If you had three wishes, what would you wish?

No. 1. That Rashid would die in a horrible car accident and we would all live happily ever after with Mummy.

No. 2. That we wake up and there is a huge box of salt and vinegar crisps under the bed which, however much we ate, would never get empty.

No. 3 is always the same. We wish for as many wishes as we want forever for the rest of our lives.

The coal-bunker is a big grey stone thing, with a wooden lid made of planks fixed together. The lid slopes down and the coal is inside. The wood is warm, damp, wet smelling and friendly. The stone feels cold to touch, granite, rough under your fingers. The lid rests on the edges of the concrete walls on the sides, but it doesn't touch the front wall, so there's a gap you can look through.

I am standing, looking out at the snow flakes that fall, fall, fall … through the narrow slit in front of my eyes. It is cold. The dry coal crunches powdery under my feet when I move. There are tears on my cheeks, drying in the cold wind that occasionally blows through the narrow slit. The world is getting whiter outside.

I am angry but he won't get at me. I bite my lower lip and fight against the tear that swells in my right eye – I feel it swell up and turn cold on my eyelid, then spill over onto my cheek. It runs down my cheek, and I try to fight the next one that comes. At least here I am safe, in the coal-bunker. I can stand and peer out, the lid just above my head. The lid is too heavy to move by myself. Outside, it looks colder. It is so black in here, so white out there. And the snow is falling, falling.

It is my sixth birthday. We had spaghetti with tomato sauce for lunch, and I was tipping back on my chair, and Rashid said to stop. He said to stop but I kept tipping backwards until my chair fell over and I fell on the floor. He picked me up and I was crying. He lifted me up in the air like a tennis ball, up from the floor where the chair was lying, my spaghetti meal still on the table, and took me out of the kitchen. He took me outside and put me in the coal-bunker.

Why are you doing that? said Mummy. She needs to be punished, said Rashid. It's her birthday, said Mummy. She needs to learn to behave properly, said Rashid.

Outside the flakes fall thicker in the garden. I can see the corner of the garden on the left where the hedge starts. The hedge is getting white too. Maybe the snow will creep up around the bunker and come in through the slit. Above me, the wooden lid must be collecting snow. Now, the tears have stopped and my cheeks feel cold where the tears ran, their lines like icy bars down my face. I watch snow through the narrow slit, drifting in the air.

And then the lid lifts, and he takes me out again.

Amy and I go upstairs and Mummy is crying in bed.

What is wrong? we ask. Are you ill?

No, says Mummy, get Mrs Willows please, as soon as you can.

We get Mrs Willows and she talks to Mummy and then she says Amy and I have to play in the garden.

Our little brother Matti is born at home. Mrs Willows tells me and Amy to go upstairs and there he is in the cot, a little baby with dark wet curly hair and eyes fast asleep. A big head. Mummy smiles at us from the bed.

Amy and I stare at Matti. Where did he come from?

This is your baby brother, says Mrs Willows.

Is he all ours? asks Amy.

He is all of yours, says Mrs Willows. He is here to stay with you.

Will he be staying long? we ask.

Of course he will, says Mrs Willows. He's your little brother.

Is that true, Mummy? we ask. We look at Mummy. She looks strange. Sleepy. Mummy nods.

Where did he come from?

The stork brought him, says Mrs Willows.

How come he arrived straight in the cot and he wasn't left on the doorstep like Baby Bear in my *Big Book of Animal Stories*? I ask.

The upstairs window was open so the stork didn't have to use the doorstep, he flew in through the window, says Mrs Willows.

Where's the stork then?

The stork came and left quickly, says Mrs Willows. It can't hang around all day. It has lots of other little babies to deliver.

Amy and I were in the garden the whole time and we never saw any stork fly through the window. We would definitely have seen it, if a stork came with a baby, I say.

It doesn't matter how he got here, says Mrs Willows. He's your little brother and he's come to stay. Your mummy's very tired, she says, you must let her rest. Why is she so tired, says Amy, she's been in bed. Just be good and help your mummy as much as possible, by going downstairs and playing quietly, says Mrs Willows.

Rashid wouldn't have anything to do with me, says Mummy to us afterwards. I told him I was in labour and he said I was making it up. He went out and left me here on my own. Then it got too late. If it hadn't been for you two telling Mrs Willows, says Mummy, I wouldn't even have had the midwife she called.

Our little brother Matti is very small, with tiny fingers. Mummy says he is a big baby and has all his hair. We stick our hands through the cot, to let him hold our fingers. Tight. Then he laughs at us. Big brown eyes. Lots of brown curling hair.

Now I know how babies are made. Two people get married then magic happens in the air and a new baby forms. Only you don't know where it will appear.

Matti is sweet. He is our little baby brother.

I am walking down the beach in South Greenstead behind everyone else. In front of me is Rashid pushing the pushchair with Matti inside, Mummy, and Amy holding her hand. The wind has knocked branches from the bushes and trees. They lie on the sand, sand-covered themselves. Some of the branches have fir cones on, small black ones on brittle leafless black twigs.

I gather the fir cones up and put them in a plastic carrier bag I find on the beach.

Hurry up, says Rashid. Or we will leave you behind.

It is a long walk. We have walked far from where we usually bathe in summer.

Are we walking to Southend? I ask.

No, Mummy and Rashid say. Southend is much further away.

We walk and walk and now we have turned around and are walking home. Come on, says Rashid, hurry up. I try to keep up with them, gathering fir cones from the sand, but, slowly, I fall behind.

I walk past a giant branch that has been knocked down from the trees by the wind. It is huge, black, covered in fir cones. I begin to fill my plastic bag. I see Mummy and Rashid walking onwards in front of me. They're not too far away to run after, so I decide to collect just a few more fir cones. I fill my bag quickly, feeling it get heavier and heavier. I decide to clear another branch of cones so I can have a full bag. Then I look up, the plastic bag heavy in my hands. They've gone.

I walk fast along the beach trying to catch up with them. I can see into the distance ahead of me but I can't see anyone. Maybe they turned off the beach onto the road. The wind keeps howling and the waves keep breaking. Where are they? There's a heaviness in the air as it starts to get grey. And colder. I keep walking on and on but I still can't see them.

Another family comes up behind me. A mummy and a daddy and three children, walking their dog. They smile.

Have you seen my mummy and stepfather and sister and little brother? I ask.

They ask me to describe them. They say, no. Do you want us to take you home? they ask. We'll drive you back in the car.

So I say, yes. Mummy says be careful with strangers, but this is a family and they don't behave like strangers, they're nice. And I don't know my way home and I don't know where I am and soon it will be dark.

We'll take you through town, say the family. Just tell us if you see them on the way anywhere. Our car is just down here. We walk away from the beach down a side road, and I get into their car with them, holding my bag of fir cones in my hands. They start driving into town and keep asking if different people on the street are my parents. But they're not.

Then we drive to a junction and the car in front of us is Rashid's car. I can see Mummy and Rashid, and Amy staring out the side window at me, and Matti in the baby seat. Amy points and waves as I peer out of the car I am sitting in with the dog and the family's three children. Amy smiles.

The people in the front get out of the car and talk to Mummy and Rashid for a bit. I hear Mummy and Rashid saying thank you to them, and sorry for the nuisance.

You must be very relieved to have her back, say the parents.

I am really sorry for the inconvenience we have caused you, says Rashid, we are very grateful. Then Rashid tells me to get into his car.

I say thank you to the nice family. I feel sorry to leave them.

We looked everywhere for you, says Mummy. I was really worried. We were driving up and down looking for you.

Mummy was really worried, says Amy.

I get into the car and sit inside its redness, on the back seat. The other family's car has gone away. It is very quiet inside the car now. Rashid drives on for a bit, then stops the car at the traffic lights. He turns around. I told you to keep up with us, he says. Why didn't you keep up?

I'm sorry, I say. I was collecting fir cones and when I looked up you were gone.

Where are the fir cones? he asks.

In my plastic bag, I say.

Give the bag to me, says Rashid.

I hand the bag full of fir cones to Rashid over the seat. He takes it in his hand. Then he rolls down the car window and throws the bag out, hard as he can. All the fir cones shoot out of the bag and spread themselves down the tarmac on the road.

You are going to bed as soon as you get home, without dinner, says Rashid. You are not supposed to go up to other families and get in their cars. They will think we can't look after you.

Well, at least she's safe and sound now, Rashid, says Mummy. That's what matters.

She is not going to embarrass me in front of other people like that again, says Rashid.

You don't have to punish her, says Mummy, she didn't mean

it. Don't you think she's been punished enough just by being lost?

Rashid doesn't say anything. Mummy is quiet, as if she's scared.

The lights change to green. As we move on, I look back at the fir cones spread all down the road. Other cars are driving across them now. I watch as the fir cones crack flat as the tyres go over them. Crack. Crack. I bite my lip. I won't cry, but a couple of tears roll down my face.

Amy leans sideways and whispers to me. It was funny seeing you in that other car with the children and the dog. It was like you were part of their family, not ours. I smile at her through my tears, but I still think of all the fir cones across the road, getting squashed. I think how nice the family was to me.

I have to go straight to bed with no dinner. I lie in bed, hungry, thinking of my fir cones and hugging Socks the cat.

Socks the cat doesn't like Rashid. When he comes in the house she runs outside. Mummy says she saw him kick Socks once and Socks is too smart to take any more. Socks is so warm and friendly, a snuggly cat with a white diamond of a chin and dark black fur. White socks that pitter-patter on their way out. Socks can tell when things are good, or sad. When things are sad she climbs into my bed and hides under the blankets with me, her paws and black fur snuggled close.

Mrs Brown my teacher says that in the nearby town the main road is a Roman road. The Romans wore leather skirts with flaps on that we colour in our colouring books, and wore helmets and only ever marched in straight lines, so their roads were always straight.

Why were they straight? I ask.

So they could get where they wanted to as quickly as possible, says Mrs Brown.

But didn't they want to stop and look around?

The Romans were just like that, says Mrs Brown. They didn't have time to look at the countryside. They were busy conquering it.

What's the point of conquering it if they don't get to see it? I ask. That's silly.

They just wanted to get where they wanted to as fast as they could, says Mrs Brown.

Rashid always walks as fast as he can, as if he is in a rush to get somewhere. And I think if he could, he would conquer everything.

I don't like Rashid. In his eyes there is evil. Hidden around the outer rims of the white parts and deep within the pupils.

And his eyes watch …

They watch me all the time.

Matti is bigger now and he can stand in the cot and look at us. He's wobbly on his legs. He wears a big nappy that pushes his legs out, so he looks bow-legged. He always pulls himself up on his cot frame, so he is standing and smiling at us when we come in the room. Even the time when his nappy fell off and we came in the room and we thought the brown stuff all over his face was chocolate until we realised he had eaten his own poo, he was still smiling, and we were caught between laughter and disgust at his smiling mouth with a brown ring all around it.

We play games with Matti. Round and round the garden. Tickly under there. Ride a Cock Horse to Banbury Cross, bouncing him up and down on our knees. And he laughs and we hug him, our little baby brother.

We are going to move, says Mummy. Now Rashid and I are married, we are going to live in Romford, close to London, close to where he works. We have to pack everything in the house into boxes.

One by one, our things go into boxes and Mummy wraps the breakable things in newspaper. Little brother Matti, who is one year and three quarters now, can walk, tottering on his chubby bandy legs. He watches as we wrap everything up and he has a go too, and laughs when we tickle him under his arms, or on his tummy. He likes to laugh.

But we made him cry.

It wasn't our fault. Not really.

Nearly everything we have is in boxes now. We wait for the delivery van.

We are waiting in the empty bedroom and there is only the bed that used to be a large cot that has had its sides taken off, so the end bedstead is very high. Amy and I are playing ten green bottles, hanging upside down from the bedstead and falling off onto the mattress when the bottle falls, and Matti is watching us, sucking his thumb. The bed sways under our weight as we swing upside down. Then we hear a loud crack. The bed starts to tilt to the side, slowly, slowly, going over. Amy and I shriek, and jump off, and the bed swings back into place with a large bang. First we laugh, then we are scared. One of the legs of the bed is broken, cracked in half with splintered edges.

Rashid comes in. He has heard the noise. He looks at the bed and us and Matti. Matti was laughing but now he starts sucking his thumb. Rashid looks so angry. I am so scared, it is like my insides have frozen into ice. *Don't hurt us.*

What was that noise? asks Rashid. He sees the bed. The end leg is cracked off, the wood completely splintered down the middle.

Rashid looks at Amy and me. Amy and I look at Matti standing by the bed, not even two years old, too young to talk or understand what we are saying. Rashid won't hurt him, because he's still a baby and he's his child, and he likes him more than us. Amy and I point at Matti. Matti did it, we say. He was jumping on the bed and the leg broke. But he didn't mean it. Matti stands, tottering on his legs, still sucking his thumb. He sees us all looking at him and smiles. But Rashid lifts his hand up high and swings it down and hits Matti on the side of his face so he falls straight down on the floor, hard sideways. And now our little brother is crying and screaming, holding his cheek, tears running down his face.

Amy and I stare at Matti. I feel so bad, I want to rush out and pick him up, but I can't because Rashid is still there. Matti is still howling, his face all red where he was hit. And he doesn't even know why, he is just looking at us like he's confused. Rashid looks at all of us. He says, no more trouble from any of you, and then he leaves.

Amy and I feel so bad, we feel terrible. We give Matti all our sweets from our pocket money and we hug him lots to make him feel better. But you know, I say to Amy, it would have been much worse if he had known we did it, Rashid would have hurt us a lot more. I know, says Amy, but I still feel horrible. Maybe Matti will forget, he's too young to remember, I say.

I still can't forget how shocked Matti looked when Rashid hit him. I didn't know he'd get hurt. He's my little brother. But we were so scared. We were really scared.

The van drivers are helping to carry our things out to the van, but Mummy goes away in the middle of all the half-loaded boxes.

We arrive at the new house on our own, just Rashid and Amy and Matti and me.

5

Moving

In the new house, boxes pile on boxes pile on boxes. And we unpack them, unwrapping things from newspaper coverings, like a giant lucky dip. Socks arrives in a special basket, with a handle at the top for carrying.

Mummy is still not here. Only me and Amy and Rashid and our little brother Matti walking upright on shaky nappy-wrapped bandy legs.

We unpack ourselves into the house. Little bits of us unpack and unroll, uncoil into corners.

There is new space to explore. We shout through the empty rooms, listening to our voices echo back at us, until Rashid tells us to shut up. We shut up. Slowly, the empty echoes get tucked away into carpets and beds and sofas and things the delivery men bring in. Rashid complains the delivery men cost too much. The boxes and packages unravel into the rooms, and we unravel too, weaving ourselves into crevices and corners, finding different spaces with every footstep.

The back garden is full of stones. At the end of the garden is a big tree, without leaves, waiting for spring. If you're bad, Rashid says to Amy and me, I will hang you from that tree. We look at the tree out in the garden. We don't go near the tree, just in case.

In the kitchen, there's a cellar, with wooden steps leading downwards. We peer in through the door, down the dark steps we can see inside. If you misbehave I will lock you in the cellar, Rashid says. When he says it, he smiles his smile with his mouth turning up at the sides, without his teeth showing.

I'm scared, Amy says to me after. What if he locks us down there? There could be ghosts and there's no light. Mummy will be home soon, I say. Just be careful for now. We become even more like mice in the house, creepy-creepying around.

We go to the hospital. Rashid parks the car and we walk up to the big strange metallic building. We go into the building, up a lift and across a corridor to the hospital ward. We see Mummy in there, in a frilly white nightie with small pink flowers on, in a bed, with lots of nurses around her. Next to her is a tiny cot on wheels with a see-through covering over it, and in it is a little baby. She is so tiny, says one of the nurses, looking at Rashid, because she was born early. She has to stay in an incubator for two weeks.

How are you? says Mummy when we see her. Are you okay? We're okay, we say. We can't tell her about the cellar or the tree in the back garden or how Rashid hit Matti or how he likes to twist our ears and arms when he talks to us, because Rashid is watching. So we just look at Mummy with our eyes, and say, we're okay. Matti is with us too, in his blue corduroy dungarees with his mass of brown curly hair and big brown eyes. He's very happy to see Mummy and is smiling all over.

It won't be long, says Mummy. I will be back very soon. They just have to keep an eye on your little sister for a few days. Your little sister has to stay in the box made of glass for two weeks, the nurse says. She is too small in weight and has to grow more, because she was born too early.

Why was she born early? asks Amy.

The nurse looks at Rashid again. The doctors say your mother shouldn't have been carrying heavy boxes around during the

94

moving and it made your sister come early, says the nurse. A pregnant woman should not be made to load heavy boxes onto a van. She must have been going through a very difficult time, says the nurse again. The nurse continues to look at Rashid, but Rashid says nothing. Your mummy has to stay here until she has had a good rest, says the nurse. She came here physically and emotionally exhausted.

Rashid still says nothing.

Amy peers out of the hospital window. You can see our car down there, she says, pointing to the car park. Why yes, says Mummy, so you can, I'll wave goodbye from the window when you go. Okay, says Amy. I'll be home as soon as I can, Mummy says.

When we leave the hospital we walk back to Rashid's car in the big car park. The cars are parked in the middle of all the hospital buildings. There's Mummy, says Amy, looking up at the building we came from. I can see Mummy's head, small, peering through the curtain at us. Amy waves and smiles, and Mummy waves back.

I'm hungry now, Amy says. Rashid reaches over and slaps Amy hard across her cheek. Be quiet, he says. Nobody told you to complain. Get in the car. Amy starts crying, holding her face as she gets into the car.

I look up to the hospital window where Mummy is and I see her looking and then her head disappears and the net curtains swing shut, swaying and dancing where Mummy had been. I look at Rashid and he is looking up at the window too. He is smiling. His smile that turns up at the corners of his mouth, without his teeth showing.

Why did he do that? whispers Amy to me between her tears on the way back. I only said I was hungry.

Mummy comes home. Our new little sister is still in the glass box at the hospital.

I saw him hit Amy, Mummy says. I saw him look up first to see if I was looking to see Amy wave goodbye, then he hit her. He did it deliberately, because he knew how I would feel because I would be too worried. He knew I would have to come home sooner.

Mummy turns to Amy. I'm sorry Amy, Mummy says, I'm sorry that happened to you. He did it to hurt me, to make me come back early, to make sure you are okay. It wasn't your fault, Amy. You did nothing wrong.

It's okay, Mummy, says Amy. He said he would put us in the cellar. And he would hang us from the tree. I was frightened. I'm glad you're back.

The empty tree stands in the backyard, staring at us through the window.

Our new little sister arrives later, wrapped in blankets, so wrapped up she is barely there. Her name is Babette and we call her Babs for short. Our little sister is very, very small. She stays small, like a tiny insect. But she's cute in her smallness. Curly ringlets of hair. One curl down the middle of her forehead, like the nursery rhyme, *There was a little girl, who had a little curl, right in the middle of her forehead.* We sing the song to her. We sing songs to Babs and our little brother Matti, and when we sing, they laugh and clap their hands, and Amy and I laugh too.

Rashid decides to clear the backyard of stones, so he can plant grass in the back. We have to fill huge cardboard boxes with stones so he can take them out the front. Soon all the stones are cleared, and he brings in big sheets of green grass like rectangular rugs and lays them in the back. I have to help him lay the big squares out in neat rows. No one is allowed on the grass, he says.

There is a concrete path down the side of the grass, next to Mummy's washing line that runs from the back of the house to the tree. Rashid waters the grass with a hose, all the water spraying out into the air. Sometimes me and Amy have to water the grass too, walking on the concrete path down the side so we don't stand on the grass.

On the left of our back garden is a low fence, and we can see into the other garden, with roses and deckchairs, where an old lady sometimes sits. Hello, says the old lady to Mummy. My name is Elsa. Mummy says we must call Elsa Mrs Lara. Sometimes another old lady sits there too. That's Mrs Lara's sister, says Mummy. She comes to stay with Mrs Lara sometimes, to keep her company and to look after her. Mummy says Mrs Lara can't walk very well, she has a special metal stick she has to hold on to. Mrs Lara's sister is almost as old as her, two frail, sticklike old ladies, but her sister is bigger. Mrs Lara is too old to get her own shopping, says Mummy, her sister says Mrs Lara should move to stay with her, but she doesn't want to, she says she likes it in her own house, she likes her independence.

When the grass is ready, Rashid says only Matti and Babs are allowed to play in the garden.

Why can't we play in the garden? says Amy, her eyes big. Please can we play there?

No, says Rashid, only Matti and Babs can. If I catch you playing on the grass, Rashid says, remember what I told you about the tree?

We stay away from the back garden. We play outside in the street, with the other kids, or upstairs, where I'm happy anyway, reading and drawing, and making things out of paper and plasticine.

I always see you and your sister going up and down the path to hang washing, says Mrs Lara one day over the fence, but I never see you two playing on the grass, only your little brother and sister. We are not allowed to, Amy says. What? says Mrs Lara. Children not being allowed to play on the grass? I never heard anything of the sort. If we do, says Amy, Rashid might hang us from the tree.

You must come around for tea, Mrs Lara says to Mummy. When your husband is out. Yes, says Mummy, that would be very nice, I will.

We have breakfast in the morning, cornflakes in a bowl. First, Rashid makes Amy and me make breakfast for Matti and Babs. Matti and Babs always eat first, Babs with her bottle of warmed milk. Then Rashid makes our breakfast. The milk always tastes funny because he waters down the milk for Amy and me. He wants to save it for Matti and Babs, Mummy says, because he wants them to grow big and strong. But don't worry, says Mummy, you get free milk at school every day. You must drink up all the milk you get at break time in the morning at school, she says, so Amy and I do.

Being eight is the smell of Mummy's ginger cake, crusted over where the edges burnt brown, earth smells, grass, leaves, the sun on hedgerows.

Does the wind smell? Amy asks. We smell the wind. No, says Amy, it smells of nothing.

No, I say, it's more than that, the wind smells of things like the lavender we had in our garden, or maybe oranges. I try to smell the blood oranges that Mummy spoke of in Mexico. I think of all the things that the wind carries. If I could smell when Rashid was approaching, then the wind would smell of evil and cruelty.

I like to watch the sun come up. The sun pops up beyond the horizon, like a rubber ball. It creeps behind clouds. Every cloud has a silver lining, says Mummy, but I haven't seen any silver linings in the clouds, only gold, racing around their edges, and yellow spilling out everywhere, all over the ground.

Mummy goes back to South Greenstead to collect some things, and me and Amy go too.

I want to see my boyfriends Timothy and John, who I'm going to marry when I grow up, I say.

You can visit your old school, says Mummy.

I meet Timothy and John. We sit outside on the grass near the climbing frame and share our sandwiches for lunch. A group of boys we don't know call out from across the grass:

Chinese, Japanese, dirty knees, what are these?

The boys pull their T-shirts out in two little triangles of cloth, like titties, and laugh and dance around and pull their eyes out and up at the sides with their fingers. What are you doing with a Chink? they shout at Timothy and John, and we are embarrassed and ignore them, but the boys do it again. Then Timothy shouts out, go away, leave us alone! There's nothing wrong with her!

The boys leave us alone after that.

Timothy says to me, they're stupid, just ignore them.

They are still my boyfriends, but when I leave it feels different, the green grass and climbing frame seem far away. When I was at school before, no one called me names. It doesn't feel like my school any more.

Amy and I share a room and a bunk bed. I lie on the top of the bunk bed, and Amy is at the bottom. It is dark. It is night. There's no light except the street lamp outside, peering through the edges of the curtains in a thin line. Amy and I whisper to each other down the side of the bed, beside the wall, so Rashid can't hear us, low enough so we can just hear each other's voices. We have a secret signal, if we think we hear Rashid coming up the stairs or outside the door, we shake the bed, it's our warning signal, so we go quiet immediately.

I tell Amy stories, whispered in the dark. I make them up and whisper them in words that travel down the side of the bunk bed into Amy's imagination and make pictures for her. I always start *Once upon a time* ... and go on from there. I start one night and then carry on the next and then the next. Amy loves the stories, especially fairy tales.

Tell me a story, Mai, she says. Please, a nice story.

I tell Amy stories of beautiful princesses, of forests and lakes, of princes who want to fall in love and go searching for adventure and romance. I make up my own stories, naughty magic goblins and wicked witches and children who grow up to be rich or princes and princesses. I make up funny stories to make her laugh too, of animals like tortoises who want to learn to fly and build themselves wings, of parrots that want to learn to sing like a canary, of lions and mice that make friends and set out together to change the world. Sometimes I make up crazy stories, just to make her laugh. The princesses are always beautiful, always alone, always have adventures and always find a prince in the end.

Tell me one about a princess, says Amy.

Once upon a time there was a beautiful princess and she lived alone high up in a big tower, far far away from everyone. She lived all on her own and she was very beautiful. And she had no one to talk to but one day a prince came to her and he stood at the bottom of the tower and said—

He said, Rapunzel, Rapunzel, let down your hair, and I will climb up and save you, says Amy.

No, I say, because this princess wasn't called Rapunzel, she was called Rosamund and she had short hair so she couldn't let it down, she just wanted the prince to unlock the door with the key outside. But the prince said, I will save you, I will kill a dragon for you, but the princess said, no you don't have to kill a dragon for me, just let me out of here. But the prince insisted he was going to kill a dragon first for her because that's what princes do – and he wouldn't listen to her. Then another prince arrived and he said he would kill a dragon too, to save the princess. But the first prince said, that's not fair, I was the first, I'm going to kill the dragon, and then they started to argue. Then a dragon came along and they said, stop right there, we are going to kill you, and the dragon said, what would you want to do that for? But the princes were determined to save the princess and they started to argue heatedly about who would kill the dragon, while the poor princess just looked down on them and said, stupid boys, why don't you just let me out?

Then the two princes started to fight each other instead of the dragon and the princess called out, why don't you just let me out, there's no point in killing that dragon. But they didn't hear her, only the dragon did, and he flew in the air (because dragons can fly, didn't you know that?) and he hovered by her window and he said, why don't you climb out of the window onto my back and fly away with me? If you want to come out, we can travel the world together.

So the princess climbed on his back and they flew off together and when the two princes decided to have a break from their fighting, because they got really tired, the princess was flying away in the distance and didn't give a damn about either of them.

Then the princess and the dragon lived happily ever after and went travelling all the time and visited lots of exciting countries and never got bored. But the two princes never got married and stayed bachelors all their lives because they were too full of themselves and always showing off so no princesses ever wanted them.

Wow, says Amy. I liked that story. What happened to the princess and the dragon after that? Did they get married? Yes, I say. Then what happened? asks Amy. Well they had a really great time after that and they had lots of babies and kept travelling around the world together. And the dragon helped look after the babies too, so the princess could have a good time as well.

Tell me the story of what happened to the dragon and princess after they got married and had lots of babies, says Amy. Please.

Okay … Once the dragon and the princess had got married and had lots of kids, they—

Creak on the stairs.

We hush quiet.

We are so quiet even the light from the street lamp outside screams through the window.

I hear the stairs creak and it's like the whole house creaks. It shudders. Fear. Creepy crawly footsteps, on the stairs.

The stairs. The stairs creak again.

I hear the creak first.

Quick. Shake the bed with your body so Amy knows. That's the signal to shut up. Be quiet, still like a mouse. Like you're asleep.

False alarm.

No, that was a footstep, I can hear it through the walls. The heavy step, the stairs creaking. He is coming up the stairs so quietly we can hardly hear him. Often, he tiptoes, trying to catch us out.

The big bad giant said Fee Fi Fo Fum. And when his feet hit the ground, the whole house shook. Shuddered.

Quiet, I say. He's coming.

The creak of feet, so quiet but so big. It's as if the house has bones and the house is creaking. We are so quiet, so quiet, we can't get any stiller, we can't freeze ourselves any more. We try to turn ourselves into blocks of stone, and the slow shudder of feet rolls up the stairs. We are waiting, hardly daring to wait. Then the feet are moving quickly, towards us.

The door bursts open, the light on. I act like I'm just waking up. Blinking. Blinking.

I heard you talking, he says.

No, we weren't talking.

I heard you.

No, really, we weren't, I say. We were asleep. I'm shaking inside. Can't let the shaking go outside. Amy must be the same. Just look tired, pretend I was asleep.

He looks at us. Pig eyes in pale face. I don't even want to think about it. The bright light, the dark, almost dead eyes, the rest of him quiet and still.

In his eyes I see something like anger, only it looks as if it is covered with mud, but you know it's there. They are muddy eyes, but there is something behind them, like the devil, Amy and I always say to each other.

I never see a person there in his eyes, only darkness. They make me afraid.

If I hear you again … he says. He looks right at me, into my eyes, holds my gaze for a few seconds, and I bury myself deep inside so he sees nothing on my face, so he can't read my eyes, my heart beating inside, all the shaking buried deep under.

He goes out, switching off the light at the same time. The room is black again. We hear him walking around nearby, in the bedroom, in the bathroom. Then he goes down the stairs.

Phew, says Amy. That was close. We'd better stop.

Okay, I say.

You can tell me the rest of the story next time, says Amy.

Soon I am lying there just thinking of nothing, all the dark night closed around me. Amy is underneath. Maybe asleep.

Amy? I whisper.

There's no reply. She's sleeping. I'm lying on top of the bunk bed, suspended in the air above her, in the dark, dark, dark. I hear myself breathing. I hear Amy breathe. Then I'm drifting … drifting … footsteps on the stairs, but I'm too tired to hear them.

Rashid invents new ways of hurting us when he tells us off. Every now and then he changes his technique. We call what he does to us 'the torture'. He used to twist our ears, but now he has started doing what at school we call burning, which we used to do as a joke, when you hold someone's arm tight around the wrist with one hand, then you twist your other hand around their wrist in the other direction, holding tight so it pulls the skin around and it feels like it's burning. Only Rashid does it really hard so it really hurts and he doesn't stop. He keeps burning and burning with his big hands, and we don't like it. When he has finished our arms are all red where his big hands twisted.

Then he finds a new way. He starts prodding us hard in the chest with his big forefinger, pressing in the middle at the front where our ribs meet, where the pain makes us breathless, or between our ribs, jabbing with his finger over and over, sometimes keeping his finger pushed in there and twisting it. Stay still, he says, as the force of his finger pushes us back, and we have to stand as still as we can so his finger can have more impact, and each time he jabs it is like he is trying to push me over, but my body isn't allowed to move. Stay still, he says. We try not to cry but sometimes you can't help it, the tears spill out eventually whatever you do, however hard you try to stop them welling up. We stare at his little piggy eyes filled with hate, those eyes that show nothing, only darkness and a light that comes from somewhere deep within, somewhere so evil we don't know what it can be – it must be worse than hell whatever it is. Even the devil can't have such blank, emotionless eyes with that little light buried deep within like a sword. Small piggy eyes staring into my eyes, like I'm fighting with them, but I know, and he knows, he will always win. He stares into me and I feel the tears coming and I see the little smile curving at the edge of his lips, the satisfaction in his eyes, as the tears break and my mouth pulls downwards despite how hard I try not to, and my cheeks are wet.

He smiles, but his eyes don't smile, they are filled with hate.

Sometimes Amy and I try to guess his technique in advance, so we can prepare ourselves better, tensing up our bodies and closing off from the pain where he's going to hurt us.

Last week I forgot to give Babs her bottle on time. He kept prodding and prodding me with his finger and then when the tears broke he sent me to bed without dinner. He does that a lot. You lie in bed and your tummy is a big hole and when it gets dark you can't have the light on and Amy can't come in to see you before bedtime.

Sometimes Socks sneaks into the room, purring. I call her up onto the top of the bunk bed, and she jumps up, high. I hide her under the bedclothes and she cuddles me. I feel her purring right through my body as I'm crying. I know that, out there in the world, she is the only one who knows what is really going on inside our house. Prrp, she says when she jumps up on the bunk bed. It's her greeting. Then she settles down and stays with me to keep me company until Amy comes to bed at eight.

We go to the seaside with Rashid and Mummy, to Southend, close to London. Bright sun on the promenade, lots of people. Pink candyfloss on sticks, too sweet for us. Amy and I eat two mouth-fuls and we both throw up on the pavement in the sunshine, on the promenade before the sea. Rashid walks on ahead. We feel dizzy. Matti and Babs are pushed around in pushchairs. It's hot. Burning hot. The sea's cold but we swim anyway, me in my red swimming costume, Amy in her blue one. We taste the salt on our tongues as we swim, the sky burning above us. We learnt to swim at school, armbands attached to our arms, floats held in front of us at the swimming pool. We are wearing the inflatable armbands Mummy bought us in South Greenstead. Rashid lies on the beach and puts on sun oil to go brown.

That night, Amy says from the bottom of the bunk bed, Mai, I feel sick.

Amy has bad sunburn and Mummy has just come in and gone downstairs to get calamine lotion to put on her red arms and shoulders.

I feel sick, says Amy again, and then she jumps out of bed and runs out the bedroom door towards the bathroom and I hear her throw up on the landing before she reaches the bathroom. Straight away, I can smell the sick. I hear Rashid come out of Mummy's and his bedroom next door.

I got sick, I hear Amy say. She starts to cry.

I climb out of bed and walk towards the open bedroom door facing on to the stair landing. Rashid is standing in front of Amy, and Mummy is coming upstairs with the bottle of calamine lotion in her hand. Rashid looks at the sick on the floor and Amy crying and then he raises his hand and hits Amy hard on her face. Whack, a big sound that goes through the house, just as Mummy reaches the top of the stairs.

Amy howls with shock, shocked at the sick, shocked with pain.

Mummy is shocked. Rashid, you can't hit a six-year-old child just for getting sick, she's got sunstroke. She's ill, she says.

Shut up, woman, says Rashid. Don't answer back. Then he grabs Mummy and pushes her backwards and I watch as Mummy grabs hold of the top of the banister just in time to stop herself falling down the stairs, her body swinging round and facing down the stairs as she catches the stair rail with one arm and grabs with the other arm onto the other side. Rashid pushes Mummy again from behind, trying to push her forwards and down. Mummy screams and topples forwards, but holds tight on both sides.

Rashid pushes harder. He tries to force her hands off the banister, and Mummy keeps screaming. She loses her grip. One hand flies up and she falls forwards. I think she is going to fall down the stairs but she grabs the banister again and pulls herself back up. The calamine-lotion bottle flies out of her hand and loses its lid as it flies down the stairs. Bounce, bounce goes the open bottle, calamine lotion spilling out all the way down the stairs, spraying pink across the wall.

Rashid stops pushing. He looks at Mummy and he looks at Amy, who is shocked and pale.

Clean the sick up, woman, he says. He walks back into the bedroom.

Mummy hugs Amy, who is still crying, but quietly. Don't worry, Amy, says Mummy, it will be all right. Are you feeling okay now? Why don't you lie in bed?

I'm sorry, Amy, says Mummy as she puts Amy to bed, I'm sorry Rashid hit you. It's not your fault, you've just got sunburn and a bit of sunstroke.

I go back to bed too. I hear Mummy cleaning up the sick on the landing. She is crying.

In the morning, Rashid makes me take a rag and a bucket of warm water. I have to go down the stairs one by one and clean up all the calamine lotion that spilled last night. I start at the top and work down. I follow the dried pink calamine-lotion trail down the stairs, left across the skirting where the bottle bounced against the wall, to the right where the stairs bend and where the calamine lotion sprayed across the wallpaper in a long arcing line. I soak the calamine with the wet rag, rubbing hard, the dissolved lotion staining my fingers, and rinse it in the water, now turning cold. The rag and my fingers become dark reddish pink with calamine lotion and dirt from the floor and walls. I watch the bucket of water turning more and more pink, step by step. I keep thinking, that could have been Mummy where the calamine lotion went, that could have been her that bounced on the stairs here. I keep thinking it as I clean each stair carpet and piece of wall, soaking up the pink into my rag, remembering Mummy hanging onto the top of the stairs, holding on with one hand and Rashid pushing her.

Rashid's a pig, says Amy afterwards. Because Rashid doesn't like pigs, I decide I'm going to start a secret diary of when Rashid is a pig.

Pig, I write in my diary. Rashid was a pig today because he told us off for talking too loud. He pushed me in the chest until it hurt, but I didn't let him see me cry. Rashid is a pig because he said I didn't change Matti's clothes fast enough today and he said I must go to bed with no dinner. He is a pig. A PIG. He says only Matti and Babs can play in the front room, we have to play in our own rooms, we are only allowed in the front room when we are baby-sitting them. He is a PIG. I hate him.

Mrs Lara, the old lady next door, suns herself in her garden in her garden chair and Mummy chats to her over the garden fence as she is hanging out the washing in the back garden that only Babs and Matti are allowed to play in. Sometimes during the day Mummy visits her and takes her food and checks she's okay.

Then one day Mrs Lara falls down in her house and she lies there in the hallway, all alone all day. She couldn't reach the door or the phone which was on the table in the hallway. Mummy finds out because she went round to say hello in the afternoon and she knocked on the door and Mrs Lara called out and Mummy just heard her, and Mummy rang an ambulance, and there was Mrs Lara lying on the floor of the hallway in pain.

It turns out Mrs Lara has broken the bone in her leg, Mummy says, your bones go soft when you are old, they get frail, and if you fall over, they break easily. I think of Mrs Lara lying down on the floor all day, the phone just out of reach, and in pain.

We go and visit Mrs Lara in hospital. I make a card, and Amy wants to give her a present so she can get well soon. Amy spends a long time in the shop trying to decide what to buy with her pocket money. Finally she buys Mrs Lara a big black plastic furry spider on elastic. It's as big as her hand with big red eyes, and the legs dangle with little funny bits of plastic sticking out of them, so they are all tingly when you touch them and tickle your skin. When it bounces, the legs shake up and down like a real spider.

What are you buying her a spider for, Amy? I say. She won't want that. I'm buying it because I want to buy it for her, says Amy. It will make her laugh and cheer her up.

Amy buys the spider to make Mrs Lara laugh, but when she shows it to Mrs Lara in the hospital and dangles it close to her, Mrs Lara shrieks, and screams, No, no! Take it away, take it away! Not so close, I don't like spiders!

Amy looks sad, but Mrs Lara says it's a nice gift, it's just that she's scared of spiders. When Amy bounces it on the elastic Mrs Lara shivers and moves her arms away fast and we laugh. Mrs Lara says she will treasure her present but now Amy is worried because she thinks Mrs Lara doesn't like her nice gift. Maybe I shouldn't have bought her the spider, Amy says. I thought it would make her laugh.

But when we visit next time in hospital, Mrs Lara has the big giant plastic spider hanging at the far end of the bed. Amy smiles and is really happy, and Mrs Lara says it makes her laugh, because she always thinks of Amy giving it to her as a present and what a surprise she got, and she knows it's not real, although she keeps it far at the end of the bed, because she's still a bit scared of it, and Amy smiles.

Then Mrs Lara comes home again in a wheelchair and her

sister Annie comes to stay for a while. Mrs Lara asks Amy and me and Mummy to visit her for tea. When we go in the house, we say hello to Mrs Lara and her sister Annie and we see that the inside of the kitchen door is covered with little toys she has stuck on. All kinds of things. Wriggly plastic things, a man with a parachute attached to his back, bangles and beads, the kind of small toys you buy in shops, toy cars and a little baby doll with starey eyes, all of them glued on the door. That's my decorations, says Mrs Lara, I started collecting all the little things in cereal packets and toys you get in Christmas crackers and then it became a hobby and then I started sticking them on the door. We keep looking at all the toys, then Mrs Lara says, okay, you can have one each, and we try to pull one off and finally we find a loose one and Amy ends up with the red and blue plastic man with the parachute on his back, and I end up with a tiny baby doll, because that's the only one I can get loose, and Mrs Lara laughs from her wheelchair.

Then we go into the sitting room and we have tea and cake and Mrs Lara's sitting room is full of more little things on her shelves and cabinets, little china and glass things and small teacups and saucers. But what we like most is a beautiful china woman with a tiny waist and skirt that goes out and out with lots of petticoats underneath. And the woman is smiling and sitting on a chair with one leg stretched forwards over the other and her arms are reaching down across her outstretched leg to tie one dancing shoe onto her foot.

That's porcelain, says Mrs Lara. I've had it a long time, and it's very special. But she lets us touch it, and the woman doesn't look stiff like the other china figures Mrs Lara has, she looks as if she is about to finish tying on her ballet shoes and she will get up right now and dance the evening away. I keep looking at her as if she is about to move. She looks so alive, even the flowers and frills under her petticoat look like they are moving. Amy and I touch her arms, and we are scared when we touch her fingers that they will break off. She's a girl getting ready to dance, says Mrs Lara. I call her my dancing lady.

Mummy used to dance, says Amy, she used to go to balls, didn't you, Mummy, and she was the best dancer. And she even has a ballgown at home, don't you, Mummy, the red satin one?

Well, I wasn't that good … says Mummy.

Granddad says you were a very good dancer, Mummy, I say. He says you were so light on your feet it looked like you were floating all over the floor. Granddad was a good dancer too, I say. He used to win dancing competitions. With his winklepickers that were so sharp you could pick winkles out of their shells with them. And Mummy used to do ballroom dancing and all the boys wanted to dance with her.

Well … says Mummy. Mrs Lara and Mummy smile.

Mrs Lara used to be a good dancer too, says Mrs Lara's sister Annie. We look at Mrs Lara and think about her hobbling with her walking frame and now in a wheelchair, dancing with the delicacy and lightness of the china dancer, and try to imagine her like that when she was young. Did she go to balls?

What about you two? Mrs Lara asks.

No, we hate dancing, we say.

I took them to ballet class and they just stood there and refused to dance, says Mummy. Twice.

It's for sissies, we both say.

And Mrs Lara laughs, and her sister beams behind her.

I brought Amy's spider from the hospital, says Mrs Lara. And I am going to stick it on the door with all the other toys, and then me and Amy smile too.

Mummy carries on visiting Mrs Lara during the day, and doing little things for her, but Amy and I have to go to school now the holidays are over. So we just say hello when we see her in passing because we can't visit in the evenings when Rashid is around and Mrs Lara doesn't come out much any more and we're not allowed to go into the garden much so we can't chat to her over the fence.

Granddad comes to visit. He watches football and Rashid lets us sit in the front room where the TV is and we have Sunday lunch with Granddad. I don't see much of you all any more, says Granddad. You have hardly been in contact!

We all go for a walk in the park nearby and I don't walk fast enough. Rashid comes to where I am at the back. Hurry up, he says, and he twists my arm until I cry. Later on Granddad slows down to walk behind with me because he can see I'm crying. What's wrong? he asks.

I can't tell you, I say.

Of course you can, says Granddad. What is it? Are you upset about something? I shake my head, and the tears are falling more now. No, I say.

Come on, Mai, says Granddad, I'm your granddad. You know you can tell me if something is wrong. What did Rashid do to you?

Nothing's wrong, I say. It will be worse if I tell you.

Just tell me why you won't say, says Granddad.

I can't, I say.

I'll ask Rashid what happened, says Granddad.

No, I say, please don't. I will be in trouble and it will be much worse. Please don't say anything to him, he will hurt me more.

Granddad looks at me, then he looks deep into my eyes as if he can see what is going on in there and he looks like he is going to say something else, then he says, okay, and he shrugs. But I can see he is worried. The tears dry on my cheeks as we walk.

I am upset with Granddad, says Mummy afterwards. He says he knew already Rashid was weird, there were rumours at work that Rashid was very strange, but Granddad never said anything to me before I got married. He said I am too stubborn to listen to him. But he could have told me. It might have made a difference to the decision I made. He never said a thing.

Rashid calls me to the bathroom. He lifts up my toothbrush.

See this, he says, and runs his thumb along the bristles.

Yes, I say. I know I'm in trouble, but I don't know why.

The bristles ping back under his thumb and little specks of water fly off. See this, he says. It's wet.

Yes, I used it earlier today.

Why didn't you dry your toothbrush? he says.

I'm surprised. People don't dry their toothbrushes, I say.

He is angry. Don't answer back. You mustn't leave it wet.

I'm sorry, I didn't know I had to, I say. How do I dry it?

Rashid runs my toothbrush bristles along the top of the towel hanging over the towel rail, then back the other way. I stare at what he's doing. It seems crazy, but even though I want to laugh I daren't because I'm too scared.

Like this, he says. It's dry now. He flicks the bristles again with his thumb. Go to bed straight away without dinner.

But who dries their toothbrush? I say.

He pulls my ear and twists it hard. I can feel it getting hotter and hotter and it hurts.

Don't answer back, he says. From now on you dry your toothbrush, not a speck of water. I want to see it completely dry. Not a drop of water, he repeats. He's still hurting me. I fight the tears that come into my eyes, but I won't cry.

I always fight the tears. It's the only weapon I have, to act like what he does doesn't affect me.

I'm sorry, I say. I should have dried it. I'll dry it in future.

Then Rashid lets go and I feel my ear go red as the blood rushes back, really hot, like it's being burnt with a hot iron, stinging like the tears that threaten in my eyes.

Straight to bed, he says.

I lie in bed and Socks comes and snuggles under the covers with me.

I put it in my diary. Rashid is mad. He makes me dry my toothbrush. He made me go to bed without dinner. He is a pig.

At school I ask my friends if they have to dry their toothbrushes. They say no. I must be the only eight-year-old who does.

Every time I run my toothbrush across the top of the towel on the towel rail in the bathroom, I feel Rashid twisting my ear. Every drop gone. Over and over.

Amy and I come home from school. Mummy is in the kitchen. She is looking at the porcelain dancing lady on the table in front of her, still tying up her ballet ribbons, leaning forwards, the yellow curls falling around her face with blue eyes that look like they're staring into the future.

Isn't that Mrs Lara's dancing lady, Mummy? we ask.

Yes, says Mummy.

Can we touch it?

Be careful, says Mummy. Amy and I run our fingers along the yellow hair piled up on her head, and her big flowing dress and the foot peeking out of the dress where she's putting on the shoe, and feel how delicate and smooth the ankle is on the foot.

Did you borrow her from Mrs Lara? we ask. No, it's a present, says Mummy.

For who?

For me, says Mummy.

Doesn't Mrs Lara want her any more?

Mummy looks at the dancing lady as if she's seeing something we can't see.

Mrs Lara passed away last week, Mummy says.

What's passed away? Amy asks.

Mrs Lara was frail and ill, says Mummy. Last week she died suddenly, from a stroke. I didn't want to tell you then, because things were very chaotic, but I suppose I should tell you now. The funeral was yesterday.

Oh, says Amy. But she didn't look ill when we saw her last time. She was smiling and chatting.

Strokes are like that, says Mummy.

Does that mean she went to heaven? asks Amy.

I'm sure she did, says Mummy. Her sister Annie brought the dancing lady round to me today. She said Mrs Lara had left it for me as a special present because I'd come round and looked after her so often. She knew I liked it.

So you must look after the dancing lady now, Mummy, we say.

Yes, says Mummy.

Is the dancing lady worth a lot of money? we ask.

Possibly, says Mummy. Mrs Lara says the figure was very old. Mummy's hands reach out and her fingers run down the arms and stroke the fingers of the porcelain dancing lady.

Mrs Lara left her for all of us, says Mummy. So you must look after her very well.

We stay looking at the dancing lady and it still looks as if she will get up and dance around the room.

Is Mrs Lara's sister going to stay in her house? we ask. No, she stays somewhere else, says Mummy. She just came to look after Mrs Lara. Other people will probably come and live there now.

Will they keep the door? we ask. With all the toys?

Probably not, says Mummy. When new owners come they want things new again.

What a waste of Mrs Lara's toys, we say. How can they waste them like that?

Mummy looks at the dancing lady for a long, long time.

Amy and I like to throw the parachute man up in the sky, and watch the plastic parachute unfurl and him spiral down, down, from the sky. And we laugh, and sometimes we tie the tiny baby doll on too, so both of them come down together, the baby doll and the parachute man in his red and blue costume, falling from the sky.

At school they call me from the classroom and take me to a room where a lady has a timer and asks me lots of questions and has things like patterned blocks I have to put in order. She keeps writing in a folder as I answer the questions and she checks the timer each time and writes it down too.

At the end the lady smiles and says, you probably thought you were playing a game, but it was a test, to see how clever you are. I know, I say. She looks surprised. How did you know? she asks. Because you kept timing how long I took to answer them. And you wrote it down.

Oh, says the lady.

Mummy says the lady was disappointed I knew it was a test, as I wasn't supposed to. Mummy says it's an IQ test which measures intelligence and that they say my IQ is very high and they want to send me to a gifted school. But if you go to a gifted school, it will be very far away and I won't get to see you, says Mummy. And also all the children will be gifted and I think it will be important to stay with normal children, it will be a better environment. Otherwise, how will you cope with normal people when you grow up? So they say although your IQ is higher than the year above you, they will put you up a year in school instead.

So I go up a year. I go into my new classroom and there is only one seat available, next to a boy. This is Adrian, says the teacher. Urgh, says Adrian to his friends. I have to sit next to a girl. Girls are stupid.

We hate each other. We are the only boy and girl sitting next to each other in the whole class.

Being nine is cold leaves against a grey sky. The taste of rain and soot, somewhere in the air, traffic fumes meshed in tree branches. The taste of apples, eaten by the bagful as I read, as I read. Being nine is when the world gets a little bigger and between here and school there are streets and in the streets are people in houses who live there and you don't know what happens inside. Being nine means I get closer to the sky.

Being nine is the smell of shoe glue. When you fix shoes, you cut the shapes out of the black leather material stuff. You scrape the old sole off the shoe with a scraping thing – it isn't always easy to get it off but it comes off at last. Then you put glue on the bottom of the shoes and the black cut-out shapes and you let them dry for a while.

Rashid says, come Mai, help me fix these shoes, I need you to assist me. We go into the front sitting room, which isn't used much. He has shoes in a row, his and Matti's and Babs'. He cuts the shapes out of the black shiny leather stuff and scrapes the old soles off. Then he puts glue on the leather shapes of the soles.

The smell of glue, the soles waiting to be stuck onto the shoes. The smell is strange, permeates the air, almost enough to make you feel sick. I smell shoes, the inside of them where sweaty feet have been, I smell sweat as he cuts out the soles with a Stanley knife, shaping the edges, I smell glue wafting over the other smells like a higher, clearer-pitched smell. I smell the carpet, the door. I smell the room sinking into me like the glue.

We must wait for them to dry a while before we stick them on, he says. We sit, waiting. How is school? Rashid asks.

I am surprised. He never asks how school is. It's okay, I say.

Rashid sighs. Yawns. The smell of shoe glue threads through the room and makes me giddy. I'm tired, he says. He stretches his arms up in the air. Aren't you?

No, I say, sitting cross-legged on the floor.

I am, he says. I need to lie down.

Rashid gets up and walks to the sitting-room door and closes it, and slides the inside bolt on the door, a little white bolt you put your finger in and pull across, and locks us inside the room. He comes back and sits beside me. He stretches, and then leans backwards onto the floor, onto his back, in his grey woollen jersey. He lies with his hands behind his head, looking at the ceiling, stretched out on the floor. I hear him breathing. He breathes loud. He says nothing.

He lies like that for a while, staring at the ceiling, and I look at the shoes.

Do you think the shoes are dry yet? I ask.

No, he says. They will be a while. He looks at me and smiles. Why don't you come and lie down beside me?

I don't want to be near him. I am afraid of him, but I mustn't show it. You must never show your enemy your fear, they say in storybooks. Or they will have power over you.

I'm not sleepy, I say.

Come here and have a rest, he says.

It's okay, I say.

I sit, he lies, and there is only breathing, breathing. I don't move.

Don't you want to rest too?

I'm fine, thank you.

Come lie down here with me, he says, patting the floor beside him.

No thanks, I say. I'm not sleepy.

He sits up with a sigh and I think, at last, he's going to do the shoes now. He lifts his arms up above his head as if stretching, then he leans forwards and next thing I am being picked up in the air and he is lying down again and he has pulled me onto his tummy.

There, he says. That's better. He sighs again. This is nice, isn't it? he says. He is breathing funny, long and slow.

I say nothing. I am lying down on my stomach and my head is on his chest and it is weird. I feel his chest and tummy move up and down and I hear his breathing getting deeper and deeper. I lie as still as I can. I have never been so close to the Enemy. Up and down, up and down, moves his stomach and chest.

Relax. Just rest. Put your hands down by your sides, he says, because I am holding them against his chest, lifting my head away. I do, but it isn't nice. I don't like the feeling of his jumper underneath me and I don't like being here. It's strange. I look at the shoe soles drying in the middle of the room. I don't like lying on top of him, arms by my sides. I lie there, lie there.

Can I get off now? I ask.

Just a bit longer, he says. I don't like the breathing. It's weird. Loud and harsh, like thunder beneath me, in long lingering gasps, his hands still behind his head, him looking up at the ceiling. I think his eyes are closed. I dare not look at his face and my face is against his chest. I am just waiting for this moment to end.

Can I get off now, please? I ask again.

Why? Don't you like it?

Not much, I say.

Why not? says Rashid. I think it's nice. His voice is funny, in bits.

It feels weird, I say.

What's wrong? he says. There's nothing wrong with what we're doing. We're just resting.

It's weird, I say.

His breathing quietens down, and he lies still. He sighs.

Okay, you can get down now, he says. He sighs again, then sits up and lifts me off him as he does so. He gets up and walks to the other side of the room, and goes to the sitting-room door and slides the bolt open again. Then he sits down. Okay, he says, we can carry on now. He starts sticking the shoes' soles down.

I sit still and quiet.

It's fine now, Mai, he says. I don't need your help any more. You can leave.

Okay, I say, and open the door.

Leave the door open, he says as I leave. The glue fumes are strong.

I go outside to play. Outside is freedom where you run around and do things and play and laugh and we roller skate on our roller skates, and outside is the sky stretching up and up forever, and no glue fumes and just trees and things and lots of clouds that whirl by. And outside is books and libraries and places where I can take other people's dreams and discover them in the pages of books. And outside is Amy and my friends down the road that we play with. I am nine, and when I go to school I play hopscotch, hopscotch on the paving stones, hopping on one foot on one in the middle then two feet, one in each adjacent paving stone, all the way to school.

There's a bully in the school, in the year above us. The other girls tell me he goes and hits girls. One day Amy and I are walking back from school and we see him walking behind us. He is catching up with us. We run up to a woman with a pram. Please protect us from the bully, we say. But she ignores us and turns the corner, leaving us on our own. The bully is getting closer. We are both scared. We have to fight, I say to Amy. We don't have a choice.

As the bully approaches, we turn around and start hitting him, kicking and pushing him against the wall. We hit and kick him until he runs away down the road, crying.

We are jubilant. We beat up a bully who is bigger than both of us. We can get our own back on boys who bully us. Maybe he wasn't going to attack us, we think afterwards. But at least we are not scared of him any more.

I come top of the year and Adrian who sits next to me looks impressed.

See, he says to his friends, girls are not that stupid after all.

Adrian's family is going to Holland and Adrian won't be coming back after the holidays. He has to pack up his desk before he goes. I want to get him a present, even though I still hate boys. I take two pence from my pocket money and buy him a small white eraser from the corner shop on the way back from school, then I wrap it in a piece of paper to give to him and write *To Adrian* on it, *from Mai*, thinking I'll put it on his desk. But I'm too shy to. So I take off the wrapper and say to Adrian, as he is cleaning out his desk at break time, oh, I have a spare eraser I don't need, do you want it? He looks at it. It's new, he says. Are you sure you don't need it? Yes, I already have another, I say. He looks at me.

Thanks, he says, in a casual way. He takes the eraser.

Then he says, now I have a new eraser, I won't need this one. He shows me his favourite big green eraser that he got on his birthday. It's large and he has written maths sums on it and his name with a pen, and he has stabbed holes in it with his compass. Go on, take it, he says. You might want to use it.

Thank you, I say, acting as casual as I can. I take the green eraser and when Adrian is gone, I treasure it with the chair empty beside me in class.

Being nine is watching the sun come up behind the horizon, throwing itself into the sky like a rubber ball. It creeps behind clouds and peeps out. Mummy says every cloud has a silver lining. I haven't seen any silver linings in the clouds yet. But I see gold, racing around their edges, and yellow spilling out everywhere, spilling all over the ground and making everything look nice. And sometimes when I am outside I forget there are any bad things at all.

6

Challenges

We are moving again.

Mummy says we are moving because Rashid is starting his postgraduate studies in chemistry and where we are going is where the university is. We are going to stay in university accommodation, she says, in a house. Once again, our lives are put in boxes. We move to another city, to a new house. When we move, Amy and I have the big room and we have separate beds.

It is dark. It is night. I am lying in bed, not sleeping. The curtains are open and I am watching the light patterning the walls. The door opens and Rashid walks in. He is naked. Moonlight glints off his body as he walks. He stops at my bed and climbs into the other end. He lies down, stretching his legs out on either side of me. I hear him sigh, loud.

I pretend I am asleep.

Mai? his voice whispers.

I don't reply. I am sleeping, but not sleeping, heart going throb throb, hoping his legs don't touch me. Why is he in my bed? I curl into a ball under the blankets, hugging my knees to my chest. Breathing, breathing. It is quiet, Amy still asleep on the other bed. I lie still. I am scared to move in case my feet touch him. I curl up in the bed. Breathe, breathe. Legs around me on either side. I stay curled up, eyes shut. He is in my bed, at the other end, with no clothes on. He lies there in the dark.

Mai? he whispers again.

Time becomes infinite and my breathing goes on forever. I daren't even move a muscle. I would hate the cold touch of his skin. Touch not the evil thing or it will contaminate you. Stay away. Amy is still sleeping. I keep sleeping, pretending to sleep, and the night is still silent. I hear Rashid's breathing, but he is still too. It is very quiet. Very quiet. I lie there, curled up, and I daren't even make a breathing sound. Mai? Rashid whispers again, but I say nothing, still pretending to sleep.

Time goes on and on and then he gets up and leaves my bed and leaves the room. The moonlight glimmers on his skin again as he leaves. It feels as if he is still in here, but he isn't. Instead, the moonlight is glistening. I lie still, still afraid to uncoil, hearing Amy's light breathing in the dark, thinking he will come back in again. But I hear nothing else. I lie still and hear the darkness. Don't bring him back again. He is strange. Does strange things. He didn't hurt me, I think, at least he didn't hurt me. And he didn't tell me off. It's strange he didn't tell me off. Usually, he does. And I lie, breathing, and the dark moonlight consumes me, and then I am asleep, really asleep.

In the morning, it feels like a strange dream. I go around with the memory of being curled up, his legs on either side of me, scared to move. Nothing is normal.

Why didn't he say anything? Why didn't he tell me off? What is he up to?

During the day, I forget. You forget what doesn't harm you. Only look out for the next thing, the next time he has an opportunity. Don't leave traces, don't leave evidence. Become invisible. Curl your legs up into a ball, hide away under the blankets, become as small as you can, like the dot on the top of an 'i'. I am now the dot on top of an 'i', hiding myself, not knowing fully why.

Days pass, and there are no more questions. There is only the next anticipated moment, and the next. For nights after, I lie still, watching the moonlight, listening to my own breaths, breathing, waiting, while Amy sleeps, hoping he won't come back, until my eyes close and there is nothing else.

Then Matti and Babs get our bedroom because it's bigger and they get a bed each, and Amy and I move to the smaller room, back to sharing the bunk bed, and I don't have to worry any more.

Mummy sends us to the Roman Catholic nuns' school down the road because she says they have a better education, even though we are not Roman Catholic. We arrive halfway through the year and everyone stares at us, all the boys and girls. But I'm used to it now, I know what it's like to be new at a school, and different. It doesn't take long to make friends.

Mummy says she went to a nuns' school and it was very good. Not everyone in the school is Roman Catholic, and because we're not, we don't have to go to confirmation classes. All the nuns wear dark cloths over their heads and white cuffs and collars and dark clothes to the ground and look very serious. Sister Mary Ann Jones, the headmistress, is the most serious of all. She never smiles, her face looks all thin and pale and has little lines on it like crinkly paper you've tried to flatten out again, she wears no make-up and her nose is as pointy as her face. Her eyes are light blue and don't say anything, and when she speaks she says, don't do this, and don't do that, all the way through assembly. She loses her temper all the time and when she does so she stamps her foot and her voice goes so high I worry it will break something, even our ears. Then Sister Mary

Ann Jones' face changes to a reddish colour and her eyes water and I feel she wants to hit someone but she can't because she's a nun, so she stamps her foot hard instead.

In assembly Sister Mary Ann Jones tells us we must all be thankful and be happy because God is there for us, but I think God must have forgotten to be there for Sister Mary Ann Jones because she is never happy and she looks all alone in the world and she is always frowning. Mummy says Sister Mary Ann Jones is probably under a lot of stress trying to run the school, but when Sister Mary Ann Jones says we must love God and Jesus is our salvation, I wonder what God and Jesus would think hearing someone as miserable as Sister Mary Ann Jones saying it, standing there in front of us all. There's not much hope for us, if that's what Sister Mary Ann Jones shows religion does to you.

There is a nice sister, called Sister Rose, who is deputy head and is very soft and kind, and you can see she wants to be nice to us. But Sister Mary Ann Jones never lets her be nice, she bosses her around, and once I saw her lose her temper at Sister Rose and stamp her foot and shout, you're not strict enough! You let them get away with far too much! And Sister Rose just stood there all quiet and looked down and looked upset and didn't say anything, but her cheeks went red.

Amy and I watch the thirteen-year-olds in the street and laugh at them. We are never going to grow up, we're never going to be like that, we tell each other as the girls clop by with platforms on. We laugh at their shaggy hair, their red lipsticks, the child faces buried in false colour. Eyeshadow. Bright blues and greens. Shaggy-dog hairstyles. Bay City Rollers trousers. The Osmonds. We are never going to grow up like them.

Amy and I hate pop music, but I have a secret fancy for Jimmy Osmond. We saw him sing once, on TV, he had longish blond hair, bell-bottomed trousers and a mike. He was a child like us and he sang about love. All the girls at school like the Osmonds. And horses. Zena, the girl who sits opposite me in class, draws nothing but horses. At art class she only draws horses. In science class she draws horses in her notebook and when the teacher says, Zena, what are you doing, she says, nothing Miss, and the teacher says, pay attention. At break time, Zena draws horses too and her friend Caroline compares their horse drawings.

What's that? I ask. Black Beauty, she says. Or, National Velvet. Zena says she loves horses, they are the best thing in the world, and when she grows up she wants to work in a stable. She says she has a horse and on weekends she goes riding in a field. It's a pony, she says. Aren't you jealous?

I don't envy her. Everyone has seen *National Velvet* at school and they all want to ride horses, well I haven't seen it and I don't like horses much. I reckon if I sit on one I'll fall right off, they're so big. Horses are the only thing I can't draw. I can draw everything else. I draw people. I draw things from my head. I create paper cut-outs from 'Make It with Paper' books and I can do origami, from the library books I borrow.

While the rest of my class are drawing horses, I fall in love with every boy in class in turn instead. I like Jason, pretty eyes and hair, he draws well too. Then I like his friend Peter too. He's nice because he's funny. Then I like Michael, because he's small and sweet. There's a new boy, Daniel, who is fair and blue eyed and he looks like the prince in Cinderella books and he knows he's good-looking and I like him because everyone else does.

But the one I really like, all the time, because I fall in and out of love with the others depending on how I feel that week, is Andrew, the boy with the eczema on his hands. His hands are red and flaky and scaly and everyone says ugh, horrible, don't let him touch you. But Andrew has a nice smile, and I know he's very clever in class and he seems to think a lot, and there's just something I like about him. His eyes are large with nice eyelashes. But I never let him see me look at him and I never see him look at me. Because I like him I never talk to him, in case the other girls guess, because I'm Mai who doesn't like any boys, they're all awful.

Do you know how the French kiss each other, Mai? whispers Amy from the bottom of the bunk bed. No, I say. What do you mean? Julie in class said French people and some grown-ups kiss differently from like they do in the films. How's that? I ask. Well, Julie says they stick their tongues in each other's mouths and wiggle them around. What, so all their saliva gets mixed up? Yes, I suppose so. Yuck, I say, that's disgusting. We giggle.

Julie says it's true, says Amy. Do you think it's true? I think about it. I try to imagine it. It's too revolting for anyone to do, I say. Think of their tongues wriggling in each other's mouths, and all that saliva getting mixed up. Think of all the diseases they'd catch. You'd have to be really sick to do it. They would throw up. Yuck.

Yeah, no one could be so stupid, says Amy. We giggle again. I reckon Julie made it up, I say. Maybe she was trying to show off.

I shape my fist into a hollow cylinder on the top of the bunk bed and put my mouth against it and stick my tongue in the gap and wiggle it. It doesn't feel like anything. I can't see what French people see in it. Then I kiss the back of my hand. I feel the warmth of my lips pressing on my skin. I like the feeling. Sometimes I kiss the back of my hand and keep my lips there, like in the films. I pretend I'm kissing Andrew with brown hair and brown eyes in class. I do it in the dark, when Amy can't see, lying at the top of the bunk bed, practising for when I grow up and get married.

Amy tells me Robert Dougall kissed her behind the blackboard once. He kissed her on both cheeks, but not like how the

French do. He did it when the teacher left the classroom and everyone gathered round to see. Then the teacher came back and caught them behind the blackboard and all the class watching and Amy and Robert had to do break-time detention and write lines for disrupting the class.

I have a dream. Andrew is a kind, beautiful prince and we are swimming together in a beautiful lake with trees all around, and we swim under and up again, our bodies gliding through the water. Then we rise out the water with our heads and shoulders above it and Andrew puts his arms around me and kisses me on the lips, like in the films, not like French people. Then we fade out like films, because I'm not sure what happens next. I don't tell Amy about the dream, because we always tease each other about who we fancy in class and I don't want her to know I fancy someone, even though we always tell each other everything.

It's sports-lesson time and today the teacher says, now you are learning dancing. All the boys snicker and the girls giggle. Spread out across the room, says the teacher Miss Taylor. We spread around the hall.

We are going to do country dancing today, says Miss Taylor, and you must get into partners of girls and boys. We all giggle but we don't move. No one wants to move first, and no one looks at anyone else. Okay, says the teacher. If you're not going to move, then the boys must find a partner. You must ask a girl to be your partner. That's the way it's usually done. We stand there and the boys are looking everywhere except in our directions, out of the window, at the ceiling, at each other, at the floor. Go on then, says the teacher, and we are all trying not to laugh – although the boys are not looking at us, we can see they are embarrassed. I'm glad I don't have to find a partner, because I'm embarrassed just standing there. But the boys don't move because none of them want to move first and be a sissy.

Then the teacher says, I am going to blow my whistle and the boys must choose a partner each and anyone who doesn't move and choose a partner straight away will be in detention and will have to miss their break time, then she blows her whistle and the boys move fast without any giggling at all. Then I look up, and there is Andrew the boy with scaly hands and he is crossing over, weaving through the moving boys and standing girls and he is coming straight towards me, curly brown hair and curling lashes, and I don't know where to look because maybe he's heading somewhere else behind me and I don't want to make a mistake and look silly. But he comes up to me and says shyly, but in a confident, friendly way, do you want to dance with me? And I try to look very cool, as if I couldn't care who asked me to dance, and I say, okay.

Then the teacher says, good, I'm glad to see you all so decisive, now you're in partners, boys must take their partners' hands. And Andrew reaches out his hand to me, little patches of scaly eczema, red and white, but it's not too bad, and I hold it gladly. It feels a little rough, but I am so happy, although I am trying not to look at him so I can still be cool. And we dance, in partners, in lines, swinging round and round. And Andrew is polite and quiet and I feel nice with him, like we're friends already, although we don't talk, and his hands are warm and friendly when I hold them, and just occasionally, we look at each other's eyes, catch each other on a turn.

After the class my friends say, ugh, how could you dance with that Andrew Bailey, you could have said no, you know, I wouldn't dance with someone with hands like that, it must have been awful. Didn't it feel all horrible?

But Mummy says eczema is just something some people get and it doesn't make them any different, it's just an allergy like some people get to pollen, like your eyes go red in summer, she says, and the person is just the same as they would be without it. And it's not going to hurt me. So when my friends ask what it was like, I just say, it was okay.

So now I daydream about Andrew, because he's not stuck up and doesn't think he's cool but was just really nice and asked me to dance and it was obvious he wanted to dance with me. Me and Andrew are going to grow up and get married and live happily ever after and maybe his eczema is going to get better or we will have lots of little children and even if they have eczema on their hands we won't care about it.

Being nine is the sound of bubbles, the smell of wallpaper, the coldness of the day, the stairs I walk, up and down, up and down, red carpet, held in at the sides by metal strips. I run my hands along the wallpaper as I walk up, one hand on the banister. I like to go two at a time sometimes. Then I stop at the little landing where the stairs turn round and go up at a right angle a short way to the top landing. The bathroom is on the left, the bedroom on the right, and Mummy and Rashid's bedroom is on the next right after that. I hear the splash, splash of Rashid in the bathroom and I hear his voice. Mai.

I stop at the top of the stairs next to the bathroom door. He is calling from inside the bathroom. Mai. The bathroom door is big and white. The smell of bubbles. Mai. Come here. I turn the doorknob.

I open the door and stand at the entrance of the bathroom. Rashid sits in the bubble bath, surrounded by bubbles. He is sitting knees up in the bath, scrubbing his back with the scrubbing brush, a wooden one with a long handle. Come inside, he says. Inside? Yes, he says. Close the door.

I close the door.

Lock it.

Lock it? I ask.

Yes, he says.

I slide the bolt across, a little round bolt you put your finger in and push sideways. Come here, says Rashid. I walk over. It is a long way from the door to the bath tub. Smell of soap and bubbles. The bath is enamel, tarnished white, like a rounded coffin.

When I get there, Rashid scrubs his back, the soapsuds spilling over his shoulders, his pale skin colour and the soapsuds merging together.

Come closer, Mai, he says, scrubbing hard. Wash my back.

Smell of bubbles. He puts soap on the scrubbing brush. With this, he says. He holds the long scrubbing-brush handle towards me, the brush end wet and heavy with soap and water. Your back? I ask. Yes, Rashid says. He leans forwards in the water, over bent knees. What are you waiting for? he says.

I begin rubbing the brush lightly across the back of Rashid's shoulders. He leans further forwards and is quiet, just breathing. I am scared, his horrible pasty back with hairs on it.

Scrub harder, he says. I can hardly feel you. I press so the bristles flatten out on the brush head, leaving white and red trails on his back. I don't want to do it wrong. I am only thinking of what might happen if I make a mistake. Rashid's skin shines under the bubbles and it makes me feel slightly sick.

Dip the brush in the water, he says. Rub it with soap again. I dip the brush in the water and Rashid passes the pink bar of soap, softly rounded by the bathwater, the soap creaming off in his big hands as he gives it to me. I rub the soap into the brush.

That's enough, Rashid says. Where do I put the soap? I ask. In the soap dish, he says. I lean forwards and put the soap in the soap dish.

Scrub my back harder this time. Lower down. He leans towards me. The bristle ends of the brush flay out where they touch his skin. The brush leaves marks where I press. Reddened lines along the creamy white soap on his back.

Go lower. Up and down. That's right.

I feel like a machine. Rashid seems impatient.

No, higher, not there, lower; that's it, across my whole back. He goes quiet as I keep scrubbing. Then he sighs. He turns round and takes the brush from me, by the long wooden handle, holds it in his hand, and puts it on the side of the bath.

Don't use the brush, use your hands, he says.

I start to rub his shoulders with the fingers of my right hand, gingerly. Wet cold slippery pasty skin ugh under my fingers, my palm, too much skin to cover at once, but I try.

No, both hands, he says. Use your whole hands. He leans forwards over his knees again, and I begin to rub with both palms. I'm scared to touch him. My hands are tiny on his huge back, and slide in the soap. I am so afraid of him. It feels scary to touch his skin, like touching the devil. But my hands have to stay there, moving back and forth, or I will be in trouble. Rashid sighs again. Is that enough? I ask. No, carry on, he says. I keep rubbing his back. More soap, he says. I put more soap on my hands, spending a long time so I don't have to touch him.

Hurry up, he says. I start, rubbing my palms up and down his back once more. His back must be clean by now, I think.

Can I stop now? I ask. He raises his head from his knees.

Why? says Rashid.

My hands are tired, I say. Your back is clean now. Can I leave?

He says nothing, only sits up. He is holding his hands between his legs. He lifts his hands up and takes soap and puts it on his hands and puts his hands back between his legs again. He smiles. No, not yet, he says. I want you to do something else first. He is rubbing his hands in the bubbles, then he lifts them and puts more soap on. I want you to wash here, he says.

Here is hands. Here is soap and soapsuds he rubs on his hands. Here is deep in the water, where a little pink bit of flesh sticks up between his legs. His hand moves up and down, mostly buried under the water.

I don't know what to do. I stand still.

Put soap on your hands, like this. The same way as you did my back, he says. Then wash here. He rolls the soap bar in his hands and rubs the pink flesh again, the water and bubbles moving around. I keep standing. Why are you taking so long? he asks. It's your willy, I say.

Yes, it is, he says. You've seen one before. Your little brother has one. When you give him a bath, you wash his, don't you? What's wrong with that? I don't wash his willy, I say. Why not? he asks. It's rude, I say. It's nice, he says. Come on, try it. He rubs the pink flesh again, faster.

I don't know what to say. I don't want to touch him any more. I pretend to joke, that it's funny. But it's wrong to touch a willy, I say.

No it's not. It's clean. I've put soap on it for you. Why is it wrong? It's nice. Come on, it's not so difficult. See, I'm doing it. You washed my back, there's no difference, it's the same thing. Don't you want to try it? He runs his hands up and down again. See? You'll like it.

Rashid is acting very nice. He is smiling at me in a nice way, like it's funny. I don't know why he's being so nice to me. Go on, he says. There's nothing wrong with it. Just try.

I want to leave. I washed his back. It's enough. And I hated washing his back. Nasty slippery ugly cold pale skin under my fingers. But Rashid is smiling, so I act like it's not serious, in case he gets angry. It's bad, I say. Who tells you it's bad? he says. I try to think of an answer.

Mummy does. She says it's bad.

Rashid stops washing. He looks towards the door. I look at the door. He is quiet for a while, rubbing more slowly. Are you sure you don't want to? he asks. Yes, I say, I'm sure. He still doesn't move, still bent forwards, feeling between his legs. Can I go now? I ask.

Are you sure? he asks.

Yes, I say.

Okay, you can go. I am relieved. I look at Rashid's back, still covered in soap. I'm worried he's angry I said no. Should I wash the soap off first? I ask. No, it's fine, he says. My hands are also covered with soap. I rinse them under the cold tap in the sink and dry them on the bath towel. I walk to the door, unlock it and open it. Goodbye, I say.

Rashid is still washing himself in the bath, bent over his legs. Shall I shut the door behind me? I ask. Yes, he says, still busy, not looking. I leave, closing the bathroom door behind me.

Why was Rashid being so nice to me? I think it's strange. I've never had to wash his back before. I hope I never have to again.

Mrs Cherry my class teacher used to be nice to me, but now she's not. At one time it looked like I was going to be head girl of the class, because I got good marks and Mrs Cherry liked me, but then Mrs Cherry did a thing in class where she talked about baptism. The project we did last week was to go home and ask our parents where we were baptised.

So, where was everyone baptised? asks Mrs Cherry. She's plump, with a soft downy moustache and orangey badly cut hair. She's quite strict, but not too much, and her body is rectangular like her haircut, and she wears an orange cardigan and brown skirt. Everyone has to stand up, one by one, round the class and tell Mrs Cherry where they were baptised.

Where were you baptised, Jane? Jane stands up. St Matthew's Church, London, Miss, says Jane. Thank you, you may sit. And you, Timmy? Timmy stands up. St Marks in Sheffield, Miss, says Timmy. Thank you, you may sit down.

Mrs Cherry goes round the class, one by one. I am on the last table in the class, so I have to wait. Our table is the biggest in the class, it has eight kids on it and everyone else has only six. One two three four five six seven eight, including myself. It is the best table in class. We have all the best ideas. Mrs Cherry gets to my table, and starts her way around the table. One two three four. I am six in line. She gets to Sally number five next to me, and Sally stands up. Where were you baptised, Sally? Sally next to me says, I was baptised at St John the Baptist Church in Lancashire, Miss. Thank you, Sally, says Mrs Cherry. You may sit down.

Now it's my turn. And where were you baptised, Mai? Mrs Cherry asks me, smiling. I stand up.

I wasn't baptised, I reply.

Come on, Mai, everyone was baptised somewhere. You must have been. You must go home and ask your mother where you were baptised and come back and tell us.

I wasn't baptised, Miss.

Did you ask your mother?

Yes, Miss.

Then you must go back and ask her again. I'm sure you've made a mistake. Everyone has been baptised somewhere.

I asked her and I'm sure I wasn't.

How do you know?

Because I was born without a father and there's no father's name on my birth certificate because my mum and dad weren't married when I was born and you have to have a mother and father when you get baptised. My mum says, if you don't have a father's name on your birth certificate, you can't get baptised.

Mrs Cherry shuffles on her feet. Her face goes bright red and kind of puffs up and her nostrils flare open and her eyes go wet looking and her mouth moves as if she wants to say something, but she doesn't. Her eyes flit around the class. Her face seems to be fighting with itself, undergoing a strange transformation. It looks like she might fall over.

Mrs Cherry says nothing, then she looks at Angela next to me. Where were you baptised? she asks Angela, in a squeaky voice.

Angela stands up. At St Martin's Church, Birmingham, Miss, Angela says.

I am still standing. Slowly, I sit down.

Mrs Cherry definitely treated me as a favourite before. But now she doesn't seem quite the same. She looks at me strangely and doesn't smile like she used to. She keeps telling us how you must love everyone, whoever they are, that God is about love for everyone, including the Holy Trinity, Jesus Christ and the Holy Spirit. She behaves differently towards me now. Not that I can help it. After all, I didn't decide where my dad's name went when I was born. I didn't choose not to be baptised. I kind of feel it is a bit unfair, because Jesus didn't grow up with his father, God, around and he didn't meet him either until he was a grown-up man and his dad spoke to him in the desert and he didn't even come out of the burning bush so he still didn't see him properly. He had his stepfather's surname like I did and his father wasn't there when he was born so maybe he wasn't baptised either. I can't see much of a difference because his mummy got married to Joseph and had other children with him, before she met someone else, and they called her Virgin Mary. Well, maybe my mummy was kind of like that too, because she had me on my own, then she married my sister's father soon after. Jesus would have understood, I thought, he never met his father too when he was a child. Where was God and everlasting love when Sister Mary Ann Jones stamped her foot down and screamed at us, and Mrs Cherry didn't seem very happy and nor did Sister Rose, and why should Mrs Cherry treat me differently just because no one had me baptised when I was little, not that I had a say in the matter anyway? All my friends know. They don't have a problem with it either.

At school, I say to my friends, I'm not afraid of boys, me and Amy beat a bully up once. My friends dare me to go hit a boy.

I run up to a boy in the year above me in the playground and I hit him on the arm. Hey, he says. What do you think you're doing? Say sorry. No, I say. I hit him again and this time he says, okay, if you want to fight I will, and he rolls up his sleeves. Fight! Fight! yell all his friends and the whole playground gathers around us and he hits me and I hit him. But I don't really know what I'm doing and after a while I say, okay, I give up, and the boy's friends yell, he won, he won! And my friends gather round and say, are you okay? And I say, yes, of course, although I'm hurting and, even though I want to, I'm definitely not going to cry.

I close my eyes and pass my fingers along the books in the library. I'm allowed to read the adult books, Mummy says they made a special arrangement at the library because I'm ahead with my reading and now I have an adult ticket.

I close my eyes and walk along the bookshelf with my eyes shut, running my fingers across the books until I decide to stop. Then, whatever book my fingers have landed on when I open my eyes, I have to take out. The books on my level are mostly science fiction, the books Mummy said my daddy from the Philippines liked. I discover Sir Arthur Conan Doyle, and Ray Bradbury and Arthur C. Clarke, opening my eyes where my finger touches. I discover the stars, and people in the future, big round moons, space stations. I read Sir Arthur Conan Doyle's *The Lost World* and discover dinosaurs, and time travel with H.G. Wells. Further on are the short-story shelves, and I discover Aldous Huxley's short stories – stories about strange goings-on between grown-ups I can only guess at, but I like the writing, and Saki's stories, that seem weird and wonderful. And further on I discover Sherlock Holmes and Dr Watson, mysteries and adventures. And then I read Agatha Christie detective stories, the ones that Mummy likes. I read a book of Mummy's from the library and it's a story about children but in the book a man in the Deep South runs away because everyone is after him, they are going to lynch him because he slept in a white woman's bed and I think, they're crazy, all he did was sleep in her bed and now they want to kill him, if he had put all the covers back properly she might not have even noticed he had been there, why would they want to do that?

I like reading. Sometimes the books smell, as if the scent of previous readers has lingered on, fingers turning, the smell of fingertips, sneezes, of someone reading over coffee, and sometimes the pages are stale and damp, as if the book got wet in the bath, and sometimes nasty unpleasant smells like sick when I open the pages that make me put the book back again. The books are heavy, solid. When Mummy goes shopping she lets me stay in the library and take out books, and when she takes hers out I take mine out too. Some of the books have big writing inside and Mummy says that's for people who can't see very well.

I take out books every week, and they go back again at the end of the week, that's also part of the game, because if I don't read them I must take out new ones. I take out craft and drawing books, and use these to make cards, origami and paper cut-outs. The books are heavy, and I must wrap my arms around their hard covers to make sure I don't drop them. When I bring my big pile of books to the desk the librarian always smiles at me. I like stories. I love reading. Reading takes me to lots of places and reminds me how big the world is. When I am grown up and I am free to do what I want I am going to explore the world like all these books. And I will be clever like Sir Arthur Conan Doyle and Aldous Huxley and I will write just like them and I will also be a scientist.

And sometimes I look up at the stars and I think of all the other worlds out there and I wonder if I'll ever meet anyone from another planet and what the children must be like. And maybe one day the aliens will come down and take me to live on their planet and everyone will be happy ever after.

It is night. It's the middle of summer and it's too hot for pyjamas so we don't wear any, just our knickers in bed. I get out of bed and I go to the bathroom at night and as I'm walking back to bed Rashid calls me – Is that you, Mai? And I say, yes, and he says, can you bring me some toilet paper from the bathroom? So I bring it into his bedroom for him where he is lying in bed, but he doesn't blow his nose like I expect him to, he just takes the tissue paper in his hand and puts it under the bedclothes and then he says, we are going to play a game. What game? I say.

We are going to play Pork and Beans, he says.

Pork and Beans is a game we play at school where you mustn't smile when someone asks you a question, you must just say pork and beans as a response, and even if they say what is your name? and what is your favourite subject at school? you must answer pork and beans without laughing, and if you laugh, you lose. So Rashid asks lots of questions and I have to answer the questions with pork and beans, and then Rashid starts pointing to different parts of me and asking, what's this? and what's this? and I say pork and beans. It's weird because Rashid never plays any games at night, especially when I'm meant to be in bed.

Then Mummy comes upstairs and she comes in the bedroom. She looks at him and looks at me funny, and she says, Rashid, what is going on? And he says, nothing. Mummy looks at me, and I say we are playing Pork and Beans. What on earth are you up to? says Mummy to Rashid. Then Mummy looks at Rashid very strangely and then she looks at me and she says, go to bed, Mai. I go back to bed, and sleep.

The next day, Mummy asks, Mai, what was happening last night with Rashid when you were in the bedroom? I tell her we were playing Pork and Beans. What do you mean? asks Mummy. I tell her the game. Was it your idea? asks Mummy. No, it was his, I say. Why were you in the bedroom? she asks. He called me there, I say. It's not normal to get you out of bed to play games. Did he wake you up? asks Mummy. No, I was awake. I was coming back from the toilet and he called me. He said I must bring him some toilet paper. Mummy looks worried. Why would he ask you to do that? she says, as if to herself. Maybe he had a cold, I say. But I didn't see him blow his nose. What did he do with it? asks Mummy. He kept it under the blanket, and he held it there with his hand.

What sort of questions was he asking you? He said, what's this? And what's this? And he pointed to different things, I reply. When I came in it looked like he was pointing at you, says Mummy. Was he? Yes, I say. Do you remember where? Different places, I say. Did he touch you? asks Mummy. His finger touched me where he pointed at me, I say. In rude places? asks Mummy. I don't know, I reply, where is rude? Where exactly did he touch you, Mai? asks Mummy. Tell me.

My nose and my mouth, I say. My ear. My eye. And my belly button. Is that rude? My chest too. Where exactly? says Mummy. I point to both sides of my chest. Here and here, I say. He touched me other places, I can't remember them all. Did he touch you between your legs? says Mummy. What do you mean? I ask. You mean my knees? I mean did he touch you where your legs meet at the top? says Mummy. Not between my legs but he touched me at the front, I say.

There's something very wrong here, says Mummy, as if to herself. Has Rashid done this sort of thing before? asks Mummy.

You mean, play Pork and Beans? No, it's the first time.

I mean has he done anything else you thought was weird?

Everything Rashid does is weird, I say. Like when he sent me to bed because I didn't dry my toothbrush. That was weird.

Other things, says Mummy. I mean, has he ever touched you in a strange way? Think hard, Mai, she says. Can you think of anything? Even if it seems silly, tell me. Has he ever touched you in any way at all that you thought was strange?

When he hurts me he touches me, he twists my ears and he pokes me with his finger in my chest.

You must think very hard, Mai, says Mummy. It's very important. Nothing else?

Does touching with his tummy count? I ask. In what way? says Mummy. How?

I tell Mummy how Rashid lay down when we were fixing shoes and put me on his tummy. That was weird, I say. But he didn't hurt me. Mummy's face looks strange. Her voice is sharp, but not at me. He put you on top of him? asks Mummy. Yes, I say. But he didn't hurt me, he was just breathing funny. Then I asked if I could get off. And he asked why, didn't I like it? And I said no. Where was I? asks Mummy. In the kitchen, I say. But he locked the door so you couldn't come in anyway. Is that rude?

Yes, says Mummy. It's very rude. Grown men don't do things like that to little girls. Tell me exactly what happened. So I tell her. Afterwards, Mummy says again, is there anything else? Any

142

other time he touched you that you can think of, Mai? I can't think of any, I say. Okay, says Mummy.

What about him making you touch him? says Mummy. Has he done that?

When I washed his back in the bath I had to touch him, I say. Does that count?

In the bath? says Mummy. She sounds very shocked. That doesn't sound right. And are you sure you only washed his back? Yes, I say. Did he touch you at all? asks Mummy. No, he didn't. And you didn't touch anywhere else? asks Mummy. No, I say.

Then I add, he did ask me to wash his willy but I said no. So I didn't touch it.

Mummy looks shocked. What? What do you mean? You must tell me exactly what happened. Everything, in detail.

I tell her.

Mummy is very quiet afterwards. Is there anything else you can think of, Mai? she says.

No, I say.

And is that the only time you have seen him without his clothes on?

I think hard. He did get into my bed with no clothes on one night, but I didn't touch him because I curled up in a ball, I say. What? says Mummy. What happened? Where was Amy? asks Mummy. She was asleep in the other bed, I say. You must let me know everything, says Mummy. Mummy makes me tell her everything over and again.

Afterwards, Mummy looks very strange. She looks pale and serious. What Rashid has been doing is very wrong, Mai, Mummy says. Why? I ask. Are those things bad? Yes, says Mummy. Grown men don't do those sorts of things. He was doing things he shouldn't do. Why didn't you tell me before he was doing all these strange things to you? says Mummy.

He always does strange things, I say. But he didn't hurt me those times, so I didn't think it was so bad. It's worse when he hurts me.

Big men don't do things like that to little girls, Mummy says. You mustn't let him touch you again, or play games like that. You must tell me if Rashid does anything else weird at all. Anything. Even if it seems silly. And if he tries again then you must tell him, no, Mummy says it's bad, and come to me straight away. Even if you're not sure.

But everything Rashid does is weird, I say.

Mummy is thinking in front of me. Then she says, you are going to Granddad's with Amy to stay for a while. We need to sort this out. Mummy looks very upset. I feel bad.

It's not that bad, Mummy. He didn't hurt me, Mummy. Not like when he twists our ears or our wrists or prods us in the chest.

Don't worry, Mai, says Mummy. You did a good thing to tell me. I needed to know this.

Here I am at Granddad's, watching the fish in the fish tank go back and forth again. Amy and I are staying here for a short while. Mummy says until she's sorted things out. I remember the time we were last here, when Mummy got married. We play our game of sneaking down the stairs on the right of Granddad when he is so busy watching football he doesn't notice. We sit behind the orange armchair as he is watching TV and we stick our heads out from behind him again. Then Granddad turns around and says, I know you're there, go to bed. And Granddad sticks his head around the back of the orange armchair and we go running up the stairs.

We go to the doctor's. Mummy is there with a strange lady and there is another lady who Mummy says is a doctor who is just going to look at my tummy, I mustn't be frightened. But now I know they're up to something or they wouldn't tell me not to be frightened, so I stand at the other end of the room behind the big sofa, between me and the two ladies and Mummy.

Come on, Mai, just come and lie on the bed.

Why? I say.

The doctor just wants to look at you.

What for?

She just wants to see your tummy.

There's nothing wrong with my tummy.

It's just a normal check-up, says the strange lady. You've been to the doctor's at school, haven't you?

Yes, I had my eyes checked.

Well, this is the same thing with your tummy. You'll be fine, I promise you.

You promise?

Yes.

Okay then.

I lie on the bed dressed in just a big apron and the doctor looks at my tummy. She tickles me and I laugh. Then she says, your tummy looks fine, I'm just going to look quickly a bit further down, but you won't feel anything.

The other lady is asking me questions like what do you do at school? Who are your friends?

Then the doctor lady says to Mummy, yes, everything looks fine to me. Thank God, Mummy says. Are you sure? Yes, she's fine, says the doctor. She can get her clothes on again.

Mummy says Rashid is going away for a while. She says what he was doing to me was very bad, that she contacted the police and they said they were definite signs that he was going to take things further, and sexually molest me.

I have no idea what Mummy means, but then Mummy says,

the rude things Rashid did, they are things only adults know about, he shouldn't do them to children. He isn't normal.

Mummy says the police wanted to arrest Rashid right away, as they were convinced there was enough evidence to prosecute him, and the only other option was to agree to treatment at the mental hospital for three years. So the next day she told Rashid the police were waiting to arrest him right away unless he went in for treatment at the mental hospital. So he had no choice but to go. And now he's going to be there for treatment, says Mummy, until he's better. It will take three years, the police say, says Mummy.

I tell Amy what Rashid did, and that it was bad.

Amy says she couldn't sleep one night when we were at Granddad's and went to sleep in Granddad's bed and he was sleeping then he took her hand and put it on his willy.

Was he asleep? asks Mummy. Maybe he was, says Amy, I think he was asleep. I think he was drunk from too much whisky.

I don't think Granddad would do a thing like that, says Mummy, could you have been dreaming?

Maybe, says Amy, but I remember him doing it.

Are you sure? says Mummy. Are you sure you didn't imagine it after you heard all Mai's stories?

Maybe you imagined it, I tell Amy. Maybe you made it up.

No, says Amy. He put my hand there. Then I took it away. But he could have been asleep.

Mummy looks shocked. Maybe he was sleeping and didn't realise what he was doing, Mummy says. Whether it's true or not, I can't let you stay with Granddad again, it's too much of a risk. I don't know who I can trust any more, Mummy says.

The Catholic school wants me to repeat a year because I'm a year ahead of my age group and they say I have to be a year older to go to secondary school, so they say I have to do the year again.

Mummy says that's a complete waste of time and it would be stupid to repeat the same year again and she won't let me repeat a year of school that I know already. So Amy and I change to Greendale Middle School. I like Greendale Middle School because it's a crazy place, you can do what you like there and it's not like home at all.

My new form teacher is called Mr Downs, but we call him Mr D for short. Mr D says chalk, cheese and chatter are the three things he hates in life. We have to be quiet when he says that. He wrote the words big on the blackboard when the year first started.

I like Mr D with his chalk, cheese and chatter, but I don't like what Robert Greene said the first day. Robert Greene is my enemy since I arrived in school, because he called me Ching Chong on my first day in class. He kept prodding me in the back at TV lesson time with his bunch of friends and telling me to go home, when the teacher went outside.

Go home, Chink, says Robert, and his friends giggle. I ignore him. He pulls my hair. Chink. We don't want you here. Go back to your country. His friends are giggling more.

Stop it, my new friend Sarah next to me says, and my face feels red and hot.

Ching Chong, says Robert.

Just stop it, says Sarah to them. Leave her alone. She's new here.

Chinky go home, says Robert, prodding me in the back again. Take your dirty yellow skin out of here. Robert keeps sniggering behind me and poking me and saying Chink and I ignore him all the way through the lesson. He carries on doing it for three weeks, especially when we watch the TV education programme. Just ignore him, says Sarah. He thinks he's special, just because he comes first in class.

Robert Bigmouth Rubber Lips, I call him because he has big pale rubber lips and a big mouth like a goldfish and shouts a lot and is stuck up, he thinks he is better than all of us. When I come first in class at the end of first term and he tries to be friendly because now he thinks I'm clever, I still hate him.

Wow, first in class, says Robert. Congratulations. I came second.

I look at him like he's mad.

The only other boy I don't like in class apart from Robert Rubber Lips is Fred Higgins, because he picks his nose in class and he smokes and he drinks alcohol out of school even though he's only ten. He's fair haired and scruffy and there's always snot coming out of his nose. I will never fall in love with Fred Higgins. Not in a million years. We ask him if it's true he drinks and smokes out of school.

Yeah, he says. Of course it's true.

Who gives it to you?

My dad. He lets me.

Mr D says we mustn't be so cruel to Fred Higgins. That it's difficult for him at home.

I get a big pack of felt-tip pens for my birthday from Mummy, and bring it to school. Everyone wants to borrow them. They queue up in a line at my desk. Robert Bigmouth Rubber Lips is in the queue and Fred Higgins is right behind him. Can I borrow a light blue? asks Lucy, who is at the front of the line. Yes, of course, I say. Here we are. Can I borrow a green and brown? asks Julian, who is next, and I give them to him. Tim is in the queue next, and wants a purple. Of course, I say. I feel special with all my classmates queuing up to borrow my felt-tip pens.

Robert is right behind Julian, and Fred Higgins with his snotty nose is right behind him. Can I borrow a red, please? asks Robert in his nicest possible voice. I look at him.

No, I say.

Sorry?

No, you can't.

Can I borrow another colour then? Orange is fine.

No.

Robert's mouth falls open. Why not?

Because I said so.

But you lent everyone else one.

Well, I'm not lending you one.

Why not? Just tell me why.

I look him straight in the eyes. You know why.

No, I've no idea. What did I do that I can't borrow a pen? I've always been friendly to you.

You've always been friendly to me?

Yes. I even congratulated you on your class marks.

I stare at him. Well, you can't have one.

I see Fred Higgins standing behind Robert and I ask, what do you want, Fred? Robert continues to stare at me with his big rubbery lips open.

Black, please, says Fred.

Of course, Fred, here we are. And you can borrow the red too.

I don't want red, says Fred.

Borrow it anyway. I give both colours to him, as Robert steps to the side.

She gave him the red! shrieks Robert. She gave Fred Higgins the red and she wouldn't give it to me! He's not even using it. See, he's stuck it up his nose!

I look at Fred Higgins, who has stuck the ends of the red and black felt-tips up both his nostrils. Look, I'm a walrus, says Fred to the rest of the queue for felt-tips at my desk, and he sniggers as he goes off back to his desk.

So what, I say to Robert. I'd rather he had them than you.

Why are you always so nasty to me? says Robert.

You know why, I say. You just don't want to admit it.

I don't know, he says. I really don't know.

Robert slinks back to his desk and stays very quiet. I have to fight with Fred Higgins after to get the felt-tip pens back again, but it's worth it. I feel a bit sorry for Robert, but he deserves it.

Why are you mean to Robert? asks Sarah. He's nice to you now.

He's only sucking up to me because I came first in class and not him. If I didn't he would still call me Chink, I say. Bigmouth Robert. His mouth is so big, if they threw him against the wall, he would stick there, I say.

Robert is always extra nice to me after that.

I wonder if I should fancy him a bit too, but I never will. Fred Higgins is dirty and rude and cruel and stupid but he has never said 'Chink, go home to your country' to me.

Mr Foley the headmaster comes to our class to tell us about the special school project. He stands at the front of the classroom in a grey suit, cut so it pokes out at angles on his tall skinny frame. He looks very smart. His bushy eyebrows move up and down as he speaks.

Mr D, our form teacher, sits at the front, filling in the class register.

Are you all listening? says Mr Foley in his aged voice. I have an important announcement to make. I need your full attention. You, boy, look at me, don't look out of the window. That includes you too, Mr Downs, says Mr Foley as he turns towards Mr D who is still writing the register.

The class snickers. Sorry, Mr Foley, says Mr D, and he abruptly puts down his blue biro with the chewed end.

Mr Foley stands tall like a lamp post. Everyone is listening.

You are going to start a Very Special Project in the name of Science, says Mr Foley, his long thin body weaving before us, and his eyes and eyebrows scanning the class. It is a science project of

Utmost Importance they are trying out for schools. A brand-new project, the First in the Country. And our school, out of all the schools in the Entire Nation, has been selected for the pilot study. And of all the classes that could have been selected, your class has been chosen. That means you must all pay attention, and work very hard on the project, as your class is very special to have been selected. The course is on the effects of smoking.

And his heavy eyebrows rise and fall as he speaks, and we can see Mr D's feet fidgeting under the desk.

The course starts, and our class watches films of old men panting up and down steps in front of doctors with stethoscopes and white coats, with the word EMPHYSEMA in big bold letters on the screen. And then we have to do experiments with strange wriggly test tubes with a cigarette at one end, and watch the smoke move down to the other end, plugged with white cotton wool that slowly turns black and yellow. We look at real grey and stained smokers' lungs with blobs of cancer, and compare them with fresh pink lungs that are brought in white plastic tubs to our classroom by women in white coats. I look at the lungs and I think that must be how Nana died.

It doesn't bother me, says Fred Higgins, my dad lets me smoke cigarettes at home whenever I want, because he says I'm old enough to be a man.

Mummy says Rashid is supposed to be away as an inpatient in the mental hospital for three years. But he is coming back again after only three months, because the psychiatrist at the hospital says he is better. Mummy says the psychiatrist at the hospital is an idiot. He's stupid, says Mummy. His name is Mr Eadie. Rashid boasts that he goes in the room and the psychiatrist says he can say whatever he wants, so Rashid just sits and says nothing. And now, after only three months, the psychiatrist says Rashid is cured and he can leave, says Mummy. He's coming back tomorrow.

Rashid comes back from the hospital, and on the same day he calls Amy and me into his bedroom one by one.

I stand in the bedroom where he has called me, and he stands opposite me.

I want to say that I'm really sorry for everything, says Rashid, and I won't ever do things like that again. I'm going to try very hard to make things better. I want us all to start again. I would like to give this to you to say sorry, it's a present for you. He holds out a fifty-pence piece.

I don't want to take it, I don't want his money, but I can't say anything, I have to take it, or there'll be trouble.

I let him put it in my hand.

Thank you, Rashid, I say.

You must stop calling me Rashid, and I want you to call me Dad like Matti and Babs do, I want us to be one family, says Rashid. I really mean it. You must call me Dad from now on, he says.

Thank you, Dad. The name rolls off my tongue like it doesn't belong there. I walk out of the room clutching the fifty-pence piece in my hand. It feels huge, a strange cold pointy sharp disc between my fingers.

Did he give you fifty pence too? I ask Amy later.

Yes, says Amy. He said we have to call him Dad. Ugh. I've already got a dad. Does that mean I have to stop calling my dad Dad? asks Amy.

I suppose so, I say.

Five weeks' pocket money. Rashid didn't look that sorry. I can't figure out why he gave it to us. Was all this worth fifty pence? It is like he is trying to buy something from me.

7

Losing

Please, Rashid, please ... please don't take them.

It is morning, two days later. Mummy is crying. Mummy is not only crying but she is hanging onto Rashid's arm in the hallway and sobbing, wailing. Get off me, woman, says Rashid, and shakes her off his arm, but she reaches out and clings to him again. Please, Rashid, cries Mummy. Don't take them from me. You can't do this. You can't do this to me. Matti and Babs are in the hall dressed in their coats and hats and look confused, and there are two packed suitcases in the hall too.

Amy and I come downstairs. What's wrong? we ask. Are Matti and Babs leaving? Where are you taking them? They are going on holiday, says Rashid.

Go to the other room and stay there, Mummy says quickly to Amy and me between her tears, trying to stop crying. We see her arm. It has a big black bruise on it. It is so big and black, and purple too, more like two bruises. What's wrong with your arm, Mummy? we ask.

Rashid looks at Mummy and Mummy looks scared. I caught it in the cupboard door, she says. But it's so big, we say. It's nothing, she says. Nothing to worry about. Please, Mai and Amy, go in the other room.

We can see Mummy through the partly open sitting-room door. She is holding onto Rashid's arm again, still begging him and crying. Please, Rashid, she says. Please. Please. Don't take my children. Please don't take my children from me. She is sobbing hysterically. You can't be so cruel. Please, Rashid, they're my children too. She is shaking. Please, you can't take them from me. We can stay together. We can make it work.

Leave off, woman, Rashid says. Do you want more trouble?

Please, Rashid. Please reconsider. They're only two and three years old … don't take them away.

Shut up, he says. I told you already. I told you already what will happen if you cause trouble. Remember what I told you? Mummy is crying very loud but she lets go of Rashid's arm.

Rashid is moving towards the door, a suitcase under his arm, and Matti and Babs are standing there, staring at everything. He takes them by their hands. We hear a car drive up outside. Rashid opens the door to look and closes it again. The taxi's here, he says. We're leaving. Any trouble from you and you'll be to blame for what happens, remember that.

Please, Rashid. Mummy is shrieking, almost screaming. Please. Please don't take them away. They're my children. She grabs his arm again, trying to hold him back. He pushes her away. I said to leave off, he says. Don't you try anything. You know what will happen. Mummy is standing very still, crying and crying, she is crying so loud we feel really sorry for her. We don't understand.

Why is she so sad if they are going on holiday? whispers Amy.

I don't know, I say.

Rashid opens the front door again, this time wide. Mummy is still pleading, quietly. Please, Rashid. Please. Please don't do it.

Why is Mummy crying so much? Why is she shaking? Why is she begging for them to stay?

Please don't. Please reconsider, Rashid. I'll do anything for you. Anything you want. Mummy is crying like she is groaning now. No, Rashid. No.

Mummy is so sad, so wild, like a wild animal, all jumpy and twitchy, with flaming nostrils. No, she screams. She tries to reach out to hold him again, but he moves his arm back. He takes Matti and Babs outside. He reaches in and takes the second suitcase.

Don't try anything stupid, Rashid says as he leads Matti and Babs to the door. Remember what I said. I mean what I say, he says.

He closes the door behind him and we hear the car drive off outside. Then there is silence.

Mummy keeps crying and crying and wailing against the wall, beating it helplessly with her fist.

Then she walks back into the kitchen and sits at the table still crying, over and over.

Amy and I go into the kitchen and hold her. Don't worry, Mummy, we say, they're only going on holiday. Why aren't we going on holiday too? They're coming back, why are you so upset? They'll be back soon. And then Mummy cries even louder, bending over the kitchen table, face buried in her arms.

They're not coming back, Mummy says. Rashid has abducted them to Morocco and he is never coming back. I'll never see my children again.

Rashid tied me up in a chair with a rope in the bedroom last night and beat me up, says Mummy between her tears. He put sticky tape over my mouth so I couldn't scream. He beat me on my head and body. Some of the time I lost consciousness, I can't remember some of it. He beat me up all night, all over my body, my body is covered with bruises, but not around my face, he said, so no one would know. He's taken Matti and Babs away from me forever and it is a punishment for putting him in the mental hospital. He hit me all over, says Mummy, all night long, on my stomach and arms as well as around my head. I have bruises everywhere.

I threw up from all the hitting, that's the only reason he took the sticky tape off my mouth because I threw up and I couldn't breathe and was suffocating.

The only way I could get him to stop hitting me was to pretend I had seen Nana's ghost, says Mummy, because Rashid is scared of ghosts. I pretended to talk to Nana, as if I was seeing her. He got scared then, says Mummy, and calmed down a bit. Otherwise he was going to seriously hurt me, I don't know what he would have done. But he wasn't scared enough to stop what he had planned.

He enjoyed it, says Mummy. He was smiling all the way through.

Mummy sees my and Amy's faces and she tries to stop crying, and she touches us on our arms and says, don't worry, it will be okay. But she still can't stop crying, and the tears and the sobs carry on down her face.

He was supposed to be cured, cries Mummy. And he comes out, with that idiot of a psychiatrist saying he is cured after only three months and not three years, then three days later he beats me up and abducts the children to Morocco. What kind of psychiatrist was that? It was all planned while he was in the mental hospital. He boasted about it to me, how he fooled the psychiatrist. He had Matti's and Babs' bags packed, the plane tickets ready. Everything was ready. Even the rope and the sticky tape.

He's not coming back, says Mummy.

Why don't you go to the police, Mummy? we say.

He says if I get the police to try to stop him before he gets to the airport he will do something terrible to Matti and Babs, says Mummy, and I know he will. He said he would really hurt me, and Matti and Babs and you two too. He's abducted my little children, cries Mummy, and he's on his way to the airport right now, and I can't do anything to stop him.

Amy and me don't know what abduction is, but Mummy says it means they will be taken to Morocco and once they are there she cannot get them back, ever again, because the law is not on her side there and there is nothing she can do about it.

I lied to you about the bruise on my arm being from the cupboard, says Mummy, because it came from Rashid and I didn't want to scare you, I didn't want him to hurt you too, she says, that's why I told you to go to the other room.

Now Rashid is gone.

It seems very quiet now we don't have Matti and Babs to play with. We don't know whether to be glad Rashid has gone, or sad about our little brother and sister. We look at Mummy's big bruise.

You should go to the doctor, Mummy, we say. But Mummy shakes her head. I can't do anything that alarms people, she says. He said he would do something nasty to them if I did so, and I would regret it. I think he would. I can't take the risk, things are bad enough already.

I don't like the idea of Mummy being tied to a chair and Rashid hitting her, hitting her. I don't like the giant purple bruise we can see covering half of Mummy's arm – it spreads out like a big blob, like the amoeba in my science book, and changes colour over the week. Mummy says it doesn't hurt much, but I think she's just saying it. I don't see the other bruises.

I don't know why Mummy married Rashid. When she married him, he wasn't our dad. He was Rashid. He came on weekends and Amy and I kept away from him. When he gave us fifty pence, he lied to us, he said he was sorry and he was our dad. He said he would be nice to us.

Amy and me spend our fifty pences, but it doesn't feel nice. It feels nice to have all that money, we've never been so rich. But that fifty pence never felt like it ever belonged to me. I just want to spend it as fast as I can to get rid of it.

Amy and I go to stay with Uncle Gregory and Aunt Celine in London. Mummy says Aunt Celine is a common-law wife because Uncle Gregory left Aunt Natasha and his children for her and that is why he is the black sheep of the family. Mummy says Uncle Gregory isn't responsible at all because he was spoilt when he was young and he spent all Aunt Natasha's money on an expensive sports car and then he crashed it. When we arrive our older boy cousins Brendan and Saul are visiting and Uncle Gregory says to them in a loud voice, hey, I forgot to give you your Christmas presents, here's ten pounds each to buy something, and our cousin Brendan, the younger one, says, why thanks Dad, are you feeling okay? Christmas was months ago. It's not like you.

Uncle Gregory lives in a council flat in London, and we meet Aunt Celine and their baby boy Abraham who is three years old and screams a lot especially when he sees sweets and nice things in the windows when Aunt Celine pushes him in his pushchair through the streets in London. Aunt Celine is a bit of a hippy, says Mummy, and she works as a waitress now she isn't at art school any more. Aunt Celine eats only vegetables and lentils and she has masses of blonde hair and is young. Mummy says she was a student of Uncle Gregory's and Aunt Celine had to leave university at eighteen because she got pregnant with our little cousin Abraham before Uncle Gregory left his wife.

Our cousin Abraham is blond with blue eyes and Aunt Celine says he did some modelling because he is so pretty, but we think he is just spoilt, especially when he screams all the time and gets his way.

Aunt Celine takes us to the cinema and it's a big pink hippo and then another film with dancing elephants and there are lots of big elephants floating around like bubbles and Aunt Celine says it's *Fantasia* and it's classical music. Amy and I don't know what to make of it, we've never seen elephants floating around to music before and we never went to the cinema before either.

When we get back I look at the bookshelf at Aunt Celine's and Uncle Gregory's and under some other books I find photograph books with lots of dark-skinned naked men in them where you can see everything and I say to Aunt Celine, why do you have all those pictures of men with no clothes on, isn't that rude? and she giggles and says, no, I don't think so, it's Mapplethorpe, I think the photographs are very artistic. I say, they are showing their willies, it's rude, Mummy says people shouldn't do that, and Aunt Celine says, you shouldn't be going through the bookcase anyway, it's only for adults.

When we get home again I'm glad to be back because we don't have to listen to our screaming cousin any more.

The anti-smoking course comes to an end. Mr D says Mr Foley is coming back to our classroom on Tuesday afternoon, to talk to us on our own, to find out how we felt about it, and whether it has had any impact on us.

Then Mr D says we are going to play a practical joke on Mr Foley when he comes to talk to us on Tuesday. It will be very funny, he says. I am going to buy thirty-six of those sweet cigarettes from the sweet shop, he says, you know, the ones that look just like cigarettes and come in a pack and the ends look all red and fiery as if they are lit, and when Mr Foley comes in to talk to the class every kid will have a sweet cigarette between their lips. It will be a great practical joke, he says.

So, when Mr Foley comes back, we each have a sweet cigarette held in our hands under our desks. Mr D got Paul, who sits in the corner, to give them out to everyone. And Mr Foley comes in again looking like a lamp post with his grey furry eyebrows and he stands in front of the blackboard and says, I would like to have your attention. I am here today to talk to you about the anti-smoking course you have just been on and what you have learnt from it.

Then Paul puts his sweet cigarette in his mouth and then so does Sarah, and the rest of us are a bit worried, but then so does Karen and so does Robert and then Jonathan, and then Jessica Strong and Marion Donalds and even Michael Stevens, so the rest of us start to put our cigarettes in our mouths too, and some of us hold them halfway up between our mouths and our desks, hesitantly, like I do.

Mr Foley stops talking. He looks around the class. Then he bends forwards over Robert in the front. What is that you have in your mouth, boy? Mr Foley asks Robert. A sweet cigarette, says Robert. It's not real, it's a sweet. He takes it out of his mouth and shows Mr Foley. And is that one you have too? asks Mr Foley, leaning towards Paul. Yes, Mr Foley, says Paul, in a small voice. And all of you? asks Mr Foley, his thin body weaving and his furry eyebrows frowning so heavily, it is as if he is going to topple over with them.

Yes, Mr Foley, we say.

Where did you get them from? he asks Paul.

Mr Downs gave them to us, Mr Foley, Sir, says Paul.

Mr Downs? What on earth for?

He said it was a practical joke, says Paul.

A joke? says Mr Foley, bending towards us.

All thirty-six of us nod. Then, for a second, Mr Foley's mouth twists up at the ends into a thin smile and a strange snorting sound comes out of the side of his mouth, which he quickly stops. I see, he says. Then he straightens up again and so does his mouth, and his eyebrows, and he stands tall like a lamp post again.

You should tell Mr Downs he should know better, says Mr

Foley. This is not funny – he is messing up the whole experiment. He will be in trouble for this.

Afterwards, we see Mr D outside and Mr Foley talking to him and we can see Mr D is being told off because he has his head down and he's saying, yes, Mr Foley, you're right, Mr Foley, just like a schoolboy, and after that Mr D never speaks again of his practical joke that could have messed up an entire national project.

After the science project, I decide I'm going to be a doctor and an artist and a writer and maybe a TV star when I grow up. Last week, we dissected a pig's eye in science class and put the lens on a piece of newspaper to make the writing go bigger. So I form a Science Dissection Club with three of my friends, Sarah, Malcolm and Lucille, so I can learn how to be a doctor.

We tell Mr D but he doesn't seem impressed, he doesn't really speak about the science project since Mr Foley told him off. Mr D says we drive him mad anyway, especially since the time we decided to collect a load of ladybirds at lunchtime and stored them in Malcolm's empty lunch box, and they all escaped because we kept the lid open a bit to give them air, and the whole class had to take all the ladybirds out, one by one, from all over the desks, even the kids pretending to have ladybirds just so they could go outside. And then there was the time we created a graph of all the times the home-economics teacher Mrs Featherstone said 'Um …' and 'Er …' in class, and also the number of times she mentioned her dead husband, which she did a lot, and Mr D said that wasn't a very nice thing to do.

So the first thing we do in the Science Dissection Club is decide to dissect something, and Malcolm says we can dissect a slug to start with, they're everywhere. His dad is a doctor so he's going to bring a scalpel, we're going to dissect out its heart. But when we look at the slug, wriggling around on the piece of paper Malcolm put it on, no one wants to kill it. We have to kill it, says Malcolm. We can't dissect it if it's alive. Even Robert Rubber Lips who stayed behind to join our group because he thinks he's clever doesn't want to kill it.

I know, says Fred Higgins, we must use salt. My dad uses it on his slugs.

How does he do it? we ask.

I dunno, says Fred. Just pour it on, I expect.

The bag of crisps I brought for lunch has a little packet of salt, says Malcolm. You could use that. I hope it's worth having horrible-tasting crisps with no salt. He opens the bag of crisps and gives Fred the small salt packet.

Fred Higgins tears off the corner of the packet. He sprinkles some of the salt over the slug on the piece of paper. Okay, he says. Here we go.

The white salt cascades out like a waterfall over the slug.

When the salt hits the slug, it starts to wriggle. Try more, says Lucille.

Fred Higgins tips the packet up and pours more on the slug.

As the salt pours down, the slug begins to writhe. Its body twirls. Bubbles appear on the salt. The slug goes mad. It shrinks. As the water from its body dissolves into the salt, it shrivels and contorts its body like crazy.

Ugh, it's horrible, we say.

When is it going to stop? asks Sarah.

Stop pouring the salt, says Malcolm to Fred Higgins. Stop.

Just a bit more, says Fred Higgins and keeps pouring until the salt packet is finished.

Horrified, we watch the slug squirm, twist and wriggle. We feel sick. The slug wriggles and wriggles, then slows down and stops, a little grey blob in a hill of salt. It looks small, hard and tough.

We stand in silence and look at the slug.

Is it dead? asks Malcolm.

Fred Higgins pokes the grey blob.

Yeah, it's dead, he says.

I feel a bit sick in the pit of my stomach. I don't really feel like dissecting it any more, I say.

Nor do I, says Lucille.

You said you wanted it dead, says Fred Higgins. I just did what you wanted.

Next time, I say. All that salt … makes it difficult.

I don't feel like eating the crisps from my lunch box any more, says Malcolm.

I'll have them, says Fred Higgins, and eats them happily.

We go off dissection after that. The dissection club disbands, moves on to other things.

Amy's father has come to visit England, says Mummy. He is visiting from South Africa. He has come to see Amy, she says.

Mummy and Amy's dad talk for a while in the sitting room. He is wearing safari-style shorts in winter and sneakers, and he has hairy legs. It's all I see, peeping through the keyhole of the sitting-room door with Amy.

Then he stands up and Mummy opens the door and says he would like to talk with Amy. Then Amy is called into the room and the door shuts and later on she comes out again.

That was my dad, says Amy proudly. He came to see me. He lives in Africa. And he wanted to speak with me specially.

Mummy and Amy's dad talk in the sitting room on their own for a long time after. Then Amy's dad leaves.

He has gone back to South Africa, says Mummy. He married someone else there a while ago, the person he met, and has a family.

Why didn't he want to talk with me too, Mummy? I ask.

Well, he didn't have much time, and he had things to discuss and he just wanted to see Amy because he knew her when she was a baby and she's his child and he hasn't seen her all these years, says Mummy. And he's going back to Africa this week. My dad says I'm special, says Amy. If you were so special, he would see more of you, I say. Your dad never came to visit, says Amy. I'm special, and one day he will come back and get me.

That's the only time we ever see Amy's dad. He's not very responsible, says Mummy.

We go to the fruit shop for Mummy. She gives us two pence for two pounds of bruised apples. The man who is usually there isn't there today. Instead it's another man, older. Two pounds of bruised apples, we say. Do you want to pick them yourselves? he asks. We start to pick out the apples, choosing the ones least bruised, with the smallest brown spots. We put them in his metal tray he puts on the weighing scales.

Is your mother going to bake an apple pie with them? he asks. No, we say. What will she do with them? he says. She cuts out the bruised parts and we eat the rest. Cuts them out? He seems surprised. Yes, we say. They're fine if you cut out the bruised parts. Why doesn't she buy apples that aren't bruised? asks the old man. Because she hasn't got enough money, we say.

The shopkeeper helps us choose. We keep adding more apples to the tray. Here's one that's hardly bruised at all, the shopkeeper says, picking out one with just a tiny bruise on it as round as my fingernail. He adds it to the tray. Isn't it two pounds yet? I ask. There's a lot of apples there. The shopkeeper lifts the tray piled high with apples and puts it on the weighing scale.

Not yet, he says. There's room for a few more. We pick out two more apples and add them to the pile. Then the man takes a shiny green and a shiny red apple from the other piles of apples on display in the shop. Here we are, he says, holding them out to us to put into the tray. But they're not bruised, we say. They are, he says, you just can't see the bruises yet, he says, but they will be. He puts them on our bruised-apple pile. He gets us to add some more apples. There, he says, two pounds of apples. He pours them into the shopping bag we have brought with us, filling it up. We can barely carry them home between us.

There seem to be a lot of apples here, says Mummy when we get back, for two pounds of apples. Usually the man at the fruit shop is really tight, he weighs everything to the tiniest ounce. I can't imagine he made a mistake.

It wasn't him, we say, it was someone else. An old man. Look, we say, he gave us two nice apples and said they were bruised too.

The next week, we go back to the fruit shop for more apples. But the nice man isn't there any more, only the young shopkeeper. He weighs our apples carefully and doesn't ask what they are for. I buy some for myself with my pocket money and I eat them on the same day, reading my library books, avoiding the bruised parts and throwing the remainder away.

Autumn is coming and the boys and girls down the road play with me and Amy in the street. Then two of the boys, Colin and Dale, say, I know where you can get free blackberries, in the old vicarage. No one lives there and there are wild blackberries growing everywhere. They take us through a hole in the fence and it's all overgrown inside and, like he said, there are blackberries growing all over the place. So Amy and me pick them and fill a plastic bag to bring back to Mummy to make blackberry jam. Where are they from? asks Mummy. They are growing wild in the old vicarage, we say, we went with our friends Colin and Dale. Just be careful there are no tramps there, says Mummy, never go inside the house.

We go back again and the next time we find a second smaller

house attached to the big vicarage garden, over a low wall. The second house has an overgrown garden too and chickens running around the yard. The chickens must belong to the tramp, I say to Amy, we have to be careful. Amy and me find a greenhouse with tomatoes growing wild inside, all overgrown and dusty, and we pick lots of tomatoes for Mummy and put them in one of the plastic bags we brought. There is a driveway beside the house, and we walk out of it into the street, next to a sign, 'The Vicarage'.

Are you sure the tomatoes are wild too? says Mummy, when we bring them. Yes, it's the old vicarage, we say, we saw the sign, and everything is overgrown. I'll make tomato chutney, says Mummy.

Amy and me go back again to get more tomatoes. We are picking tomatoes in the greenhouse when a small black car comes into the driveway. A thin man with black hair gets out.

The tramp! screams Amy. Quick! Get out!

The man sees us and comes running.

Stop! he shouts. Stop right now!

Run! I shout to Amy. Don't let him catch us! We leap back over the low wall and into the vicarage garden and run through the blackberry bushes, then out of the hole in the fence and into the street. But the man comes round the corner, driving in his black car. So Amy and me run through an alleyway to our street, but the man appears again, driving down our road as we bang on our front door. Mummy, we shout, it's the tramp, let us in, the tramp is after us!

When the man gets to our door he knocks loudly and Amy and I hide in the cupboard under the stairs while Mummy opens the front door. We are crying.

You can come out now, says Mummy, when the man has gone. That man wasn't a tramp, he's the new trainee vicar. The place you were in with the sign is the real vicarage, next to the old vicarage, the vicar and his wife have been away for a long time, and the trainee vicar looks after the property. The real vicar and his wife are back next week, says Mummy – we will have to replace the tomatoes.

Mummy sends me and Amy back the next week with a bag of bought tomatoes. Nobody answers when we knock so Amy and I decide to leave the tomatoes on the doorstep, but then the door opens and we are looking up at a lady who is asking us what we are doing putting tomatoes on the doorstep, and we say it's to replace the ones we took for Mummy. Why did you pick the tomatoes? she asks. So Mummy could cook them for food, we say. Do you have more family? she asks, and Amy and I say yes, a little brother and sister, but we don't have them any more, because they were abducted. Abducted? says the lady. Yes, we say. They were taken to Morocco and now Mummy has to manage on her own.

Oh, says the lady, and she asks us where we live.

You know, says Mummy later, it's strange how things work out. Because you took the tomatoes, the vicar and his wife came to see me the other day, and they are helping me out, and they have put me in touch with Social Services and we are getting some support.

Weren't they angry? we ask.

No, says Mummy. In fact they thought it was very funny, because the trainee vicar is very full of himself, and you both thought he was a tramp. So sometimes things work out unexpectedly, just when you don't think they will.

I win third prize in the painting competition in the city and they put my work in the city art gallery. It's joint third prize and I share it with a six-year-old's painting of a fat ballerina with thick legs. Mummy comes when they give me my prize, an oil-painting set. And now I start painting at home, creating pictures in colours.

167

It is the end of the year and the teachers put on a pantomime for the students, which they do every year. This year it is *Peter Pan*. Mr D is Peter Pan and Mrs Featherstone is a bad pirate who keeps saying a bottle of rum. And then Mr Foley our very serious headmaster with bushy eyebrows appears.

He is Tinker Bell the fairy, wearing a pink tutu and shining tiara and a glittering star on the end of a stick, and he has little wings attached to his shoulder blades and his long skinny hairy bare legs with bony kneecaps extend down from his wide-skirted pink tutu. I am the fairy Tinker Bell, your wish is my command, he says in a high-pitched voice, and he bounces onto the stage with one skinny leg bent high in the air, like a pink flamingo with bad balance, and the whole school is shouting with laughter and rolling on the floor and I laugh so much, tears come out of my eyes.

Mummy gets us Christmas presents. Amy and I wait all night for our presents to arrive. Mummy brings them at midnight and we pretend to be asleep. She brings them in two big paper bags. We know what they are. Mummy said she would get us tennis racquets to play with. And when we open them in the morning, there are the tennis racquets all wrapped up.

Amy and I got each other the same present from our pocket money – a packet of mint toffees each. While we were waiting for Mummy to come with the Christmas presents, we ate all the mint toffees, one by one. But when we open the Christmas packets we find a big piece of caramel toffee each that Mummy made for us. We like Mummy's toffee and eat it all by lunchtime.

But this time, there's no Matti and Babs to share it with.

Christmas seems very quiet without them.

8

Darkness

Rashid has come back from Morocco with Matti and Babs after being away. Mummy says she has no idea why Rashid has come back, after all these months. He told her it was going to be forever.

Rashid never gave an explanation, he never said why he came back, says Mummy. When he left he definitely said he was taking them forever, and I am sure he meant it. I don't know why he changed his mind. I think maybe his mother sent him back here, because he had taken his children away from their mother. If his mother told him to, he would have to do it because she is very strict and everyone obeys her. Mummy says Rashid's mother is very powerful and very controlling and anything she tells him, Rashid will do. At least, that's what Rashid tells her.

Matti and Babs say they liked Morocco. They talk about their grandma and we don't know who she is. We see a picture and she is wearing black. She looks old.

Rashid's father died when he was seven and since then his mother has been the head of the family, Mummy says. Rashid's family is very powerful in Morocco, they are elite. One of Rashid's brothers is very high up in the army and the other in the police. They have servants. Rashid told me when he was beating me that when he was a boy he and his brothers used to do bad things to the live-in servant girl, up until she was about twelve years old, and she couldn't do anything about it because she had no power. He boasted they could do anything they wanted to her. Nobody says how Rashid's father died, says Mummy.

I think his mother must have sent him back, Mummy says again. I can't think of any other explanation, and from the way he's speaking it seems that's the case. Or maybe he needed work. But for all I know, says Mummy, he might go again. I need to be very careful about what I say and do. Otherwise he might take Matti and Babs again. I can't risk losing them again, and I can't risk anyone being hurt.

We are still not allowed to call him Rashid. We still have to call him Dad. At first, it's difficult. Then we get used to it.

I like reading but Dad says I mustn't read any more. He calls me to him and says, from now on you are not allowed to read books at home. You are not allowed to get library books out. Why? I ask. What did I do wrong?

Because I said so, he says.

When Dad says no we don't question.

I don't see what is wrong with reading books. Mummy says maybe it's because he is jealous I do well at school and he wants his own children to do better, so Dad thinks if I read less I won't be so clever. So now I can't read in the evenings, or weekends when Dad is around.

She is supposed to look after Matti and Babs, he says to Mummy. She is not looking after them if she reads.

I'm used to reading and looking after Matti and Babs at the same time. I always do my homework sitting on the bedroom floor or on the bunk bed with Matti and Babs playing in the room. Sometimes I write short stories while everyone plays around me. I have five short stories I wrote. I am making a collection of them, all in one book, a pink exercise book that I've nearly filled with stories and I'm really proud of. I make up little picture books for Matti and Babs, of Pickles the bird and the worm he always tries to catch, with drawings. Matti and Babs love reading the stories, with big pictures of the worm and bird, turning the pages excitedly. Every time Pickles tries to catch the worm, the worm outwits him, in every book. Matti and Babs always laugh when they reach the end.

Sorry, Mai, says Amy. I know how much you like reading.

It's okay, I say, I'll make things instead. But it's like Dad has taken away the thing inside me that makes me feel alive. Pig, I write in my diary. Dad is a pig. He won't let me read any books.

Amy says, don't worry, I'll get you books out on my library tickets and you can read them secretly, before he gets home. Amy is in the children's library. Amy gets me some library books off her card and I read when he is out of the house, but I mustn't let Matti and Babs see me reading in case they say something to Dad, so I do it very secretly.

Amy's books, from the children's library, are very different from mine, but she finds me compendiums of fairy stories – Hansel and Gretel, Cinderella, the gingerbread house, Irish folk tales, the Brothers Grimm. I also read *Pollyanna, Anne of Green Gables* and Professor Branestawm, who is always losing his glasses.

There is a street lamp outside the window of our bedroom. I find I can read at night by the light of the street lamp, if I lift the thick right-hand-side bedroom curtain and tie it to the top rail of the bunk bed where I am, so the light can shine onto the top of the bunk bed. That way, Rashid doesn't know. I've set up a system with Amy that if she hears footsteps creak on the stairs she shakes the bottom of the bunk bed with her body, our secret signal, and I feel it at the top of the bunk bed. Then I pull the curtain loose and let it drop back into place and hide the book under the bed-clothes by my feet, and if he opens the bedroom door we pretend to be asleep. I read by the lamplight, once we are in bed at 8 p.m. When the moon is out, it is even lighter. Especially the full moon.

Sometimes Amy wants to sleep. Hurry up, Mai, she says. I want to sleep. I just want to finish this chapter, I say. I'm sleepy, she says. Please, Amy, I say, just let me read this. It won't take much longer. Okay, says Amy. But not for much longer. Amy understands I can't read in the day and how much I love reading.

During the day I look forward to going to bed, so I can read in the dark.

At school, our friends say, only babies call their mummy Mummy. You should use the word Mum. So now we call Mummy Mum. Mum doesn't like it much, she says it isn't as nice. You just don't want us to grow up, Mum, Amy and me say. We're big girls now. And to prove it, we keep calling her Mum.

Amy and I call home prison. We call school freedom. There's prison and school and the journey in between and the streets around us where we play on weekends and holidays.

It's prison especially when Dad is home – usually he comes home about six o'clock.

Because it's still winter, our fingers and feet get cold. When we get home from school we sit around the fire with Mum, drinking tea and holding hot-water bottles because Rashid won't let us put the fire on before he gets back home and it gets very cold. Dad doesn't allow us to put on any heaters because he says it's too expensive. So Amy and I wrap up in jumpers and scarves and woolly gloves.

When Dad comes home he puts the fire on full in the front sitting room, all three bars, and sits in front of it. Matti and Babs are allowed in the front sitting room, but Amy and I are not. He leaves Matti and Babs to play in the front sitting room with the fire on weekends, and he sits there too, but Amy and I are not allowed in unless we are babysitting. Usually Amy and me and Mum are freezing cold.

Upstairs, in Amy's and my bedroom, it can get really cold, so we wear jumpers and coats and hats and sometimes our gloves to stop us shivering. It's funny to sit upstairs and try to turn the pages of Amy's library books with gloves on.

Sometimes when Dad is out, if it is early enough, Mum sneaks on just one bar of the electric fire in the dining room for a short while, and we all sit around it to get warm. Matti and Babs play beside us. Then we chat around the fire, like we used to do in South Greenstead. Mum switches the single bar off again a long time before he comes home so he can't feel the heat in the room. He always checks the electricity meter when he gets home. That's why we can only have the fire on for a few minutes.

One day, we are sitting around the single bar of the fire and suddenly we hear the sound of the key in the door.

Oh my God, Rashid's home early, says Mum. She jumps up to switch off the fire. Then she says to herself, as her hand touches the switch, no, better to leave it, and she switches the fire on again.

Shouldn't we switch it off, Mum, won't he be angry?

No, she says. He'll feel the warmth in the room anyway. Better to leave it, says Mum.

Dad comes in the room. He looks at the fire. The fire's on, he says.

Yes, I put it on, says Mum. A short while ago. I thought I'd warm the room up a bit for you before you came back. It's minus four degrees outside. It's only one bar.

I said the fire's not to go on before I come back, Dad says.

Sorry, Rashid. It was just this once. It's below freezing point. Matti and Babs were getting cold.

Well, you're not to put it on again when I'm not here, says Dad. Okay, I won't, says Mum.

After that, we're more careful. It only goes on if he's definitely away for a whole day in the week. Mum has to be very careful, because it might show on the bills. So we only get a bit of heat sometimes.

Our ears become sensitive, tuned in, always listening for the sound of his key in the door.

The sky today is ice, freezing, icy rain on cold grey and dark concrete. It's well below zero, says Mum, it will snow soon, I think it will snow today, she says. She goes to cook supper in the kitchen.

Dad comes upstairs to my and Amy's bedroom where I am babysitting Matti and Babs.

Come outside, Mai, he says. I have a job for you. I pause to get my coat, gloves and woolly hat off the hook on the bedroom door. No, Dad says. Come as you are, you don't need to bring your coat. But it's cold outside, I say. It doesn't matter, he says. Come as you are.

I follow Dad to the front door and he opens it. A blast of cold wind hits us both, iced air blowing in. Step outside, says Dad.

I step onto the cold grey paving stones of our front garden path, hugging my arms around me to stay warm in the chilled wind. I watch his face, wondering what he wants me to do. He is smiling again, that strange smile that twists the corners of his mouth. My mind jumps, leaps around. The smile is a warning, it isn't really a smile, it's a mask. All I see is the indentation on the side of his jaw where the muscles pull in tight, as if he is pressing his back teeth hard together, as if he is angry at the same time. I look at his eyes, strange orbs that have no feeling behind them, except a pinpoint of evil coming deep from within. All his anger, hatred, cruelty and evil are focused in that intense pinprick of evil.

I have a job for you, says Dad, still smiling. He points to a cardboard box on the step. I want you to clear the garden path of leaves, he says.

A large tree hangs over the side of our garden, over the tall wall that separates us from next door. The wind is blowing wet autumn leaves down from the tree, yellowed and browned. Our garden path is covered with a thick half-frozen blanket of leaves, flattened out on the wet paving stones. The wind constantly blows down more leaves, landing on the pathway and rectangular concrete area that make up our front garden, with a thin border of earth around it, behind a low wall next to the pavement where pedestrians walk. The front area is thick with wet and half-frozen leaves. More are being blown down as I watch.

I'll get the broom, I say.

No, Dad says, you don't need a broom, you must pick them up with your hands, like this, he says. Dad bends down and scoops up a handful of wet, half-frozen leaves from the garden path with his big palms, and he places them in the box. More leaves from the tree flutter down around him, blown by the gusty wind, filling the space.

I want to see you do it, says Dad.

So I crouch down on the pathway and place my child palms on the pavement and draw them towards each other, gathering half-frozen leaves in each hand as they come together. The ground is freezing cold, and my fingers are momentarily numbed as they gather the leaves that are crisp with ice. I place the few leaves I am able to gather in the box.

Okay, Dad says, you must clear the whole front garden, including the earth, of all the leaves and put them all in this box. You can't stop until every leaf is cleared.

I look up at the branches of the tree above me, and it still has lots of yellow and brown leaves. Several more leaves drift down as I look up, severed from their branches by the cold and the fierce wind, and land on the pavement.

It would be quicker to use the broom, I say.

I told you to use your hands, says Dad.

Can I get my coat and gloves first? I ask. It's very cold.

No, says Dad. You must stay as you are, and you can't come back in until every single leaf is in the box.

Dad goes back indoors, closing the front door, locking me out in the front garden. I begin to pick up leaves with my small palms and fingers. I try to scoop layers from the path and garden earth, but the wet leaves cling stubbornly to the ground. The iciness of the half-frozen leaves and the wind running across my fingers quickly numbs them and I rub my hands together to keep them warm. I can feel myself getting colder without a coat and I huddle my chest into my knees to keep warm. But the leaves keep falling from the tree faster than I can pick them up, and I can't keep up with them. It's getting colder. I have to pick at the leaves with my fingertips, which get colder and colder, my movements get slower and slower. The ends of my fingers feel raw and sore with the scraping of the cold concrete against them, like touching the icebox of a refrigerator. Time passes. The early afternoon is becoming late afternoon and the sky is getting greyer. There is white frost forming on the ground. White mist evaporates from my mouth as I breathe, chilled and cold and silent in front of me. Nobody is out on the streets today.

Dad comes back out and looks at the now thinner layer of leaves in the path and garden, leaves still falling from the tree.

You haven't finished yet, he says. Look, there's more here. And here. He picks up a few leaves from the earth and drops them back down on the earth again.

Please can I get gloves or a coat, I say, I can't pick the leaves up because my fingers are too frozen.

No, says Dad. You must clear the garden completely. He looks at me, smiling at the corners of his mouth. The door closes behind him again.

I carry on picking up leaves, but my hands are too cold and numb for my fingers to close properly around their edges, and the leaves keep falling back onto the pavement. It gets harder and harder to pick up the leaves. I blow on my fingers to get feeling back into them, but it hurts. When I rub my fingers together, they feel warmer, but they hurt more. My feet are numb, my hands are numb. I shiver hard. My job is futile – the more I gather, the more leaves fall. A sudden stronger gust of wind scatters even more leaves from the tree into the front garden and I look at it in despair.

Small flakes of snow start to fall from the sky. If I weren't so cold it would be beautiful, large pale flakes drifting down from a dark mottled sky.

My fingers are red at the tips. I can barely move them, and the frozen ground feels like fire when I touch it. The veins on the back of my hands swell into little bumps, painful when I touch them. The more I scoop along the path, the more my fingers burn from its iciness, and the harder it becomes to pick up a single leaf without dropping it. I crouch down to stay warmer. I can't stop shivering, but I must keep working, because I can't go inside until the garden is free from leaves. My teeth chatter hard as I work, and tears roll down my cheeks.

I have been crouching on the ground picking up leaves in the front garden for hours now. More tears start falling down my cheeks, and I brush my fingers against them. They feel hot against my icy-cold face. It is getting dark now. I am so cold. My teeth chatter and my body is shaking. The sky is even darker now, and the street lamps come on. Snowflakes are still gently falling.

A small group of people pass by on the pavement, heavily wrapped in thick coats, scarves, gloves and hats. My teeth are chattering loudly and I try to clench my jaw tight to stop them hearing me, and pretend as if I'm playing in the garden. I can't move my hands at all now because the swollen veins and my fingertips are too painful so I am trying to get the leaves by bringing the edges of my two hands together. I sense the group of people looking at me in the garden, and tuck my head down, ashamed. I hear one of them comment to the rest of the group as they pass.

That's a pleasant job that child has, someone says, and they snicker.

She doesn't even have a coat or hat on, says another voice, a woman's voice. She must be freezing.

I pretend I don't see them, and, from the corners of my eyes, watch them in their thick warm winter coats disappear past the house.

The front door opens and it is Mum. There you are, Mai, she says. I've been looking everywhere for you. What are you doing out here? She looks shocked, because she can see when I lift my face that something is wrong. Why aren't you wearing your coat?

Dad says I have to fill this box with leaves.

Why aren't you using the broom?

He said I had to do it like this, I say.

At least put a coat and gloves and hat on. You'll freeze like this.

He said I couldn't.

What?

He said I couldn't put a coat on.

That's ridiculous. It's well below zero and it's snowing and it's nearly dark. You'll get hypothermia. Go put a coat on. It will be fine.

He said I can't. I look, helplessly, at her. My hands are so frozen I can't pick up the leaves any more, I say.

Dad comes to the doorway.

What are you making this child do? says Mum. She's out here without any warm clothes, in the freezing wind, picking up leaves in the snow.

She's clearing the front garden, Dad says. She's not coming in until she's finished.

But, Rashid, you're making her do it with bare hands and no coat, not even a proper warm top, says Mum. How long has she been here? You can't put a child out after dark in the freezing cold dressed like this. She'll get hypothermia. Can't she even get her coat? Mum asks.

Go back inside, woman, says Dad. Or there'll be trouble. I warned you before not to interfere, you know what can happen. He looks at Mum, and she looks scared. She is quiet.

Mum says nothing, but she looks at me as if to say, be brave, be strong. I can see how upset she is. And the door closes behind him and her.

But I'm happier because someone cares. Mum's caring makes me feel warmer. I know Mum can't do anything, he might even make it worse for me if she tries. I'm still freezing, and shivering so much my teeth chatter loudly, I can't stop them. I carry on picking at leaves, looking at the lumpy swollen veins on the back of my hands, the big icy bumps where the veins join together.

Shortly after, Dad comes out again. It is completely dark now and I'm using the street lamps to see the leaves on the path. He looks around the garden.

How much have you done? he says. He looks in the box, which is two-thirds full. More leaves are still falling in the garden.

Okay, you can come in now, he says. I go inside the house. The warmth outside my skin hits me like an oven. I go upstairs to the bedroom. I'm so cold it's a while before I begin to feel the warmth inside me again.

Dad was going through our room, says Amy to me afterwards. For ages.

I think he might have read my diary, I say. Afterwards, I take the diary out and throw it in the rubbish bin in the street. It's too dangerous to try to write a diary.

It's my birthday tomorrow and I will be ten and Mum says I can have a birthday party. I have invited all my friends at school, and Mum is making my birthday cake. It's late afternoon, and we are upstairs playing.

What's this? I hear Dad's voice downstairs in the kitchen. I'm making Mai a birthday cake for tomorrow, says Mum. She's having some friends around tomorrow. You'll be working tomorrow and I thought …

Big crash in the kitchen.

Dad has smashed the bowl with the cake mixture in it. You never asked me if Mai could have a birthday party, he says. There is silence. Then Dad says, she's not having any party here, and he goes out.

When I go down to the kitchen, the cake mixture and Mum's favourite cake-mixing bowl are all mixed up on the ground and Mum is picking up the pieces of the bowl from the floor. I hear the pieces scraping as she picks them up, and the dull clink as she puts them into what is left of the base of the bowl. What shall I tell all my friends I've invited to my party? I say. Don't worry, Mai, Mum says, I'll think of something. At least Rashid isn't here tomorrow during the day, he's working.

The next day, when the parents bring all their children to the house, Mum says, it's such a nice day, I thought we'd have a birthday in the park. Mum has a sponge cake she bought from the shop with icing powder sprinkled on the top and we use it as my birthday cake, and she has made sandwiches. I look at it, thinking of the cake mixture on the kitchen floor. I don't say anything to my friends. I'm glad it's warmer today. So we all walk to the park. When we get there, we play games and have fun. And we have a lovely day.

Being ten is the sound of trees rustling at night and the sound of the moon hanging in the sky. I like that sound best because the round full moon just sits and the clouds drift across it like slow ships, and you can hear in the quietness imaginary sounds and stories, sirens calling to sailors, the splash of waves, the cry of an owl, the sounds of the millions of voices in the world, the creak, creak as the world turns, the sound as a bird's wings flap against the sky, all in the quietness of a night sky and a full moon. I like the moon when it is quiet and light, with the clouds sailing by like dancers, taking my sad feelings away.

9

Hiding

I'm reading in bed. The curtain is pulled back and tied to the side of the bunk bed. There's a big full moon in the sky, shining behind the lamp post. Dad comes home later these days, sometimes about nine in the evening. Mum says it's because he is finishing his postgraduate degree at the university, he is doing it in one year less because he is so clever, she says, and the time is up now. She says his behaviour is getting worse because of the pressure. It's past the time Dad usually comes home so I assume he is downstairs.

Suddenly, I hear the key in the front door.

Mai, Mai, whispers Amy. She is shaking the bed violently. Dad's outside. He's only coming back home now, he might see our bedroom curtain open.

I fling the curtain back. I throw the book under the bedclothes and lie on it. The front door opens and we hear it close and we hear Dad running up the stairs, fast. His feet sound very heavy. I close my eyes and I feel my heart beating, loud.

I try to control my breathing. Slow it.

Dad's feet pound on the stairs, and I hear them reach the landing and our bedroom door flies open and the light goes on. He's standing there, in the doorway, at the end of the bunk bed. I pretend I'm sleeping, peeping from the corner of my eye first, to see if the curtain has stopped swinging. It has. I pretend I'm just waking up.

What is it? I say, half raising my head from the pillow. Dad looks at me. He looks angry. He looks around the room. He looks at the curtains. He waits. He says nothing. Then he switches off the light and closes the door and his feet go down the stairs again.

We both breathe out with relief. My chest is pounding.

Do you think he saw? says Amy. I don't know, I say. Why did he come in like that then? says Amy. I don't know, I say, maybe he did see. Why didn't he do anything then? asks Amy. Maybe he didn't see, I say. Maybe he saw but he wasn't sure, says Amy. I hope he didn't, I say. Well, he didn't say anything. Maybe it's okay, says Amy. I hope so, I say.

We lie in bed, waiting.

He doesn't come back in.

Probably he didn't see, says Amy.

I suppose so. He'd have said something, wouldn't he? I say.

I'm nervous all the next day. Dad says nothing. In the afternoon, we're in the sitting room, because Dad has told me to look after Babs and Matti. Then Dad calls me over to the armchair where he is sitting. My heart sinks. I want to talk with you, Mai, he says, did you have the curtains open last night?

No, Dad, I say.

You did have the curtains open, didn't you?

No, Dad.

I saw them open. What were you doing? Tell me.

No, Dad. Really I wasn't. Really.

Dad takes my ear and twists it so it burns. Tell me. Did you have them open?

No, Dad. No. He keeps twisting my ear.

My ear is burning red now, I feel its heat.

I know you were doing it, Mai. Just tell me and I'll stop.

No, Dad, no, really, I didn't open the curtains, I don't know what you mean. I was sleeping. You saw I was in bed sleeping.

Dad keeps twisting. Tears come in my eyes. I feel them, and bite my lip. I am too scared to tell him, because I don't know what he'll do. Then he lets me go.

Carry on looking after Matti and Babs then.

Later in the day he calls me to him again. He smiles. Mai, he says, I saw the curtains open last night and I know you did it. Just tell me you did it and I promise I won't punish you.

I'm so scared I'm like a wooden board.

No, Dad, I didn't have them open.

Just tell me, Mai, really, I won't hurt you.

I didn't do it, I say.

If you tell me, I promise it will be fine.

I look at him.

Are you frightened to tell me? Are you frightened I will hurt you? says Dad.

I nod.

I promise you, Mai, if you tell me the truth, I won't be angry with you. I just want to know. I won't hurt you. I won't punish you. I promise. Just tell me. Just tell me the truth. I promise I won't hurt you. Tell me the truth. The curtains were open, weren't they? I just want to know.

I look at him. He's being nice. Speaking to me kindly.

You really promise you won't hurt me?

I give you my word. It's okay, don't be frightened.

I look at him again. He is smiling. I promise you will not get punished, he says.

Really? I say.

Yes, he says, nicely.

Okay, I say. The curtain was open.

Why? he asks.

185

So I could read my book. Because I'm not allowed to read any more, so I was reading by moonlight and the street lamp.

Dad looks at me and his face and voice change.

Go to bed, he says. Straight away. Without dinner. Right now.

I go upstairs to bed. I'm crying as I change into my pyjamas. I'm crying as I climb into bed. I'm crying as I lie there, waiting under the bedclothes, for his footsteps on the stairs, until the tears start drying on my face. Then I hear his footsteps creep up the stairs. I hear them clearly through the wall, beside the bunk bed, because the staircase is just behind the wall. I hear each foot as it treads on the staircase. The door opens.

Dad closes it behind him.

Sit up, Mai.

I pull myself up, slowly.

No, sit up properly. Right up. So I can see your face properly. He comes closer, up to the side of the bed.

I sit up straight. Dad reaches back and swings his fist back, then forwards, and punches me on the side of my face.

Sit up, he says again. He reaches back his other arm and punches me again, this time on my chin. I cry. Sit up. Stay still. His teeth are clenched. This is for reading books, he says. As he punches me, his expression changes. He looks angry at first, and he's frowning, then I see his face change as he keeps punching. He's smiling. He's smiling as he hits me, and I keep crying. His face is smiling at me, piggy eyes, piggy eyes, cold and hard and hateful, and I can't believe he is smiling, while I am screaming inside, but outside I am crying quietly.

And this is to teach you not to lie to me, he says. I am crying through the tears and the punches and his ugly face haunting me and the shock of him smiling through the pain and hurt.

Then he turns and leaves.

My cheeks are red and sore and burning and a bit swollen, but he didn't hit me hard enough to bruise me. I bury my head in my pillow, and cry tears for all the books I have ever read.

Socks comes up later and joins me, and I hide her under the bedclothes with me while I hug her and cry quietly. Socks the cat knows when I am sad, when I am in bed and hungry. She finds me, all alone, and soaks the tears away with her warm fur. The bed is like a cocoon: safe, hidden. And Socks is the centre of it, protecting me and taking my sad feelings away.

Spring comes, and summer comes, and it is hot again. Amy finds a fat green caterpillar in the street. Poor thing, she says, maybe it's hungry, it's going to be my pet caterpillar. She brings it into our front garden and puts it on a leaf on one of the weeds growing there to give it food.

What's this? says Dad, seeing her bending over the leaf. It's a caterpillar, says Amy. It's hungry so I'm giving it some food. Dad reaches his hand back and slaps Amy hard across her face. She cries. Her big eyes are full of tears. Get rid of it, says Dad. You are not allowed to bring animals into the garden. Amy takes the caterpillar down the street. I found another bush for it, Amy says to me, a long way from the house, so Dad can't find it and he can't kill it. It can't be my pet now though, she says.

Dad does the shopping now. On Saturdays I must go with him to the large supermarket at the bottom of the series of long winding steep roads that go down from our house to the bottom of the hill that ends at a park that small children catch tadpoles in. Him and me. We bring two pushchairs with us which get loaded with boxes for the week, and Dad pushes one and I push one too. This Saturday we take Babs with us. She has to use the pushchair because she's still two and she can't walk far yet. All the super-market boxes are piled high in Dad's pushchair, and I am pushing Babs in her pushchair.

Hurry up, says Dad as we start up the hill. Babs is heavier than I thought. My hands barely reach the tops of the handles when I push her up the hill. Each step is an effort to push her. Dad is walking up very fast, pushing his big cardboard box of shopping. He marches along with strong strides. Faster, he says. Tall trees pass overhead. Sky passes overhead. I concentrate on each step, going up, but my arms are getting tired, my legs are getting tired. Faster, faster, he says, and he walks even faster.

One step at a time. Up and up. Beyond each step is another. I am struggling with the pushchair. It does not want to go up, it wants to stop. My feet scramble for the ground. I feel my heart beating, fast. I feel my feet pounding on the gravel pavement as it swoops upwards. My heart goes faster.

Hurry up, Dad says, do you want a beating? And he walks even faster, beads of sweat appearing on his forehead.

My legs feel weak. My arms feel weak. Babs gets heavier and heavier. I am almost running, leaning forwards hard to keep the pushchair going up and up, scared to stop. I ascend never-ending crescents of hills as one road leads into another, and another, each one going upwards. All I can think of is the hard pavement under my feet and the hill that goes up and up.

Can I rest? I ask. Babs is heavy.

He stops until I catch up. He prods me in my ribs, hard, below my right shoulder. I hate that feeling of his finger against my bones, poking hard. Then he twists my ear.

When I say you keep up, you keep up. Or there'll be trouble when you get back.

He starts walking again, straight away, as fast as before.

So I keep up as best I can. It is hot. The sky is hot. The black tarmac I am walking on reflects the heat. My cheeks feel hot. My little sister doesn't know what is happening and she is laughing at the speed, brown curly ringlets shaking with laughter as she goes up. Dad's legs are so much longer than mine, I take three steps to his one. The pushchair sticks a little, catches on bumps and pieces of paving, then moves on. And he is sweating heavily from the speed he is walking, big beads of sweat dripping down his forehead. His face is getting redder and redder from all the effort. And I am trying desperately to keep up, pushing Babs on the steep hill. I feel my heart pound in my chest boom boom like a big drum.

Keep up. Keep up, walk faster, he says, still far ahead of me, and he turns his head to look back at me, and it looks like his mouth wants to smile.

I keep pushing, gasping for air. My heart is beating so hard it feels like it is in my head.

When we finally reach the top and the ground levels out, we don't slow down. My arms and legs are shaking, and I am still gasping for air. We carry on full speed back to the house.

When we get back, he opens the front door and pushes the shopping in. Mum is in the hallway, and Amy, come to take the shopping out. As I push Babs in her pushchair in over the door-step, I feel my body fall forwards, trembling all over. I gasp for air, like a fish. Mum asks what is wrong, but I cannot speak because of the gasping, and she has to hold me up, because I am so tired I can't stand up. What is wrong? What is wrong? Mum keeps asking. I just keep shivering and crying and gasping for air like I have been winded.

What have you done to her, Rashid? Mum asks. She can't even speak to me. What on earth have you done to her? The child's exhausted. She looks terrified.

Nothing. She's just pretending, says Dad.

I wish this crying and shaking would stop, so I don't get into trouble – I am frightened. It's nothing, I'm just tired … from the hill, I gasp.

She's just lazy, Dad says. She's trying to get attention.

No she's not, she's suffering from exhaustion, says Mum, holding me up. She's only ten, she's just a little girl, Rashid, she hasn't got the strength of a grown man.

Amy is staring at me in the corridor like she is shocked. I can't do anything. I just gasp for air and look at her, ashamed to be like this. It is as if the world is falling over and my heart is falling with it.

Take the pushchair, Amy, says Dad, and he pushes Babs into the hallway.

We are playing in the road and there's a little passage with small gardens in it and our tennis ball goes over the fence and we can't get to it. So Amy and I go round to the front and knock and ask the plumpish lady with greying hair in a bun who opens the door, please, do you mind if we get our ball, and she says, let me get it, just you wait here, have a seat. And then we wait on two of the kitchen chairs and there's a table and a kitchen sink and the TV is on and it's *The Waltons*. And the lady comes back and says, is this your ball? and we say yes, thank you very much, but then she sees our eyes are on the TV screen, watching *The Waltons* even though we're standing up again to leave now, and she says, do you want to carry on watching? It's no problem for me, I'm just doing some cooking while the TV is on. It won't bother me. And we smile at her and say, yes please, and sit down again. Just make yourself comfortable, says the lady, and she asks our names and she tells us she is Mrs Smith. And then Mrs Smith finishes her cooking and she says, I would like a nice cup of tea, wouldn't you?

Amy and I nod and say, yes please, and smile again, then Mrs

Smith makes us all tea and sits on the armchair and watches TV with us, drinking cups of tea. And she says, don't you watch TV at home? and we say not really because it's in the sitting room and Dad rarely lets us, so we don't get to see the TV much but Dad lets Matti and Babs see the kiddies' programmes.

So now we go round to watch *The Waltons* every Sunday.

We knock on the door and say, hello, and Mrs Smith with twinkly eyes and grey hair in a bun stands there and says, hello, how are you? And Amy and me say, fine, thank you, are you busy today? and she says, no, I'm only making some tea, would you like some? And we say, if you don't mind, because Mum says she knows Mrs Smith and it's fine to visit her when she asks. And then we say, are you watching TV? and she says, yes, come in, you're just in time to watch *The Waltons*, and we go in and she pulls a chair up for Amy and a stool up for me to sit in front of the TV because I like the stool. And then she makes cups of tea in proper cups made of china with saucers because she says we're her guests and we all sit and watch *The Waltons*.

Sometimes Mrs Smith shows us the frozen fruit in her freezer, raspberries and strawberries and things. We've never seen frozen raspberries before and it's such a big freezer you can lean forwards and nearly fall in. And if we reach out far we can reach the strawberries which look fat and juicy but they are rock hard, like marbles, all in little plastic bags. Mrs Smith is keeping them for winter. They're nice for winter, she says, because when you defrost them they are just like fresh. I do them all myself, she says. I buy in bulk, then I freeze them.

One time we come round and Mrs Smith has a bowl of tomatoes on the table ready for freezing. Ripe. Juicy. Round.

Mrs Smith peels the tomatoes. You boil them first, she says. Quickly. It loosens the skins. We watch, fascinated, as her fingernails dig up thin sheaves of tomato skin, leaving the flesh raw and a rich red. The peels come off paper-thin and her fingers peel quickly, as if they are used to it. Freed from the tight shiny skin, the tomatoes take on new, flatter shapes, bulging at the sides. One of the tomatoes has split and we can see through to the seeds.

Whoops, she says, as a piece of tomato flesh breaks under her pull. Here, you have a go.

I hold the tomato carefully in my hand. It feels soft and warm and pulp-like. I peel slowly as Mrs Smith finishes five more tomatoes. Amy has one too. When Amy and I finish our tomatoes they don't look round and perfectly smooth like Mrs Smith's. Ours have holes and dented surfaces, and breaks where our fingers dug in too deep.

That's perfect, says Mrs Smith. You girls have done such great jobs.

Amy and I look at how different our peeled tomatoes look from Mrs Smith's, and know that we haven't, but we smile anyway.

Now, we pop them into plastic bags, like this ... Mrs Smith takes a wire tie encased in white plastic, then twists them closed. Then they go straight into the freezer. And in go our tomatoes with the raspberries and strawberries.

For the next few Sundays, when we visit, Mrs Smith puts tomatoes in the freezer. It's tomato season, she says. Then, continues Mrs Smith, when the season is finished I still have tomatoes and strawberries and raspberries. All winter.

We sit on our chairs and chat.

I look at the books on Mrs Smith's shelves. They are children's books, and Mrs Smith says they are there for when her nieces and nephews visit. She lets me look at them. I start reading one, and she says, do you want to take it home and finish it?

No thank you, I say, it's fine. I'll read some more next time I come round. Really, says Mrs Smith, take it home and read it. No one else will need it if you keep it for a week and bring it back next Sunday. My nephews and nieces won't be visiting for a long time.

I look at the book longingly. No, it's okay, I say.

Take it home, says Mrs Smith. I want you to.

She can't, says Amy.

Why not? asks Mrs Smith.

She's not allowed to read books, says Amy.

I shuffle uncomfortably on my feet.

Why's that? asks Mrs Smith.

Our dad said so, says Amy.

And if she does?

She'll be in trouble, says Amy.

Go on, take it anyway, she says to me.

I can't, I say.

Why can't you just tell your dad you want to read? Mrs Smith says.

I don't know what to say. I don't want to say anything. I know she can see my face says I want to take the book, but she looks into my eyes and she sees I can't.

If she reads books he'll hurt her, says Amy. Or she'll go to bed with no food.

Are you sure? asks Mrs Smith.

Yes, says Amy.

Why doesn't your mother say something about it then?

He will hurt her too, says Amy, like when he tried to throw her down the stairs, and he bruised her arm. Or he'll take our little brother and sister away to Morocco like he did before and they'll never come back. And if you talk to him it will be worse.

I never heard of a child not being allowed to read books, Mrs Smith mutters to herself. She puts the book away on the shelf again. You can read the book here any time when you come around, says Mrs Smith.

I feel sorry for Mrs Smith because I'd like to make her happy by taking the book and I can see she wants me to.

Mum says Mrs Smith knows there's something wrong at home because she came round and asked Mum about the things we are not allowed to do. That's why she's always so nice to you, and you can go to her for tea, says Mum.

Mrs Smith is our friend.

Mrs Smith is like the lady in the corner shop. Whenever we go down to the shop and buy half-penny Black Jacks, then the corner-shop lady always gives us a little more. We like her. She is kind and has the type of understanding Mrs Smith has, like she knows us.

Then one day the shop lady isn't there any more and Mum says she was fired from her job for stealing from the till. Mum says, pity, she was such a nice lady. We say, she was always giving us extra sweets and she always smiled at us, and Mum says, the shop owner probably didn't like her giving sweets away either.

Maybe she needed the money badly, we say, and Mum says, could be. She was a good person, says Mum. Maybe she was very desperate.

When I look at Mrs Smith I see a good person because she does a lot by doing little things, like cups of tea on Sundays. Mrs Smith's place is like another home and she is like how an auntie would be if we had one, only she has her own nieces and nephews. She sits and chats to us and watches *The Waltons* with us. We wish we were her nieces and nephews. But we know we're not.

One day we come back a bit late from Mrs Smith because we were having a nice chat and Dad says, where were you, I was out calling you to come in from the streets and I never saw you. And we say, we didn't hear because we were visiting Mrs Smith, and Dad says, who's that? And we say, she's a lady who lives nearby.

What do you do there? says Dad. We have tea and she lets us watch the TV sometimes, we say. And Dad says, no, you're not to go any more, she should mind her own business. And we say, but she's nice, she's a friend, and Dad says, if I catch you even close to there again, there'll be trouble.

So we go to Mrs Smith's the next Sunday. Amy and me check first that no one is looking and we knock on the door. When Mrs Smith opens it we say, sorry, we won't be able to come any more to your house, not ever again. And Mrs Smith asks us, why not? And we say, we can't say.

Then Mrs Smith says, is it your dad? and we nod. And she says, I'll talk to him about it. And then Amy and me go really still and we say, no, please don't, because if you do we'll be in trouble, he'll be really angry, we told you, we're not even meant to be here now, and it will be much worse for us. Please don't. And Mrs Smith looks at us and she understands.

And I say in my best voice, I am sorry we can't come any more and we really enjoyed watching *The Waltons* and having cups of tea with you and reading books, and we just wanted to say thank you for everything.

And then Mrs Smith says, well I'm very sorry about it, and I really enjoyed having you around, and I say, well you can still have your nieces and nephews round, it won't be so bad.

And Mrs Smith says, yes, that's true, I will. I will miss my little friends, says Mrs Smith.

So she closes the door again and we go off and we never go into Mrs Smith's again. Once I saw the door open up and Mrs Smith put a milk bottle on the doorstep, but she didn't see me. Sometimes I'd like to go up and just knock at the door, and say hello, but I'm always worried Dad might find out, so I don't.

One day in the holidays Mum says the social worker is coming around, she is meeting in the front room, and Amy and me must keep Matti and Babs upstairs playing, because if they see her they might tell Dad. We play upstairs with Matti and Babs and keep them busy. Downstairs, Mum talks with the social worker for a long long time. After the social worker has gone, Mum talks with Amy and me in the kitchen.

The social worker says it's mental cruelty, she says we need to do something about it, says Mum. Things are getting really bad, says Mum, and I think Rashid might try to abduct Matti and Babs again, especially now he is finishing his degree. It gets harder and harder with Rashid every day, she says. He doesn't give me any housekeeping money, and all I have is your child allowance to get one or two extra things. He won't even let me leave the house now, apart from taking Matti to school, and I'm not allowed to go anywhere else. Rashid even gets all the shopping on weekends now, with you, Mai, so I can't even go out to the shops. He says I must stay in the house all the time. I'm not even allowed to have the front sitting-room curtains open in the daytime, because there is a garage opposite, and he says men will look in and see me through the window. It's getting worse and worse. I have to get permission to go out in the day. And I can't do anything about it, because I'm scared he will take the little ones away.

Amy and me and Mum keep talking about the bad things Dad does and how weird he is. Mum and I are seated at the far end of the kitchen. Amy is standing near the open door leading into the hallway. And then suddenly Amy leaps up and dances around the room.

La la la la la la … she sings at the top of her voice.

What are you doing that for, Amy? says Mum. We are both laughing at Amy. She is dancing and singing loudly but she looks scared.

Are you crazy, Amy? I ask. What are you doing?

La la … la … sings Amy. She grimaces and widens her eyes, points her finger discreetly in front of her body to the door.

Then we realise. We hear the sound of the front door closing and Dad walks down the hallway into the kitchen.

Afterwards, Amy says, I heard him at the door and you didn't. He opened the door and was coming into the hallway and he could have heard everything you were saying if he had come closer, so the only thing I could think of was to do something silly to stop you talking. And you still didn't realise. I couldn't say he was here, because he could see and hear me from the hallway. So I danced and sang to cover up your words and I don't think he realised anything. And it worked, says Amy. I saved us all.

We thought you'd gone completely mad, I say. We have to be more careful about talking about this in the house, says Mum. You must never mention anything to anyone. And we can only talk about these things when we are outside the house.

Later, Mum speaks to me on my own. The social worker says the only thing we can do is run away, says Mum, before things get much much worse, because now Rashid's finishing his degree, he might abduct Matti and Babs for good. She says we have to go to a battered wives' home, says Mum, it's a place where women run away to when their husbands are abusive. There are only two battered wives' homes in Britain, and we might be able to get a place. The social worker says the one is so crowded there are two families sometimes to a room, and whole families staying in the corridors and bathrooms, so she will try to get us a space in the other one, but we don't have much choice. You mustn't repeat anything I told you just now, says Mum, not even to Amy, you mustn't say anything to anyone, absolutely no one should know.

We are walking Matti to school. Mum and I are walking together, Mum pushing Babs in the pushchair. Amy is some way ahead of us, skipping over the paving stones with Matti. It is a sunny day.

Then Mum says in a low voice to me, we're going to run away today, Mai. I want you to remember that, when I come to school later today, you must go get Amy immediately and come with me. You're not to say anything to anyone. Not even Amy. It could be extremely risky if you do. If Rashid has even the slightest suspicion, I don't even want to think of what he might do. Do you understand that, Mai?

Yes, I say.

I couldn't tell you before, says Mum, in case Rashid found out. But I have to tell you now because I need your help to make sure Amy goes too. You have to make sure she comes with us.

Yes, I say, I understand. Amy and Matti are still skipping over the paving stones ahead. Where are we going? I ask.

It's a secret, says Mum, everything depends on no one knowing. It's too dangerous otherwise. Rashid mustn't find anything out, even after we've gone. He mustn't be able to trace us. Do you understand?

What time will we leave? I ask. I don't know yet, says Mum. You must just be ready. I am packing a few things, not much, I can't bring everything. Is there anything you and Amy like more than all your other belongings you want me to bring?

Our tennis racquets, I say. And my writing book of short stories.

All morning, my head is numb. I do my classwork in slow motion. I stare at my new class teacher, Mrs Henry, to see if she treats me any differently, but she doesn't. I hope Rashid doesn't find out. My best friend Sarah chats to me. I am trying to say goodbye in the way I talk to her, but I'm not allowed to let on to anything. Only I know. Only I know what is going to happen. I keep thinking of Mum saying it could be very dangerous to tell anyone. I am sad I can't say goodbye. I do my maths class and the teacher gives us work for the next class lesson, but I know I won't be doing it. It seems silly to pretend to work, but I have to. Every time the door opens I think it's Mum coming to get us. But it isn't.

In my desk I have my *Strand Magazine* omnibus that I bought in a jumble sale with my pocket money, which I brought in yesterday to show to Mrs Henry, which I love and I am going to bring with me. It has all the *Strand Magazine*s one after another, bound together in a green cover. There are people in long skirts and jokes from *Punch* and it has a photograph of a lady in a long dress standing next to another lady made of snow, because the Thames River froze up and everyone went skating on it. Very nice, Mrs Henry said. She didn't understand when I showed her it had all the Sherlock Holmes stories in. The very first ones. I've read all the stories and articles. I know the book is old. Mrs Henry didn't seem to think it was very important, but it's precious to me. I place it carefully in my desk, at first break, to take it with me when I go. Ready, on top of everything else.

First break ends.

We start lessons again. When is Mum going to come? I look up every time the door opens.

Mrs Henry smiles at me. I don't think she knows.

At school dinner Amy sits at the same table as me, like she usually does. There's eight to a table, grab a seat where you can. My best friend Sarah is also at my table. We eat liver stewed in gravy, cabbage. The liver is hard and chewy because they cooked it too long. Then dessert comes, chocolate pudding and chocolate custard. I think they are trying to make up for the liver, says Sarah. Amy is happy. It's her favourite dessert. We cut the chocolate pudding into eight pieces and serve it.

We are passing around the chocolate-custard pot when I see

Mum. She is standing with Mr Foley the headmaster in the dinner hall, and they are looking at all the tables. Then they see us and he points at us. Amy stares back at them.

What's Mum doing here? asks Amy. Mum beckons to us, waving her right arm.

Come on, I say to Amy. We have to go.

Where are you going? asks Sarah.

I remember I'm not allowed to say anything. Um … I say. It's not important, I say.

Good, says Amy, looking at the steaming bowl in front of her, I can finish my chocolate pudding and custard first. She grabs her spoon.

No, Amy, I say, we have to go now, immediately. Come on.

Amy is so surprised that she gets up at once. I look at Sarah and inwardly wish her goodbye. I take Amy's hand and we walk over quickly to Mum and the headmaster. They look very serious and we walk quickly out of the hall. What is happening? asks Amy.

Mr Foley takes us to the main door of the school. A lady is standing there and holds Mum's arm. I'm Mrs Andrews the social worker, says the lady to me and Amy.

There is a policeman standing a bit further away outside the main school door and there's another standing by the school gate outside, who keeps looking around.

Mr Foley speaks hurriedly. I'm very sorry you are leaving us, he says. I just want to wish you both good luck, and he shakes our hands. Then he turns to Mum and wishes her good luck too and he and Mum and the social worker all talk quickly in low voices.

What does he mean, we're leaving? whispers Amy.

I'll tell you later, I say.

Come on, says Mrs Andrews the social worker, and she walks with us into the schoolyard where a small van is parked, facing the gates. Mum looks very nervous, she's shaking. Don't worry, Mrs

Andrews says to Mum, holding her arm, you're in safe hands now, she says, there are policemen all around to protect you.

We walk up to the back of the van. It has two doors at the back that close down the middle and a window you can't see into. A lady comes out the front of the van. She says hello to Mum and Mrs Andrews, and Mr Foley. We need to move fast, she says. She opens the back doors of the van quickly. Inside we see Matti and Babs sitting on blankets with a second lady holding them close. Matti is sucking his thumb and when he sees us he smiles. The second lady climbs out of the van. I'm Mrs Jones the social worker for where we are going to, she says to me and Amy. Jump inside, she says, smiling as if it's fun, but I can see from her eyes she is not smiling, and she looks around too. Come on. Get in, says Mum. We don't have time to waste. Amy and me climb in quickly.

Thanks for everything, Mum says to Mr Foley and Mrs Andrews. You'll be fine, says Mrs Andrews to Mum, and she smiles. I wish you the best of luck in your new home. Mum climbs in after us and she takes Babs on her lap. What's happening? whispers Amy again. Why are we getting into a van?

Mrs Jones closes the doors fast behind us, and we hear the lock go on the outside, and we can tell everyone else is nervous too, and we hear Mrs Jones go around to sit with the lady at the front of the van and then the motor starts up. Don't worry, says Mrs Jones from the front through the hatch. She points to the driver. This man's with us for security. It might be a bit shaky inside but the journey's not too long, less than a couple of hours. Just hold onto the sides if there are any big bumps. We will drive carefully.

The van pulls away with a clanking sound. The small rectangular window across the two doors has grid marks on it but we can see through them. I see Mr Foley and Mrs Andrews waving as we drive out of the schoolyard, past the policeman who is still looking around, up and down the road. I see our school getting smaller and smaller, the grey road vanishing behind us, and then it is gone.

I look around the inside of the van. There's our pink laundry basket, my height, with its pink plastic lid, bulging with clothes hastily thrown inside, and two suitcases. And in the corner is Socks' wicker basket, and Socks is meowing inside.

Where are we going? asks Amy. What's happening? You have to tell me.

We're running away from Dad, I say.

Forever?

Yes, forever, I say. We're not going back.

Where to?

I don't know, I say.

Where are we going, Mum? Amy asks.

You'll see when we get there, says Mum.

I don't know where we are going. Take us away. Take us away in the back of the van, the road disappearing behind us. We're hiding in the back of a van, the five of us. The pink laundry basket, some belongings, not much, the two suitcases and Mum's sewing machine, and some blankets, and Socks. I see our tennis racquets and I know Mum brought my storybook. Mum doesn't talk much. She's very serious and very quiet and holds Matti and Babs, who are also quiet. I see the roads pass outside the van, and we pass familiar places and then they become less familiar and then I don't recognise any of the roads at all. And then there are big roads that we pass down and lots of other cars and I wonder if any of them out there know that there's a family trying to escape in the back of our van. I can hear the two ladies in the front of the van talking and a man's voice too.

Mrs Jones smiles at us through the window. Just hold on if there are any bumps, she says. It won't be long now.

202

We travel on and on, and we start to get bored. Not much further now, Mrs Jones says cheerfully again.

Then I remember. My *Strand Magazine* omnibus book. I left it in the desk. A sinking feeling is in my stomach. I think of it there, in my school desk. Mum, I forgot my book. The *Strand* one, with the Sherlock Holmes stories.

I'm afraid there's not much we can do about it now, says Mum. Can't they post it to me? I ask. They're not allowed to know where we are, says Mum.

Not even to post something?

No, not at all. I'm sorry, Mai, we can't get it.

I sit, thinking about my book I can't go back and get, not ever, and I listen to Socks meowing in the basket.

Where are we going, Mum? asks Amy.

To a battered wives' home, says Mum. We're hiding from Rashid.

Are we going to the overcrowded one? I ask.

No, Mum says, we're going to the other one. They are giving us a room.

Are we going to school there? asks Amy.

Yes, you'll be starting a new school.

Almost there now, says Mrs Jones.

Now, says Mum, we all have to have new surnames, so Rashid can't find us. We're going to be called Roberts.

What, like Amy Roberts? asks Amy.

Yes.

Can't we have a better surname? Roberts is boring, says Amy.

We need one that doesn't stand out as different, says Mum.

We practise our surnames. Elizabeth Roberts. Mai Roberts. Amy Roberts. Matti Roberts. Babette Roberts. Socks Roberts. They sound funny and we laugh.

You have to practise saying your new names until they become natural, says Mum. You really have to remember. You must never let anyone know your other surnames, not ever.

Not even Granddad? I ask.

Not even Granddad, Mum says. He mustn't know where we are. Just in case. You never know what Rashid can do. If anyone finds out, Rashid could trace us. It's crucial to make sure no one knows where we are, says Mum. From now on, Roberts is your surname.

We've started going up a narrow road. The van is bumping a lot now, and we have to hold the washing basket and Socks' carrying basket to stop them falling over, with Socks meowing loudly inside. We keep saying our new names on the tips of our tongues.

This is the place, says Mrs Jones, as the van turns another corner. There is a long concrete wall with a gate in it. We pull up to it and stop. Behind the wall, a large house rises up, with white walls and a sloping roof.

Is that it? says Amy. Is that where we're going to live?

Yes, says Mum.

We stare at the house and the concrete wall. We drive up to the gate and Mrs Jones jumps out and rings a bell and the gates of the driveway open and the van drives in. Then the gates are closed behind us. You can come out now, says Mrs Jones. We're here. She opens up the back doors of the van.

We climb out, stiff from the journey. It's cold, and Amy and I shiver, because we don't have our coats, they're still hanging on the pegs in the classrooms in Greendale School where we left them to get dinner.

Welcome to your new home, Mrs Jones says to us.

Hello, say a man and a woman who are standing on the inside of the gate.

They smile.

This is Mr and Mrs Browne, who look after the house and whose house it is, says Mrs Jones. Mrs Browne is a social worker, and they donated the house as a battered wives' home. They live in the area out the back, in the small building attached to the house.

Is that their real names? asks Amy.

No, says Mum. No one has real names here, so they can't ever get traced. Everyone has false surnames, like you.

They take us to the big wooden front door and open it.

The other lady from the front of the van comes out and more ladies from inside the house, and they start to take our pink washing basket and suitcases from the van down the path and inside into the hallway of the house. Mrs Jones and Mum are talking with Mr and Mrs Browne.

Come in, says the first lady who came out. My name's Anne and I live here.

There are more people standing inside the front door. More ladies and big and little children are standing inside the hallway and they watch us walk up the path, me, Mum, Amy, Matti and Babs in her pushchair with Mrs Jones pushing it after us, and our pink washing basket, Socks, Mum's sewing machine and the two suitcases and the blankets and our tennis racquets, carried by Mr and Mrs Browne and the people from the van and others who come from the house.

Wait upstairs until we have moved everything in from the van, say the ladies to the children, who move out of the corridor and climb the stairs as we enter.

The hallway is wooden and our feet go clop clop down the passage and the children watch us from the stairs, peering through the banisters. One of them, a girl about our age with freckles and straw-yellow hair, leans forwards against the banisters and says, hello, I'm Shelley.

Shelley, we're busy now, says one of the ladies in the corridor.

You can chat later. We told you children you must stay upstairs until everything is in.

Shelley climbs back up to the landing at the top of the stairs and makes funny faces at us, so Amy and me laugh.

We don't usually use the front door, says Mr Browne to Mum. It's only when new people arrive and we need to take in belongings. Usually we come in through the back way, through the side door that leads into the kitchen. Mr and Mrs Browne are the only ones who open the front door, says Mrs Jones, to make sure there is enough security.

They take us into the kitchen. In the kitchen there are some more women, some sitting, some standing. They are looking at us. We look back at them. They smile at Mum.

Hello, they say to her.

I have to go back to the office now, says Mrs Jones. I wish you all luck, she says. You are in safe hands now. She walks out into the corridor talking with Mum.

We will take you up to your room now, say Mr and Mrs Browne, and they start to walk up the carpeted stairs with our things.

10

In flight

Now we are free. Bounce, bounce … Ball hits the wall hits my racquet hits the wall. Over and over, I get into the repetition of the movement, the repetition of my thoughts. The wall forms the outside of the kitchen, in the yard inside the big outer wall of the house. There's just enough room to hit the ball back and forth. The house wall is made up of brown-red bricks with concrete in between. It's a strong wall. All the tennis balls hitting it won't even leave a dent, I think. I think of the wall, everyone inside. I think of locked doors. I think of people squashed inside, the pounding of the ball over and over, thinking … ball … hit … wall … ball … run … hit … wall … ball … hit … over and over.

I watch the bouncing of the ball, and I keep hitting it over and over. Now we are free. We are free.

Socks the cat is with us. Mum put butter on her feet and kept her indoors for three days because she was worried Socks would run away and try to go home.

The kitchen door has lots of locks. It has a latch which closes when you close the door, it clicks in, and then you can fasten it with a little button so you can't undo it easily. Then there's a bolt beneath that slides across. There's a metal chain with a button that goes into a metal slit thing on the door frame so you can only open the door a little bit. Sometimes that's done up and sometimes it isn't. Then there's a big bolt at the top of the door and another at the bottom that we do up at night. Mum says that people who don't know the place always knock at the front door, so the kitchen door's always fine, when you hear a knock you can open it for whoever's there.

The kitchen door leads into the backyard, and the building at the back where the owners Mr and Mrs Browne stay. The side entrance is through a narrow passageway along the side of the house and a tall wooden gate that clicks open and shut, and we use it to go into and out of the house.

Kitchen smells. May is cooking in the corner. She reminds me of a tank, guns raised, grey metallic shiny oven surface, a big woman with a large chest, her thick arms like tree trunks, lifting saucepans like teaspoons. She wears a floral-print dress that hangs down, sack-like, from her square frame, as she lifts the boiling pot from the stove.

These spuds are taking longer than usual, she says. I got them down the market, but I don't think much of them.

She lifts the lid, a swirl of steam enveloping the upper half of the kitchen. Her hair – short, brown – stands on end a little, she keeps ruffling it with her steamy hands.

Fuck, says May. It's hot in here.

She leans forwards and opens the window just a little. It's pitch black outside. It's winter, dark by four, and I have just got back from school, and have my homework book out on the kitchen table.

As May opens the upper part of the window, a gap opens to the outside, a space where the outside world can creep in and envelop us. Outside is bad. Outside is where husbands lurk and hunt us out, they're stalking the streets peering through half-opened, narrow-slit windows in kitchens, where women open them because there's too much steam. The trickle of cold air has pierced the steam and sends a cool tongue-like shiver down our necks. I feel it on my arms as I write in my schoolbook, and on the back of my hand. Everyone is watching the window, because it lets the outside in. In here it's cosy, it's protection, with everyone checking the kitchen door is closed properly and locked all the time. The slim gap is like an open mouth. It feels as though, if you put your fingers out of it, it might snap them off.

I feel the same thought wriggle around in the women in the kitchen.

No one can get through that, says May jokingly. They'd have to be built like a beanpole.

Close it, May, says Shelley's mum. It's too cold.

So May leans forwards and closes the window and all the women's shoulders sink down a little again, not that you would have noticed they'd gone up, but I reckon it's like cats, when they're sensing danger, and in the cartoons all the fur stands up on their backs.

The radio is on faintly. May is cooking and Shelley's mum, Anne, is cooking too. Shelley's mum has been here the longest, and she's a kind of weasel woman, thin, with short spiky bright yellow dyed hair. I think the women like her because she's funny, but Mum says she doesn't quite trust her because there's something sly about her. Shelley's mum is cutting up some bread, and May is cutting up some corned beef, and Mum is getting some food out of the fridge they all share. Shelley's blonde with freckles and the same age as Amy. What's strange about Shelley is that she has an extra-short third finger with a short stumpy nail and she says she was born like that. She says her toes are webbed too, but she won't show us.

Bloody hell, says May, my potatoes have disintegrated now. Look. She digs a fork into the pot and pulls out a crumbly piece of potato, bits of it dropping off on the sides. Everyone laughs. The potato at the end of May's fork sends a white column of steam towards the kitchen ceiling. They weren't cheap, neither, says May. Maybe I should make potato soup instead, she says, and they laugh again.

Shelley's mum looks in the fridge and is angry because May's kids have been using her butter, and May says, don't accuse my kids of stealing, because she's in a bad mood about her potatoes which cost her twelve pence a pound and disintegrated. So Mum says to Shelley's mum, have some of my butter, it's okay, and Shelley's mum says thanks, but she glares at May.

I'm sitting doing my homework on the kitchen table as usual. I'm allowed to work in the kitchen because it's the quietest place in the house, not like the lounge and playroom with all the kids in, and the bedroom is a bit miserable and cramped with all the beds in it and there's no table there, so the mothers say it's okay as long as I stay quiet.

My homework is biology and it's about plants, where the liquid goes up the plant stalks by osmosis until it gets out into the open air, and there's oxygen that goes out too, and the women are chatting and laughing to the sound of the radio in the background, and every time I look up from my homework, Mrs Simpson's face is across from me.

Mrs Simpson is nearly as invisible as I am in the kitchen. She doesn't ask to be seen or heard, and the others often ignore her, as she wishes. Click, click. In the corner of the kitchen, where the light stays dim, she knits, and says nothing, burying herself in the wool in front of her. I watch how she hides behind the rhythmic sway of knitting needles, the beige wool thread that pulls taut, then dangles loose again on her knees, how the ball of wool twists and turns, shrivels smaller and smaller, as she weaves each new stitch into the one before. Mum told me Mrs Simpson had a very tough time with her husband and tried to kill herself several times. She was very depressed for a while after, and then she had to have antidepressants. She's still a bit down, Mum told me, which is why she doesn't talk much.

I watch how Mrs Simpson hides behind the wool, and I think to myself, Mrs Simpson must have had a really bad time if she can't even talk about it. She never talks about her husband, ever. She knits a brown meaningless shape, burying the pattern in her knitting basket. All her words are turned into stitches. Needle over needle, one stitch over the other, stories in every twist of the thread. The only sound she makes is the sound of needles clacking, like the metronome in music class, clack, clack, and the bobbing of her head when she occasionally responds with a yes or a no to the conversation that ebbs and flows around her. She buries an element of secrecy in every thread – stories that are never heard. As I watch her needles, row after row, and do my homework, line after line, I feel our shared silence, me hiding in my homework, her in her knitting. But both of us are hearing and seeing everything that goes on.

Is that something you're making for your son? asks Shelley's mum.

Mrs Simpson looks up slightly, raising her eyelids briefly. She has a child, a boy, who is five years old and has started school, and a little baby, and is waiting, like the other women, for her new home. She smiles timidly and nods a quiet yes. Then her attention falls back to her knitting.

The atmosphere in the kitchen is lighter now. The women are animated and their conversation is lively. I'm trying to study my biology but there's a lot of laughter going on. The leaves of the plant take the sunlight and use it to break carbon dioxide into water and oxygen with their chlorophyll, which is why the leaves are green, I write. I'm drawing a picture of osmosis. I've got the leaves done and I've done all the veins and I'm very proud of them, then there's the stalk, like it's cut in half with water going up one way and other things going down. I used a ruler, so I've got a very straight plant with clean lines, looking like a machine, not a plant really, when you think how plants move and wriggle around in the wind.

The women are talking about the prices in the supermarkets, and how potatoes have gone up again. Everyone is speaking about it, and how difficult it is to feed a family with the money they have. And I'm thinking how we turn plants from what we see into these strange flat diagrams that don't really look like plants at all, and there's no shade and light and any of the things you think about when you think of plants, and no colours either, and isn't that interesting?

Then Mrs Simpson lifts her head and says, yes, it isn't easy to manage on Social Security, it doesn't last. Then she looks back into her knitting, almost apologetic for speaking. The other women look at her, surprised. You're lively today, Lucy, says Shelley's mum.

Mrs Simpson's head doesn't move but I can see she's half smiling across the table, and her eyes look up, and quickly down again. The smell of cooking, the soggy potatoes, the laughter and animation seem to have affected even her too. We should have a party, Lucy, says Shelley's mum. An evening for the ladies? What do you think?

Yes, very nice, says Mrs Simpson.

Then the women start talking about their husbands, joking about them, and comparing stories. Mrs Mitchell tells us a story of how her husband threw the electric fire at her and he missed and hit the wall instead and the fire smashed up to pieces so they were cold after that, and the women laugh and say, fool, he should have been a bit more practical, they always throw things they shouldn't, then they regret it after. Mrs Mitchell is new, and she's upper class. She has a very neat voice, like all the words are tidied up, and she moves around in a tidied-up way, kind of controlled, she doesn't swear fuck and shit and bloody like the others, specially May. May swears all the time and has a loud laugh and Mum says May used to fight just as much as her husband, they both drank too much and that's why her boys are problem kids, and I'm a bit scared of May, although Mum says she has a good heart. Mrs Mitchell is definitely frightened of May and you can see she's not very comfortable around everyone else, like she feels maybe the others should have tidied up their voices too, and she's pretty alone, but all the others are friendly to her, it's like they're all in a big band together.

Mum says Mrs Mitchell is posh because she's from a very rich upper middle class family, and her husband is a well-known solicitor, and they lived in a really big house and they had everything they wanted in a material sense, it was cushy, and it just goes to show how violence happens across all families really, Mum says.

The next time, says Mrs Mitchell, he threw the iron at me, but he didn't miss that time. I ended up in hospital. I lied and said I fell over. Then Mrs Mitchell says her husband used to beat her for next to nothing, he used to get drunk and he threw the kitchen table at her too. She went to hospital four times, and the fourth time her head hit the wall and he knocked her out and she couldn't lie, it had become too obvious, and that's how people found out about it, and the social workers sent her here.

They found out about me when I ended up in hospital too, says Shelley's mum, nodding.

While the other women talk of their husbands, the fights, the problems, their anxieties, Mrs Simpson becomes even more quiet. Slash slash. Her needles slice nervously, like lightning bolts. Her knitting has become faster, angrier.

Her hands tremble, and the stitches go wobbly, and she drops a stitch and she picks it up again. The clack clack of her needles has sped up, like when you switch a metronome from slow to fast and all the music has to speed up to follow, as if the needles are attacking each other, they cross and weave like swords duelling, leaving a trail of twisted thread behind them, as her knuckles whiten and the circles of wool loop in and out of each other. And now she's not smiling any more, her face is set like concrete. She says nothing, her eyes looking downwards, her mouth held tight around the edges.

I've never seen anyone more scared in my life.

Isn't your kid a bit late from school, Lucy? Shelley's mum says to Mrs Simpson. Shouldn't he be back by now?

Just half an hour, says Mrs Simpson. I reckon he'll turn up soon. Sometimes he plays with his friends on the way back. Then Mrs Simpson hides behind her needles again and it's like the knitting she's making is a mask and she's not going to take it off.

I look up and see Mrs Simpson knitting, and I smell the potatoes' boiling smell get stronger as May drains them into a colander and then tips them into a bowl to add butter to them and mash them, and Shelley's mum is buttering her bread with my mum's butter, and I think God, Shelley's mum has taken a lot of my mum's butter, and Mum is making some tea and is cutting some malted loaf to toast and I can see her looking sideways out of the corner of her eye at Shelley's mum taking half our butter but she doesn't say anything. Shelley's mum seems less angry now, but every time May walks across the kitchen, which isn't very big, Shelley's mum steps away from May who is much larger than she is.

Then there's a knock on the kitchen door.

Mrs Simpson looks up and sees that everyone's busy. I'm not allowed to open the kitchen door anyway because children aren't allowed to, so I don't move. So Mrs Simpson gets up, carrying her knitting with her, and goes to the door and opens it just a little, because as soon as she has opened it a crack, she looks out and lets out a big scream and slams the door shut tight, BAM, and her knitting falls on the ground and the needles go clatter clatter and everyone stops what they're doing, and they look at Mrs Simpson who is frantically doing up the bottom bolt on the kitchen door and then the metal catch and she's trying to reach the big bolt at the top, and her hands are shaking and slipping and sliding on the bolts, and her feet are treading all over her brown knitting, and she's shivering and crying and shouting, it's my husband, it's my husband, it's my husband …

All the women look shit scared and they rush up to Mrs Simpson and they hold her and Shelley's mum says, are you sure? and Mrs Simpson cries, yes, yes, it's him, it's him, how did he find me, it's him, how did he get here? like she's talking to the air.

And all the women are shrieking and trampling on Mrs Simpson's knitting now, and they're all shit scared because Mr Browne who owns the place and his wife are out tonight and there's no one here to help them.

Shelley's mum runs out into the corridor and I hear her tell all the children in the playroom they must go upstairs right away, and she comes back in again.

Mum says, Mai, you must leave the kitchen and go upstairs too, so I start to get my things together to go out.

But then the knocking starts at the door again and the women jump and I stop moving. Mrs Simpson shrieks and this time it's really really loud, and she doesn't stop, and all the women are standing around holding Mrs Simpson and don't know what to do.

Then May says, I'll talk to him, he can't come in, we're all here, we won't let him in, he doesn't know me, I'll keep the chain on the door.

May puts the metal chain on and unbolts the bolts and opens the door just the smallest bit, with all the women standing behind her and Mrs Simpson huddled up crying in their arms, and May speaks through the gap in the door and says in a big loud voice:

Go away, you're not wanted here.

Then a voice says something quietly on the other side and May stops still. She says, just one moment, and closes the door again and locks it, and she looks a bit strange, and she looks at Mrs Simpson who is still shaking and crying.

May says, he says he's got your son. He took him from school and he's got him in his car. Unless you go outside and talk, he says he will do something to your little boy.

And May is normally a big strong woman and Mum says she's sure she gives what she gets, but this time May is white as a sheet and her face is cold and solemn and shocked and her eyes – gleaming and moist and helpless – say everything to Mrs Simpson that her face doesn't.

And now the women shriek and go around in circles again and Mrs Simpson starts crying really loud, saying, he's got my baby, he's got my baby, my little baby boy, he's going to hurt my boy, it's all my fault, why didn't I collect him from school, why didn't I fetch him?

Call the police, says Shelley's mum, but Mrs Simpson shrieks out, no! No, you can't call the police, please don't call the police. You can't call them. They won't help me, they won't help. Please don't call the police. And Mrs Simpson sobs loudly and clutches at the women around her.

Why ever not? says Shelley's mum.

They're on his side, he'll say I ran with the kids, they're on his side, sobs Mrs Simpson, they're on his side …

The women stare, astonished, as Mrs Simpson clings to them.

216

You're in shock, says Shelley's mum. You're hysterical. Why would they be on his side? Of course it's okay to call the police. They'll arrest him for kidnapping your boy.

Of course we can call the police, says May.

No, no, you can't go to them, it's the police, don't you see, screams out Mrs Simpson, don't you see, why don't you understand? and she is crying and wailing.

What do you mean, Lucy? asks May.

You're not making any sense, says Shelley's mum.

Mrs Simpson is still crying loudly, but we can hear her say between breaths, don't you see, there's nothing you can do, he's high up, don't you understand … they won't help, he's high up … don't you see?

But the women just look at her blankly, and then Mrs Simpson screams out, IT'S THE POLICE … MY HUSBAND … HE'S A POLICE-MAN.

Oh my God, says May. He *is* the police.

He's high up, sobs Mrs Simpson, he's in charge, he's the head of police, he's in charge of the whole district, that's how he found me. There's nothing I can do, they're on his side. And then she starts crying hysterically, really really loud.

And now the women go silent, and then they panic and they are screaming too.

Then Shelley's mum says, Lucy, it's their duty to protect us. You have to call the police. There's nothing else we can do. He's got your son.

No, says Mrs Simpson. It's useless.

What area is he head of? asks Shelley's mum.

Leicestershire, says Mrs Simpson.

Well that's a different county, says Shelley's mum. He's got no power over this region. He can't touch you here.

Mum sees me still standing there in the doorway with my

school stuff in my hands, and says, I told you to leave, Mai, go upstairs, but don't say anything about this to the other children, we don't want to scare them, just tell them to stay upstairs in their rooms.

I go out into the corridor, closing the door behind me, and Shelley and Amy are there leaning over the banister halfway down the stairs and I say, don't worry, it's a grown-ups' thing, it's just something that happened, but everyone must stay upstairs.

I sit at the top of the stairs with my homework on my knees.

Then Mum comes out and she goes to the pay telephone under the stairs and starts dialling and she speaks to someone then she waits.

I say, what are you doing, Mum? and Mum says, quiet Mai, I'm phoning the police. Then Mum says, I've agreed to meet him outside in a street with his son to negotiate. I'm telling the police where we're going to meet so they can get there quickly and get the child. Is that safe, Mum? I say, and she says, what else can we do, he's got Mrs Simpson's son and he could do anything. At least it delays things.

I'm a stranger to him, says Mum, I'm safe. The only person he wants to hurt is his wife.

What if the police take too long? I say.

Go into the bedroom and close the door, Mai, says Mum. I need to finish this call.

I sit in the bedroom with Amy and Matti and Babs playing around me, and I hear Mum talking on the phone, and then shortly after I hear the kitchen door open and close again, then everything is quiet. I start to do my homework again, but it's very hard to think about plants and water coming out of leaves when Mum's talking to Mrs Simpson's husband in a street somewhere and it's dangerous, but I try to do it anyway, it keeps me calm.

A bit later I hear a knock and the kitchen door open and shut again and lots of talking and Mum's voice. A short while after Mum comes upstairs into the bedroom.

Mum says, it was fine, the police were very good, even before I got there, they were there already, and he had her son there in the car and they arrested him straight away, so Mrs Simpson has her son back safe and sound.

Mum sounds calm, but she's tense, a bit on edge, I can hear it in her voice.

I think to myself, my mum's a real hero, she's really brave, the only one who knew what to do and had the courage to do it. And I'm proud of Mum and I think the other mothers must respect her a lot for what she did.

When Mr and Mrs Browne the caretakers get back they are shocked about it all and say, we came as soon as we heard. The police are there talking too, and they discuss security with the women in the corridor in lowered voices, maybe because of all us kids trying to hear from the top of the stairs.

After that the kitchen door always has the metal chain latch on and one bolt. And there's a special signal, knock-knock … knock-knock-knock … knock-knock, to say it's okay, it's only one of us, so the women can open the door safely, just like in the detective films on TV.

And now if Mr and Mrs Browne go out, there must always be a policeman on duty around the house.

After that Mrs Simpson has to leave because now her husband knows where she is, and she has to go to a new place. No one says where, because it's all secret, and Mrs Simpson will have to change her name again.

Mum says because Mrs Simpson's husband is a policeman, that's how he found her, through the police, not anywhere is safe really, especially when your husband's in the police and can track you down. And now I know why Mrs Simpson is always so scared, because wherever she goes, her husband can find her.

And now it's quiet in the kitchen where she used to be, because the needles clacking and clicking had become part of the kitchen, and she always nodded to what was being said, so even though she was quiet, she was like a kind of cushion in the room where all the sounds and arguments and noises and laughter bounced off. I miss her, because me and her always used to sit at the kitchen table working together and now I have to do my homework alone.

When we kids play in the hall, the big double wooden front door is like a huge barrier to the outside, keeping us safe. The front door has big bolts too and only the owners of the house, Mr and Mrs Browne, can open it, and they only do it if they really have to, like when a new family arrives or leaves and they need to carry boxes and suitcases and prams through, so it stays shut most of the time. Us kids, we can't play out in the streets, it's forbidden, most of the time we're inside running round the house. Mum says we mustn't undo the big wooden double front door, even as a joke. Sometimes me and Amy and Shelley, the girl who greeted us when we first arrived, linger in the porch behind the door and it feels very dangerous, like we shouldn't be there, and we know on the other side of the door is Outside.

Inside, there's a TV room and a playroom where there's space and toys for the young kids. Us older ones sometimes escape to the backyard because it is quieter, more unused, where you can think a bit, whereas the TV room with its old armchairs and sofas feels crowded, with its red-patterned carpet that has been eaten up by too many feet running across it, and the TV on all the time, and May's three boys racing around making a racket. Mum says, don't get too involved with May's boys, they're bad boys.

So I stay out of the way, but I fancy the older one a bit, he's fifteen and his other brothers are thirteen and ten, and he has mousy-brown hair just above his shoulders and a kind of interesting energy, a bit restless, a bit wild. I reckon he's not as stupid as he acts, he's pretty sharp, he just plays the fool because that's all he knows what to do, it's like an escape for him. He doesn't do his homework like me, but I bet he'd like to find out things, like I do. I've seen May's kids boss the young kids around a bit, but no one here is really bad, nobody is really cruel to each other. Us kids running up and down the staircases, we're like a team, we protect each other. We don't always get close, we know how to keep our distances and how not to get too involved, we're well trained in it, but we're kind of bonded by that. We all move around each other, but we're all in the same situation, we kind of respect it in each other.

When new people arrive, the front door is opened wide and us kids like to stand and stare at the belongings coming through the door like a little procession, and usually there's not much, just what could be grabbed at the time, I reckon, just blankets and clothes and a few precious things, and bank books if they have one, because Mum brought hers, and things people's families gave them, like a special book or something, but it's nice to guess and to watch the boxes and the suitcases come in. Our special things were a box of Matti's and Babs' toys and Mum's sewing machine which she says she will never leave behind, and the dancing lady from Mrs Lara, and our tennis racquets from Christmas and our schoolbooks. When new people arrive, there's usually a pram of some kind; sometimes it's big and blue, like Mrs Simpson's, who arrived with her baby and little boy, with her narrow face with not much meat on it and mousy permed hair.

Then the family arrive, emerging out of the small van where they've been cooped up all those hours with the windows blacked out, and they always look completely numbed like they don't know what's going on, they're shit scared and sometimes the kids are playing up to show they're not shit scared of anything, but we know really they're pretending, but usually the mums don't, they say, behave yourselves, can't you see you've got to behave? or shut up, will you, but I can see the fear in the kids' eyes even if their mums can't, because their mums are even more shit scared. And it's like people arrive without their whole house wrapped around them and whatever abusive relationship they had that, whatever it was like, gave them some sense of belonging, even if it was a false security, and if you want to see people really naked, that's how the families look, they haven't got a bed, house, belongings, father, home, school, street, future or past, and not even their names.

We watch the families come in after their belongings, and as they come in the door they look emptier and more fragile and more pathetic than even their few belongings that preceded them, and their mums talk with Mr and Mrs Browne of the house, the kids play up, and all the other women gather round in a group to greet them and I can see they're trying to be as warm as possible. Once the new woman's put her stuff in her room and they've helped her settle down a bit and shown her around so she knows where things are, like the larder and the laundry room, and the kids' playroom, they draw her into the kitchen. Then they sit her down in the kitchen and that's where the stories begin. I wasn't allowed in at first, but after a while they got used to me sitting at the kitchen table to do my homework, and I spend so much time there, I get to hear things.

Sometimes the new woman is really, really scared, like Mrs Patel, the Indian woman, she's got a baby and she wears a sari and has a red mark on her forehead and she's really young and I don't think her English is that good, she's really shy and doesn't come in the kitchen that much and lots of social workers visit her and she has a big long beautiful plait hanging down her back. She's very polite and always smiles but I think the other women find it hard to talk to her because she doesn't understand them very well. So she ends up a bit like Mrs Simpson, not saying anything and being very quiet, but they say they are going to move her soon to a place where people can speak her language.

The new kids that are old enough get to meet us, and we have our own thing outside the kitchen, we don't bother with conversations like the women, we say, what's your name? or do you want to play? and then they say yes, so we play games, and sometimes, like when Mrs Mitchell's children arrived, the children go straight upstairs and we don't see much of them. I guess Mrs Mitchell's worried about the effect us kids will have on her own children, because they stay very separate from us and don't mix much, like they've been told to do that. Mum says Mrs Mitchell's two boys went to an expensive private school before they came here, and they seem nice, but I reckon Mrs Mitchell warned them not to hang around us in case they get influenced or something.

We don't see much of Mrs Peters' two teenage girls who are fourteen and fifteen, much older than I am, because they are nearly grown up, and all they talk about is boys and lipstick and sometimes they come and do homework too, but they don't do much of it. They go to secondary modern school and, even though they are fourteen and fifteen years old, two years and three years older than me, they are still doing fractions, and Mum says it's not fair, because you can do a fourteen-plus examination to get into grammar school later but if they're not teaching you anything, what chance have you got?

To get into the grammar school I have to do an entrance examination. There is only me and one boy who is applying for the year above me, because we are both starting the year late.

We finish the exam early and the secretary comes out and takes our papers.

Are you sure you have both finished? she asks. You've still got lots more time.

Yes, thank you, we both say.

You'll have to wait here, says the secretary. The headmaster only gets back later and your parents are coming at the end of the exam time.

We wait. What's your name? says the boy, after we have been sitting silently on our own for a while. Mai, I say. Mine is Anthony, he says. Where are you from? I tell him the county we lived in before. That's a long way to walk, he says.

I laugh. Yes, my legs wore out getting here, I say.

So how did you get here then, without legs? he says.

I got bionic ones as a replacement.

Did they wear out too?

Yes. But there are plenty more available. They keep them in a pile out at the back.

Anthony tells me his dad is a professor of philosophy at the university and that is why they have moved here. We chat and chat and chat until the headmaster comes back and we say we finished already, and he replies that was quick, well, thank you, you can wait outside where your parents will collect you and we will get back to you at a later date.

We wait, sitting in the foyer of the office. When Anthony's parents come to collect him they seem very important and are dressed very smart and are very nice to him, and his dad puts his hand on his shoulder and says, how did it go? and Anthony says, it went fine thanks Dad. The car's parked in the school parking, says Anthony's dad. It's just a short walk from here.

Then Mum comes to fetch me and we take the bus back to the battered wives' home which is an hour's journey.

The local authorities don't want you to go to this school, says Mum, because they said it's not in your catchment area. But I argued you need to go to a grammar school and not a secondary modern because you were going to go to a gifted school before. The nearby grammar school is full so they said you could sit the exam and see.

I get in.

Before I start the first day at the grammar school, Mum says the headmaster wants to welcome me to the school and she leaves me at his office.

Anthony is there already.

Hi, says Anthony to me, and smiles. You made it too. That's good.

I smile back.

You both did exceptionally well in the entrance exam, says the headmaster and he puts his hands on both our shoulders. It's rare we get two students of such promise coming in at the same time, he says. I hope you will enjoy your time with us. This is a good school. We expect a lot from both of you, and he smiles again.

At school they say I can learn the violin. Mum has my great-grandfather's violin, it was his personal one, she says. She brought it with her when we ran away because she always thought it would be good for us to learn it. It's very big, it's almost a viola, says my teacher. My teacher is very old and used to play in an orchestra. He looks at my hands and bends my fingers back gently and says, very good, her fingers are double-jointed, that's a good sign for a violin player. And when I start playing my teacher's very nice to me and I practise at home, in the room with the door closed because Mum says I mustn't disturb everyone. Amy laughs and says I sound squeaky, but sometimes we play recorder together, because they taught us the basics at Greendale Middle School, in music class. When I practise my violin I forget everything else and just hear the music soar up and down and sometimes the music is happy and sometimes it is sad.

My best friend at school is called Selina. Her dad is training to be a priest, she's part of a Christian Union thing and there's lots of them living in little houses by a big priest school. Selina believes in God, and she says you must love everyone and it's bad to tell lies because it's against God's will and you won't go to heaven. I think how lots of things seem to be against God's will, after going to school with Sister Mary Ann Jones, and it's not what God thinks that I'm so worried about, but the thing about telling lies bothers me, because Mum's strict about that and says we must always be honest and I've always thought it was wrong to lie and I think how Selina doesn't know my real surname. It's on the tip of my tongue to tell her but the only reason I don't is because I promised Mum I wouldn't and I'd be breaking my promise. But I know we're all lying and when I tell Mum, she says, well, Mai, sometimes it's all right to tell white lies, sometimes you just have to. She says I mustn't tell Selina, even though I feel bad about it, but I mustn't worry because in this case it's okay to tell a white lie. Our false surname, Roberts, is quite easy to remember and only once I made a mistake and began to say my other surname at school but I made out I was talking about something else and no one seemed to notice. But I feel a bit guilty when Selina talks about honesty or mentions my name, and sometimes when I say my new surname it comes out slow, slow, like it's stuck inside me.

Selina believes God is there for the good of all.

I don't know if I believe in God, I say. If there was a God, then why does he let the world be the way it is? and she says the bad things exist because of the devil.

I still don't believe her, but I think of Rashid and I think if there's a devil, it must be Rashid, because his eyes are so evil it's like the devil is sitting there ready to jump right out.

Selina believes in love and kindness, and her whole world seems to be based on that, on her happy family and her father and mother and sister who love her, and it's strange because I believe in evil and unfairness, it's just there in my life.

Selina doesn't know I live in a battered wives' home because none of us kids are allowed to say anything about where we live, in case we ever get traced.

Mum goes to Parents' Day and she says, your teacher at the grammar school never understood why you had free dinners, she was really surprised to find out we were living in a battered wives' home and we were all living in one room. She thought you were from a middle-class family, because you speak well and because your marks are so good.

Mum seems proud. I don't like having free school dinners much. It makes me feel funny, because I have to put up my hand in front of the whole class when the teacher asks so she can count them, and everyone looks.

This year I catch tonsillitis three times. I go to the doctor's and my temperature is soaring, the room spinning, my face hot. Thirty-nine degrees, says the doctor, and prescribes penicillin.

I get a rash all over my body. The doctor is called back and examines me in the kitchen of the battered wives' home. He checks my throat, listens to my heartbeat under my top. The women are gathered around. They think it's measles.

It's not measles. She's allergic to penicillin, says the doctor, and prescribes erythromycin, and I get better.

At the battered wives' home, Mum says one of the social workers has suggested I enter for a scholarship at a very good boarding school, and that I will do a maths and English exam and the best results of all the people who take the exam will get the place at the boarding school.

The social worker says it's worth a try, says Mum. She says you will definitely get to Oxford or Cambridge if you go to that school. Mum gives me a maths book which says *Math 3 and 4* and says, they said you should study this because the maths you are doing right now is not as advanced as theirs.

So I sit inside and work my way through the book like it's a puzzle book, triangles and angles and shapes that you calculate numbers for and something called algebra where you use letters instead of numbers, and that's fun.

Mrs Mitchell goes home again. Mum says she missed her home comforts, the house and the lifestyle and the posh school her children went to.

Mum says Mrs Mitchell's husband told her he wouldn't do it again, but she'd left twice before and he'd done the same, and he still carried on doing it, so Mum reckoned it wouldn't get much better, Mrs Mitchell would probably end up back in hospital again. But, as Mum said, what future did Mrs Mitchell have with two kids and no job and no qualifications, she'd never get a house or lifestyle like that. At least she had a house and a home and respect from the neighbours, and her kids could go to a really good school, and sometimes you don't really feel you have a choice, because despite what's going on at home, you have security and something, rather than nothing and nowhere to go and no future to look forward to for your children.

I think of Mrs Mitchell talking about when he threw the fire, and the iron, at her, and I wonder what will be thrown this time, and where he'll hit her, and if she'll go back to hospital even worse or if the kids want that, or if they suffer, but they never say anything about it to us anyway. None of us kids talk to each other about what it was like before we came here.

I know what Mum means. We didn't have much to give up, but we still have to all live in only one room, it's one room per family and in our room we have four beds, one for Mum, one for me, one for my sister, a smaller one for baby brother Matti, and a cot for my baby sister Babs, and what with our washing basket and the suitcases that doesn't leave any room over. We don't spend any time there, except Mum says we have to make our beds in the morning, so we always do that, and I like to fold my bed really neat, with the sheet tight under the mattress, but most of the time we're outside the room. Once in a while I go inside and shut the door to have some peace from the kitchen and the kids and the noise and the women chatting and the radio and the smells from the kitchen and the TV on full volume and May's kids fighting over what programme to watch because us younger ones never get a say, and the sound of toys clacking in the playroom, and I sit on my bed and look around me at the other beds and the cot and smell the smell of my family. It's all crowded in here, all our life and our dreams and everything we have, but at least it's us and for once we're really free to be what we want to be and no one's telling me not to read books and we don't have to scuttle around like scared mice any more, and no one's going to try to throw Mum down the stairs, and I'm happy being here, it's a bit crowded and one hell of a lot of people in this house, but for once our family is itself, and we all live in this little room but we get on really well together and Amy is doing well at school and for once we're free.

Two new women, Mrs Jones, with a little boy and a little girl, eight and four years old, and Mrs Williamson, who has a nine-year-old son, arrive as soon as Mrs Mitchell leaves.

Mrs Patel leaves about this time too. Mum says she's been there long enough, now she's got a home to go to, this is only a place of safety, and temporary, there's a long waiting list of more battered wives, and the women wait there until they're rehoused. And Mum says we're lucky, we could've gone to the other home, they were the first in the country, there are only two, and that one is so crowded now they even have two families in a room, and women in the corridors, at least, that's what she's heard, so I say, how long are we here for, Mum? and she says she doesn't know, it will be a few months at least, until they find a new home for us, we're on a waiting list. And I say, what, will we have our own house to live in? And Mum says, probably, yes, when one becomes available.

11

Dancing

Christmas is coming, the goose is getting fat … and all that.

Why they say goose I don't know. I've never had goose at Christmas. I don't know anyone who has. Christmas makes the goose grow fat, but only if you have a goose.

Please put a penny in the old man's hat.

There aren't any old men here. There aren't any men at all, only Mr Browne who lives round the back of the house with his wife in the little separate bit added on, and he's not old enough. Mum says it's very kind of him and his wife, they had this big house and they donated it to the battered wives when they could have had it all to themselves and they chose to live out in the bit at the back.

When it's Christmas there's lots of pictures on the playroom telly of homes with Christmas trees and all kinds of presents you can buy for your children. I like to watch the ads, there's always interesting toys and nice cartoons, and the music's fun, and you can watch the families gathered round opening up their presents after Father Christmas comes down the chimney and leaves presents – of course it's always an actor dressed up, and anyway it's lucky you can't come down the chimney really because it's bad enough having to lock the windows and the front door and the kitchen side door without having to lock your chimney too, to keep the husbands out. But I like the idea of riding a sleigh across the sky, with presents on.

Once, when I was very little, I sat on Father Christmas's knee in a department store and he said something nice to me and he asked me if I wanted a nice present and what did I want, so I told him and I thought he was going to reach into his sack and pull a present out right there and then, so I was a bit disappointed when he just said, Merry Christmas, write a letter to me, and didn't give me a present right there and then, I thought it was a bit of a con, seeing as he led you on to think you were going to get something and then you didn't get anything. Christmas Day was a hell of a long way away and by then I might have changed my mind about my present anyway.

The battered wives decide we're going to have a Christmas party.

The first one to hear about it is Shelley, who comes flying down the corridor into the TV room where we're watching TV and she shouts, we're going to have a Christmas party, we're going to have a Christmas party! and then we go ask, will we get presents?

And the wives say, yes, you will, Mr Browne says he will donate some money towards the party and we will raise the rest.

So the wives get together in a meeting in the kitchen to see how we can raise money and who's going to cook what, and May says she'll make a Christmas cake because that's what she's best at, and they say there'll be two parties at the same time, one for the kids in the playroom and one for the mums in the kitchen and the room next to it, which is kind of like a big larder and washroom, and all us kids talk of nothing except how we are going to get presents and everything.

Then the wives say we are going to go carol-singing. You must wear your best clothes for the carol-singing, they say, and everyone must get dressed up smart. We say, can't we get dressed up like Halloween, it's more fun, but the wives say it's best clothes or you don't go.

So we all get dressed up and then we put on scarves and coats and hats and gloves and we giggle at each other because all the jumpers and coats we're wearing make us look fat.

Everyone's there, there's a lot of us when we're all together – there's Mrs Jones and her two kids, and May's three teenage boys who are saying it's baby to do this, but they're there anyway because May says if they don't do it, there's no Christmas party for them and no presents, and then there's new Mrs Williamson's boy, and then there's me and Amy and Matti, and Shelley. And Babs is there, Mum has her in the pushchair, and Shelley's little brother who is the same age as Matti, five, and it's a lot of us. There's another brand-new family, two boys of about eight and seven, and of course there's all the wives too.

So we all go out in our big group and walk down the street together.

May and Shelley's mum are at the front and May has a big plastic bucket that's bright orange and she's Sellotaped a big piece of paper on it that says Collection For Homeless Children and she has a special badge she wears. Mum is at the back with Mrs Williamson and Mr Browne and his wife, they're making sure none of us get lost on the way, and Mrs Peters stays back home because she says she's not up to it, she's feeling unwell. There's more mums in the middle, including the new one, and even another new one with short hair who doesn't have any children but is still a battered wife and Mum says she is very young. We keep walking and now we're in wider streets and Shelley's mum and May say this is the area we want to be in, they're posh here, we're in a posh area with big houses because they have lots of dosh. We walk up to the first front door and we're a lot of people, a big crowd of us. And we all stand there on the front path feeling a bit funny.

Shelley's mum says, sing, then, but we don't do anything except look at each other nervously.

And then Shelley's mum says again – Sing! – and we still do nothing.

So then Mrs Jones says, I'll start, and she sings 'Away in a Manger' because we don't know many Christmas carols except parts of 'Silent Night' and Glo-or-or-or-ia and 'Little Town of Bethlehem', and we all know 'Away in a Manger' because it's one we all have to learn at school. So we all join in and Shelley's giggling with Amy and they keep nudging each other to stop giggling. May's three boys are looking embarrassed and are not singing, so May gives them a look and they start singing, and May keeps looking at them, so they don't stop. They know when May says, any trouble from you three and you've had it, May means it, and they've been well warned.

Matti is trying to sing the words too, but he doesn't really know them, but he likes it and is smiling, and Babs doesn't know any words at all, she's in the pushchair in a big woolly hat with a red bobble on and a thick coat and her cheeks are all rosy and she looks kind of cute and pretty, and Mum is in her red coat with the fur on the inside to keep her warm, the one she got married in, because I saw the wedding photograph.

Then the door opens and a woman comes out and says thank you and puts some money, quick, into May's bucket, and then she goes back inside and closes the door again.

May and Shelley's mum look in the bucket and say, two pence, these posh people are stingy.

Then Shelley's mum turns to us and says, she probably gave us that to go away, can you sing up a bit you lot, you need to sing louder, you sound like you're half dead, I'm sure you're not that bad, and your singing's all over the place too. May says, Shelley and Amy, you two stop giggling this time or I'll split you both up, and she gives them the look she gives her boys, and Shelley and Amy stop grinning immediately.

So at the next house Amy and Shelley don't giggle at all, and we all sing really really loud, and Shelley tries to sing louder than Amy and I try to sing louder than them and May's three boys look at us and try to sing even louder than us lot, and Mrs Mitchell's kids also join in the game, and then Shelley and Amy sing even louder than May's three boys, and the competition's on …

I can hardly hear anything except a big noise of us singing and shouting, and Babs is banging the sides of her pushchair and clapping her hands and I look at Matti and he's jumping up and down with a big grin on his face, he's so excited, and the other little ones are jumping up and down too and enjoying it and it's really funny, we're all smiling and laughing.

And then May knocks at the door and someone comes out, and the money goes clink in the bottom of the bucket, and May and Shelley's mum go, thank you, Sir, for your help.

This time when the door closes May says, when I said loud I didn't mean scream the place down, I never heard such a racket, it's a lot better, but stay in tune, five pence only, stingy buggers, next time we leave the posh areas alone.

And Shelley's mum says, just enjoy yourselves, kids, but May's right, you could be more in tune.

When we get to the third house we're still singing loud but our voices are a bit sore from before, so it's quieter. Afterwards May says, any kid who was away in a manger would be dead by now with the racket you were making at the last house, but that was an improvement. But she's laughing and there's a pink glow to her cheeks, and Shelley's mum goes, look we got 50p, it couldn't have been that bad, keep it up kids. And now even May's three boys are laughing and they don't seem to mind singing at all.

So we go from house to house singing and it's great fun. Usually the door opens when May knocks and May says, we're collecting for homeless children, and then the money goes clunk, and sometimes it goes clunk clunk clunk when there's lots of change, and sometimes the person goes no, thank you.

And sometimes no one answers at all but you know they're there because the TV's on, and May goes, stingy buggers, I hope they have a shit Christmas, and all the women go, yeah. But usually we get money and people are very nice and we feel good because we're collecting for homeless children.

Then we get to a large house with a big front door and lights on at the sides and when it opens there is a little old lady with silvery hair and a big thick warm coat on and she stops in surprise to see so many of us there all stretched down the garden path and out the gate, because there's not enough room for all of us on the path because May says we mustn't step on any people's flower beds because they'll get angry and won't give us any money.

And the old lady looks at us and says, what is it you're collecting for? and May and Shelley's mum say, for the homeless children, and the little old lady looks down the garden path and says, are all these the homeless children?

And May and Shelley's mum say, yes, they are. And the old lady looks out at all of us and says, aren't they lovely?

Then I look at Amy and Amy looks at Shelley and Shelley looks at me and Amy whispers, does that mean we're the homeless children? And we're shocked because somehow we thought when you collect money for charity you collect for other people at school, when you collect for homeless people or the blind or the poor or the refugees, they are never yourself, and we never thought homeless children was us.

Then the old lady says, do they want some sweets? We all look at Shelley's mum straight away and she says, I'm sure they wouldn't say no, the cheeky buggers, and the old lady goes, just one minute. She goes away inside and we wait and she comes back out again with a metal bowl and it's full of sweets. We come up one by one and take one and say, thank you. The sweets have plastic wrappers on and they're fruit flavoured and they're quite big and Matti's one is so big it makes his cheek stick right out and he looks really happy.

And while we are eating the sweets the old lady chats and asks, what is the money for? Is it for something in particular?

May and Shelley's mum say, it's for our Christmas party and the little old lady says, that's lovely, would you all like another sweet? And we all say, yes please, and she holds out the bowl and we all go up in a line and take another sweet one by one like the mothers tell us to, and the old lady goes, what lovely children they all are, I hope you have a wonderful party. And then the old lady gives May and Shelley's mum a five-pound note and their eyes nearly stick out of their heads and they say, thank you very, very much, it's really kind of you, then the little old lady says, goodbye, Merry Christmas, and we all say Merry Christmas back and the old lady goes back in and shuts the door, and we're left chewing our sweets and holding one extra each in our hands, except May's three boys who took two sweets each the second time around and they think they're clever.

When we get back to the house again all the women gather round the table in the larder and count up the money and they make a lot of noise and all the coins go jangle jangle when they tip the bucket out on the table and then May says, we made thirty-two pounds thirty-seven pence, and everyone cheers.

The Christmas tree arrives, it's big, two people have to carry it, and they put it in the TV room because that's where we're going to have the party. Then we all get to put up decorations which come in a big box and later there's going to be presents because Mum says they wrote to Boots the chemist's factory for free presents and they are going to send us some extra stock and seconds, which are nearly as good as new things, only a little bit different.

When the tree is up it looks great, except May's three boys knock it over the next day because they are playing chase, even though you're not meant to run in the TV room, it's forbidden. May's youngest boy runs into the tree from behind the TV, and he falls into it and the tree goes right over in front towards us, crash, and all the coloured shiny things fall down, and the angel at the top goes skidding off across the floor to the other side of the room, and all us kids scream and laugh, but the mums don't think it's funny at all.

So May's boys are made to put the tree up again, but now one side's a bit squashed and scruffy where the floor hit it and there're needles all over the floor because some branches broke, and the boys are not too good at decorating so the decorations are a bit skew, and now the tree looks like it's leaning over to one side. May's boys get banned from the TV room until the party, but sometimes they come and sneak in and sit at the back because the women are too busy preparing to notice.

And all the wives these days are doing nothing but talking about who is going to cook what and do what and May is getting her Christmas cake ready and Mum is going to do the roast potatoes and the sausages and there are two huge turkeys and all the decorations go up and there's lots of balloons.

The boxes donated from the Boots factory turn up and there's lots of them, big boxes. But it's all secret, us kids aren't allowed to look, say the mums, but we peep through into the larder room and see the mums going through the boxes and there's toys in plastic packaging and all of them are being looked at oooh and aaah and there're things for everyone, even the mums, and then they shut the door clunk and we can't see what they're doing.

Well, this Christmas for once we have a goose, it's a fluffy cuddly toy goose that comes with the presents that Babs gets, with dangly orange legs. All us kids are in the TV room opening our presents around the tree and all the presents are everywhere in the room in a big mess of wrapping paper and plastic.

I get a new school satchel in brown leather and an oil-painting set for my drawing and painting and some silly pink girly stuff, a plastic mirror and hairpin, and I reckon I got that because there's no girls near my age, only Tina and Sally, Mrs Peters' two teenage daughters, who get make-up because they are almost grown up. Matti has a big bouncy plastic football, he's really happy and he's kicking it round the TV room, which he can do today only because it's Christmas Day, and all the kids are running around the room screaming and making noises. We're all really happy, because we all have three or four or five presents each, and the mums have presents too, and they all got a present for Mr Browne and his wife. I've got a book to read from Mum, and Shelley got a ruler she didn't want so I swapped it for one of my girly things.

They're the best presents we ever got, except for the tennis racquets and toffee Mum gave us before.

For the party, there's a lot of food and cakes and big turkeys and May's giant Christmas cake. Mr and Mrs Browne come and some men and women from the Social Services and there's some friends of Mr Browne's, and other men and women, maybe they're Social Services too, or maybe the police who guarded us, and there's a lot of noise in the room next to the kitchen where the grown-ups' party is.

The wives bring a huge pile of food into the TV room and there's a big table where we can help ourselves. Then the women shut the door to the larder room while we're watching the Christmas films on the telly, and they're drinking and laughing really loud and talking loud to the men, and they have the radio on and they're dancing, and the noise they make is more than the kids.

Shelley says, God, those grown-ups are making a lot of noise, I can't hear the bloody TV, and she gets up and shuts the TV room door.

Some of the little ones have fallen asleep because they've eaten so much. Every now and then the playroom door opens and a mum sticks her head in and says, is everything all right, are you having fun? and we say, yes, all of us glued to the TV, except some of the little ones who are still awake and are playing with their toys. So the mum goes out again like she's worried she's missing something and can't wait to get back to it, and I wonder what makes an adult party different from a kids' party and we can hear the laughing and shrieking from the room next door, and sometimes I wonder if their party is even better than ours.

12

Rediscovery

Christmas is over and it's our turn to move to a new house. Mum says it's in a part of the city called the Streets, it's by the big wide river which travels through the city and we all learnt about in school. Is it pretty there? we ask, and Mum says, well, the other side of the river is. And when we get there we see why she said it, because it's all terraced council houses and little roads on our side, but on the other side it's big houses and big gardens, and when you walk along the river edge you can see the houses on the other side. Between the two sides of the river is a big concrete bridge, and on both sides of the river are grey concrete walls with steps down the sides.

Mum says we live on the poor side. It's called the Streets but it's more houses than streets. You can see the water passing through between the concrete borders like a murky grey snake, fat and ugly, like a python trying to wrap itself around the houses. Sometimes there are shows on the river, like boat displays and parachutes falling like cherry blossom from jet planes passing overhead, and all the people sit on the concrete steps that go down on both sides of the river and watch everything that happens. Like the time the queen came to visit, and there was a car, and an arm in a green woolly sleeve waved a hand in a white glove out of the window.

That's the queen, said Mum, but it was all very quick and I was a bit disappointed that was all we got to see of her, an arm and a hand, nothing like the storybooks that have the queen sitting with all the crown jewels sparkling and a big red robe.

I like to watch the river when the sun sparkles on it, then it's like scales on a snake's back, all the little ripples like separate scales, reflecting the sun.

The other side's where the snobs live, say the local kids. I don't tell them we joined the tennis club on the other side because Mum is going to play tennis like she used to when she was young and she's going to teach us. The other side has big beautiful houses, not crowded like on our side, with toilets on the outside as well as the inside, all hemmed in together. It's like we're a pack of playing cards, all tight against each other, and the big houses are paintings hanging on a wall, all spaced out. I like to look at the houses when we go past on the way to the tennis club, like you look at paintings.

When we first arrive at our house we all stay in one room because Mum only has one big mattress and a couple of blankets the battered wives' home lent her, so we all share the mattress, me, Mum, Amy, Matti and Babs, all in a row. Mum says it's fun, because we are all sleeping together, it's an adventure, like camping. We giggle, because we haven't slept like that before, with Babs and Matti and Mum and Amy and me, all pulling the covers this way and that way because we have to share the blankets, and we spend a long time pulling the blankets back and forth, until Mum says, stop it now, we all need to sleep.

The battered wives come around with the Social Services people to visit and wish us luck. There's a lot of them. They bring some biscuits and they come in and walk through the rooms one by one, in a long file, going very nice, very nice and nodding their heads, and looking around from side to side at every room, and joking with Mum, saying how will you get used to this space, after living in one room, this is luxury, what are you going to fill it with? All the rooms are empty because we don't have any furniture, but we do have a stove and a fridge, and a table where the women put the biscuits and the tea. You're going up in the world, Elizabeth, they say to Mum, looking around at the empty rooms, and Mum laughs back. Then they all stay in the kitchen and chat while we go outside to play.

I'm going to get beds with a lady from Social Services, says Mum a few days later, because they have a grant for me. We're going to the auctions at the nearby cattle market. We go to the market with the lady, who is very serious, and there are cows and animals being auctioned, and rooms with furniture with tickets on with numbers. Mum says you choose the number of the item you want, and then you bid for it. We go to the auction and the man is talking, talking, and the lady gets Mum to put her hand up and we get two beds and then in the middle of the week Mum goes back with us and puts her hand up, and we get another bed. In the cattle market Mum also gets sausages, she says they make them specially here, with good meat and nice spices.

We go another time and Mum says she's going to get kitchen utensils. There's a big box of kitchen things and there are men snooping around in the boxes. Those are the dealers, says Mum. They're looking for things to sell in their shops. The auction comes and the man is talking, talking and Mum puts up her hand for the box of kitchen utensils and gets the box. Mum is pleased. Now we have cooking things, and pots and pans, she says. But when she goes to collect the box, it's a different box.

It's all rubbish, says Mum. I can't believe it. It's not the box I looked at, and I know I got the number right. The dealer must have switched the numbers. We see the dealer collect the box we should have had and he looks sideways at us. He cheated us, says

Mum, and she looks really angry. But we can't do anything, the number's on the box, and I bid for it.

When we get home, Mum goes through the box we have. There's nothing of any use, says Mum. Only a teapot that looks silver, it's a bit dented, it might be pewter, with silver plate, with a long fine spout, it's the only thing I can keep. Mum polishes the teapot with Brasso and it looks very nice, and Amy and I call it our silver teapot and pretend we're rich. Mum is very disappointed. That man who changed the numbers is a crook, says Mum. He's stopping people who really need the things getting them.

Near our house we have a fish and chip shop. It sells very greasy chips, because the oil is never changed, says Mum, but sometimes Mum lets us buy some as a treat. Hers taste better, but it's nice to go to the chip shop, because the chips come wrapped in newspaper, and half the thrill is coming back with the heat of the packet and the grease seeping through to your fingers, and stealing a chip or two before you get home.

Next door there's an old lady and she makes friends with us and she gives Mum a cake and we eat it, and it's a bit like chewy moist gingerbread and the old lady says it's called parkin, and it has molasses in. Then she says when she was little they used to say, up t'wooden hill and underneath t'eaves for when she went to bed, so we say it too.

I learn to paint with my oil paints and set out to do a painting of my violin. I do it slowly, checking all the different hues and colours, shades and lights, my violin and violin case in a corner of the room. I've got my own attic room here in the Streets, at the top of the house, with a slanting roof, and it looks out over all the back gardens of the other houses of the street at right angles to ours. I have the big blue mattress we all slept on the first night, as the others have the beds, and during the day I roll it up and turn it into a settee. It's my own space, my first room of my own ever. In the corner I have my schoolbooks on the floor and I do my homework sitting on my home-made settee or downstairs in the kitchen. Sometimes Socks comes to visit and sits on my mattress and watches me paint, and sometimes she tries to catch my paintbrush as I use it.

We've got a small back garden, and Mum plants potatoes and tomatoes in the back. She digs away with a spade from the market and heaves the earth around – it's poor earth, she says, full of stones, and gets compost to add to it. The potatoes start growing, little round blobs at the end of roots. Mum yanks up her potato plant from the ground, fresh earth clinging to the roots, breaking away as she pulls it.

We have potatoes, she says, but they're a bit small. I watch as Mum pulls more potatoes from the ground, uprooting them. She tends her potatoes carefully, lovingly, watering them daily, and the other things she grows too start to sprout. Soon we'll have a vegetable garden, Mum says.

Matti has started school now and is learning to play the recorder. He's very musical, says Mum. The teacher says he has a lot of promise.

Across the fence behind the alleyway that leads to the back of our house stay two boys our age, and they make their way down the alleyway between the gardens and shout things at us and we shout back. One of them is a bit older, and dark haired, and I wonder if I should fancy him.

Let's make cakes, says Amy when Mum's out and we're in, and we set out with flour and sugar and butter. We know how to make fairy cakes because they taught us in school. We make the cake mixture and put it in the cake pans. It looks pale and creamy and soft.

They look boring like that, I say. Let's put food colouring in them.

We pull all the food-colouring bottles out, in a little rack – blue, magenta, bright yellow, green. We put drops into each of the cake mixes in the little cake pans in the trays – each one a different colour, sometimes mixing the colours. We put them in to bake and the cakes come out bright blue, bright green, bright red, bright yellow, bright purple, and dark brown. We try eating one, but the colours put us off. Or maybe we tasted the cake mixture too much when we were making them.

Mum comes back and asks us what on earth we've made. We say we thought they'd be nice but they came out looking a bit wrong. They look too revolting to eat.

Let's give them to the boys next door, says Amy, and we shout over the fence and ask if they want any. The boys gobble them up.

Mum saves and gets some more crockery from the market. I need a good knife, says Mum, and she buys a large knife from the market with an orange plastic handle. It's new, and it's really strong and sharp, says Mum, it's a proper butcher's knife, and it can cut anything. It's even shaped so you can hold it properly. It's the only knife we have that's big and sharp, and Mum's very proud of it, and Mum sharpens it regularly and always uses it when she makes the food.

Mum says she still needs a frying pan. I see a frying pan in the sale basket they keep at the end of the row of groceries in the small store a few streets away where Mum sends me on errands to get shopping. It is large and deep with an enamelled outside with orange flowers and a lid, and doubles up as a stewing pan. I tell Mum, and she says, okay, I'll take a look. We get to the shop and the frying pan is still there. Mum looks at it and says, it's very nice, Mai, but it's too expensive. I'm disappointed. But it's on sale, I say. It's really good quality. It's still too much money for us, says Mum. It will need to be about half the price it is for me to afford it. Maybe they'll reduce it more, I say. Would you buy it then? I ask. Yes, says Mum.

Every time I go back to the shop I go to the end row and check if the frying pan is still in the sale basket. It is. Every time I go, I see it's reduced a bit more. The price keeps going down and down over the weeks that pass, but it's not half yet. I look at the new red stickers every time they appear on its side. I'm worried some-one will buy it before it gets to half price. The price gets lower and lower, and now I go in daily just to check if the frying pan is any cheaper. The more I look at it, the more beautiful it seems. Finally, it gets to half the original sale price.

I go racing back to Mum and tell her it's half price now. Hurry, hurry, I say, someone might buy it. Okay, says Mum, we'll go get it.

I hope it's still there when we get there. We walk to the shop. I am almost running, I'm so keen to get there. We go to the sale basket at the back of the shop. You're right, it's half the price, says Mum. We'll buy it.

Mum buys it and I'm so pleased – I feel clever, getting her a quality bargain frying pan.

We talk to Mum about when we grow up. When you all grow up you'll want to live your own lives and you'll live in your own homes, says Mum. I'll be on my own then. No, we won't, we say. We'll live with you. No, says Mum, you won't want to – you'll want to do your own thing and be far too busy living your lives to the full to want to look after me. It's normal. No, says Amy, I'll have my own house and I'll always have a room for you to stay in, you can live there. And I say, no, Mum's going to stay in my house, with me.

But you'll have your own families, says Mum. You think you'll want me around now, but when you grow up you'll think differently. Everyone is like that. Everyone wants to live life to the full, you don't want an old sick person staying with you. You'll send me to the old people's home, like everyone else. No, says Amy. Never. And I say never too, and we argue over who is going to have Mum in their house. Then we decide maybe we'll share a big house and Mum can stay there too. But I won't want to be a burden to you either, says Mum. You won't be a burden, I say. We'll have a big house and you can own part of it. No, it will be different when you are grown up, says Mum.

I can see Mum is thinking about it and imagining it in her head, because there is a small frown between her eyebrows and her eyes are looking somewhere else as she speaks.

It can be very lonely when you get older, she says.

I look at Mum and I think deep down, I don't really ever want to grow up. Growing up means you turn into a woman and you have to get married and then you have a husband and you can never be free.

Mum takes me to a place where I do a mathematics and English exam and she says it's for the scholarship to the boarding school. When I come out I say, I don't think I did that well, I couldn't answer some of the questions.

But then they call me back and say I did much better than the other competitors and I will be going to the boarding school.

We always lose the best, says the headmaster of my grammar school when I leave the school. He shakes hands with me.

I look for Anthony in the last week to say goodbye. On the last day of school before the summer holidays, the bus passes down the road away from the school and I hope at least I will see him in the street as I leave. But I don't see him. Ever again.

I am getting ready to go to boarding school. I have to pack everything in a suitcase, and Mum bought me one that is all my own. Mum says she must go to the bank, but because we are doing everything hidden, under a false name, she can't go to the bank here, because then Rashid could trace her, so she is going to go to another city instead. She takes the train to the other city, travelling with just her handbag. When she comes back she is late and talking fast. You wouldn't believe it, Mum says. I bumped into Rashid. In a street in the other city, as I was walking back towards the train station, I bumped into him. What kind of coincidence is that? Of all places, I go to another city for one day to use the bank, and he is there too.

I was so shocked when I saw him, says Mum, I didn't know what to say. So I thought I'd better act as if I lived there and be as normal as I could, so he wouldn't be suspicious. He said hello and I said hello. He asked what I was doing there, and I said, I am just going shopping in town. He said he was there for a job interview, which he had just finished, and was on his way to the train station. He walked the same way as me and I didn't know what to do. He suggested we talk and asked if I could take us to a nice local café for coffee. Well, I couldn't go back to the train station to catch my train back, so I said yes, there's one this way, down this street. I led him down the street but there was no café. So I said, I'm sure there was one here, it must be the next street. We walked into the next street and there wasn't one there either. We kept walking through the streets, with me going, I'm sure it's around here somewhere, going round and round in circles for ages. I'm sure he realised straight away I didn't live there. It was so embarrassing. I was trying to pretend I lived there, but I had no idea where I was. I said, the café must have closed down and moved. I'm sure he guessed I was lying, he must have realised I was totally lost. Finally I found a place, it was hardly a café, but at least they did tea and coffee. So we had coffee and he said he wanted to get back together again, that he was really sorry about everything. He said he loved me and missed you all and realised he had done wrong.

I didn't know what to do, I couldn't leave, as I couldn't walk back to the train station in case he followed, so I just waited and talked about anything I could think of. Finally, he said, well, I'd better be catching the train back home. So I said, I'll walk you there. So I walked him back to the train station, and he bought me two boxes of chocolates at the station and he said sorry again. He got on a train and I said goodbye and made sure I saw him leave the station, and then I caught my own train back. I was so shocked, says Mum. I don't think he has any idea where I really live, but I'm sure he knows I don't live in that city. He never saw me get the train back here, I made sure he waved from the carriage as he left, I doubt he knows I live here. I really must have fate against me, says Mum. What kind of coincidence is that, that on the only day I go to another city, and the only day he goes there too, we both meet in the street? Maybe I'm destined never to get away from him, she says, I still can hardly believe it, even now. And I must have looked such an idiot, because it was clear I didn't know my way around, I didn't even know my way back to the train station properly. I said I didn't normally go to that part of town. And nobody knew I was going to the bank except me and the bank manager, how could he have known? It's impossible. I really must have fate against me, says Mum.

I go to boarding school. The boarding school is far from home, a train journey of one and a half hours. It's a girls' school and lots of people get to Oxford and Cambridge from here, says the headmistress. It's the first time I've been to a school where there are only girls and not boys. I start in the beginning of the second year, but because I'm new the schoolgirls say I have to sit next to the first-years at mealtimes. In the boarding school we are all cooped up like chickens in a cage in school uniforms. On Sunday a sixth-former has to take us for a walk outside the school. She does it at a hundred miles an hour. The fifth- and sixth-formers hate us because they are grown up and we are just kids, and they just want to get their duties over with. We have to run to keep up, round the block, past the local shops so fast we can hardly see them, and then back into the school and it's all over.

One of the sixth-formers is a bad girl because she hates the school, and our housemistress says she is a rebel. She ran away on Guy Fawkes night to a fireworks party with her boyfriend and now the housemistress says she has been sent to Coventry for a month, which means no one is to speak with her, not even one person, or they'll be in trouble. Later we see the girl, looking very sad and alone. It's not like the Enid Blyton books where they are always solving mysteries and having midnight snacks.

On weekends we write letters home and get our mail. Mum writes that Matti is still doing extremely well at the recorder and that the teacher says he is very gifted. Amy is upset because people at school call her Paki because when it's summer she goes brown and Mum says it's because Amy's great-great-grandmother on Amy's father's side was Indian, the one her great-great-grandfather married when he was in India. Dear Mai, writes Mum, we all miss you and are looking forward to you coming back for the holidays. We are getting more furniture now and a settee from the auction. Don't worry, I haven't heard from Rashid again, I think that was just a coincidence, and there's no way he can trace me. But it was a narrow escape. Babs and Amy are well and we still get parkin cake from the next-door neighbour and she sends her best

251

wishes. Amy wants to write to you too, so I'll let her say what she wants underneath.

In Amy's letter she writes: Dear Mai, I am having fun at school and my best friend is Sindy. Everyone calls me Paki because they say I look Pakistani even though I'm not, but Mum says I have the blood of an Indian princess. I miss seeing you. Me and Sindy had a talk at school about periods and we sneaked off with a sanitary towel that we stole from Sindy's mother. We hid in an alleyway and pulled the sanitary towel apart to see what's inside. But it was just cotton wool. That's all it was. There wasn't anything else inside. Don't tell anyone. It's secret. Love Amy.

At boarding school, the English teacher says she never ever gives an A for creative writing, the highest she has ever given is a B plus. For my first creative-writing essay I get an A minus, and I'm very proud. Very good, your writing shows promise, writes the teacher. I also learn the violin, because I brought my violin with me. The music teacher gets the head of music to listen to me and another girl, a first-year whose sister is in the National Philharmonic, play together, then he says, you both show promise and smiles at us. But I know with music I'll never put the hard work in, in order to succeed, but I write all the time and draw and I like science, and one day I want to be a writer, and a doctor, and an artist.

The other girls at school are from posh families. The girl at the end of the dorm I am in says she's the daughter of a lord and she speaks very loud about how when she grows up she will be a lady. I don't like her much. The older girls think I'm weird because I don't know how to lay a table like they do and don't know how to behave around the boarding school because it's all so new to me. Once the headmistress came for tea in the house dining room and sat at my table. I didn't have a teaspoon and I was too shy to get up and get one from another table, so I stirred my tea with a knife. The housemistress called me in and told me off afterwards and the older girls think I'm stupid because of it.

At the end of the term I get the highest marks in my class, and as the results are read out I see a sixth-former in front of me nudge another sixth-former and say, Mai? She's stupid, I can't believe she got five stars.

I don't like being cooped up, and I don't like all the rules, they seem silly.

Half-term comes and I go home for the holiday. Now I can walk freely again and go to the fish and chip shop and hug Socks, and take the knives and forks out the drawer only when my plate of food is ready and then sit to eat without laying the table all square with spoons and glasses, and I can do what I like when I like.

One evening we're at home and there is a knock on the door. Mum is puzzled, and gets up to answer it. She returns with an envelope in her hand. She opens it. She is looking at the piece of paper in her hands and she is pale and shaking.

It's an affidavit, Mum says. He knows where I am. It was delivered to my door. He traced us. Rashid wants to take me to court to get Matti and Babs back. And he had me going round and round in circles looking for that café. He probably knew, that time we met. He probably knew where we lived even then, and he had a good laugh to himself about it afterwards.

Mum bursts into tears. He always wins, says Mum, he always gets his way.

And Mum keeps crying, holding the piece of paper in her hands, her head bent over as she sits on our new second-hand sofa from the market.

Don't worry, Mum, Amy and I say, we can run away again, somewhere else.

I can't keep running forever, Mum says. There're only two women's refuges in the whole country. We've already stayed in one, and that only leaves the other, and Rashid's already traced us to where we are, in only a few months. He'll find us again in no time, wherever we go. There's no way out. He could abduct Matti and Babs again, now he knows where we are, and run away with them to Morocco for good, and there's nothing I can do to stop him. Where can I hide? says Mum. If he can find me now, so fast, after all our efforts, he'll always be able to find me. If he abducts Matti and Babs a second time, he will leave the country and I will never ever see them again.

We can go to the police, says Amy.

The police delivered the affidavit, says Mum. How are they going to protect us? If Rashid wants to take your little brother and sister, he can. He'll have them out of the country before the police even realise. He's too clever for the authorities, says Mum. He always wins.

The next day, Mum says Rashid contacted her by phone through the authorities and says he wants to meet her and talk about things. Just a meeting, he said. In a neutral, safe place.

Don't go, Mum, says Amy. Call the police.

I asked him on the phone how he traced us, says Mum, and he said through the Salvation Army. The Salvation Army are meant to help people. He told a whole lot of lies that I had run off with his children, and they traced us through the police. The authorities were meant to protect us, says Mum. What kind of protection is that? How could they tell him? There's just no way out, says Mum. I just can't trust the authorities, they don't know what they are dealing with. The only thing I can do is go to talk with him, to see what my options are.

Don't go, Mum, says Amy. Please, Mum, you mustn't go. He'll persuade you to go back. I know he will.

Maybe I can talk him out of the court case, says Mum. What else can I do? He says it looks bad because I ran away with his two children, that I'll lose the case, he'll make sure of that. And what if he does win? Where could we run to? We'd have to go to the other refuge, and we'd have to change our names again and start all over once more, and we've only just settled in here. And he'll find us, like this time, and then where? I can't see a way out, says Mum. If he traces me there's nothing to stop him abducting the children for good, and there's nothing I can do to stop him. What else can I do?

We don't mind running away again, say Amy and I. We'd rather run away than go back to him.

But don't you see, says Mum, he'll find us again. If he could find us now, with our names changed and all the police protection, he'll still find us. And next time he might just take the children with no warning. What other choice do I have?

I can't lose my children again, says Mum. I won't be able to take it.

And her face is white and her jaw clenched and her eyes are filled with tears.

I have to talk with him, says Mum. It's the only possible option I have.

Mum goes to talk with Rashid and comes back with boxes of chocolates. Rashid says he's really sorry and he wants to start again, she says, and he won't prosecute me for taking his children if I go back to him. He says he'll be nice to us all, like a proper family. He says he'll never be cruel to me or any of us again. He says he loves me. If I go back, maybe there's some hope, she says. Maybe he'll be better this time. He kept buying me more and more chocolates. He seemed really sorry. Maybe he really means it. Maybe it's the only way, says Mum.

You're mad, Mum, says Amy. I'm warning you, it won't be any different.

I don't have a choice, says Mum. What else can I do? The only way there's any hope is to go back. Either I keep running forever and I risk losing my children for good, or I give it another chance. Rashid seems to mean it. Maybe it will be different this time. What other solution do I have?

I have to go back to the boarding school because half-term is over. I go back to the timetables, prep time, the girl at the end of the dorm who boasts about being a lord's daughter, the rebel student who is in trouble all the time. The first- and second-years have to do a house Christmas Nativity play and I volunteer to direct it and I write a script. It's a lot of work. The other pupils don't treat me so badly, now I'm directing the school play.

A month passes.

While we are rehearsing, and Joseph and Mary are meeting the three kings, the headmistress comes up to me and says Mum has come to see me. We go to the headmistress's office. Mum takes me outside and she walks around the school with me. I'm going back to Rashid, says Mum. I've decided to give it another chance. I know you and Amy don't agree, but it's the only realistic option I have right now. I thought it all through very carefully. The job interview that Rashid said he went to when I met him was to work for an oil company in Libya, in North Africa. It means we will all have to go and live in Libya.

You have the choice to come with us to Libya, or to stay at boarding school, says Mum. Here, everyone says you will have a good education, and the headmistress says she is pretty sure you will do well and get to Oxford or Cambridge, and you have a very bright future. If you stay here, you will do very well, says Mum, and everyone says it is the best choice. But ultimately, it has to be your decision.

How can I see you if you are living far away? I ask.

Rashid says he will pay for you to fly over in the holidays, says Mum.

What if he doesn't?

Rashid promised me. I'll make sure you come, says Mum.

We walk back to the office. You will do very well if you stay here, says the headmistress. Your future will be assured. It's in your best interests, says the headmistress to me. It's important you get the education you need to support you.

It's the best choice, she has top marks in everything, says the headmistress to Mum. And we will look after her well.

Are you sure I will be able to come over in the holidays? I ask Mum.

Yes, says Mum.

Okay, I'll stay here at the school then, I say.

You don't need to rush, says Mum. We won't be going for a few weeks. You have time to think it through carefully, she says, before she leaves.

Later, I think, what if things go wrong in Libya and I'm not there? What if Rashid refuses to pay for the air ticket to bring me over and I'm cut off from my family forever? What if things get very bad and I don't hear from anyone, and I can't be with the people who matter to me, just stuck here with the housemistress and the girl sent to Coventry and the girl at the end of the dorm who's the daughter of a lord and never stops talking about it?

I think very hard about it. A week later, I go to the headmistress and say to her I've decided to leave after all, I'm scared I'll lose contact with my family.

Are you sure you want to give up your education here? says the headmistress. You know you're guaranteed a good future here.

I don't have a future if I lose contact with my family, I say. It's very far away and I have no idea what might happen. What if I never see them again?

And I'm sure about it. Even though I'm now beginning to enjoy it here, as it's my second term, I don't want to stay cooped up like a chicken in a chicken run, not being able to walk around the streets freely. But most of all I want to be with Mum and Amy and Babs and Matti, because I am scared I will lose them all. I don't want to lose them, ever, and I don't want to be stuck here in England if Rashid refuses to get a ticket to fly me back.

When I see Mum again, she asks, are you sure about this? You're giving up a lot, you know.

Yes, I'm sure, I say, I thought hard about it. I want to be with you all.

Rashid says you will have good schools, says Mum. The oil company pays for it as part of the job. I don't say I'm scared Rashid will never fly me over and I'll be stuck in England at twelve years old with no family.

I can see the relief in Mum's eyes and, deep down, I know it's the right decision.

Rashid is there when I get back from boarding school.

Rashid's being very nice, says Mum, when she and Amy meet me at the train station. He says he really wants to make a go of it and we must be a proper family. Maybe he really means it. So you must keep calling him Dad, like before.

I don't want to call him Dad, says Amy. I told you, you're mad going back to him, Mum.

I told you I don't have a choice, says Mum. The authorities have failed to protect us. He found us after only three months, and I hid everything, our names, bank accounts, everything. He's too clever for them all. Do you want to lose your little brother and sister forever? And Mum's face is white and pale and her eyes are watery and her fists clenched. If you can't do it for him, do it for me, says Mum. I have to make it work, she says, I just don't think I could cope if I lost my children again.

Okay, says Amy, I'll do it for you, Mum. But you're making a big mistake, I've warned you.

What other choice do I have? asks Mum. Do you really think we can run away again and he won't find us? You don't understand, Amy, Rashid will always find us – it's the only chance we've got.

And I look at Mum and Amy and I think of ladybirds, when we released them from our hands when we were little, and they went up, up in the sky, travelling the world, and we had no idea where they went.

We are flying tomorrow. Mum has packed everything for Libya. There's not much, just a few suitcases, the sewing machine, our tennis racquets. All our beds and everything from the market are being left behind.

Socks can't come with us to Libya because of all the quarantine problems, says Mum, and she's too old to go to anyone else, no one will take her. The best thing to do is to put her down, says Mum.

Mum takes Socks away to the vet in the centre of the city, to have her put down. Mum is crying, and Socks is meowing inside her worn wicker travel basket, with the worn leather straps that smell of Socks, and Mum is hugging the basket close to her as she crosses the road and takes Socks away. And when Mum gets back the wicker travel basket is empty but the smell of Socks is still there and Mum is wiping away tears and says nothing, except, it was just like going to sleep, and Amy and I don't know what to ask.

Mum's making a big mistake, says Amy to me. At night I lie in bed, knowing I have a family again, and knowing I'm with them, even if things go wrong. And sometimes you never know the future until it happens, and then you realise maybe you did know, and maybe you didn't, and all you can do is fly in circles, but however bright you shine, sometimes you are not sure if anyone is ever seeing you at all.

13

Desert

Out of the aeroplane when we arrive, into a night that hits us with its warmth. Strange odours. Strange sounds. Unexpected heat in the blackness of night, as if the stars have warmed it up, like a fire in the air. Desert dryness. Heat we feel being breathed into our mouths, drying them out, filling our lungs.

Straight out of the cool air conditioning into the harsh dryness, and cries that seem to come out of nowhere, stars that are brighter than the cries and continual shouting, shouting that never makes any sense because we can't understand the language. Cries that Mum says are Arabic but that to us are only cries, which wrap around our throats, pulse inside them and force us into muteness. The language is all around us, in the clattering, the screeching trolley wheels, the suitcases piled high, the hum of the aeroplane engines, voices bouncing off each other and volleying out into the night, into the desert sand.

It is as if the aeroplane were a cocoon, and we have re-emerged on the other side of the ocean in a foreign land. Ali Baba. Abracadabra. Men in long white gowns with dark waistcoats hold up signs in Arabic script, unintelligible to us, except as calligraphic patterns that sweep across the bent cardboard, their dark male hands holding the signs in front of their chests or in the air, clutching at them uncomfortably amid the screeching of trolleys and airport porters clamouring for attention. Hussein! Abdullah!

they call out, names of those they search for in the crowd. They jostle. They shove.

Someone should be here to meet us, says Dad. He steps forwards with our trolley. Looking. Looking. The noises eat him up. Someone is supposed to meet us, he says again. He approaches one of the dark moustached men standing around the arrival point holding a card and says something to him. We are shocked. It is the first time we have heard Dad speak Arabic. It sounds strange to us. Suddenly, he merges into the surrounding confusion, steps out of familiarity into strangeness, swiftly joins the realm of desert sand and fezzes.

The man Dad speaks to shakes his head.

We stand still in the airport, wondering who is supposed to meet us. Dad seems as confused as we are.

Taxi? A group of men hovering, darting back and forth like flies around prospective customers. They swarm around us and we cling to our trolley island of suitcases and bags. Dad waves them away. I'll phone, he says. He disappears into the volleying voices – people pointing him this way and that. He comes back a short while later. There's no one there. They're out. I left a message.

Perhaps they're on their way here, says Mum. Time passes, and there's still no one to meet us. We stay quiet and wait, holding onto the trolley with our suitcases, staring at the unknown faces around us, hoping for some form of recognition amid the avalanche of voices. The airport begins to clear of passengers from our plane. The crowd disperses, and now only the taxi drivers are hovering around us. Tripoli? they say. Sabratha?

There must have been a mistake. Perhaps we can get there on our own, says Mum to Dad. Maybe we should find out if where we are staying is far from here. Dad speaks to the taxi drivers in Arabic. They reply, guttural sounds, harsher than his. It's hard to work out what they are saying, he says. Their Arabic is very different from Moroccan, it's a different dialect. He speaks with them again.

I look out and around at the stars. I can see beyond the wide doorway to the aeroplanes outside, sense the warmth that seeps from the desert floor, warmth that flows up and around long after the sun has gone. I can taste the warm breath of the air in my lungs. It feels different, heavy.

Dad is still talking to the taxi drivers. He pulls an envelope from his breast pocket and unfolds a piece of paper inside. He holds the paper in his hand and they are all pointing to the writing on it and talking. He walks back.

It seems the company accommodation is not far from here, Dad says. He is now speaking mostly with a larger man who has followed him back, with a fat moustache over his upper lip, a face like a dark rotund balloon, arms and eyes that gesticulate, arms one way, and eyes the other, like clockwork, in different directions. But every now and then his eyes stop and watch us, to see our response.

I don't think the person who is meant to meet us is coming, says Dad. I think we should take a taxi to the place we are staying in.

Where are we staying? we ask Mum.

In a villa provided by the company, Mum tells us. They say there is a swimming pool. I saw a photograph. It is very nice.

The taxi driver, seeing his opportunity, is making attempts to move our trolley of suitcases forwards, towards the exit of the airport. Dad says something to him angrily, and the taxi driver lets go.

Dad speaks with Mum for a while. Okay, we're going, Dad says. He waves to the taxi driver to go ahead, and our trolley and cases move forwards with us clinging around them. Dad keeps speaking with the taxi man in Arabic.

We walk out of the large exit of the airport and suddenly find ourselves swept into the space of the outside sky. Men in long white clothes flow around us into the night, with cloths or white hats on their heads. They stare at us occasionally. The taxi driver keeps talking, gesticulating, smiling. Hello, he says. How – are – you? His words sound forced, like a tape recording gone slow. He grins at his display of English, and our surprise. He waves his arms in a welcoming gesture in the direction of the hot night sky and the stars. Welcome – to – Libya, he says, with pauses between the words. He opens the boot of his station wagon and begins to pile the suitcases in. Get in the car, says Dad. We climb in the back seat, sit taking in the strange new smells and scenes around us. Mum gets in next to us.

We – go, says the taxi driver, climbing into the front seat, with Dad sitting beside him. We – go home – now. He turns the engine on, begins to drive. He speaks to Dad in Arabic, leans over, and turns a switch on the front panel. Music blares out, tinny, loud. We listen to its harshness – alternating waves, gliding from one note to another, slippery. We look out of the car window. We see palm trees. They flash by as dark silhouettes against the street lighting, some short and bushy on top, some tall and slender, just like the pictures in magazines. Even the sky seems different, a warm bluish-black, behind the palm trees that seem to reach up and become part of the sky above them.

Here – is – Tripoli, says the driver, grinning and waving his arm in a big arc out of the window. He hoots his horn to another driver and shouts something out of the window in Arabic. Someone shouts back. A car flashes past in the opposite direction. Unfamiliar music from doorways. Men grouped around food vendors in narrow doorways. Smell of bread, strange flat breads being sold, the smell of meat cooking. Flowing white clothes in the dark, voices breaking harshly through the night. And blocks of flats, everywhere, poking up into the night sky.

We arrive. A dusty road. Tall blocks of flats. Darkness. The driver stops in a small dusty street beside a large yellow wall and we peer out into the dark street to see our villa. No villa. Only a yellowish block of flats. Dad asks the driver where our villa is. They speak in Arabic, checking the address. The taxi driver points to the flats and speaks with Dad.

He says this is the place, says Dad. We stare up at the block of flats. Balconies that look like prison cells.

Our new home. We're busy smelling the new environment. Clean air, with the smell of people. Dusty, sandy road. Everything smells so different. Amy and I are very tired. Matti and Babs are fast asleep in the back of the taxi. People come out of the flats, walk up to us, speak to Mum and Dad. They are talking, talking. Now there are more of them arriving, and they are talking too. The new talking people have come from the block of flats. Their sentences in English stand out from the Arabic. We were told we were getting a villa too, says one of them. The villas have been under construction for the last year. This – and he points to the flats – is meant to be temporary. It's been temporary for the last year, and there's no sign of any change. They didn't meet you? It's not surprising. They're so disorganised ... Where's the swimming pool? we ask. There isn't one. But they said ... We are too tired. Somehow, we arrive inside our flat on the fourth floor, and fall asleep.

At six in the morning, the voices start calling, like echoes. They pulse out from loudspeakers, the lilting sound of prayer, loud, then soft, loud, then soft, again and again. The noise disturbs Amy and me from our sleep. We wake with the sounds reverberating around our ears, listen to the battle of voices. We don't know they're for prayer. The voices sound like strange alien singing, the humming of bees, cries of pain, the chanting of sirens, not like the type of prayer we're used to, people muttering softly into their hands. We listen to the voices all around us: one moment on our left, then another voice to the right, then two more joining in until the whole world is calling out around us. Sometimes it sounds like one voice is being tossed across town and is being caught up and hurled out again. We stick our heads out of the window into the early grey-pink rising of the dawn, followed soon by the bright glare of sunlight. All the mosques have loudspeakers, pointing four ways outwards. They poke up and tower above the faded pastel orange and yellow apartment buildings in the capital, conical towers with small gleaming silver crescent moons on top. Every morning, the mosques whine, whirr into action. We hear the motors warming up, a dull fuzz, louder, then louder, and the voices peal out. They call like lost voices, calling out for attention in the early morning light, like voices crying.

I think they're competing to see who can be loudest, so more people come to them, says Mum.

The caretaker of the flats downstairs comes out of a small hut-like building in the space next to the basement, surrounded by high walls, and he pulls out his mat, unrolls it, and kneels at the end of it. Then he bends forwards and places his hands at the front end of the mat and begins to pray. We don't understand what he is saying. Mum says we must respect what he is doing, and we must not interrupt him. He looks very busy, leaning his head continually on the front of his mat. It is as if he is eating the mat with his forehead, hands placed beside him like table legs, supporting the sides of his body, his round stomach with clothes stretching across it, shirt with buttons pulled tight, small fez cap on his head. Salaam, he says as we go by, salaam alaikum, and grins.

The flats are tall, like a mountain, rooms on top of each other, yellow-painted stone, faded by the harsh sun and dried and cracked by the wind. We live two-thirds of the way up the block. Everyone, we are told, is waiting for their accommodation. Villas. Villas that never appear, and, instead, each family in a small flat. The Indian man who lives downstairs, who came outside last night, greets us. Hello, I am Dr Indira. I am a civil engineer. He introduces himself, his wife and his son, Kuzi. His son is two years older than me, fourteen years old, nice looking, with intense dark eyes and white teeth. His wife Mrs Indira is elegant, in a long sari. They tell us they are Indians from Kenya. There is another Indian couple, Mr and Mrs Padri – your neighbours, they introduce themselves as – also with children. This time a little girl, three years old, and a little boy, four years old, almost five, the same age as Matti. They speak perfect English, says Mum. When we hear the little girl, Ameena, speak, she speaks English better than her brother, Youssef, in full sentences. Apparently, the little girl is a genius, says Mum.

Mum seems to like talking with Kuzi's mother, Mrs Indira. Mrs Indira looks kind and gentle. She's very intelligent, says Mum. She has a degree too, but gave it up to be with her husband, as she is not allowed to work here.

In the flat opposite us in the same corridor lives a Polish woman and her Iranian husband. They are very quiet.

We start living. We start breathing the hot air and grow accustomed to it. It fills our lungs with its warmth. The sand, too, becomes pleasant, always a dry dusty feeling in our mouths. Cold drinks and more cold drinks. They make a strange sort of fruit squash here, with very little flavour and bright purple or bright orange, a sort of sweet coloured syrup. We get used to that too. Much of the stuff is imported: biscuits from Europe, soft drinks from Europe. Each packet with several languages on, but always the Arabic in unfamiliar styled letters, little dots and squiggles we cannot understand. The olives that are grown here, says Mum, are exported to the Italians. They turn them into olive oil and that is imported back again. The olive-oil tins have a mixture of languages on them, including Arabic. The olives fall from the trees and rot on the ground, there are so many, always. It seems strange to think they go all the way to Italy to be pressed. Why aren't they pressed in Libya? we ask Mum. I don't know, she says, and laughs.

Amy and I share a bedroom in the flat. We look out over the pastel rooftops from our window and see people passing up and down the narrow, sandy street. Cars. Children. We see women wrapped like packages in thick white sheet-like cloths, holding them around their faces, with only one eye showing. Men who blow their noses in the street, no handkerchiefs, and their fingers slicing the mucus hanging from their nostrils so it falls onto the ground. There are trees by the roadside that are trimmed to form canopies, with branches that grow outwards like umbrellas, that spread outwards in a way we've never seen them do before. For the shade, says Mum, it keeps the pavements shaded from the sun. Trees like rectangles, squares. Foliage tightly packed. Dark green leaves. Flats going up and up into the air. New flats being built.

Look, says Dad. He is driving us down the road. It's the new leader. Kaddafi.

Kaddafi's photograph on every lamp post as we go down, multiple Kaddafis smiling out at us. Lamp posts speed by. Kaddafi salutes us from each lamp post, in smart uniform and hat. His face floats by. Every lamp post has a face on it and a hand. He stares out everywhere. It makes a strange pattern as we drive down the road, like an animation picture that doesn't change. He's only just got to power, says Mum. He took the place of someone else. He makes speeches in the square, near the medina where the souk is, the big marketplace in Tripoli near the sea, with narrow streets, and metal beaters hammering large copper and tin plates into decorative trays, square and round, patterns on them, piles of coloured material.

The car moves on. Amy is in the back seat with me, Matti and Babs. Faces, coverings, drift by. The hammering in the souk in the medina, and the dried shrivelled orange-brown fruits Mum says are dates from the palm trees, on dry twigs, piled up high in the streets. We don't know why people buy them, and puzzle when we see people crowding around the sellers. We don't know what they taste like because we don't eat them. And watermelons. The vendors cut them up with big steel knives, as long as a forearm, the red richness of the watermelons bursting out of the green shells. Mum says they grow them here along with oranges, although they need so much water and there is a water shortage, because they know people like them so much. The oranges are watery, no taste at all, a pale orange colour, and hardly any smell. And there are apricots too, we buy some by the roadside and they are delicious, and we eat half of them before we realise they are full of maggots.

Libya is oil wells, dust, desert, dryness. People wrapped in cloths, rows upon rows of bleached flats one after another, and children and stray dogs and cats, and meat hanging, dripping from hooks in butcher shops. The flies cluster on the rails and the light fittings in the butcher's, especially on the thick white electric wires hanging from the centre of the ceiling, where the flies are so close together they look like black fur on the wires, on the hooks where the meat is hanging inside, and on the hooks with the cow's head hanging outside the shop entrance in the street, eyes closed shut with tight lashes, ears like leather, stuck on hooks pointing outwards. Mum says they hang the meat to get all the blood out. The butchers cut the meat from the carcasses anywhere they like. Stray dogs sit outside the doorways of the butchers', clustered on the pavement, hoping for scraps, and slink out of the way when people come close. The cats are there too, but they stay under the cars, hidden away, kittens and cats, lots of them, all shapes and sizes. You must be careful with the dogs, says Mum. You can get rabies here.

Mum says there's too many potholes. We're not sure what she means. They sound deliberate. Not another pothole, she says. Why don't they fill them in? Dad swears at them when he drives over them in the small car he has bought. We wonder why they dig holes and don't fill them in. And what would be the point of filling them in if they spent all that time digging them? We imagine lots of people employed digging these strange holes in the road. Potholes. And they never fill them up again.

14

Sand

I think I am seeing things. Camels pass in a line in front of me, at the end of the narrow street, head to tail. They are all tied together by loose ropes that link them one by one to each other. I watch them pass one after another after another, across the far end of the narrow street. They never seem to stop coming. Occasionally a man with a thick cloth wrapped over his head and long white clothes walks past with them, holding the bridle of one of the camels. They stride past slowly, sometimes side by side, camel after camel. They look dignified, solemn.

I walk halfway down our street towards them and stand and watch with the Libyan children, always in the streets, watching too, a dusty face among dusty faces, harsh dry heat and stag beetles and termites crawling in the sand. The camel train is orderly, quiet, peaceful, made up of ropes, hands, feet, robes, headscarves, the humps wobbling by, and colours. Colours. Deep dark heavy colours, long white robes, coloured cloths on the camels' backs and over the heads of the men. The camels smell of dust, and sun, and the dryness of many days. They pass one by one, their owners guiding them, everyone in silence, patient. The line goes on and on. Their feet move slowly, as if they are marking time, like water dripping from a tap – halting, waiting, then thud, the foot falls. The strange men, dressed differently from the people here, in thick scarves and long white robes, look dignified too. It seems as if hours pass, camel after camel. They move slowly, consistently, step by step. As if time doesn't matter, there is no need to hurry, time will pass anyway and they will, step after step, slowly move towards the place they are going to, and, just as slowly, arrive.

As the camel train draws to an end, the camels get smaller and younger, linked with long ropes and then there are more men wrapped in thick flowing clothes. The baby camels stumble at the end, less self-assured and elegant than the adult camels, less sure of where their feet are going.

And the long train ends with the very smallest camel, and more men, and then they are gone.

Mum sweeps the sand away, out of our home. Too much, she says, too much sand. Where does it come from? she says. Our shoes? the air? the sun? out of the corners of the walls?

I look around at the bare walls and ache for Socks, something to hug, some warm darkness that isn't bleached walls – but that time has passed. That was before. Now, it is now. Outside, large termites carry big boulders of sand, grains rolled in their jaws, rolled up tight and neat like parcels, and pile them up high in little towers on the ground. Little mounds of perfect round balls, in their big pincers. Sometimes I see small ant nests in the ground, small bodies scurrying around, compared with the big-jawed giant ants that build the mountains of sand. I watch the big jaws gripping sideways.

Amy and I play outside by the faded yellow flat walls, beside all the other faded flat walls. The caretaker always leans on the wall and watches, smiling. Or he takes out his mat and prays. Forever praying and watching. In the afternoon, when he is very hot, he sleeps in his little wooden hut by the entrance to the flats. We play out on the road that runs down along the flats, alongside other blocks of flats, to the road that crosses like a т at the other end. We call it a road, but it is narrow and made of sand, fine dusty sand, not like beach sand, but grubby and powder-fine on the surface. The sun bakes it crisp, and we watch the giant ants crawling out of the cracks on their unending journeys across the terrain.

Up on top of the flats is a flat roof with a low wall all around it, just high enough for us to peep over. We can climb up the stairs to the top and look out over the wall. We can see the caretaker down below, like a distant miniaturised version of himself, walking around or praying. We see him from the top of his balding head down, his round stomach protruding around him, an old faded tweed jacket buttoned tightly around his white cotton shirt reaching to his knees over his loose white trousers. He seems small, his wooden hut seems small. We see the neighbours going to and fro. They look different too from this perspective, like watching television.

We're not really meant to go up here. This is the place where Youssef, Ameena's big brother, took a street kitten and threw it down from the top and killed it. But it's safe for us because there's a wall around. We can look over and see the city around us, spread out in blocks of faded pastel flats, and the minarets of the mosques with their loudspeakers circling us. It looks the same all the way round. The end of our street looks like the end of every other street.

A snake lurks in the company building where Rashid works. It's kept in a small empty aquarium tank. We go to see it. A cobra, says its owner. I found it here, in the company grounds. It's had its poison removed. We stare at it, dry sandpaper skin, coiling its way out of the glass tank its owner keeps it in, watching it crawl around his hand and arm, mouth gaping, the hood that rises around its neck. It can't poison me now, says the owner, and puts his large fat brown finger in its gaping mouth. See. I told your father he should bring you to see it. See, it's a cobra. Touch it. But we won't touch it, just in case – the gaping mouth, the flapping hood, rising and falling again.

It's not very big, says its owner. It's a medium-size one.

Wah'ed. Ethnayen. Talata. Arba'a. Khemsa. Setta. Saba'a. Tesa'a. Tamania. A'shra. But I don't remember more. Just up to ten. I start again. Up to ten only. The sand is hot under my feet. It catches. In my toes. In my sandals. I'm used to it. The sand is hot, but there are still puddles on the road. Large puddles, after the big rain. Rainy season has started, says Mum. She says that means lots of rain over the next few months.

It rained hard for the first time this morning. Now the rain lies in big shapeless puddles between the bumps in the sand. A'shra. My Arabic is limited. Only because I don't learn it at school, and the caretaker of the block of flats taught me up to ten. And the word for button. But I don't remember it now. I swing my basket, square-shaped, plastic, red and blue stripes with wire handles. Down the end of the road. Turn left. Then you get to it. The baker's. Where the bread comes tumbling out from huge trays into baskets and onto the big wide shelves. Sometimes they have round loaves, sometimes short thin loaves, like short French baguettes marked with diagonal lines across the top.

Mum wants twelve loaves of bread. But I only remember up to ten. There must be a way around it. The sun has already baked the sand dusty in parts, hot under my feet, furrowed by the odd car that has passed, the street near deserted. Potholes, rain, bumps and lumps of puddles and sand. The outside of our block of flats is whitewashed dim yellow, bleached and weathered down by the sun, as if the sun has been scrubbing it. The high walls that border the block also look weathered, washed over in white

274

bleached paint that peels. The huge empty sky stretches above me. The sand creepy-creeps between my toes, in my sandals.

As I walk past the end corner wall of our block of flats, I see Youssef, Mr and Mrs Padri's four-year-old son, in the middle of the road around the corner of the wall. He's a short stubby boy. Strong. His face is kind of big, and square. He is holding one end of a huge heavy stick in his hands, thick, more like a log, the other end dragging on the ground, and is staring at the giant stag beetles, big huge things with sharp claw things on their heads that have come out after the rain.

Youssef is too preoccupied to notice me.

Inside the baker's it's hot and dark. Smells of hot bread, and cold dough waiting to be heated. It is small inside, but feels big because it is dark compared to the glaring sun outside. There's just enough room for me and a few other people: a man in white, the baker, and the dark kid peering in at me from the doorway, with his friends behind him. He's curious. But polite. At first, because the glare of the outside sun has made it hard for my eyes to adjust, I just see hands and bread. A big tray comes in and the bread slides off plop plop. Then my eyes get used to the darkness and I see the baker, in his white loose cotton trousers and shirt, and waistcoat. A'shra, I say, and point to the loaves. A'shra khobza. The baker counts out ten and places them in my basket. Then I point again. Ethnayen. The baker adds two more. I feel the weight of them, and the warmth pressing against me. I hand him the dinars Mum gave me for the bread. Shokran. Thank you. The bag full of hot loaves seems large and heavy, and makes me feel small. I walk the loaves home.

Youssef is still on his own at the corner of the flats. I carry my basket towards him, because I have to pass him to get to the main gate. The rain has beaten the sand down so it looks smooth. The ground smells fresh-washed. He still doesn't see me and is staring at the ground. His face has a darkish hue to it, it's the expression, or the impression, of a sort of fixedness, a focus that comes from something unpleasant inside, that makes me believe it when Mum says he and another boy found a stray kitten and took it to the top of the flats and threw it off so it died. One of the many wild cats in Tripoli, crawling out of cars, drains, under flats. Splat. I see it die in my mind.

Youssef is killing things now. The huge stick he holds is longer than him, and he is standing at the corner on a stretch of dry sand and killing the giant stag beetles. The stick is so long and heavy he can barely lift it. But he does. He pulls it over his head. He brings his arms down. Down the stick goes. Yeaargh! Yeaargh! he shouts hard as the stick crashes down in front of him, a young boy's shout. He doesn't speak much – his is more a guttural response to the world around him. Thud. The ground shakes.

Stag beetles run all around him. They are all out, huge black beetles after the rain. I have never seen so many before. They must have come out of the sand. There are not a lot of people around. Maybe all the beetles are out instead of the people.

I think he is afraid as well as angry, enjoying it maybe. Fear and anger and brutality coming together. Yeaargh! shouts Youssef again.

Smack. Youssef's stick falls hard, but he misses. Ugh! He stomps and snorts. Alone at the corner of the road, he is trying to kill all the beetles. They run and scatter in all directions. One beetle stands in the middle of a big puddle, on a large stone, and Youssef aims at it. He pulls the huge stick over his head again, but it is so heavy he can't control it. Brown water flies everywhere and hits Youssef. He is playing big but I think he must be scared.

The caretaker passes by the gate. He stops and looks out. He laughs when he sees Youssef, killing the beetles with the stick. He laughs, and says something in Arabic. He's probably going to pray.

Seven times a day, Mum says. Salaam, the caretaker says to me. I smile. I'm shy. I'm walking down the middle of the road. Youssef is now to my left. The caretaker goes to a small open space at the bottom of the block of flats and unrolls his prayer mat, then he kneels down and bows his head and prays.

Youssef is in the middle of the puddle now, standing on the stone in the centre like an island, where the beetle was, and he is still hitting the beetles. Another beetle comes running towards him and he brings the stick down fast. Crack. Then crack again as he hits it a second time. Crack. Over and over. Five or six times. He leans forwards and checks it is dead. Flattened out. I hold the bread basket between my arms, and when I hear Youssef's stick hit the ground I jump, and squeeze the bread tighter, and I hear the bread crack too. Yeaargh! Youssef yells again. The beetles run and scatter, scared.

Mum says Youssef's going to be a bully. He's out there with his stick, rescuing the world from beetles. Laughed at by the care-taker. But I don't laugh. I don't like him killing all these beetles. I'm not scared of them. How can I be? They're just beetles, run-ning out after the rain. Maybe they're just trying to dry off. I like things that live. Better they crawl around than to have nothing coming out of the dry sand. Better there is some life down there. They're not up to much. They're just wandering around, like anyone else. And, as much as he's scared, Youssef's enjoying it. He likes the crack of the stick on their backs, he likes it when he makes the ground shake and all the puddles ripple from the shock. It is as if I can hear the beetles dying, whispering, whimpering. Like broken glass fragments, I hear their shells crack, over and over again. And as I turn the corner that leads to the entrance to the flats, bordered by dilapidated and whitewashed walls, I remember the camel train.

Youssef crashes the stick down and the beetles run. I smell the scent of the sand. I turn towards the flats, holding the bread, keeping it warm. I see the caretaker pass by in the yard, returning from prayer. Salaam, he says again. Behind me, I hear the thud of Youssef's stick, his grunt as he crashes it to the floor. As I enter the gateway, I turn back to look at him, the big four-year-old with the huge stick, on his island surrounded by water, the beetles racing around him as they run crazily everywhere.

Dad buys a watermelon. We eat pieces of it, half is left. He sticks the big knife in the remaining half, leaves it in the kitchen on a plate, under a chair. You mustn't remove the knife, he says. Why not? says Mum. You can't leave that big knife in there, she says. The watermelon has to have metal inside, he says, a metal blade. If you don't, evil spirits will enter into it, says Dad. He won't let us take the knife out, so the watermelon stays with the big knife handle poking out of it, in a corner of the kitchen.

We don't understand. We think it's funny. Dad's mad, says Amy. Why does he think there's evil spirits? I'm worried he's starting again, says Mum. Starting what? we ask. Starting again, says Mum, starting to do weird things. It could be cultural, but he doesn't normally do this, I'm worried.

We are going to see the Roman ruins in Libya, says Mum. Two of them: Sabratha, and Leptis Magna, and maybe some other ruins called Cyrene. We are going to see the closest one today, Sabratha, then the other one, Leptis Magna, another day, on a cliff beside the sea. Cyrene is quite far away.

Babs and Matti are in the back seat with me and Amy. We drive across mountains away and out of Tripoli, across roads with big potholes which Dad swears at when we pass over or around them. The road curves thin around a tall rocky sandy mountain, spare shrubs and cactus springing out of it. There is a group of women among the shrubs bathing in a river and washing clothes, still wearing their clothes, brightly coloured, children playing around them. Unlike the city women, the women in the country areas wear colourful clothes, their faces uncovered, only a multicoloured cloth over their heads. We pass above them, curving up a mountain, and they don't see us. We climb higher and higher up the mountain. It's very hot.

Drive carefully, Rashid, says Mum. But Dad is in a bad mood because of the heat and the potholes, so he drives faster. Please, Rashid, drive slower, says Mum, you're frightening me. Don't tell me how to drive, woman, Dad says, and he speeds up even more. We go hurtling over potholes and sliding around mountain corners, the sky getting closer and closer, and valleys disappearing below us. We sit in silence, saying nothing, until the road once again begins to descend, then levels out.

Medusas look down at us. Carved Medusa heads with stone snakes curling around their cheeks, mouths snarling with sharp-toothed grins, on every column. We stand in the centre of the town square, in the glaring sun. Their eyes are of stone, staring blankly out at us. They surround us, snarling, from many, many years ago. Some of the columns are broken, many are whole. The Medusa heads that are broken lie on the ground around us, stone snakes spilling out on the stone paving.

The Italians were restoring the ruins when they were here, says Mum, as a tourist attraction, but then they left and the rebuilding stopped and it stayed like this. A rusty train track runs along the streets around the Medusa square, half covered in sand, then vanishes into deeper sand further down the street. The place is empty, just one Libyan man in trousers and a white shirt and waistcoat also walking around, occasionally watching us. We walk through the ruined town. Empty streets. Empty skeletons of houses.

We go to the other Roman ruined city another day. Another day of mountains and driving. This time the town is at the top of a mountain, with a cliff looking out to the sea crashing below. For defence, says Mum. We walk along the clifftop surrounded by the ancient ruins, the sea spray misting the air, waves crashing on the rocks below, and our feet tracing paths where Roman sandalled feet had also traced their patterns on the wind-and-sand-worn stones. We walk the streets. The mosaics and buildings are half made, floors with mosaics, faces of women and children we never knew. The Roman baths, with central heating built in around the edges, with a surrounding stone ledge for people to sit. I feel the breath of the Romans in the streets. An amphitheatre, deserted, the statue of a woman holding a child staring from the top of the steps.

I will take a photograph, says Dad. We stand on a stone pedestal near the woman-and-child statue. I have to hold Matti while Mum holds Babette, but Matti is heavy and I struggle to hold him up, so Dad hurts my arm because I'm not staying still, and in the picture we are standing in the Roman ruin town and my face is red because I don't want to cry, and everyone is smiling because Dad said we had to, but I'm not really, and if you look close into our eyes you can see no one is smiling at all.

We go to the American oil companies' school, where the children from the oil companies and the university go. I am in a class a year above my age and am allowed to study a higher grade's mathematics book, because they say my mathematics is more advanced. My sister is in the upper class of the primary school. There are lots of Americans there but also children from all over the world. All my friends are from different countries. Su Li, a Chinese-American girl, Tasneem from Pakistan, Heike, a Hungarian girl, Marleen, a Canadian with short blonde hair and big thick glasses, and Cara, who is Welsh. We make a nice team. We hang out at lunchtimes. I decide I'm going to form a club.

At school we must learn about Russia. *A Comparison Between the East and West.* It's a book with chapters with writing and pictures and then questions. It teaches us how bad the USSR is. The teacher says it's compulsory in every American school for children of our age. We have to learn a chapter every week. Then we have a quiz on it. Lenina Valera always gets the answers right. She has big blue eyes, golden-yellow hair and perfect legs. She flashes her legs at the boys and her big blue eyes at the teachers with her perfect teeth, and answers all the questions just right. She sounds just like the answer came out of the textbook, in perfect English, word for word. But she doesn't get our jokes. And she doesn't fool around like us. She doesn't bother talking to us either. It's because she thinks we're not good enough for her, says Tasneem my Pakistani friend. Her father is very high up in the American embassy, says Cara. She gets on the honour roll every year. She's a cheerleader too. What's a cheerleader? I ask. They jump around with pompoms and do the splits and shout things, says Cara. She's the All-American Girl, says Tasneen. Everyone likes Lenina, but we don't like Lenina much.

Why are they so nasty to the Russians? I say to Amy. They say in my book that the Russian children are brainwashed to think Russia is great, and they are made to march around the school-yard shouting Russian slogans. But the Americans think America is just as great, they're just as brainwashed, and they do cheer-leading. My teacher doesn't say Soviet Union, says Amy. He says Soviet Onion. That's not nice, I say. What if I called Americans names?

I am walking up the stairs and I see Mrs Indira's son, Kuzi, going into the door of his family's flat on the level below. He is fourteen, two years older than me. He is short, sporty looking. Like me, Mum says, he is also in the year above his age as he is clever at school. His father says Kuzi has been on the honour roll at school three years in a row. Kuzi's family is from Kenya, but he has a slightly North American accent because his parents worked in Canada and he grew up in Canada. It grates when I hear it. I see him looking for keys in his bag, about to open the door of his family's flat. He looks round when I come past on the stairs, and his large dark eyes under heavy eyebrows look back at me. A moment. He looks at me for a second. I look back. A glance in a corridor. Then he is gone, vanishes into the depths of his home, as the door closes behind him.

I don't know what this feeling is but when I say hello to him after that, in corridors, doorways, school corridors, I am webbed in shyness. But I hunt his eyes out and try to hold them with mine, as if something else is in there. Something about him fascinates me. The intensity of his eyes perhaps. His dark skin, like rich chocolate, that makes his cheeks, neck and arms like velvet that I could reach out and touch. I turn red when I see him. I imagine bumping into Kuzi in the corridor. *Oops, sorry.*

Sorry. His brown eyes looking back, velvet skin melting before me. We stand, staring at each other. His hand touches my arm. Lips brush my face in a light kiss. Like a feather duster.

I love you.

I learnt sex education in school in England in science class. I learnt it three times, once in middle school, once in grammar school and then in boarding school, because the schools I went to covered it at different times in their syllabus. Little diagrams in textbooks. A sperm and an egg. The teacher's face red as she/he described the reproductive organs. I learnt all the diagrams and got an A. It had something to do with men and women. It probably has something to do with Kuzi, but I'm not sure.

In the Norman Wisdom films on TV they kiss. A brief kiss, lips to lips. The music starts up. They stare into each other's eyes. Then there is fade-out. Something is confusing me about what happens after fade-out. I try to figure out what happens in the gap between fade-out and sex education, but they are disconnected. I give up. The two haven't a hope of ever fitting together, textbook and real world. In the real world, there's a look, a deep burning look from dark eyes – *I love you.* Beyond that there's no beyond. The teacher said nothing about dreams where he kisses me like a feather duster. Or looking into his eyes. Or feeling the heat in my cheeks and my body when he says hello. In my daydream, we stare into each other's eyes and kiss. Then there is marriage. Kuzi and Mai. In this case, the caretaker, the Libyan desert, and the blocks of flats. The music starts, and then there is fade-out. The film credits. Happy ever after.

When we get married we are going to fade out, like in the movies.

Mrs Indira, Kuzi's mother, is tall, willowy like a charcoal stick, bendy, fragile, wrapped in fabric drifting like sails over her arms, the side of her waist revealed, her hair long and tied into a black plait like a rope down her back to her waist, her nose aquiline, regal. She glides like a full-masted ship, in a red silk-like sari with gold trim billowing around her, red dot in the middle of her forehead, dark-wrapped eyes, eyelined in kohl. She is from Kenya. Her face is like the silk she is wearing: smooth, young, redolent of spices that have seeped in. She stands at the door of our flat, which Mum has just opened. She holds in her arms a jar, filled with a brown liquid, and in it are suspended round things, browny orange, ping-pong-ball sized, soft looking, sweet looking. They float in there like little doughnuts and we peep out at them. She holds the jar out to Mum. For Diwali, she says. Diwali, festival of lights, of sweets, of giving, her arms hugging the jar, the little balls of dough sailing in their soft sticky wet syrup. It's a Hindu celebration, a bit like Christmas. We give food to our neighbours. Please, have some. Mum takes the jar, hugs it to her, gingerly, tentatively, precious in her arms, and I sense the friendship between them. She smiles. Mrs Indira smiles back, Mum holding the sweets in her arms, Mrs Indira standing tall, willowy and regal in the dim corridors of the bare-boned flats, among the sterile anonymous streets and the pale lace-like yellow sand drifting into passageways, doorsteps, again and again.

That's so lovely, Mum says. And Mum unscrews the jar and smells. They smell delicious, she says. So lovely, I think, knowing that Mrs Indira drifts in holding Kuzi in her body, Mrs Indira who gave birth to the apparition in the hallway, the same dark skin, the same flowing limbs, only Kuzi is darker and shorter, like his father. They're gulab jamun, says Mrs Indira, a traditional sweet, we cook them in syrup, soak them overnight, so all the syrup goes in.

Mum and Mrs Indira let us take the round dumpling balls out. Amy and I reach in, say thank you, trying not to drip syrup. The balls float up to the top. They are soft and squashy, and the syrup melts when our tongues touch them. They dissolve on our taste buds, melt like pancakes in our full mouths. So delicious, I have never tasted such a delicious sweet. Sweet, journeying, the dough releases the syrup and the rest flakes in delicious crumbs. I love the taste, almondy, nutty, they are nothing like anything I have ever tasted before. Come around for tea some time, says Mrs Indira in the doorway. Thank you, says Mum.

The jar of gulab jamuns is a real gift, treasured by Mum like a precious jewel, and in it, the gulab jamuns bob up and down, drifting like Mrs Indira's sari after she has gone. I think she wanted to come in for tea, says Mum when the door closes. But Rashid is going to arrive any time now and I couldn't ask her.

We are doing our cleaning tasks. I am helping in the kitchen. I hear shouting from the hallway. We run out to see.

Amy has picked up the broom she was sweeping the hall with and is crying and shouting and waving the end of the broom at Dad. You pig … You pig … she is shouting. Just you dare hit me, just you dare hit me!

I am frightened for her. Dad grabs the other end of the broom and tries to hit her with it, but Amy grabs the top end and clings on with her whole body weight, so he can't lift the broom to hit her, and she won't let go. Let go, shouts Dad. You'll be punished for this.

You just try to hit me with it, screams Amy through her tears, I'll get my real father on to you, I'll contact him and get him on to you and tell him you hurt me, and he'll come over and stop you.

Dad lets go. He looks around at all of us. Amy is still scared. Go to bed, Dad says. Immediately.

Amy goes into the bedroom and gets into bed. She has to stay there without food, Dad says, until he says she can come out again. Later, I go into the bedroom, and ask what happened. I was sweeping the floor, and he said it was no good, says Amy. And I said, you can't get the sand up, it blows in, I'm doing my best, and then he said, don't answer back, and he tried to hit me, but I held the end of the broom up at him and I shouted at him not to hit me. So he grabbed the other end of the broom. I knew if I let go he was going to hit me with it, so I held onto my end with all my strength so he couldn't. All I could think of was to shout that I'd get my dad on him if he hit me. And he stopped. When I said I'd get my father on him, he was scared, I saw it in his eyes. Or maybe he thought someone might hear me shouting because I was in the hall next to the front door of the flat. But I think he thinks my father is still in contact with me. So he sent me to bed instead, and I didn't get hit. Amy seems proud. I know he'll get his own back, but I won, she says.

I don't have a father to get on to anyone, I think. In a way, Amy doesn't either. She's only seen hers once, years ago. But she talks about him a lot.

Dad says Amy has to stay in bed for three days without food. She can only drink water from the bathroom tap when she goes to the bathroom. We are not allowed to go in to talk to her, except when I go to bed, or when I have to fetch something from the bedroom.

Rashid, she's only ten years old, says Mum. You can't starve her. Can't she even have a glass of milk? No, says Dad. She's not allowed anything. If you try, it will be worse.

It's the weekend so Dad is there the whole time. Mum sneaks me a banana while Dad is in the bathroom, to smuggle in on the second day. Tell Amy to hide the banana peel, says Mum. You can go and fetch it later. Keep the banana peel in your nightie, I say to Amy. He mustn't see it or we'll be in trouble.

I'm so hungry, Amy says. It's like my stomach is a big hole.

I come back to collect the skins later when Dad is in the sitting room where he plays with Matti and Babs. I buy three chocolate wafers with my pocket money. I smuggle those in too. Eat them bit by bit, I say. I smuggle the wrappers out too.

At the end of the third day without food, Dad says Amy can get out of bed and join us for supper. I was so hungry, Amy says to me afterwards, I was so hungry, you wouldn't believe it. All I could do was think how hungry I was, I've never been so hungry in my life. I kept drinking more and more water from the bathroom tap to try to fill myself up.

Dad picks Amy and me up from school every day, and it takes a while to drive back home. One day he stops the car shortly after we leave school. Dad says Amy is making too much noise in the car because she is talking.

Get out the car, he says to Amy. You are going to walk home as a punishment. Amy gets out, and Rashid drives off, leaving her in the sand-filled street in Tripoli, people going to and fro.

When we get home, Mum says, where is Amy?

She is walking home, I say.

What? says Mum. She's ten. She doesn't even know her way home.

Dad says nothing.

We must go and look for her, says Mum.

She must find her own way back, says Dad.

It starts to get dark, and Mum is worried. Then Amy turns up.

I knew he was going to make me walk home one day, says Amy. I knew he would do it. I think Dad has it in for me, now I fought with him. I think he was hoping I would get lost and never come back. But I was prepared. I memorised the route home carefully every day so I would remember if I had to walk home. And I walked really slowly and then I hung around a bit in the street just so he would start getting worried, and then I came in.

A man comes round one evening for dinner to talk with Dad and Mum. Mum says he's a Libyan high up at the oil company come to visit us, he's something to do with business or work or something, and to see how we are settling in. We have to look smart and be good, Dad says.

Dark shapes. Not much to see through the door. Only dark shapes. Chit-chat. Dad calls us in and we sit opposite the man on a mattress on the floor when the food comes, all of us, Matti and

Babs, Amy and me. Dad and Mum and the man sit on chairs opposite. We are so shy, we don't talk. The men chit-chat, chit-chat in Arabic. We don't know what about. Mum is cooking most of the time. She brings the food and says, sorry everything is so simple. We are waiting for our villa and our furniture. We sit, scared we might do something wrong, so we say nothing. Amy giggles. Be quiet, says Dad.

Mum and Dad and the man talk. After dinner they carry on talking and we go outside to play. The man leaves. Mum and Dad are talking with each other afterwards. They are laughing.

What was so funny? we ask afterwards.

He offered to buy Amy as a wife, Mum says, laughing. He said he would pay a lot of money for her. A good price.

Amy and I look at each other. Are you going to sell me? asks Amy, her eyes big.

No, says Mum. Of course not. When you both came and sat and ate with us the man thought we were displaying you to him as possible wives.

But I'm only ten, says Amy.

He can't marry her, I say to Mum. She hasn't grown up yet. We make faces and giggle.

How old is he? we ask. In his thirties, says Mum. He wanted to arrange it in advance for when she got a bit older.

Why Amy and not me then? I ask. I'm older. Mum pauses before she speaks. Well, Amy's looks are more typically English, she says. An English-looking wife is considered very special here. It would make him feel important among his friends. He said he would pay a very big dowry.

But he doesn't even know Amy, I say. She's a child.

I don't want to get married, says Amy. I don't love him.

Don't worry, it won't happen, says Mum. It's the way things are done here, a different way of doing things. Here, when a girl

288

reaches twelve or thirteen, about Mai's age, she has to stay inside and she cannot walk around and see people or go places on her own. She's kept like that until she's married. They shut them away, and they don't go out. That's why you don't see any young girls your age in the streets. Then they stay in the house, until some-one comes and marries them. They think we should be covering our faces too.

Does it happen to all the girls here? we ask.

Yes, says Mum.

I think of all the little girls in the street, and the women with the white sheets wrapped around their faces.

I don't want to be sold, says Amy. She looks worried now.

Don't worry, says Mum. Dad didn't take it at all seriously. He just thought it was funny. He won't sell you.

Amy comes to me afterwards. I'm scared, Mai, don't let Dad sell me to that man. Do you think he will? I don't want him to. Especially now I've argued with him. I really don't. I'm sure he'll sell me and I'll have to marry that man and I'll never see you or Mum or Matti or Babs again.

No, I say, don't worry, I don't think Dad took it very seriously, didn't you see how he was laughing too?

Maybe he'll want the money? says Amy.

Mum would never let him anyway, I say.

Dad comes to us later. He says, don't sit on the floor with your knees up to your chin when people come round, the visitor could see your knickers.

Now Amy is scared Dad will sell her. The next few days we are very quiet.

He won't sell Amy, says Mum.

Maybe he will, says Amy, maybe he will. I'm going to stay extra good from now on.

But Dad doesn't mention it again.

Mum's Polish friend, Ilse, comes round to our flat quite a lot in the daytime. Her husband is Iranian. She cries and cries.

Her husband beats her up badly, but she can't leave him, says Mum. She's covered in bruises, but she can never go back to Poland, because the country is communist, and she married someone from outside, and left. So now she's banned from going back.

Ilse is much younger than Mum, and thin, her hair short light brownish yellow, hanging around her cheeks. She looks worn, her eyes swollen from crying, when she comes around, and she and Mum sit together and chat in the kitchen while we play in our rooms. Ilse has a tiny little baby, so she never stays for long. She goes back to her flat, which is on another floor of the block. She's worried her husband will come back and see she is not in.

He doesn't let her go out at all, says Mum. The poor thing, she's completely trapped. She's not even meant to visit me. You mustn't tell people you saw her here.

Amy seems different, now someone has offered to buy her. I still don't understand why the man preferred Amy to me. Amy must be prettier than me, I think, I must be ugly. I think of all the women walking in the streets, covered up, one eye peering out. I think of Amy like that, of being shut away. I imagine I couldn't go out any more, I imagine being locked inside, only my books and my studies around me.

There aren't any young girls like me in town, only very little ones. The women cover their faces so well only one eye shows, like cocooned insects peeping out. All you can see are their sandalled feet peering from the bottom. One hand permanently holds the white cloth up to their eyes so they only have one hand free. Sometimes they hold children beside them, shopping. I can't even see if they laugh or smile. And when the wind blows, they hold tight, so nothing blows up. Is it dark inside?

When I walk past all the houses and blocks of flats I think of all the twelve-year-old girls my age, locked away. Amy and me can't imagine being locked away like that, peering out over the rooftops.

Hello baby, say the men to us from their cars, or when they are passing in the street. How are you? Sometimes they beckon us from alleyways, or into their cars. Mum says we must never follow them, and to ignore them. Mum says it's the American films the men watch in the cinemas here. The men here put Western women down, but they are the first to try to chat you up, says Mum. They think Western women behave just like they do in the films. It's not surprising though, says Mum, when you see how Western women behave in the films. I think of when the Libyan children throw stones at our feet from the corners of houses, hiding behind the walls. Maybe that's why.

They think Western women are bad, says Mum. Because we don't cover our faces. Who knows what we mean to them?

The housing estate where we live is close to a barren piece of land, a square where the odd small patch of threadbare grass lingers. This is where little children play, small dark children with dirty cotton dresses and snotty noses – always caked with lines of green and yellow snot, the trail on their upper lips. Large dark eyes with curling lashes, and rounded lips, the boys with short curled hair. Some have reddish hair, lighter. So many red-haired children, says Mum. You see a lot of them here.

The children's eyes get bigger when they stare. They open up like cameras and stare at me.

I stoop down and scoop sand up in my fingers. It's not sand you can build with, it's too smooth and soft and impossible to shape. On this sand have trodden camels, people, children in bare feet and broken shoes, all tracing paths across it, I think. All the footsteps of people are in there, large ones, small, little peaks and troughs, not shaped like the soles of their shoes, because the sand is too dry and soft and fine; instead, it stays in little dents and mountains where the shoes have been. I play with the sand in my palm, letting the sand where feet have marked themselves over and over trickle through my fingers, holding the sand footsteps of the world, knowing this is time passing, like an egg timer, trickling footsteps from my palms and through the sides of my fingers.

Sandstorms come sometimes, they tell us. You have to close all the windows and doors tight, so the sand can't come in. The world becomes alien: sand sweeps its way into buildings and around us, people are like sandcastles, walking, sand-swept women's coverings like thick white sheets held around them. Children cling to the edges of their mothers' robes, holding tight. Their eyes follow us. Sometimes stones follow too, chasing our feet, words in Arabic.

A small girl runs up and looks at me, clear pale brown eyes, windswept hair, clasping her fingers together before her face, then runs away again. For a brief moment, we stare at each other as equals, then pass out of each other's lives.

Sky and buildings, vast expanses of sand and nothingness. More buildings go up, they are going up everywhere. The new government is busy building them for the people. Flats with washing lines on balconies. Washing drips down from each balcony. It drips from ours too. Washing on lines on balconies, like rows of white smiles above and below each other, like packs of cards piled up, like dominoes.

The dust blows and mixes with the sound of Arab voices, flat-baked bread like pizzas, khobza, gibna, processed cheese in the supermarket. I look at the mosques' white smooth outsides, blue-painted domes, with minarets on top, crescent moons.

Mystery houses. Noises come out; people go in, rows of shoes outside tracing their footsteps like forgotten memories. Somewhere I can't go. Parts of Libya stay hidden from me, like the twelve-year-old girls who are cloistered away until the bride-price is offered, kept away from childhood wanderings once the blood breaks out between their legs. I sense a key: a prison that locks away the childhood I still have like a treasure; I sense something lost once the dark faces disappear behind doors, only to emerge later as white sheets around bodies with children in tow. And I wonder what can happen behind closed doors.

We are playing, Amy and I, with our tennis racquets, and Kuzi says can I join you? Your mum says you are quite good. I am plunged into mute shyness. Amy gives him her racquet and we hit the tennis ball up and down the yard. Neither of us speaks. It goes on for a long while. My face is red with embarrassment. Afterwards, he says, thank you.

We don't talk. And in the corridors, I still ignore him from shyness.

We are going shopping with Mum. We pass a fence low enough just to see over into a yard. There is a big black cow standing in the middle of the yard, with three men standing around it.

We pass the fence again on our way home. Now, they are slicing the cow up. It's lying on its side now, dead. Black hide with rich red welts where they have carved away the flesh. One of the men calls my mother over by the fence. He hands her a white plastic bag, full of fresh, dripping meat. Waves his hand at the bag and then her. For you, he says.

Mum says, no, thank you.

The man waves his hand again for her to take it. Ramadan, he says. Eid. He is smiling. And the other two men are smiling. Mum says, thank you, takes the bag full of moist meat. It's warm still, warm with the life of that huge black cow. She takes it home and cooks it. Before Dad comes home, Mum gives Amy and me a huge piece of meat each to eat first, because Dad doesn't give Amy and me much meat at supper. He won't know, she says. Don't let Matti and Babs see, they might tell Dad. Matti and Babs get a piece of meat each too, but afterwards. When we eat it, Mum says, he gave us a really good cut.

Someone comes around. He's from Joulou, an island in the Caribbean. A dark brown man. He says he's Indian-Joulouian mixed with African, like many Joulouians. He says how much he likes Joulou. People dress up there, he says. They like to go out. The colours. The sea. Palm trees and hibiscus. Hummingbirds. And the parties. Dancing and carnival. He gets excited about it as he speaks, leaning forwards on the chair, hands clasping together and his eyes open big. I miss Joulou, he says. When I retire I'm going back there.

He stays for only a short time because he has to go somewhere.

Thanks, say Mum and Dad. Thanks for your information.

Dad got another job, says Mum. The company here never lived up to its promises, so Dad looked for another job in another company. We are going to move again, says Mum. We've been here a year, and we still haven't got our villa, as well as other things. They didn't honour the contract. We're going to a place called Joulou. In the West Indies. Dad's decided.

When we fly this time, I am saying goodbye to Kuzi in my mind. We will meet again in the future I am sure, and he will fall in love with me and we'll get married. Maybe he'll turn up in Joulou. I imagine us meeting one day when we're grown up. He sees me in the street, and he says, aren't you Mai? and I say, yes.

And he is so happy to see me, and we kiss and live happily ever after. I see him in the corridor once more, but I am too shy to say goodbye.

So I guess this is fade-out. Kuzi probably hardly noticed me anyway.

15

Tropics

Joulou is big red sky, honey dripping out of gold molten sun burning drops from the sky. It is birds in trees, butterflies and parrots, the throb of life and living humming in the earth, hummingbirds droning into deep petal-cups with long beaks. There are red flowers, hibiscus, big and red and wide and open, everywhere. I turn thirteen the week we arrive.

This country has a wild feeling, like the hibiscus, an underlying energy that emanates from the land, the vegetation, something in the soil. The soil is a deep dark brown; it holds banana trees, avocados, butterflies, scorpions, decayed vibrant carcasses of tropical birds, scarlet ibis, giant spiders. And there are bachacs, large ants that walk on cuticle-covered legs, holding big leaves and colourful petals, six times their own size, in their teeth, and the praying mantis praying with his hands cupped to his face, and the insect that's a stick, more still than a twig that shakes in the wind. The leaves are green, so green, rich in greenness. In the streets there is dark skin everywhere, polished nut-shell gleaming, beautiful, like wood sculptures, like trees. People here shine, and they are the most beautiful I have ever seen in the world.

We have company accommodation, a large flat old house, one storey high. It's on stilts! we say when we see it. The stilts are low thick concrete blocks that lift the house above the land. Mum says it's cooler that way, to let the air go underneath. If we want we can climb underneath the house. But we don't, because we would have to stay crouched over, and it's too dirty and dark, because the space underneath is lower than ground level. There's a lot of garden, like a wilderness, all around the house; in front is a small area behind a fence, with the driveway to the left and at the back there is a big expanse of overgrown garden, not large but enormous to us. It has weeds as high as ourselves.

Look, a jungle, we say. The jungle is so high. We stand and stare at the tangle of leaves and flowers. Butterflies, all colours, racing around the garden; hornets, bees, all in the air; snails, woodlice, worms, slugs in the soil. You can smell the insects.

As I stand, the blades of grass shift a little. Out of the grass comes a butterfly with big blue wings as big as a book. It lifts itself from the grass, blue wings large and slow, stunning, bright bright blue, shining like jewels, like water glittering in the sunlight.

The butterfly rises up, surrounded by the brown-yellow-white and orange-red of the other butterflies and the dry yellow-green stalks of grass up to my hips, wild, in their own paradise. The tops of the wings shine more brightly than underneath, so when its wings open up and part, the blue shines out. It goes up and up, its wings flapping as if in slow motion. It rises in the air and circles slightly. In the trees behind it, there are parrots sitting, peering through the leaves.

The butterfly is flapping its wings, saying goodbye, it can't stay here any more. I fly up with it, sailing and skimming with it, up into the air, with the birds and the trees and the parrots, and the whole world circling up there beyond me. I wish it could stay here with me, but I would rather give it freedom, I would rather it travelled around the world, the sky, the trees, the hills, to be part of everything beautiful, the sunlight, the bright fresh air and the puffed-up clouds. I want it to sail away and travel far, forever. I hold its memory with me, like an echo. It is the only one like that I ever see in the garden. Mum tells me it is probably a Blue Emperor butterfly, one of the largest in the world.

There is a huge tree in the back garden near the fence. It has giant dried bean-shaped pods hanging from it like giant runner beans, which fall to the ground. The bean pods are as long as our arms. We invent a new game, bean hockey, with Matti and Babs, using a tennis ball and the dried-up bean pods. Amy is with Matti, and I am with Babs. We hit the tennis ball back and forth between the two ends of the path that act as goalposts.

When one bean pod breaks, then we must pick up another immediately, and carry on the game.

As we play, day turns to sunset. Golden-red lava drip-drops out of the sky and fills the spaces between the tree branches where the seed pods grow. I stand and watch. The redness consumes the tree branches as if a huge forest fire has caught the world and is tearing it between its teeth and all the blood is falling out. I watch the sunset run through its hues, the reds, the oranges, the crimsons, the golds. I am amazed that the world can produce such beauty, just in one go. Everything takes part: the tree branches that darken and become charcoal silhouette smudges, bird calls that strengthen and swell within the oncoming night.

The sun burns up like a huge cinder. Then the sky is a fire put out, the coals burning, dimming. It makes me think of the fire we had at home when we were little, the flames licking around the coals as if they were hungry for the chestnuts we held at the end of the toasting fork. The sun has become the fire we had at home, and, with it, all the stories we shared, tucked around the grate, of Mexico, of my sister's father in South Africa, the hot toast and currant buns that sometimes blackened at the sides, the woollen mittens and shoes wet from the snow, and wellington boots left on the porch, slippery with white crusted snow melting in puddles below it. I want to dive into the sky and become it; I am taken home, transported to our warm fire. But I am home here too, because the sky is the fire I loved, and the fire the sky, and even my heart is out there, pulsing, all its little veins running like the black branches crossing the sky.

What are you doing? asks Amy, coming up to me.

Looking at the sunset, I reply. But the light is darkening now, the fire is dimming, hiding itself, the best has gone. The sky plummets into purple, then a warm black. But we watch, none-theless, until the bean tree casts itself into shadow and there is nothing to make out any more, until branch by branch it is con-sumed by darkness. I can only hear the breathing of the trees now, the plants, the scratch of insects, the crunch of our shoes on the soil as we shuffle our feet back and forth.

It's like blood, I say. It's like a fire gone out.

Matti and Babs are disappointed. They were playing bean hockey, and the world went dark.

We lost our ball.

Leave it till the morning. We won't find it now.

Dark sets in amid the heat and warmth; the outlines of the hills suggest themselves softly in the blackness like a moan, gut-throat moan.

In the morning, the tennis ball is found in a bunch of grass near the bottom of the tree where the roots lift out of the soil.

We smell something from under the sitting-room floor. We smell something nasty.

When we walk in the house through the kitchen, fleas jump

on our legs. We think we have fleas, but Mum says no, they're only coming on our legs, it must be something under the floorboards. Dad looks but he doesn't see anything. He jumps down under the house. He looks around. He says, dead dog. We see the poor dog, all skeletal, smelling and smelling, lying on its side far under the house, between the pillars that support the floor. That's where the fleas come from, says Mum. Dad drags the dog out. Pooh, we say, the smell gets worse, so we hold our noses.

Poor sick dog, Amy and I say, why is he under the house? How did he get there?

He probably went there to die, says Mum. He crawled under because he was sick or starving. He probably starved, because he's so thin, his ribs are sticking out. He was probably starving and crawled under the house to die.

After that, Mum disinfects the floor and the fleas stop. Mum tells me that Dad told her after that when he was working and living in London, the man living in the flat opposite him died – he had locked the door on the inside and nobody knew he was in there. Only after the flies started collecting, Dad said, more and more of them coming from under the door and no one could work out why, they noticed the smell and the police broke in and all this time he'd been dead, behind the door opposite Dad, just down the corridor.

It was like he enjoyed it, says Mum, the idea of the flies being there and the man dead, like a macabre enjoyment of living opposite the event. Mum says then Dad told her his first girlfriend committed suicide. She killed herself because she was pregnant with his baby, and he said he would have nothing to do with her once he found out about the baby. He boasted about it, says Mum, I am sure he was boasting. How can you enjoy telling someone your ex-girlfriend killed herself with your baby? She must have been very alone. The way Rashid said it, it was almost as if he was threatening me, says Mum, almost to herself. Something's not right. He's behaving very strangely.

I am standing in a sea. Around me are mermaids, fish, octopuses, creatures that exist and yet do not exist, moving and swaying as they move towards the centre of the capital.

A burst of noise. A loud burst. We are at Joulou Carnival, happening shortly after we arrive, just before my birthday. Mum says Joulou Carnival is like Rio Carnival in Brazil. Around me, the sea dances, multicoloured, multi-faceted, multi-peopled. I see Neptune with trident and mermaids; I see half-dressed people dancing and swaying around me. The river moves down the street – fish and serpents – and gives way to dancing Indians, to people of the world, Chinese and Indian and European and Arabic and all other nations.

Before me is a huge big-bellied Chinese man bearing a flag with the title of his section of the carnival band written on it. But he has lost his band and is in the wrong section. All in green, dressed in a long silken green robe with tassels draped over his large belly and reaching to his feet, and a mandarin-style hat, and a moustache hanging down from his face, he is grinning and drunk – waving a long black flag as large as himself, its pole large and unwieldy in his hands.

Because he is drunk, he cannot hold it properly. Every time he lifts the heavy flag in the air and moves it to the other side, its weight pulls him sideways and he lurches towards the other side of the road, eventually rolling on the ground along with the flag, or catching himself just in time before the flag, toppling to one side, reaches the ground. The din of carnival sways around him, and at every failed sway of the flag, others carrying huge flags, banners, crowns, cloaks move past him in a sway of colours and the beat beat of music. But the man is laughing and smiling and drunk and happy; I have never seen such happiness as in the moments when he lifts his flag and falls sideways, swaying towards the other side of the street, occasionally landing on the pavement between passing dancing feet. There are two rivers: the rivers of costumes that pass, and this man, moving as if in slow motion in the opposite direction, toppling from side to side, inching his way along in flashes of deep green silk, his large grin over double chin and rounded cheeks reaching ear to ear. Clearly, they chose him as flag bearer because of his size and strength. But now he has lost the carnival band he was in and sways and dances to his own tune instead, and others sway and dance around him in equal happiness.

I turn my face to the sky, and under the white puffed-up conical island clouds, colours pass above me, colours and music and movement, and I, in my head, am dancing with them, a bemused Chinese-looking thirteen-year-old standing in the middle of the street with carnival bands moving around me, and the large-bellied Chinese man in green tottering from side to side, losing his balance, over and over.

Dad starts to clear the garden that runs all around the back and right-hand side of the house. He starts cutting down all the leaves and grass with a big knife and a lawnmower he borrows from the neighbours. He cuts the long grass, and all the butterflies rise up like a yellow and white curtain from the green blades of grass and fly away. He chops at the leaves and bushes with a huge scythe, slicing through the undergrowth so the branches fall flat on their sides, the blades of grass heaped one on top of another. We have to carry the grass to a wheelbarrow, where he piles all the vegetation up at the other end of the garden at the back.

As Dad cuts, I see two parrots in the tops of the tall trees at the end of the garden. They fly away, startled, with big green wings, colourful yellow and red feathers and bright beaks. The mound of cut twigs and grass blades gets bigger and bigger and starts to dry out and go brown in the sun. We cart the leaves back and forth.

Dad clears all the grass and plants from the garden over the next few days. We find giant snails under the sliced large blades of grass. They are big, like your fist curled up, and live under the house and in the garden, under the long wild grass and the butterflies. We race them, fascinated by their size, on the garden path.

He clears the parrots and the butterflies. Then the animals and insects evacuate, leaving only earth and dry twigs. The last butterflies drift off out of the garden as the last plants are ripped out of the soil. The snails stay on for a while, but they slowly disappear as the grass and plants disappear. Then all the snails are gone too, and leave the house and garden like the other creatures, a few weeks after the butterflies and parrots.

Soon, the whole area of long grass and plants is completely cleared along the path under the bean tree and in the garden round the back. Only the hibiscus and a few other bushes are left around the front of the house. All there is left is brown earth, no butterflies, no spinning whirling insects among them. I stare at the brown earth. It looks sad – empty, soulless, lifeless. I don't know why Dad had to clear it.

Our neighbours, Mr and Mrs Kincaid, come back from their holidays. They chat over the fence. Mr Kincaid works as a zoologist, says Mum, and Mrs Kincaid teaches in the junior school. She is Matti's teacher.

Mr Kincaid used to have a crocodile, says Mum. He doesn't have a crocodile any more, he used to keep it in a bath. Really? we ask him, over the garden wall. Yes, he says. Just a baby crocodile, says Mrs Kincaid.

One day Mr Kincaid says we can come round to see his tarantula, he found it inside his garage, on the wall. We go into the garage with him and Mrs Kincaid, and there the tarantula is, high up on the wall, in the corner where the roof meets the side of the wall – a furry black blob with thick hairy legs. It's a baby, says Mr Kincaid. They get much larger. He grins, like a schoolboy. Is this the same place you had a crocodile? we ask. In a bath? Yes, he says. It was a while ago. A small one.

Mum says Mrs Kincaid is a good teacher. It is a good school, Mum says. The kids get good marks and go on to good secondary schools, which are competitive for entries. The standard is very high.

The other neighbours, Mr and Mrs Naidoo, in the house immediately joined to ours, are shy. They never talk to us much. They usually just say hello and goodbye. They have a daughter, Vaneshri, with long curling hair who is pretty and Amy's age, but she's very quiet too and doesn't say much either.

Mum said Mr Kincaid told her and Dad yesterday there are dangerous scorpions here in Joulou that live under rocks, and large poisonous millipedes that can kill you. He said there are probably lots of scorpions in our garden because no one has lived here for a while, so we must be very careful.

Dad takes me to a large cardboard box at the edge of the garden where he has weeded and cleared the earth flat. Dad says, fill the box. To the top. When you are finished, bring it to me.

Fill it with what?

Earth. I am moving the earth from here to the other side of the garden.

Why?

Just fill it.

I stare at the box and the soil.

Go on then. Start.

How am I going to get the earth in there?

Use your hands, he says. Do what I say. You must dig with your hands and fill up the box.

But can't I have a spade?

No, you can't have a spade. Dig the soil with your hands and fill the box. Look. He squats down on the concrete path beside the garden and scoops up a handful of soil and throws it in the box. See. Do what I did. Dig up the soil with your hands and fill the box. Get on with it.

The box is huge. It will take ages with my hands. My hands are much smaller than Dad's.

Start now, says Dad. Or there'll be trouble. And no stopping. I squat down on the concrete path with Dad watching me, rubbing the earth from his hands. I reach out one hand, dip down, and dig up a handful of earth in front of me with my fingers, feel it sticky wet in my child-size hand. Worms and squashy things, maybe scorpions, that's what I'm afraid of. I look at the soil. I hope there's no worms. Or scorpions. I try not to think about them. Little insects that wriggle out when I lift the earth up climb over my fingers and drop back to the ground. I can't hold much.

It will take really long with my hands, I say.

Use both hands, not just one, and scoop up more earth.

I reach out my second hand beside the first. Two hands scoop up a bit more. Squidgy warm cold sticky wetness. I think of all the slimy things in there.

Dad leaves me there, after my first handful, and I carry on.

The soil is rich, black, like the night. I watch the stars at night, all that black out there, well now it's like I'm digging it up with my hands, the soil as mysterious and hidden as the night sky. Tiny white minuscule stones like stars that catch under my nails, little insects that run and scurry about. I dig with my fingers, my palms. At least the earth is soft, spongy. At least it's warm. Tiny woodlice curl up in tight balls when they are discovered and scooped up and land in the cardboard box.

Time goes on and on.

Finally, I fill the box, my hands dark and earth-covered.

Dad comes over.

I filled it, I say.

He takes the box of earth and carries it to the other side of the garden and tips it onto a heap of piled-up leaves and stones. He brings the box back.

You must fill it again, he says, a slight smile curving at the edge of his mouth. I crouch down, squatting, then lean on my knees, as I keep adding more and more dark earth to the box. Dad goes inside the house. But I know he's still watching me, because occasionally I see his silhouette like a shadow as he stands behind the living-room window and looks out, thinking I can't see him there.

Why? I ask myself. But it is not for me to question why, just to do it. He does not have reasons, he is always illogical – but I am puzzled, what could I have done to cause this? Filling the box becomes more tolerable. Unpleasant, because I don't know what creatures I'm going to feel next against my fingers, but at least I can feel in touch with the earth, the insects, the garden. Warm earth: it's different. I try to be friends with the insects. Parrots fly in the trees overhead. I watch them momentarily, out of the corner of my eye, appear and disappear. But I can't pause in case he sees me watching them.

Amy comes up to me.

Mum and I were looking for you. We thought you were in-doors. She looks at the box, my hands and the hollow space in the garden earth. What are you doing? she asks.

Filling this box with earth. Dad said I had to, I reply.

Why?

I don't know, I say, still filling the box, tears threatening at the corners of my eyes.

Why don't you use a spade?

Dad said I can't use one.

That's really weird, Amy whispers.

She goes back inside the house and comes out again with a large metal spoon that Mum uses to serve vegetables in the kitchen.

Mum sent me out with this to help you. She said you should use it to dig with.

I can't, I say. He said I had to use my hands. Tell Mum I can't, or I'll be in trouble. Take it back before he sees it.

Amy goes back inside the house. Then Mum comes out with the spoon. I see her holding it in her right hand, holding it in the air towards me.

Mai, what are you doing? Why don't you use the spoon to dig with?

I can't, I say.

Don't worry, Mai, says Mum. Take the spoon. I'll sort it out.

Dad said I had to use my hands. I can't use a spade.

Come on, don't be silly. Use the spoon. He didn't say you couldn't use a spoon. Only a spade.

I'll get in trouble if I do.

Come on, take the spoon.

No. It's fine, I say.

Dad comes out of the house. He comes up to me, Amy and Mum.

Mum says, what are you doing, Rashid? You can't make her fill a box with her bare hands.

She has to fill the box, says Dad.

But at least give her the spade. Why can't she use a spade? Or this spoon? She won't even take this spoon. What are you doing to her? She's so terrified of you she won't even take the spoon. Let her dig with something, not with her bare hands.

No, she has to use her hands.

Mum looks at him. Are you crazy? she says.

Shut up, woman, says Dad. Go back inside. Or there'll be trouble.

Mum looks at me. I can see in her eyes, she knows it will get worse for us both if she stays. Don't worry, Mai, says Mum. I'll sort it out. She goes back indoors, and Dad glares at me, then follows her. I carry on filling the box with my bare hands.

Dad comes out when the second box is filled, and tells me I can stop. I think Mum said something that worked.

He watched the whole time from the living room. I saw his shadow through the net curtains, standing there. I think he enjoys it.

Mum washes clothes every day in the washbasin, white suds soaking around her fingers. I wash my own. I've got the two skirts I wear and two tops. I've had them since Libya.

Mum says, Mai, you need a nightdress. She finds an old sheet to make my nightie because Dad won't give her money to buy one. She makes a simple nightie from the sheet, cutting it up, using her sewing machine to sew it. Another part of the sheet she makes into a cord that goes around the neckline, where it ties over my shoulders to form straps. It's not perfect, she says, but it does the job.

Ha ha, Mai's got an old sheet as a nightie, says Amy.

Quiet, Amy, says Mum, you're not to make jokes like that. It's the best I can do. Dad won't give us any money for clothes. It's better than not having a nightie at all.

But I don't mind. I like my nightie. It's made by Mum. I wash it often and hang it on the washing line and watch it blow on the breeze, hanging with my other clothes, the piece of sheet ribbon threaded through the top. It seems so creative, to make it from a sheet.

White sheets and clothes hanging like patchwork in the garden. The wind blows at them, they toss like the leaves, coil themselves occasionally around the white cord and wooden pegs, like Swiss rolls in a row. Washed nappies, patchwork sheets, my nightdress. Parts of ourselves hanging out in the garden, bits of our lives hanging out there, as if our bodies had not soiled them. Trying to distance themselves from our excrement, our sweat, our tears, yet soaked in them nonetheless, the feel of us.

I watch my nightie flap, the sheet cord looped around the neck as shoulder straps, I look at me out there on the washing line, Matti's T-shirt, Amy's shorts and Babs' pink dress, Dad's large white Y-fronts and string vest and shirts and trousers, Mum's yellow dress with small blue primroses she made with her sewing machine, and her brown corduroy dress, and our sheets.

Dad's clothes are larger, dominant. They swathe the other clothes into submission through their size. I wish he were like his clothes, could be tossed by the wind. I would like to take his clothes and pour red paint on them, destroy them with scissors, but when Mum says, take in the dry washing, Mai, I hold Dad's clothes with the tips of my fingers at the far edge and quickly drop them in the wash basket. Touch not. Touch not the evil items. They will contaminate you. They will cast a spell and you will be held by them. Stay away, as far as possible.

The glowflies dance, the lower ends of their bodies fluorescent and skimming the plants. We laugh when Matti and Babs try to catch up with them, racing up and down the garden excitedly. You can only catch glowflies if you wait until they stop and then clasp them quickly in your hand. We watch their tail ends pulse and coil, with their strange greeny-yellow colour, flickering in the night.

Making patterns in the sky, I sweep my hands in the air. If I sweep my hands up across the stars, I know I can pull one of the dancing stars out of the sky and put it in the jam jar, little wings flapping, green bottom twitching up and down in the base of the glass, legs scratching around the sides.

The stars are so bright. When I sweep my hand across, I blot them out temporarily, so they seem to flash at me. And, however many times I wave my hand across, the stars are still there. Only the glowflies dance around, weaving in and out of the stars. Like all my thoughts. I give each one of the glowflies a thought to take with it. It captures it and takes off and away with it. Soon the sky is dancing with my thoughts.

Amy comes with another glowfly to put in the jar. She pops it in with the one I have already caught and we look at the two of them.

You haven't caught many yet, Amy says. I thought you said you could catch much more than I can.

I was watching them, I say. Flying around.

Me too, she says.

As she speaks, a light lights up from a nearby leaf, emerald green flashing like a torch, on and off. We look at the two glow-flies in the jam jar. One of them is also flashing its light on and off. We are catching them and putting them in a jar to make a lamp, because I read they make lanterns out of glowflies like that in China. If you catch enough, you can make lanterns, like the Chinese. Then you have another set of stars, then you have all the lights of the universe in your jam jar.

Here's one, say Matti and Babs, running up excitedly with a glowfly on a leaf. Babs has curly hair, a round face and grey eyes.

Our nana had grey eyes. Matti is smiling, curly brown haired, with freckles, a lot of them.

I don't think we'll catch enough to make a lamp tonight, says Amy. They don't make enough light.

Not tonight. Maybe another night.

Should we let them free?

I think so, I say.

We tip both the glowflies out of the jar, but one keeps climbing back into the jar from the rim. Eventually they are both on the ground. Babs and Matti watch us excitedly. And when we look down again, they've flown away.

Another night, says Amy.

Another night, I say.

But there isn't another night for catching glowflies. The glowflies disappear, along with the grass and butterflies and plants that turn to dark brown earth.

16

Dusk

Amy and I go to secondary school, and Matti and Babs go to the primary school. When we start school the headmistress says, we do O levels here, and because you came from an American school, you must go to the beginning of O levels. So she puts me and Amy down a year below our ages. Mum says, but Mai is clever, she was already up a year in class, now she loses two years. But the headmistress says the academic year has started in O level, so she has to start the year below. She says the American school is bad and we need to catch up to their standards. She says if I come first in my class at the end of term, I can go up a year. I come first, but she still doesn't let me go up a year.

So now Amy and I are both a year down in school. All the people around me have brown or dark skin. My best friends Lucille and Samira have Afro hair but it's light, and African features but their skin is light. And Kerry Ann, she's dark and pretty, she has slightly Chinese eyes and a flat beautiful nose and she can stay out in the sun without burning. I don't burn too easily but I prefer the shade.

Moon-face, they call me, and laugh at my round Asian face. You have a face like a moon. But nobody here is cruel.

My school friends say, you should meet Corinne, she comes top of class too, she's in your year, but class 2x, so I say okay, then they introduce me to Corinne. She's short and has a big grin and we get on fine, I just know we understand each other. I form a group with seven friends: they are Violet, Georgina, Patsy-Anne, Joanna, Corinne, and Lucille and Samira. At lunchtimes the group must meet and sit at the Spot, which is a small tree with a tiny bit of shade on the grass by the playing field, and we must divide our sandwiches into eight and share them. Everyone ends up with eight little tiny pieces of different sandwiches, which makes lunch more exciting because we all have variety.

Corinne and I become best friends.

Under the tree we talk about lots of things. We act out plays for class, and think of practical jokes. Sometimes my friends compare who has the best suntan. Look, I'm darker today, says Corinne, I sat out in the sun yesterday. She shows her arm, which is dark brown. See. Today I look more black. Not as black as Samira, says Patsy-Anne. She doesn't have to tan, says Lucille. She's black already. No, says Samira, I do get darker in the sun. Look. My arms are darker than the rest of me.

Everyone else around me has brown skin or dark skin.

Mai, you'll never get a tan, says Patsy-Anne. Look at you next to the rest of us. Look at your pale skin, it will just fry up in the sun and go red. They laugh, but inside, I wish I could turn dark like them, and become smooth and brown and beautiful when the sun shines on me.

Hey, Patsy-Anne, you sunburn too, says Violet. Remember that time your face peeled? You looked like a rag carpet. Lots of bits of skin hanging down.

Hey, says Patsy-Anne, quiet about that. I don't want to be reminded about it. We giggle. Patsy-Anne did look funny the time she burnt. All feathery with little fringes of skin that kept peeling off her forehead and nose. She laughs. Okay, okay. Hey, Mai, you sit in this shady part, and you won't burn. You too, says Violet.

Go on, Patsy-Anne. Patsy-Anne sits beside me. Anyone for a piece of tuna and chilli paste? she asks.

We go round for dinner with Mr and Mrs Shahiz. Mrs Shahiz is English and is also married to a Moroccan, Mr Shahiz, and Mum and Dad chat about lots of things with them. Mr Shahiz works at the same place as Dad, says Mum, but in a different area. Mr Shahiz wears glasses and is thin and scrawny and always nervous, not quiet and reserved like Dad. Mrs Shahiz has brown curly hair, is nervous too, and has two tubby young children, ages four and two, who are very noisy and are always eating, and Mrs Shahiz has a look like she is trying to keep control but is always losing it, especially with her children, who she shouts at and they don't listen to her.

At the end of the meal, everyone says they will stay in touch.

There's a rat in the kitchen. Mum says it's eating the food. It leaves droppings. She can hear it. The rat is scampering around the kitchen. Dad's going to catch it. He gets a big red bucket and he tries to catch it. He chases it around the kitchen. He catches it on the sink's steel draining board under the bucket.

Fill the sink, he says. Dad is going to drown the rat. Fill the sink, quickly. He puts the plug in the sink. Mum turns the tap on. Water pours from the tap.

Dad slides the red bucket across the top of the draining board. The rat falls into the sink as it fills with water. Dad keeps the bucket over it. The rat is struggling, swimming inside the bucket, it's frantic, he can hardly keep the bucket over it. Dad slides the side of the bucket over the rat's neck and holds it down in the sink. The rat struggles hard. He keeps the rat's head under the water, but it still keeps struggling, the water splashing. Dad is fighting with the bucket, forcing it down. He doesn't seem to mind.

I watch Dad holding the red plastic bucket over the rat, listen to the struggling hammering in the water, see his hands pressing down firmly, his arms moving every time the rat tries to push the bucket away. It's a strong rat, but Dad is stronger. I would rather let the rat go free than feel it struggling under the bucket, it squeals, squeals, and still he holds it down. Frantic, the rat kicks and kicks, drumming under the bucket, its claws hit the steel sink, thump thump. Then it dies. Suddenly. The kicking stops, one or two feeble thumps.

When the rat is dead we are all silent.

Dad puts the rat in the bin outside. We are all very silent for the rest of the day. I wish we'd never mentioned the rat.

The rat's death makes the house very quiet. It scars the house. Somehow the dead dog and the rat feel like a bad omen.

At school we are told to collect things from nature for science class. I find an old piece of hornets' nest and leave it on my desk at school to look at, at the front of the old wooden desk, next to the unused inkwell.

In the middle of my history class one of the little cells in the nest starts to cut away. I watch as a small hole appears at the side of the hexagonal cell, then the paper-thin covering slowly opens up, like the inside of a can being opened by a tin opener. I watch, fascinated.

The paper-thin top is being cut by a hornet's mouth as it is being born from its cell. It cuts away, slowly, with its small razor mouth, until it has gone all the way round. Then it pushes its head upwards and pulls itself out of the cell, its body all shiny and new. Its wings are small and thin at first, but then I see it pump its wings out, and they start to fill up and get fatter. I'm scared it will sting but am fascinated at the same time. Its wings get bigger and stronger and drier. Then it perches on the edge of the nest and flies away out of the window. Nobody sees it except me. I am fascinated, more than by any class I have had. I feel close to the hornet but now I'm scared the other cells will hatch too and I'll have hornets all over my school desk. But they don't.

After the lesson, in break time, I take the hornets' nest out and leave the nest outside on the grass, carefully, wondering if the other cells will hatch. I glance quickly at the sky before I go back to lessons. Somewhere, outside, the hornet I saw being born is flying.

The flying ants begin. Hundreds of them. They flutter around on little wings, scattering around the windows. The crickets and locusts fly too, in straight lines – when they get in the house they go in a straight line, they don't look, they hit you and crash on your body and fall on the ground and sometimes they fall under your feet and scrunch as you're walking, they get sickly sickly squashed into pieces, smudgy pieces that stick to the floor.

I hate them most because I am afraid they are going to fly into my mouth. The flying ants are brown and hard-shelled like the ones in Libya. Their legs hang down in funny droopy useless dribbling positions when they fly. The hornets are very big huge things with wings and legs, they skate through the air effortlessly. They never seem to want to sting us, though.

There is Diwali in Joulou. Out go the small diyas, the tiny clay lamps filled with oil and a string wick, out along the walls and fences of the houses. We watch the neighbours, Mr and Mrs Naidoo, put them along the walls of their garden at night. One by one, they carry the diyas out, the small flame burning and reflecting off their hands, flickering on their faces, giving warmth to the garden plants and the hibiscus flowers in the early evening. As the sky darkens to a jet black, the diyas slowly spread their light outwards, as if growing from the tiny pinprick of a wick end to fill up the space of the night. The diyas remind me of an ant trail, a trail of bachacs carrying lights, suspended in time. Along the roads, trails of lights spring up, added to one by one as each diya is added on. I follow the path of them with my eyes. I watch the lights flickering as if they should be leading me somewhere, outwards, onwards.

We always put lights out at Diwali, says Mrs Naidoo. All the Hindus do that. It's our Christmas, Mr Naidoo says. Vaneshri, their daughter, stands and smiles at us. She's always too shy to say anything, and she wears braces. When she smiles, she doesn't show her teeth. She's the same age as Amy, but in a different class.

Aren't they beautiful? says Mum. Like glowflies, says Amy. Shining in the dark. I just watch them and stare. I watch Mum's face as she looks out at all the lights. I remember Mrs Indira and the jar of gulab jamuns. I wonder if all the candle flames bobbing and flickering up and down in the night breeze remind Mum of the gulab jamuns in the jar, and Mrs Indira, and Ilse the Polish woman who Mum said was married to an Iranian who beat her up, and couldn't go back to Poland because she had left and Poland was communist.

Happy Diwali, we say. I look at Mum's eyes, and there are the Diwali lights, sparkling inside them.

I feel sorry for Matti. He is in the sitting room trying to do his maths homework and Dad is teaching him. He has to stand by the dining-room table while Dad sits with his homework book. Every time Matti gets the answer wrong, Dad hits him on the back of his hand with the ruler. Matti is getting all the answers wrong. There are tears running down Matti's face and he is crying. Dad is getting angrier and angrier. Fifty-six divided by four, says Dad, what is it? Seven, says Matti, and this time Dad hits him on his upper arm with his hand, so Matti is pushed sideways by the blow. No, says Dad. Get it right. Put your hand back on the table. Then Dad hits Matti on the hand with the ruler again.

Everyone in the sitting room is very quiet. We don't know what to say. I sit, pretending to read my book, Amy too. Babs is sitting on the rug on the floor, playing with her dolls. Mum comes in from the kitchen. She has come to ask Dad something about dinner, but has to wait for Dad to finish with Matti. Matti is crying, crying. It hurts inside when I see him cry. It is like when I saw Dad hit him when he was two years old, when the bed broke.

Why are you hitting him, Rashid? says Mum. I can see Mum is scared too.

He has to get it right, says Dad. If he doesn't, he doesn't get to the good secondary school.

You're hurting him, says Mum.

I know what I'm doing, says Dad. If you don't shut up, I'll hurt him a lot more.

Again, says Dad to Matti. Keep your hand on the table. Matti is trembling, his pencil stumbling through his maths book, with his other hand on the table in front of Dad. Matti is eight now, and they have end-of-year exams coming. Twelve, says Matti. No, says Dad. Dad hits Matti's hand again. Every time Dad hits Matti, I jump inside, but I show nothing. None of us shows anything. We have learnt not to. But our eyes probably show it, and we don't let him see inside them.

Matti is standing upright by the table trying to work out the sum, stumbling with the pencil through his tears. He's very stressed, Rashid, says Mum. When you hit him he gets more stressed and he can't think straight. I can see Mum wants to reach out and touch Matti, but she can't.

Every now and then Babs looks up from the rug in the centre

of the floor, then away again before Dad sees her. I realise even Babs has learnt not to show anything either. She is six. When Dad hits Matti like this the whole room feels like breaking ice, as if it is about to crack. And with every crack of the ruler, Matti's tears melt the ice a little more and expose us to our fear, fear in our eyes, in the way Babs holds her dolls, in the way Mum stands with her dishcloth twisted between her hands, trying to change Dad's mind.

He has to get it right, says Dad, and hits Matti again and glares at Mum defiantly. Mum keeps talking to Dad about the oven in the kitchen and the temperature control she thinks Dad should take a look at, and Matti keeps working.

I'll look at the oven another time, says Dad.

Fourteen, says Matti, looking up from his paperwork.

Okay, says Dad. Go sit over there, and do the next sum.

Matti sits on the chair, doing his homework. But I can see he is trembling when he writes. He looks anxious, glancing up and down at Dad to see if he is looking. Dad is going through some of his own work now.

I would like to do the sums for Matti, but I can't.

Corinne's dad says she must get a lift from school today, and that she must ask our dad because he lives closest. After school, he arrives in his red car, and I must go up and ask, Corinne by my side, Dad, can Corinne get a lift back with us please? Her dad can't come tonight.

Dad says, yes, of course.

He drops Corinne at her home and her mother says, thank you very much. Then we go home. When we reach home he says, go to bed straight away, Mai. You are never going to put me in that situation again. Mum says, but it wasn't Mai's fault. Her friend Corinne asked her during the day, and she couldn't organise it before. But

Dad says, you are never going to ask for a lift for your friend again. And I go to bed without supper. When I'm in bed, I cry.

The next day I tell Corinne she can't get any more lifts. That my dad was annoyed because we asked him. Then Corinne laughs and says it must be a joke, what did we do wrong? So I just say, my dad's like that. But you have to tell your parents not to ask again, or I'll get into trouble. Corinne says, what kind of a dad is that, to get you into trouble for giving me a lift home? I'll explain to him next time I see him. But I say, no, just leave it, it will make things worse. And she says, what kind of a dad do you have to do something like that? Is he crazy? and she laughs. But I say nothing. What can I say? Instead, I change the subject. Corinne realises I'm serious and says, well, I think it's very strange. He's like that, I say. After that, we don't talk any more about him.

It gets hotter and hotter, the air thick like you could stir it, heat gathering on our arms and legs, sticky in our clothes.

Rainy season's here, says Mum.

Smell of rain-washed leaves swollen with heat, leafy surfaces shiny like gold in the sun, harsh hot sea breeze, snails and worms in the earth, the sunshine like gold dust on my skin, my hair, soaking into my eyes, everything golden. Gold in the songs of the birds.

Quiet in the sky. Dry electric sharp quiet, crackly.

The first breath of thunder, like a stick snapping, like a plank of wood tearing apart. Then a boom. A dull thud shaking the earth. Boom. The sky breaks open. Dry clothes; wet clothes. Dry hair; hair that streams like a wet rat tail. No time to run for cover, just feel the rain pour down, clothes soaked in seconds, wet rain on my skin, feel it run down my face, through my light clothes onto my body, feel its fingers tingle my skin. Even my underwear is wet, shoes are wet, toes and heels are wet.

At night I wait for the patter of rain, the boom of thunder, the rain on the corrugated-iron rooftops, pattering, then drumming its dancing feet, then thundering down so hard you can't even hear the thunder.

In my mind I see all the water swirling down the garden path, whisking away leaves, the insects, the spiders from their webs on the plants, breaking leaves and bending branches, the trees swaying wildly in the wind, the glowflies being knocked out of the sky, the dark heat swirling around like the rain, the stars being washed away.

The night world comes alive. Glowflies that light up and spin through the undergrowth. Crickets that croak and chirp like alarm bells ringing – wake up, wake up – the din of drumming buried in their calls, the rain that beats rhythms on housetops, that knocks branches and leaves flying, breaks flowers from stems, bachac ants still holding their piece of leaf or petal, swept in rivers of rain by the sidewalks like ships with sails, sailing down, spinning helplessly as the dark turbulent rainwater runs like a river down the garden paths.

Black night, black mountains – at night, they stare down, shapeless, formless, blurred at the edges, but solid nonetheless. Silently, I call across hills and ground, soil and feet, I see the world stir. If I pull the sky down, like a blanket, will all the clouds and stars and hills come with it? I can reach up with my finger, and with its tip obliterate each star, one by one, as if it had never existed, as if all the life that encircles it never existed. In my head, I silently scream up to the stars. In my head, I hear them scream back. Everything, everywhere, that screams, I feel it.

A scream doesn't have to be loud. The strongest screams are the ones we hear within us, the ones that twist our organs up and run like a fist through our intestines and ribcages, the ones that have no voice. Yet it comforts me, because I know I am alive.

Sometimes, I watch the rain when it drips from leaves, thudding on the soil with wet spreading patches, causing them to spring back with the lost weight. When the soil quiets its rapid pitted dimpling, and the leaves stop bouncing, it's as if my own heartbeat slows to their drip, drip.

Mum says Matti's marks are dropping at school. Mrs Kincaid is his teacher and she says he is starting to behave badly, to play around at the back of the class, to be disruptive, to cause havoc. Mrs Kincaid asked if something is going on at home, says Mum. She said Matti is a lovely boy, and is very bright, but his marks have fallen dramatically and he is not paying attention to anything; his focus has gone. I said he was under a lot of pressure at home, from Rashid, says Mum.

Matti is always anxious these days. And always doing his homework. Sometimes I feel glad I'm not Dad's child. At least he doesn't care if I do well or not at school. None of us wants to be hit while doing our homework. Now, when Matti is hit, Babs has learnt to joke.

Babs behaves like a baby with everyone – although she's six, she's like a little child. The smallest in her class, says Mum. Everyone thinks she's really cute, and she's clever. I can see Babs is a survivor. She's clever enough to understand people, to figure out how to get her way and at the same time get through the hard things. Babs uses her charm to survive, and acts the baby too. Maybe she thinks like us, if you never grow up, it will be easier. I somehow feel Babs will be all right. But Matti, says Mum, is the sensitive one. He is sucking his thumb in class, Mrs Kincaid says, and he is eight. He feels things. Amy and Matti are very close, and Babs is close to me. Be careful what you say in front of Babs, says Mum. It might get back to Dad. She has Dad's brains, but fortunately, I think, neither Matti nor Babs has his character, his cruelty, his insanity.

I feel so sorry for Matti when he trembles and shakes as he does his homework. Babs just smiles and lets her smile light up her face. But her eyes often meet mine, and even though she is six, I can read them. We'll get through this, won't we, Mai? her eyes say behind her smile. I should know. At school I smile and laugh a lot and do well, like Babs. At school, I enjoy and make the most of every good moment I have. School is freedom, and home is prison. We are lucky we go to school and don't see Dad much, and he is only there all the time at weekends, when we stay very quiet. Sometimes, I hold Babs on my lap, and we chat and laugh and hug, and I play with the ringlets of dark curling hair. And Matti and Amy play out in the garden, and chat and talk as they climb trees and look at the blue blue sky. Only when Dad's not around.

When Dad is around, the house is quiet like death, death hanging around our house like a cloud: a heavy inert cloud, threatening. We are all scared of Dad. We are scared of what he did to the rat, scared of the story of his ex-girlfriend, of what he has done to Mum in the past. Dad can do anything. Even when you run away and change your name, he finds you. He goes to a mental home for three years and comes back after only three months. He can take away your little brother and sister to Morocco forever and tie your mother in a chair and beat her up so in the morning she has large black and blue bruises on her arms and is crying, no, no, don't take them away. Dad can punch you for reading books and doing well at school, throw Mum down the stairs because your sister has sunstroke and has thrown up, can hit you all over for saying pig to him, put you to bed for three days with no food when you are ten years old.

Rashid controls the money, says Mum. We depend on him for food, for clothes, for everything. I have a small amount of savings, from what I sold before we left England, mostly from Mrs Lara's dancing lady. If I do anything against Rashid, it will just get worse. If I stand up to him, he'll punish all of us – it will get worse for Matti and Babs, and you and Amy and me. The only thing I can do is get away again. I have to try to sort something out. And Mum has a determined look in her eyes, a look that comes from desperation and determination when there is no other choice.

I'll work on something, says Mum, don't worry, I'll sort something out. I have to. You won't have to wait too long. Then Mum laughs. Remember, she says to me and Amy, if it can't get any worse, it can only get better. We hug Matti and Babs to us when Dad's not around and they hug us. I love my little brother and sister. And I love Mum too. But I could never love Dad. He's a million million miles away from me – so far away I could never come close. Around Dad, I am closed, closed, hidden away from his eyes that stare into you, yet have no soul. Dad has hurt us all. Dad has tried to make Amy and me hate Matti and Babs by treating them better, with lots of toys and privileges, but we still love them. It's not their fault. They are his children, but first of all they are our little brother and sister. The only weapon you can have is to carry on nevertheless – to still be able to laugh and smile; to persevere. Because all you have is your spirit, the part of you that dreams of a future, where life is bright and full of roses and colour, and butterflies rise from the long blades of grass under a sunlight-streaked sky.

The sky spreads over the mountains as Mum and I walk in the street. The market women sit on the ground, cloths spread in front of them – vegetables, coconuts, potatoes, different kinds.

He's been behaving strangely again, says Mum. What do you mean? I ask. I'm worried he's started doing strange things again. Maybe it's nothing, but I'm planning to get us away from here. He's just being strange, says Mum. And I'm suspicious. I'm worried he'll do something to Babs, like he did to you. What do you mean? I say. When I was out on the weekend, Babs says he said she was dirty from playing in the garden and he took her and gave her a shower. But he never baths Babs, I always do. Maybe it's nothing, but Babs said when he was hosing her down, he spent a long time washing her between her legs. I asked if he was just rinsing her, but she said he went on and on for a long time. She showed me how, says Mum, and it didn't look like he was just washing her. Mum clenches her fists. We need to get her away. He might do something very serious to her very soon.

Are you sure he wasn't just washing her? I ask. It seems the only thing I can say. Yes, says Mum. Can't you see, Mai? He was molesting her, like when he was in the bath with you, it's the same thing, and she's getting close to the age you were, don't you see? But I don't really understand much about what she's saying. I had to wash him, I say, not the other way around. It's the same, says Mum. The same way it started with you. Exactly the same way.

I'm trying to get away again, says Mum, away from Rashid. We need to leave.

Where will we go? I ask.

Back to England. I don't have any money, Rashid never gives me any, so I'm trying to get the British embassy to get us tickets back. I've explained Rashid's past, and why it's important, and that I'm frightened he's starting again. But the ambassador is being very slow about it, and he keeps saying the British embassy doesn't deal with domestic disputes. He said Uncle Gregory has to get the tickets for us, and he wrote to Uncle Gregory for money a while back but Uncle Gregory says he doesn't have the money. And I wrote to Granddad, but he has retired to somewhere rural in France and the mail is very slow, so I haven't heard anything. I think the ambassador is a bit stupid. I've told him all the problems of before, he knows we stayed in a battered wives' home, and

Rashid has a history of abuse and went to a mental home and then abducted the children, but he says he wants to try other ways before he gets tickets for us. He says that the embassy will only take us back to England if it's a real life-and-death emergency situation. I told him it could be an emergency, Rashid is dangerous, but he keeps saying it's a domestic dispute. He says he'll try other methods first, then if that doesn't work, they will send us home. The problem is, I don't have any proof.

It's taking so long I'm worried that time is running out and Rashid will find out. I know Rashid is getting suspicious, says Mum. He knows how he's been recently and he knows I'll try to get us all away. I'm sure he suspects something. We have to leave very soon.

Don't say anything to anyone, says Mum. Not even to Amy. He can't find out. It just has to happen soon.

When do you think the ambassador will sort it out? I ask.

I don't know, says Mum. I don't know if he really believes me. He's so arrogant. And her lips tighten. Her cheeks tighten. I just hope it's soon. If Rashid finds out I'm planning to leave, things could get very serious. I think he knows I'm trying to get away. He hasn't said anything, but I think he knows. He said something the other day and I think he's guessed. But I'm not sure. I'm worried the ambassador said something to him. I just think that time's running out.

We need a backup plan if things go wrong, says Mum. If there's ever a problem, and you need to get out of the house fast, get out through the bathroom window. There's room to jump. If you need to get out to get help. Just remember, she says, if you need to escape, use the bathroom window.

And now, instead of Diwali lights, all I see in Mum's eyes is fear and when she looks at me her eyes seem somewhere else.

These days the leaves and flowers in the garden seem tense, hanging from the tips of their stems, tautened by the wind, ready to break. The ants move, mechanistic, carrying pieces of debris on their backs, thin carefully serrated pieces of red hibiscus petal, smooth-edged semicircular bite marks, like cut razor blades. At night, the sunset falls and brings strange noises, crickets, cicadas, the quiet swish of branches in infrequent breezes. I lie in bed and listen to the noises, hear them breathing with me, as if the whole house is breathing. These days I pin the washing out on the line and watch my sheet-nightie flap back and forth, drying hard and crisp in the hot sun, as if waiting for something. Mum is preoccupied, lips tight over cooking dinner. The dry heat feels as if the ground were tightening up, and the garden and house were about to crack in two. Matti and Babs play in the garden, digging in the soil and running behind the bushes, and I watch them outside. I am studying for end-of-year exams, and everything seems to be waiting, a moment in time, suspended, held tight, waiting for something to happen, something to snap.

17

Fear

At night I don't feel so sleepy. It is past bedtime. Amy is asleep. I lie in bed, thinking about the day, looking at the white-painted ceiling I can see dimly in the moonlight, trying to unravel the cracks with my thoughts in the darkness. I can just make the cracks out, thin spindly lines that vanish back into the ceiling. I hear Amy's breathing, my own, the stillness of my body under the sheet, lying in my nightdress. I listen to the noise of the insects outside, their whirring and clicking.

Thud. I hear a noise.

Murmurs. Murmuring voices.

Thud.

Scraping, slithering sound from Mum and Dad's room next door. Like the bed moving.

Don't, Rashid. Don't do it. Mum's voice. She's scared.

Another thud. Don't, Rashid.

A scream. A long loud scream.

Then silence.

I sit bolt upright in bed. Is Mum okay? And more silence.

Is that a faint sound of voices, of movement, from far away? Then I hear him walk out their bedroom, down the corridor, past our door. To another room? I don't know which. I'm sitting up in my bed, in the dark, my ears like sharp razors, trying to catch another sound from Mum. I only hear my own breathing. I listen for Mum again, but hear nothing.

What has he done to her?

Only quiet.

Where is Dad?

It is so quiet. I can't hear anything over the sound of my heart beating. It is too quiet. Why isn't Mum screaming any more? Did he kill her?

He's done it, I think. He's done it. He's killed her.

The fear pierces hard, catches my breath like a needle sewing through me. Should I run in there to see if she's okay? What do I do?

The kitchen back door opens. It's still quiet. I'm listening for sounds in the room next door. I daren't move. Amy is sleeping on her bed on the other side of the room. All I hear is dark. Voices. Out the back. Must be the neighbours. I hear Dad. He's talking loud. He's calling to the neighbours. They must have come around because they heard Mum scream. The back door must be open. Here, noise carries far. It's okay, it's okay, he calls. Elizabeth saw a mouse. He laughs. She got a shock and screamed. It's okay now. It's all right, he says again. Elizabeth saw a mouse, that's why she screamed. Everything's fine now. No really, thanks, everything's fine. You can go back now.

But where's Mum? Why can't I hear Mum screaming any more? Why is it so quiet? Where is Mum? There're more voices, quieter now. The neighbours' voices drift away. I want to shout out, no don't go! But I can't say anything, I'm too scared. I sit up in bed, not even moving, mind darting like a frightened glowfly around and around the room.

I should run in there, to see if she's okay. But then I hear the kitchen door close and lock and his footsteps coming back again, down the corridor. My breath is fast, like his footsteps. My heart is jumping around in my chest like the rat under the red bucket. It is still quiet. His feet walk past our bedroom door into their bedroom. As soon as his footsteps go in, I hear them come out again. Fast. His footsteps pass quickly down the corridor, into the sitting room, then the hall, then I hear him open up Babs and Matti's room next door, the click of the light switch going on and then off, then the door closing again, then he goes back into the kitchen. Then the kitchen back door opens again. More silence. It closes. Back inside the house. I hear him going from room to room again and back into the corridor. Quickly round the wooden floors of the house, rummaging. Towards our room. All this time, I sit bolt upright in bed, listening for Mum. But I still hear nothing.

The latch on our door clicks. I throw myself quietly back down on the bed and close my eyes, trying to stifle my breathing so it seems calm, pretending to be asleep, like we always do.

Mai, Amy.

I rub my eyes, blink at the light, as if half dazed.

Get up, he says, standing in the open doorway.

Sorry? Heart beating. Heart pounding.

Wake Amy up and both get dressed.

Amy is stirring, wondering what is going on, opens her eyes. What's happening? she asks.

Don't answer back, says Dad. Just get up and get dressed.

Okay, I say. I'm frightened. He has something in mind. His voice is tense, but I can see he is trying to act like everything is normal. That's when he frightens me most – I know he's planned to do something to us because he's half smiling. I don't know what he's planned. It doesn't feel good. I'm scared, because I can't hear Mum and I don't know what he's going to do. My head is racing. What should I do?

He goes out, closing the door behind him. I hear his footsteps go outside again, and he's speaking over the garden wall to the neighbours, Mr and Mrs Naidoo again, from the balcony. I can't hear what the neighbours are saying but I can hear him.

She's mentally unbalanced, he's saying over the wall. She isn't thinking straight. Don't listen to her. She had a nervous breakdown before in England, went to a mental hospital. She used to be on medication. It's not true. She's mad.

Shock cold fear anger fill me. *Don't believe him*, I want to scream. *Please don't believe him. It was him who went to a mental hospital.*

What's happening? Amy asks, rubbing her eyes.

The emergency plan, I think. The bathroom. I need to get us there. No suspicion. Must be careful.

We have to get dressed, I say. I'll go change. Get your clothes and follow me. Amy and I always take it in turns to change in the bathroom. Mum taught us to always change in the bathroom with the door locked.

Okay.

I collect my clothes together and go to the bathroom to change. My head is spinning, my ears open to all the night sounds. I am trying to work out what has happened. I can't hear Dad talking any more. Why is it so quiet? What's going on? Where's Mum? What is this panic? This helplessness? The feeling I must keep under control but I can't. I can't. How do I do it? I open the bathroom door and step inside. Quickly, I lock the door behind me as I usually do, my fingers trembling as I turn the key in the lock, head racing – what to do? What to do? I'm trying to work out what has happened. I pull on the light cord. My head is spinning, open to all the night sounds. I turn round and lean against the door as the light comes on.

In the centre of the bathroom floor, shocked by the sudden bright light, is a huge cockroach, the biggest I've ever seen. Its feelers quiver, twitch on its head. It doesn't know where to turn so it stands facing me, big brown back, feelers upright, legs frozen in jagged fear. I look at the cockroach, him trapped in the shock of the sudden light, me trapped in the bathroom. I realise I am shaking uncontrollably, trembling all over, and we stare facing each other, me trembling, the cockroach trembling too. The shaking is so violent that I lean against the door, holding my arms around me to steady myself.

Usually I hate cockroaches, but I recognise my own fear in the way it holds itself so still, so rigid, the light encasing it like a shell, both of us trapped, shuddering. It's so small in comparison to me, but right now I feel no bigger. Maybe it can hear my heart beating.

Then the cockroach turns and runs and I am left alone as it slithers into a crack in the wall. I have no crack to slither into. At least you can get away, I think. What to do? Oh my God, what do I do? We should leave by the window. But what about Amy? And Matti and Babs? What to do?

I stand, holding myself, trying to make sense. Must stay calm. Must stay calm. Amy might be here any minute. I am still shivering, and I can hear my breathing, short and shallow, but I can't waste time. I start to pull on my clothes. My head is working full speed and I pull them on automatically, like a reflex, I'm not even aware I'm dressed. As I dress, I feel my whole body still shaking, shivering all over, even my hands as I pull on my clothes.

I can hear them still talking outside, a blur of voices. I stay quiet. Got to get Amy in the bathroom too. I stand still, shivering, leaning against the bathroom door for support, thinking. I think. I still don't know what to do. Should I go back, pull her in here?

A knock at the door. I jump. It's Amy.

Mai, are you going to hurry up? says Amy. Why are you taking so long?

Do you have your clothes with you? I ask. Yes, she says. Wait a minute, I say. I open the door quietly, hastily, turn the key in its white paint-flaked socket.

Get in, quickly, I whisper. Before he comes.

But you're not finished yet …

Amy looks at my face and grins, holding her clothes. What's wrong? Why's your face all pale …? Get in, I say. Now. GET IN. I take Amy's arm and pull her inside. I close the door quickly behind her. I can still hear Dad talking outside. Then they stop talking and I hear him enter the kitchen and the back door close again. It is quiet outside. No time.

Amy is staring at me. What's wrong? Why's your face so white? It looks funny.

Get dressed. Fast.

Amy still grins. Your face looks like a ghost, she says.

Get dressed, I say again. It's serious.

What is it? What's happened? she asks, her face changing.

Dad was trying to beat Mum up. I heard noises. I think she ran out the house, she must have gone to the neighbours, because Dad is trying to convince them to send Mum back. He's saying she's mad.

What do you mean? says Amy. Is she hurt?

I don't know. He wants us to get dressed. I don't know what he's going to do to us. I don't think it's safe for us to stay here. We have to get out. We have to jump out of the bathroom window. Like we planned. Put your clothes on.

Amy's eyes are wide, startled now. She starts pulling on her clothes. What about Matti and Babs? Amy says. We can't leave them here.

There's no time, I say. We can't do anything else. We can't get near their room. If we wake them up, Dad will hear us and he'll catch us. He's planned something. I know he has. He won't hurt them, they're his children, but he can hurt us.

Amy's dressed.

Have you finished?

Yes.

There's a knock at the bathroom door. It shakes. Dad tries to open it, but it's locked. Are you ready yet? he says.

We're just changing, I say, trying to sound normal.

Hurry up.

We hear his footsteps go towards his bedroom.

We've got to get out quick, I say. Before he gets suspicious.

We walk to the far end of the bathroom, where the window is. Quietly, I release the bathroom window catch, trying not to make any noise. Heartbeat. Heartbeat. I can't hear anyone outside any more. I inch the bathroom window up slowly, making no sound. We peer out. The back garden is empty, silent in the night. Everyone is inside again. It's quite high, but not too high for us to jump down.

Quick. We don't have much time, I say to Amy. I'll go first. Then I'll help you out. I climb out of the window, scrambling out feet first, hanging from my arms from the windowsill, then push myself out from the wall. Out of the window onto the concrete below. Into the warm Joulouian night air. The smell of earth, the trees rustling, the warm air. The breath jolts out of me slightly as I land.

Amy, get on the ledge, I say. Amy jumps after me, me holding her arm, helping her down as she jumps.

Quick, I say. Now, run. To the neighbours. Then we run like crazy. We run together, me holding her hand. Ducking, we make our way along the edge of the house, over the low fence to the neighbours' house. We reach the patio and their back door.

I can see Mum inside through the glass doors. She is sitting on a wicker chair, and holds a cup of tea in one hand, her hair in a ponytail, in her blue trousers. The neighbours are there, in their dressing gowns. We start banging on the door, beating on it. Let us in … let us in … before he comes.

Mrs Naidoo opens the door. We fly inside to where Mum is on the chair.

Mum!

We both run to her. Relief floods over me. I start trembling again and now the tears come and I can't stop crying. I'm crying and crying and shaking and shaking. Mum holds me and Amy. Breathing hurts, I'm gulping air, like the time I pushed the push-chair up the hill, and all the words are falling out at once, I thought you were dead, I thought he'd killed you, you're all right, you're all right, and all the tears are falling out at once and mixing up with the words and I'm not even sure what I'm saying any more. And I feel bad I left Matti and Babs behind, but what could I do?

Did he hurt you? I ask.

I'm okay, Mum says. Then she says, I'm sorry I ran out the house and left you behind. I had to get out. He was planning to do something very bad, I could see it. He's been behaving very strangely the last few days, says Mum. Maybe he found out. I think he guessed something. Or he knew something. Maybe the ambassador from the embassy told him something. Today he knew Mr and Mrs Naidoo were going out for the evening. They said they were all going out to the theatre. He moved all the clocks in the house an hour forwards so you went to bed early. I know, because my watch was still an hour behind. He thought I wouldn't notice. Then he came in the room and said he knew I was up to something, and he said he was going to get the infor-mation from me, whatever it took. He said I was going to get very, very hurt. I was very frightened. I could see he meant it. He tried to grab my arm, and I jumped across the bed. He pushed the bed against the wall, at me, and I pushed it back, trying to keep him back. I knew I was going to get very hurt. Just like last time, or worse. He came around and grabbed me again, and this time he caught my arm, and then he hit me, and I screamed. As loud as I could. He thought Mr and Mrs Naidoo were still out at the theatre, but luckily they decided to come home early tonight instead, and they heard me scream. I heard voices and movement next door so I screamed loud again. He heard them moving around and talking loudly next door, so he went out to tell them it's okay. I ran down the corridor and out of the front door while he was talking with them and I hid under the house. I waited until he came back in, then I came under the house round here, says Mum. He tried to get the Naidoos to bring me back, but they kept me here.

How did you get out? asks Mum.

We jumped out of the bathroom window, like you said, the emergency plan, I say, and start to cry again. Matti and Babs are still in there. I couldn't bring them. I was scared he'd catch us, and I'd have to wake them up. I couldn't get them.

That's all right. Don't worry.

The neighbours watch, Mr and Mrs Naidoo and Vaneshri, their daughter, horrified.

What will we do? we ask. What about Matti and Babs?

We have to get them out, says Mum. They can't stay there with him.

Don't worry, you're safe now, say Mrs Naidoo. Have some tea.

No, I have to get them out, says Mum. It's not safe for them.

Well, there's nothing you can do now, says Mrs Naidoo. Mr Naidoo has tried talking to him and couldn't get anywhere with him and no one can get in the house without keys. He won't hurt his own children. What you need to do is rest and start fresh in the morning. You're safe here. Nobody is going to hurt you. Mr Naidoo will lock all the doors, won't you? And her eyes move to

Mr Naidoo's eyes and he says, yes, of course, and he locks the patio door with a key.

We have a spare bed for you, says Mrs Naidoo, and a mattress for the girls. Vaneshri, go prepare them. Things will be better in the morning.

I need to get them out, says Mum. It's not safe.

There's nothing you can do right now, says Mrs Naidoo. Vaneshri, take the girls to the spare room.

It's strange how when you think you're not going to sleep at all, that in no way can you fall asleep, that there's so much on your mind you won't sleep a wink, it's just pointless to try, you're just going to toss and turn all night, there are times when exhaustion is just so strong that it takes over and wins anyway and sends you into sleep the minute your head rests on the pillow.

18

Wandering

After we sleep over at the Naidoos' they tell us Mr and Mrs Shahiz will let us stay at their place for a while, while we sort things out. You can move there today, say Mr and Mrs Naidoo.

I must get Babs and Matti out first, says Mum.

He doesn't want to give them to you, say Mr and Mrs Naidoo. We asked him, we argued with him. He says he won't.

We must go to the police then, says Mum.

Why not move first, then sort things out with the police? say Mr and Mrs Naidoo. You need a rest. You've been very stressed and hardly slept all night.

No, says Mum, the children are at risk. I know he's going to start molesting Babs, if he's not already. She's at risk. I must stop him.

Mum tells them Babs said Dad had been behaving strangely. That's why I was trying to get us all away, she says. Maybe it's my imagination, says Mum, but Babs says Dad was behaving strangely with her. But she wouldn't say what. He could be abusing her right now. He already took her in the shower and he never showers her. We must go to the police station now, says Mum. She looks at Mr and Mrs Naidoo.

Why don't you rest today and then my husband can take you to the police station later, when he gets back from work? says

Mrs Naidoo. I'm sure it will all calm down and you can sort something out.

No, I must go immediately, says Mum. If you won't take me now, I'll go on my own.

I really have to get to work, says Mr Naidoo.

Mum takes a local taxi with Amy and me to the police station.

Waiting in the police station. A big queue. Want it to move fast. Waiting. It doesn't seem very busy here. There are lots of people sitting waiting around, some of them with friends, some with policemen, at the wooden tables with wooden chairs that fill the room. People are taking a long time. No one is hurried. They seem hot and sleepy. Amy has to sit down and wait at one of the tables while Mum and I queue. Mum is nervous when she reaches the front desk, trying to talk with the policeman behind it. But she's at risk, I hear Mum say to the policeman at the desk. I wait among the smell of sweat, people moving in and out. It's important, says Mum. There's not much reaction. It's urgent, says Mum again. You will have to wait, says the policeman. But a child could be at risk, says Mum. It's an issue of child safety. He has a history. He went to a mental hospital because of it. The policeman looks at her. I need to speak to someone in charge, says Mum. It's very important. I insist. If a child gets hurt you will be responsible. He has her completely on his own.

I'll get the detective, says the policeman. The policeman goes to someone in another room, behind a door, then he comes back. The detective says come to his office, says the policeman. Wait over there, says Mum to us. Mum goes off behind the counter to talk in another room.

I sit at one of the small wooden tables across the room, Amy beside me, in the corner of the police station, full of other people sitting waiting at wooden tables. We stay sitting at the table.

Nothing seems to move in here. Just lots of people sitting around. Then Mum comes back with two different policemen. They walk up to where I am sitting.

Tell them, Mai, says Mum. Tell them it's true what he did to you. That he tried to molest you, it happened to you. Tell them what your stepfather did when you were nine. So they believe me, Mum says. Tell them, Mai, that it's true. You have to tell them, Mai. What he did. What, here, Mum? I ask, looking at the two policemen and around the police station.

We have to. They don't believe that he might do the same thing to Babs. They think it's just a domestic argument. They don't realise she's at risk. They need to know it's true. Yes, it's true, I say to them. He tried to molest me when I was nine. See, his own daughter is in danger now, says Mum to the two policemen. She's reaching the same age as when he tried to molest Mai. He could be molesting her right now. You could be responsible for the risk you are exposing them to. We need to get the children out.

The policemen stand opposite and stare at me. Smell of police station. I don't even look at their faces, only their uniforms, the buttons on their uniforms, the guns slung around their hips. Can she give a statement? says the first policeman.

Is it necessary? says Mum. Isn't this enough proof?

It might help. It could come in useful if there is any sort of court case as a result.

Does she have to do it herself? says Mum. Can't I do it? We need the statement from her if it directly involves her, as a witness, says the policeman. Why are you wasting time? says Mum. We need to get them out as soon as possible and you are wasting time getting a statement. Well, says the first policeman, technically you left the house, which means that technically you abandoned the children. But I was in danger, says Mum. But technically you still abandoned the children. You should have taken them with you.

You left the parental home. I couldn't, says Mum. How could I? He was attacking me. I ran out for my own safety. You still should have taken them, says the policeman. In court, that's how it stands. How can the law be so stupid? says Mum. So you see, we need a statement that the children are at risk, and then we have to proceed from there, says the policeman. We can't do anything without it. But you need to get the children away *now*, says Mum.

If she gives a statement, it will be faster, says the policeman. Otherwise we can do nothing.

Okay, says Mum. Take a statement from her.

How old is she? asks the policeman.

Fourteen, says Mum.

The policeman looks at the other, who nods. That's fine, says the policeman. She's old enough.

Mai, you have to tell them everything that happened, says Mum to me. In detail. So they can write it all down. And don't forget anything. The more they know, the easier it will be to get the children out.

Take a statement, says the first policeman to the second. You need a second witness. Then bring it to me.

The first policeman goes away.

I'll just get some paper, says the second policeman. He goes to the desk and comes back with a clipboard with paper on it and a pen. He calls another policeman to join him and they both sit opposite me.

Tell him, Mai, says Mum. Tell him what happened to you when you were nine. Don't leave anything out.

The hot sticky sweaty day makes me feel dizzy. Swirling around me. Fat sticky hands hold the board and piece of paper. I don't feel well, Mum. My head swims.

Tell him. You have to. You don't want the same to happen to

342

Babs, do you? We have to tell them what he is capable of. It's the only way.

I sit at the table, and like an automaton, blurt it out. It sounds like a shopping list. And then he … and then he … The words come out like they don't belong to me.

What about the time you were fixing shoes? says Mum.

And I have to tell them that one too. The policeman, with the other one next to him, keeps writing, writing as I speak, as Mum sits with Amy. When I finish he pushes the paper towards me. Sign this please. I sign it. I'll take you to the detective again, says the first policeman to Mum.

What do Amy and I do? I ask.

Just wait here, says Mum. I won't be long. Mum and the policeman walk off with the board. Amy and I sit. The policeman who was writing the statement comes back on his own without the board and paper, and stands next to the other policeman who was the witness. They both lean against the wall next to me.

I look around the police station. I don't feel good, my head is swimming, hurting, the people and uniforms swirling around me. I rest my head on my left hand, my left elbow on the wooden table. I feel detached, as if I sit here in the centre and everything moves around me, separate from me.

There's something not quite right about her, says the first policeman to the second, so I can hear, and they both snicker.

Their words sting through the blur of the police station. I don't look at them. I pretend I don't hear. It hurts, but I switch off, just let it swirl around me, mix up with the nauseous feeling I have.

Then Mum is back. She looks upset.

Come on, Mai. They still can't do anything. They say we have to wait. They say, effectively, I left the house and abandoned the children. So he gets to keep them and there's nothing they can do for now. I can't believe we wasted all that time giving a statement.

At the end of it they tell me they can't do anything, it has to go to court. I can't do anything. They refuse to help because I ran out of the house. There's nothing else I can do to get Matti and Babs back.

Mum's mouth is clenched, taut. Her eyes look nowhere, straight ahead. It is as if she is looking inside herself instead.

Amy and I walk out with her, out again into the bright sunshine, the heat, the people, the taxis. I feel dizzy, I say, but Mum doesn't hear. She walks ahead of us.

We need to find a taxi back again, Mum says. Mum's walking fast, doesn't turn around, her back to us, weaving through the people to the taxi stop. As if she doesn't want us to see her face. At one point we nearly see it, but she turns away quickly. I walk behind, dragging my heels.

Hurry up, says Mum. She sounds tense, angry, upset. I feel dizzy, sick, nauseous.

I hate this. I hate this. I hate all of it and the more I hate it the more sick I feel. There's something not quite right about her, I hear the words ringing in my head, and I feel worse. I think: I told my story, and that's what they say.

Fareed's cry starts like the thin hum of a whistle. Mrs Shahiz covers her ears. Please, Fareed, don't start now. Don't start to cry. Fareed's thin shriek gets louder and his mouth falls open. Now it's more like the twanging of strings, up and down, up and down. Fareed sounds like a steam engine. He hits his mother. No Fareed, she shouts, please, Fareed, stop behaving this way.

We have moved to the Shahizes', who live in the same area, who have agreed to put us up. Mum is out trying to sort out things with the police and the courts, and Amy and I have to stay here during the day with Mrs Shahiz and her two children.

Fareed is plump. So is his sister. Fareed is four and his sister

Fatima is three. Fareed, no, says Mrs Shahiz. I can't give it to you. You're making too much noise.

I want my fire engine! shouts Fareed. Give me back my fire engine! The fire engine is at the top of the cupboard where Mrs Shahiz has put it, because he's driving her mad.

Fatima is riding a plastic toy car down the corridor, and she sees her brother crying so she starts too. When Fatima starts crying, she opens her mouth and screams. Her scream is louder than Fareed's. It is so loud I have to block my eardrums. It's louder than Fareed's fire engine.

How about some sweets? asks Mrs Shahiz. I've got chocolates.

No, screams Fareed, and hits his mother again. No.

Fatima is still screaming.

Quiet, Fatima, says Mrs Shahiz. I can't stand it any more.

I feel as though Mrs Shahiz is going to cry.

Then Mrs Shahiz says, okay, Fareed, have your fire engine, and she reaches up and gives it to him. Fareed grins and starts playing with it.

But Fatima carries on. What's wrong with you, Fatima? asks Mrs Shahiz. I want chocolates, screams Fatima, and Mrs Shahiz, now totally deflated, goes into the kitchen and opens the kitchen cupboard and gives them both chocolates.

At school I have missed one set of end-of-term tests because of all the chaos of last week. All my schoolbooks have been left behind at our house and I don't have any to revise from. So I just go in and complete the exams. But I do okay, because I remember most of it and the exams I missed just bring my class average down. So I haven't done too badly.

One afternoon we are working in the classroom at school, in our white blouses and tartan dresses. It is hot, but a breeze blows through the windows that are always big and open, because there are no window panes in them. I am just going out for a few minutes, says Mrs Joy our teacher, please keep working on your exercises, so we carry on working.

Then Chandra sitting by the window says, there's a man out there, and all the girls get excited and get up out of their seats to look out the window, except me. What is he doing? Fixing something over the windows. They are all pushing and shoving at the window, and giggling hysterically. I think they're silly. Haven't they seen a man before? Right now I don't want to look at anyone.

Now it's going to be holidays, with longs stretches of days for doing nothing spread in front of us.

19

Slipping

We have a room at the end of the Shahizes' house while we sort things out. Mum says she will have to take Dad to court to get Babs and Matti back. She has been told she must put in a claim of domestic abuse, saying that Babs is at risk. This week, Mum's been sorting out a lawyer.

There's a lawyer, Mrs Chanderpaul, says Mum, who says she will do it for free because even though I have no money, she says we will win the case because here the woman has automatic right to the children. Rashid will have to pay the costs if he loses, says Mum, so Mrs Chanderpaul says don't worry about fees. It takes so much time though, says Mum. We have to prepare a court summons. I'm trying to do everything as fast as possible.

It is afternoon. Mum is inside the house with us, in the lounge, and so are Mrs Shahiz and Mr Shahiz. Mr Shahiz is reading the paper, Amy and I are reading books Mrs Shahiz gave us to read, and Mum is writing notes down for the lawyer. Mrs Shahiz is sitting reading a woman's magazine and her two children are in their bedroom playing. For once, it is quiet.

The phone rings in the lounge. Mr Shahiz picks it up.

Hullo, he says, Shahiz speaking. Yes, he says. Yes, it's fine. He looks round at us as he speaks and then says, I'll just go out to the extension in the hall. Excuse me, says Mr Shahiz. Mrs Shahiz looks up from her magazine briefly as Mr Shahiz goes into the hallway. He speaks in the hallway for a short time and then comes back into the lounge. He sits back down again and picks up his paper.

Not long after, there is the sound of a car and the doorbell rings. Mr Shahiz leaps to his feet and Mrs Shahiz raises her eyebrows like a question mark as Mr Shahiz gets up and goes outside.

I'll get it. Excuse me, he says. Then Mr Shahiz comes back into the lounge again. He says to Mum, someone has come to speak with you. They're at the gate.

Why not invite them in, Ali? asks Mrs Shahiz.

No, says Mr Shahiz, they just want to see Elizabeth quickly.

Mum and Mrs Shahiz look surprised.

Who is it? asks Mum.

Mr Shahiz fidgets on his feet. I don't know, he says, just a man. He says it's important to talk with you.

Is it about the children? asks Mum. She looks worried. Has something happened to them?

Yes, it's about the children, says Mr Shahiz. Why don't you go outside to speak with him? I'll come outside with you.

Mum gets to her feet quickly to follow Mr Shahiz, and so do Amy and I and Mrs Shahiz to see what is happening. Mrs Shahiz's children have also heard the doorbell and come out and follow after their mother. We all walk down the corridor out of the back entrance of the house and around to the driveway.

In the road outside the front gate is a shiny blue car, with the engine still running and a driver and another person in the front.

Who is it? asks Mum.

Someone who has to speak with you about your children, Mr Shahiz says, you must go talk with him.

Mum quickly walks towards the big wide white metal gate that divides the road from the Shahizes' front garden. As she does so, a man steps out of the front of the car, a stranger, a biggish man, in a brown suit and wearing thick-rimmed sunglasses. The man beckons to Mum to come closer to speak to him. Mum walks right up to the gate. He says something to Mum we can't hear and then gives her something in her hand. Then the man gets back into the front seat of the car and the car drives away. As it drives past, we see Dad sitting in the back of the car. They quickly drive away from the gate, down the road, and round the corner.

Mum is left standing at the gate, staring down at what she is holding in her hands. It's a white envelope.

She opens it.

Inside is a piece of paper which she pulls out. I see her hands. They are shaking as she reads, behind the white metal gates at the end of the driveway. Mr Shahiz, thin, scrawny, slightly bent over, walks up to Mum. He doesn't say anything, but looks at Mum and the white piece of paper and the white envelope.

Mum looks up at Mr Shahiz. Mrs Shahiz is behind me, further down the driveway, with her two children and Amy.

Mum looks at Mr Shahiz, and her face is white, almost as white as the envelope, the corner of which is trembling in the breeze and glistening in the sun, and the wind blows at Mum's shoulder-length brown hair and that trembles too.

Mum stares at Mr Shahiz and Mr Shahiz shrugs his shoulders and opens his mouth as if to say something, but he doesn't seem to have found any words to say yet.

You knew about this, didn't you? says Mum.

Mr Shahiz's hands flutter like the piece of paper that Mum holds. Mum is slowly walking away from the gate towards Mr Shahiz, holding the piece of paper.

No, says Mr Shahiz, his hands still fluttering. I assure you, I didn't know this was going to happen. All I knew was that Rashid wanted to speak to you and it was important. That's what he told me. I knew nothing about it.

Yes you did, Mum says. You know this is a court summons. You had to have arranged this with Rashid. He's accused me of deserting my children. You knew the summons had to be delivered into my hands, and you knew I was going to be here at this time today. You know it's harder if he serves the summons on me, if I have to defend myself, and you knew he would have the advantage if he did it first. Don't pretend you don't know anything. You even made sure you were here to be a witness.

Mr Shahiz makes a face like he is swallowing a piece of string, but then says, I didn't know about it.

Yes you did, Ali, says Mrs Shahiz. Don't lie, she says to him angrily. You're a bad liar. Things are bad enough already. She puts her arm around Mum. You thought I was asleep, didn't you, Ali? But I heard you. I'm sorry, I should have said something to you, Elizabeth, but he's been making late-night calls to someone all week, whispering in the hallway. I didn't say anything, because I thought it wasn't anything serious, and it wasn't my position to interfere, but I should have realised what was going on. Now I realise he's been on the phone to Rashid every night this week. Last night he was on the phone again, and it was a particularly long phone call. I thought I heard Rashid's name. Go on, tell the truth, Ali. I wondered why you were whispering on the phone so long. I didn't realise they were planning something like this. I'm really sorry, says Mrs Shahiz to Mum, I had no idea.

Mum looks at Mr Shahiz, whose mouth is opening and shutting and he's saying, calm down, calm down everyone, it's not that bad.

You crook, says Mum. How long have you been telling him what I've been doing, acting as his spy? You knew he was planning this, says Mum, and you knew I was going to take him to court, and that it would be much worse if I'm defending rather than summonsing a court case. And you let him know what I was doing so he could serve a summons first. You allowed him to plan this and you collaborated, and you let me stay in your house and you never told me. You didn't even warn me. How could you be so two-faced? If you supported him, then why did you put me up in your house, and act like you wanted to help? Whose side do you think you are on?

I didn't realise … says Mr Shahiz.

Yes, you did realise, Ali, you knew all along, says Mrs Shahiz.

Mr Shahiz just stares like he doesn't know what to say, like he's confused. But underneath all that he doesn't look so confused.

It was my wife, she wanted you to stay, says Mr Shahiz. What could I do? He's Moroccan, we're from the same country. He said it wasn't a very serious thing. He's my friend, too.

Mum glares at him. If that was how you felt, you should have been honest about it, and not put us up. But you put us here and spied on us, and told him everything we've been doing. And you lied to me.

I'm sorry, says Mr Shahiz.

So am I, says Mrs Shahiz. I'm so disappointed in you, Ali. And I really apologise, on behalf of both of us. And she puts her arm around Mum's shoulder again and glares at her husband. I'm ashamed of you, Ali, really, I'm ashamed of you. I am really sorry about it all. She starts to walk Mum inside.

It will all work out all right, says Mr Shahiz. I'm sure it will work out fine. It's only a court case. Aren't you being a bit over-dramatic about all this?

They're my children, says Mum. How can I be over-dramatic about my own children? How can I be any less dramatic? This means nothing to you, doesn't it? Don't you realise what you're doing, there are children at risk here, my youngest daughter could be getting abused right this minute as we speak, and you say I'm being over-dramatic?

Mum's face looks pale and she looks like she's going to cry.

Now, now, calm down, says Mr Shahiz. All I did was call you over to the gate.

Ali, says Mrs Shahiz. Just shut up. Her voice has gone high like when she shouts at Fareed. I'm ashamed of what you have done. You should have known better. She's your guest in your house. So much for being Moroccan, you've always gone on about being hospitable to your guests, is this how you treat them? I am so ashamed of you.

Mr and Mrs Shahiz's children are just staring at us. Mrs Shahiz takes Mum inside to her room, still holding the piece of paper. She tells Fareed and Fatima to go play in the garden and, for once, they seem to know they have to behave and do what they are told. Amy and I are left sitting in the lounge with Mr Shahiz, who takes up a newspaper and makes like he is reading it. Only he stays on the same page far too long so we know he's not really reading it. All we hear is the tick tock of the clock on the mantelpiece, and the slight rustle of the newspaper between Mr Shahiz's fingers, as Amy and I sit and pretend to study, while looking at each other every now and then across the room.

I should never have trusted him, says Mum to me after. I should have known better, after all, they're both Moroccan, and of course he would be on his side, and Rashid's such a charmer and so convincing, I should have realised. I shouldn't have been such a fool as to stay here.

So now we move to Mrs Rey's, a friend of Mrs Shahiz's, while she goes away to work abroad for a few months. We get to stay in her holiday cottage which she lets out to guests next to the main house. Mum says Mrs Rey says we can stay there rent-free as we are keeping an eye on the house while she is away, so it works out fine.

Mrs Rey comes to visit us before she goes away and she seems a nice lady, with short curly hair and a smart suit, and she has a loud voice and says things just as they are. You are doing me a favour, she says, because I need a house-sitter while I'm away and my daughter Petal who is seventeen is studying away in Miami, but she will probably come and visit later in the holidays and stay in the main house and check how you are.

So we go to Mrs Rey's. It's in the capital, near the top of a huge hill, more like a mountain.

See what a nice view it is, says Mrs Rey. You can see all over the town from here. Mrs Rey's house is behind and our cottage is in front. We look down on one house after another.

Here is the holiday cottage, says Mrs Rey. We rent it to people sometimes, but no one is renting it now.

There is a bedroom with two small beds and Amy and I get to stay in there, and a bedroom for Mum.

The cottage smells clean. Empty. Too clean. Like a hospital.

Mrs Mac cleans, says Mrs Rey. She comes to do small things around the house and the garden while I'm away, and will come more often when my daughter comes. She lives just up the road.

Mrs Mac is dark and gawky and wears a headscarf and she smiles at us from a wrinkled face with a big grin and missing teeth, and makes me and Amy laugh. She is very friendly, and scruffy.

Poor Mrs Mac, says Mum, she's old and simple. They gave her lots of electric-shock treatment in the town mental home, says Mum, I think it destroyed her brain cells. I think she had postnatal depression when she was very young, and she had to go into the mental home. Her child was taken away from her, because that's what they used to do in those days and she never recovered from it. It was a long time ago.

Even though Mrs Mac is simple in the head I think she's got

it more right than most really; she's a nice person, she's a lot more real than other people because she finds lots of things funny and she always seems happy. And Mum is always nice to people like Mrs Mac and on Mrs Mac's birthday Mum makes a birthday cake and we celebrate so Mrs Mac can be happy, and I think that's why Mrs Mac likes her.

Mr Mac, Mrs Mac's husband, is also friendly, and he breeds fighting chickens.

Come see them, he says.

Mr and Mrs Mac live just a bit up the road, in a small shack-like house. Out in the backyard are small sheds with the cocks in cages.

Each cage is separate, or they'll claw each other to bits, says Mr Mac, who is toothless like Mrs Mac. Then he shows us the metal claws they put on their feet. He seems very proud of them. They are all mine, he says. He shows us a big bird, which pecks when we come near.

That's my prize cock, he says. He's won many fights for me. He never loses.

My lawyer, Mrs Chanderpaul, has offered you some work over the summer in her office, Mai, says Mum. That will give us some money to survive on while the trial happens. She would like to meet you first.

Mrs Chanderpaul, Mum's lawyer, is large, Indian, with curling black hair and a flowing red sari that looks more like a pompom than a sari when she walks. When she talks she smiles and shows large teeth between deep-red lipsticked lips.

Mai can work for me during the holidays, says Mrs Chander-paul. We need a filing assistant. There's a lot of filing to be done, and general help around the office, photocopying and so on. It will help you manage on your own as you must need the money, says Mrs Chanderpaul to Mum. And Mrs Chanderpaul smiles her big smile that stretches across her face like an advertisement.

Thank you, says Mum. We are really grateful. Mai is very bright. She'll work fast.

Work hard, Mai. It will help us a lot, says Mum. I have hardly any money left for us to live on and at least we can buy food.

I start working for Mrs Chanderpaul, filing and helping the secretaries in the office.

20

Climbing

Mrs Chanderpaul's office is in the centre of town. To get there, I have to go down the big hill. On the way back from working at Mrs Chanderpaul's, I walk uphill. It's a very steep hill. It's one of the steepest roads in Joulou. I know some people stare, they're wondering why I don't take a taxi because the hill is so steep. But I save money by not taking taxis, even though Mum said I could. When I reach the main starting point of the second part of the walk where the road levels after the first hill, and then gets even steeper, I grit myself for the climb.

That's where the Rastas are. I walk past them every day. At the top of the first hill, in the grass clearing beside the road. The Rastas seem to be everywhere, spreading through Joulou.

At the front gate of a house at the side of the clearing stands a golden-brown Rasta, holding a staff clasped in both hands in front of him, the bottom of the staff resting on the ground between his feet. He has a strong broad chest, muscles on his abdomen, long golden dreadlocks. He stands at the gate and stares out, his long mane cascading from his head, down across his body, wearing a cloth only, wrapped around his hips

Look at the white Rasta, says Amy the first time we see him, giggling. But he's not white, he's golden brown. Golden brown and delicious, and I, fourteen years old, feast on him with my eyes, curious, from the other side of the road, watching but not watching, from the corner of my eye. I think he is beautiful.

In the clearing, the other Rastas sit with black dreads, darker, smoother, equally beautiful. They smoke a sickly sweet substance that flattens them out on rocks, drapes them like growing grass under trees, with arms and legs extended, also with cloths only wrapped round their hips. All I see are their chests and arms, earthy legs rooted in the earth, and the slowness, oh the slowness, of their movements. It is as if you reach out to touch the bark of a tree with your fingers and you try to explain the feeling. I envy their sitting in the green patch at the junction of the road, their stillness as I pass by and the cars pass by. The rest of the world evaporates into spent energy and only the Rastas, through sitting still, seem to have meaning as I walk by, temporarily slowing my footsteps to coincide with their time.

The sun beats down on the standing golden-brown Rasta every day and burns his golden-ness darker. Perhaps he is white or perhaps he is brown, but where did those golden-brown dread-locks come from? He stares only into empty space, disturbing no one, and we are all sure he is mad, we laugh at the leopard-skin loincloth and the big thick club, carved from a tree root, with a large lump at the end. Secretly I sense a longing for something I do not quite understand. And the smell of sickly sweet smoke drifts across.

Stay away from that, says Mum, it's hashish.

But the smell is somehow comforting as it drifts up from the lower part of the hill and over the garden fence at night. It reminds me there are other people out there, existing in a different reality from mine. It makes me think of warmth and hair and brown bodies, and I imagine they are all resting, peaceful, quiet, with leaves and earth and the hot night warmth. The smoke pours over my path like hands reaching out and comforting me. And the

Rasta children, arms and legs sprouting with the flowers, running around between the adult Rastas, are at home among the tree roots in the patch of grass beside the roadway. And I too want to find a home among the tree roots, bury myself among flowers and watch the leaves fall from the trees, slowly, slowly, floating, drifting down like the dandelion parachute seeds we blew from their stalks when we were little children.

At the lawyer's office, there are files everywhere. The secretaries work hard, and I photocopy what they write, then I put it in files. And when a secretary wants a file, she asks me to get it from the room where all the files are in alphabetical order.

Our file is there too. When Mum hears that she asks me to photocopy her handwritten documents for her, so she has a copy of her records too. I need to know what is going on, she says. So I do it, and bring it home piece by piece, in my bag. No one notices, and no one seems to care.

At the lawyer's there's sometimes spare time in the filing room and I read through Mum's handwritten notes, which are photo-copied and are all in her file. I read what Mum has written in them. Nobody tells me to, but nobody tells me not to. There are pages and pages of them, and she keeps adding to them, as Mrs Chan-derpaul has told her to put down everything she remembers, because anything could be useful.

The first time she realised something was wrong with Rashid, writes Mum, was when he threw the bowl of soup at her when he was working in the garden. Mum writes he often forced her to have sex against her will and without her consent. And she writes that he used to take long walks for hours in the evening in South Greenstead and she never knew where he went, and at the same time there were a number of attempted rapes in the area, by a masked man the same height and build as Rashid, at the same times Rashid was walking. It may not have been him, Mum writes. But they were very long walks, and she had no idea where he went, and, although it seems crazy, there is just a slight possibility, it was just a feeling she had, and she wondered about it. She has no evidence he may ever have been responsible, but they never caught the man, and after we moved from South Greenstead the attempts stopped, at exactly the same time.

Mum also writes that when she was pregnant with Matti, Rashid refused to get her medical help when her waters broke. He left the house and she had to get Amy and me to go next door and call a midwife. And when she had our little sister, Rashid had forced her to lift heavy boxes because we were moving, even though she was pregnant, and the baby was born very premature and the nurses insisted Mum stay in the hospital, because she was physically worn out and couldn't breastfeed, but she had to come back early because she was scared for us. She writes that after he came back from abducting the children to Morocco without any warning, he would refuse to give her housekeeping money and bought all the shopping himself and she wasn't allowed out of the house.

And she writes that soon after they got married some strange things happened in the house, strange electrical things – she came into the sitting room in the evening and was about to switch on the light, but just before she did, she looked, and the front of the light switch had been removed, and there were just bare wires. And she looked around and she found the front of the light switch, with all the screws neatly next to it, in the kitchen, and she asked Rashid to put it back on again, and he said he was fixing it although she didn't remember it being broken, and at the time she just thought it was a bit strange. And when she went back in the room the light switch was back on the wall again. Mum also writes that in South Greenstead, she came home once and the kettle wouldn't work. She plugged it in and it didn't work, so she turned it off at the socket and took it to the shop and the man said, it's lucky you didn't fiddle with the kettle switch while the plug was still in, you might have been killed, someone has taken a piece out of it, it's live wires, and if you had fiddled with the switch it would have electrocuted you. The man was convinced someone had fiddled with the kettle, says Mum, but at the time I didn't believe him.

Then the electric fire wouldn't work one day and Mum was suspicious. She switched the plug off and looked at the switch and she could see there was a part missing just like the electrician had shown her. Then Mum went to Rashid and said, can you put the missing part of the fire back in again, Rashid? I know you have it.

And he got up and fetched it and put it back in again and said nothing.

Mum writes that at first she thought it was her imagination, and maybe she was just being paranoid or something, but the thing with the fire was so obvious that she wondered if Rashid had tried to kill her. But she was struggling with a little baby to breastfeed and young children, with no help from Rashid at all, and at the same time they were moving house, so she put it out of her mind. Now, she writes, she looks back and really thinks he was trying to kill her at the time, although she doesn't understand the reason, there were just too many strange coincidences. And now she wonders, even though Rashid said his previous girlfriend had killed herself when she was pregnant with his baby, who knows what really happened, maybe he had something to do with it, he had seemed so threatening when he told her about it, as if he was trying to tell her something, as if he enjoyed it.

Mum buries her head in her hands. She sits on the bed, in her yellow cotton dress with flowers, legs outstretched, the big blue folder of case notes on her lap. I sit further down the same bed, and Amy at the far end.

Shut up, shut up, the two of you!

Mum puts the blue folder she has been writing in – writing, writing, for days onto pieces of paper – down on her knees. She shouts so loud and her face is so angry.

For God's sake, can't you two be quiet? Can't you see I'm trying to work?

Amy and I stop punching each other at the end of the bed. Amy just hit me. I just hit her back. We're playing. We don't hit to hurt. Just enough to annoy each other. We're bickering, fighting between ourselves.

Then Mum is crying. The bed blankets are crumpled, and Mum's face crumples in her hands like the blankets.

Hey Mum, you're meant to be strong. Aren't all adults strong, made of steel, for me to rest my head against, and they're there, always there?

I watch the tears break out and watch them run down Mum's cheeks. I don't want to see them. I pretend they're not there.

Amy and I look at each other. We sit in silence as Mum sobs on the bed; tears race down her face, her hands shivering.

Catch the tears. Catch them before they fall. They don't belong there. Mum wears tears like they don't belong to her, like a shroud over a dead person. Take them away.

And now Mum is crying and banging her fists on the folder, still holding the pen, and she's saying, will you please both stop fighting? I have so much on my mind, so much to do. What am I going to do? What am I going to do? Don't you realise the pressure on me to get things done? Don't you realise how serious things are? You could lose your little sister and brother forever and all you can do is make it worse by fighting. I don't even know what to do. I'm under such pressure from the court case, nothing's going right, Mrs Chanderpaul's doing nothing constructive, I've hardly got any money left, I don't even know how we're going to eat next week. I keep writing and writing to people in the UK to get evidence, but everything is so slow, and so hard. How am I going to get through this? What am I going to do? How am I going to cope?

Amy's and my faces are white, white like clear smooth plastic, no emotions, no emotions. We have learnt to mask feelings. We know how to look blank, like the dead, like paintings on a wall. We both don't want to look. We don't even look at each other.

Silence.

Don't blame us, Mum, don't blame us.

God, I think Mum's going mad. She's losing it.

Sorry, Mum, I say. Sorry for fighting.

We won't do it again, says Amy. Please don't cry, Mum.

What do we do now? We feel guilty. We shouldn't have been fighting and making a noise. Maybe Mum's going to have a nervous breakdown.

Don't look at Mum. Her eyes are scrunched up and there are tears. Don't look. Her mouth is tight and taut. Her mouth scrunches, her eyes scrunch, she is angry with us and she's not my mum. She's someone else who isn't a steel pillar to cling to.

The tears are clearing.

I'm sorry, says Mum. I'm sorry, I didn't mean to shout at you both like that. I know it's hard for you too. It's just the pressure that I'm under right now. It's okay, she says. Don't worry. It's not your fault. I'm sorry. It's really not your fault. I have to get the court case ready and time is running out and it's hard to do work if you're noisy. I'm just under so much pressure, says Mum. If you want to play, you can go outside. Or else, please, bear with me and be quiet.

Then Mum is okay again. She wipes her tears, tucks in her lips between her teeth, blinks so the tears go away round the side of her eyelids, into the corners of her eyes, straightens her face out so it looks calm again.

But I feel guilty. I feel we're losing control. Control is slipping through our fingers, like we're trying to hold onto a big blanket hanging over a cliff but it's slipping out of our hands, as if a big force we can't see is taking it away.

Mum picks up the pencil and starts writing again. She is calm. But now I'm frightened. Now, her mask has slipped and with that the tears that held it on have come unstuck, and for a moment the world shatters, crumples up, tears itself apart and in the crevice all I see is broken glass. And I start to wonder when this will all finish, before that crevice opens up and cracks open and tears us all apart.

We love our mum. When she cries, we are broken up, we are scared. Mum says nothing more about it. We say nothing about it. I hold the silence inside me, and stare at the folds in the bed blanket, as if they hold all the answers. Amy stares at her feet. Maybe there is a better answer to be found there. The blanket slips as my sister moves her legs. I look at the crumpled blue wool blanket on the bed and I reach out and try to pull the corner straight, smooth it down.

Don't worry, says Mum. It's fine. We'll be fine.

But I sit there and realise we're not so fine. I look at Mum. She has grown thinner. So much thinner. And her hair seems thinner too. Her eyes seem stressed, tired. There's not enough money for food. Is that why Mum's so thin? And I'm scared. What if it gets too much for her and she really does go mad? She looks stressed and ill with stress. And I can't do anything.

The absence of Matti and Babs fills the room as Mum writes. In the silence, Mum's pencil goes scratch, scratch over the surface. There's not even their laughter or talking to fill the empty spaces. All these words gathered together for her legal statement, all these notes that I photocopy in the office and put in files like all the other files, where they just become words among words, among photocopies, among a jungle of pleas and cries and disagreements. I think where her words will end up, and how they try to explain her life, what has happened to us. But no one can explain the silence the room holds when Matti and Babs are not there and Mum has just finished starting to cry.

So, at the lawyer's office I just work harder, I just do my filing more diligently and I just look forward to my money at the end of the month, so I can give it to her.

Not long before that, Mum tells me she has a period that hasn't stopped for three weeks. She says she's worried about it. She's still bleeding.

I say, why not go to the doctor? She says she doesn't know if she can cope with it, what if it was something serious, how could she cope with it and all this at the same time? And she hasn't even got enough money for hospital bills and doctor's bills anyway.

Maybe it's not so serious, I say.

She doesn't know. It could even be cancer, she says, like your grandmother. I say, what do you think it could be? The only thing I can think of is cancer, she says. Whatever it is, it could be serious. Maybe it's not that bad, I say. But you should see a doctor. No, she says. I'll wait a bit longer and see. But, Mum, you should see a doctor. Not yet. I'll wait. We don't have the money anyway.

So maybe that's why she's getting thinner. I don't know what makes you bleed and bleed from inside. All that blood being lost.

And I just work harder and harder at the lawyer's. Every day I walk down the big hill from town. I walk past the Mother Earth Rastas, lying under the trees in a grass clearing at the top of the road, smell the strange smell they are smoking, down past the big tree with no leaves that they cover in electric light bulbs at Christmas. I pass groups of young men lounging at the side of the road who call out to Mum, me and Amy when we walk to town to get food – Whitey, whitey, can't afford to catch a taxi.

In the early evening I walk back from work, up the hill, step by step, the steepest hill I know in the town, resting as I go along. Sometimes I feel I won't reach the end, it goes on so long. Sometimes I walk backwards, to rest my legs. And when they laugh because I don't catch a taxi, I just ignore them, or look at them and then turn away. Taxis slow down beside me, and then go on when I don't stop. Mum says I can catch a taxi if I need to, but I know I don't need to: I can save her the money.

21

Fighting

The court has given Mum access to see Babs and Matti. Mum has to go with police protection if she visits them. Last time Mum tried to get police protection, the police said there was no one free to go with her, so Mum couldn't go. Now they are coming to visit us. Rashid must drop them off and collect them later.

When Matti and Babs come in the door, Mum hugs them, tight, to herself, as if she doesn't want to let them go. Matti and Babs look a bit bewildered and confused, then Babs sees me and calls out my name and runs over and hugs me. And Matti grins, he thinks he is a big boy at eight years old, so he's not going to hug anyone, but his grin is all over his face under his curly hair. Then Mum takes them into a room and talks to them on their own and then she comes out again looking worried, then she sits and writes notes while they come and play with us.

Mum calls me over.

You have to ask her, Mai, Mum says. She won't tell me because she's promised Rashid not to tell me, but I can see it's on the tip of her tongue. And Matti's too scared. You're closest to Babs and I'm sure she'll tell you. I know it's hard for you, but please ask Babs for all our sake. We have to know in order to have a chance.

Babs is smiling, her eyes beaming and her dark ringlets bouncing up and down, and Matti runs around excitedly, playing with Amy.

So I take Babs with me and next we're playing and she's laughing and then she's sitting on my lap and I hug her warm against me, her curly ringlets tickling my cheek. Then, while Amy and Matti are playing outside, I ask –

Babs, what is the name of Daddy's lawyer?

Then Babs stops laughing and says, Daddy says I mustn't say.

Babs, please tell me, I say. If you want us to be together, you have to tell me. Do you know the lawyer's name?

Yes, she says. I know the two people who come to Daddy.

Can you tell me?

Daddy says I mustn't.

Did he say you mustn't tell me?

No. Only Mummy.

So you can tell me like it's a secret, I say.

Will you keep it a secret? she asks.

Yes, I say.

Promise you won't tell Mummy, says Babs. Daddy says Mummy mustn't know.

And with my heart in my mouth I say, yes, I promise. And now all my feelings are mixed up and I feel sad, so sad.

Okay, I'll tell you only because it's you, and you're my big sister and you're special, she says. But it's a secret. Then she turns and whispers in my ear, Mr Sawyers and Mr Thomassen.

You'll keep it secret? she asks.

Yes. And you mustn't tell Daddy you told me. You must keep it secret too. It's our secret, I say. Promise? Promise, she says.

Then I hug Babs close to me, holding her tight, and she hugs me. I miss you, Mai, she says. Are we going to be back together soon? I hope so, I say.

When they go, Mum turns to me and says, did you get the name?

Yes, I say, thinking of Babs holding me close. I did.

What is it? asks Mum.

There's two names, I say, and I tell her.

And I feel like it's one of the worst things I've ever done, knowing that although I had to do it, I betrayed Babs. And I hate all of this, having to lie to my sister, having to be part of any of this. And then I think I'm doing it for Matti and Babs, for Mum and for all of us. But it still makes me feel lonely, lonelier than I have ever felt before.

I'm hoping Rashid's scared to do anything he shouldn't because the court will get him, so I think Babs is okay, says Mum, at least she seems so for now. But I don't know how long she'll be okay for. Although it's hard to tell – she won't say anything to me, she just clams up every time, I think he's told her she must say nothing to me. Either way, if he hasn't done anything to her already, I'm sure he will soon. I'm very worried about them both. I need to see them more often, she says, to make sure they're okay. Time's running out. I need to get them away from him. I've thought of running in and grabbing them if they were in the garden or something, but it might jeopardise the court case. Anyway, he guards them really carefully, he doesn't even let them out of the house and he doesn't have to, now it's the holidays.

I'm confused. Everything seems to be spinning out of control.

I'm sitting under Mrs Rey's house. It smells of old concrete, spiderwebs on the pillars and corners of the concrete floor. I've found a nice stone, a safe stone to sit under, near the edge of the house, on the side, so I can look out at the sky. I feel a bit like one of the stars floating there in the blackness. I feel important. All the noises of the town are around me. It's strange how noises hug the heat, and somehow smell is part of the heat, the smell of sweat, and the day's heat still emanating from the soil, and the curve of the wind around the pillar of the house and, underneath, the distant smell of hashish from the Rastas, the slow exhalation of smoke drifting out into the air and slowly creeping across the garden wall where it reaches my nostrils, my lips, and I inhale. And I can smell the sharp excreta of the hens, Mr Mac's cockerels with sharp claws and angry beaks.

I sit under the house among the night noises, and then I hear Mum shouting out of the door, Mai, come back, please come back, don't run away like that, don't do this to me, I've lost two children already, please don't let me lose another. And I can hear she's crying. I can hear Mum crying and, deep down, now I am happy because now I know she really loves me, and part of me says, yeah, you deserve it, because you upset me. I ate some of the food from the fridge and Mum said, you're not being responsible enough because we can't afford to just snack on food, there's not enough money, you just don't care about what's going on right now. And I replied, well, you don't care about me, you don't care either. And I'm thinking you haven't asked me once how I am, and how my exams went and what's going on in my life, you only care about Matti and Babs, and inside me I think of the job with Mrs Chanderpaul and the big hill every day, and saving the taxi fare, and the guys calling out, look whitey can't pay the taxi, and laughing, and I got up and I ran out of the house. And I think I will run away, then I realise it's scary out there and I'm not that irresponsible, I'll just sit under the house and think it out a bit.

Mum stops shouting and she closes the door again, still crying, and it goes quiet. But I feel awful too because I made Mum cry, and after waiting a while, I go back. I knock at the door, and Mum opens it, and I say nothing, and she hugs me very hard, and she says, I'm sorry, I'm really sorry I upset you, and I don't say anything because I don't know what to say, but I just look at her. Mum says, I'm sorry, I didn't mean it, Mai, of course I care about you and Amy too, it's just that things have been so difficult with Babs and Matti recently and I've been under so much stress, I'm just glad to have you safe with me.

Now I know Mum cares, I can dedicate myself to helping, because now I know I really do matter to her. But part of me still feels, God, here I am in this big world and I can feel it all changing around me, and Mum can only think about getting Matti and Babs back, and here I am shouldering everything else, Amy and Matti and Babs and Mum's worries and work, and who am I among all of this? And in that half hour under the house, I felt alive, breathing, close to the earth and soil and stars and there was the whole world out there and somehow I felt I knew who I was. I'm fourteen, I don't have a thing in the world, only two skirts, two tops, a school uniform and a sheet nightie, and my legs and arms and my brother and sisters and my mum. But somehow I'm glad I have them, they are more special to me than anything else I could ever have.

Amy comes up to me after and says, how could you run away from home like that, you made Mum cry, and I just look at her and say, of course I didn't run away, I just went and sat outside for a bit, and Amy says, that was really bad of you, Mai, she was really upset, and I don't know what to say, except all I know is that when I was outside, I felt free.

We sit in the courtroom. We are here so Mum can start the pre-liminaries. Something to get the official court case started, to set a date. It will be very short, says Mum.

We sit on wooden benches at the side of the courtroom. It is packed and where we sit it is also packed, people squashed up together. A bench faces us and people sit directly opposite, so their knees almost touch ours, and an old man with a big strong face, a square chin, big strong shoulders and body, sits directly opposite me. People are waiting, like at the doctor's room. The judge prescribes fines.

They are dealing with small claims, says Mum. Simple robberies. One man is standing and speaking and then the judge hits a wooden hammer on his desk and says he has to pay fifty dollars.

The courtroom smells of sweat from the people in the room and warm air that has soaked into the benches, fresh air coming in through the big open windows where sun pours in and heats the place up.

They're just going to read our case out, then pass it through, says Mum. This will be simple.

Mr Sawyers, Dad's lawyer, and his partner Mr Thomassen appear, and slide into the courtroom. Mr Sawyers is skinny, with a weathered moustache, cheeks that sink in slightly at the sides. He looks like a crook, we whisper to each other. He says nothing. He just looks thin, while Mr Thomassen looks smart, with a small paunch.

Mrs Chanderpaul isn't here yet, says Mum. She's late. Where is she?

We wait on the bench at the side of the courtroom for others to finish. We don't know who is good and who is bad. Two people are arguing about a fence, over who agreed to what when. The judge says something, hits his hammer again, then it's all over. When the case ends people leave and more people move up. A new case is called, and people stand up and change places.

It won't be long now, says Mum. Mrs Chanderpaul had better arrive soon.

Amy and I wait, sitting on either side of Mum on the bench. I swing my legs beneath me, look at my toes sticking out of my worn dusty sandals. The large-faced man still sits opposite. His features are strong and his skin is dark, as if he has spent a lot of time in the sun. Dark like the darkest blackened tree stump after a fire. He is old, but you can see how he must have been very strong once, and he still looks very strong. The man is staring into space. He looks directly across at me, his face a couple of feet away, looking straight at me, and he's staring into my eyes. I try to look away, but he keeps on staring at me. His eyes get wider and bigger. I can see the red rims around them, redder and pinker against his dark skin, and the whites look whiter and they have red veins. I feel frightened. Why is he staring at me like this, so hard? His eyes widen more. They look like they are popping out of his head. His mouth grimaces into a snarl, showing his teeth like a wide flat line on his face. Then he is moaning, with the same fixed expression, and his eyes seem to pop out at me even more. His moan starts small, then gets bigger and louder. Mum notices and leans forwards in front of me to protect me. His moan gets louder and louder and soon it's just one big, loud moan and he is still snarling at me. By now, the whole courtroom has heard his moaning. I am still staring at those frightening eyes. The people stop talking and shuffling around, the judge looks in our direction.

Come here, Mai, says Mum and pulls me towards her. I have moved away but the man is still staring at the place I was sitting, with the same expression, and that loud, loud moaning sound coming from his large mouth, from deep inside him.

He's having a stroke, someone says from a nearby bench. The echo of the person's words passes back along the courtroom and ends in murmuring.

Clear the court, says the judge. The courtroom starts to clear. Mum puts her arms around Amy and me and leads us out together. We all flood from the exit down the corridor, as uniformed people rush the other way.

You know, Mai, Mum says outside, I thought he was staring at you at first, that he was a bit mad or something. You must have had a bit of a shock, Mai. Poor man.

I say nothing. I still remember his eyes and the grimace confronting me and the moaning welling up inside him and filling me with fear. Perhaps those eyes had tried to ask me for help, perhaps the moan was a shout.

The courtrooms are large, balconied, so people can pass along open outside passageways from room to room. We walk around to the front upper balcony with the other people from the courtroom, to be out of the way of the people walking in the passageway.

I can see out across the balcony to the large square of green grass in front, around which hawkers sell young coconuts, with the tops hacked off for coconut milk. It is humid and hot, and lawyers and clerks wipe sweat off their brows as they rush by in the passageway behind us with papers – lawyers in black, suffering with the extremes of heat, flapping their wings in order to air themselves, trying to substitute court papers for coquettish fans.

The humidity hangs heavy, and the tension of suspended rain waiting to break wraps us all in its heat. Rainy season has been approaching again; we have felt its oiliness grow day after day. Each day new drops fill the atmosphere until it feels as if the air is one big wet cloud waiting to burst.

I stand on the law court's balcony with Mum and Amy, peering out across the grass square. The sky suddenly grows dark, and the sunlight is blotted out, and the world around us acquires an eerie grey-black dimness. There is a brief cold stillness, a dip in the temperature of a few degrees, as blackness gathers ominously over the square.

A single cool raindrop lands on my face.

It's raining, says Amy. She puts her hand out over the balcony and I follow suit. Another raindrop on my palm. Then, after a pause, another. Then, suddenly, two together, then three, a triplet, dancing. Instantly afterwards, my hand is filled with water, as rain pours down.

The onslaught of rain creeps like a mist across the square, across the few trees, and the large patch of clear green grass, veiling it.

Look, says Mum. She points to the right. Through the rain, I see brown figures crossing the square. Brown arms, brown legs, brown chests.

It's the Rastas, says Mum. I see heads of thick hair, appearing and disappearing among the sheets of rain. Dreadlocks hang from a small child's head, from all their heads.

It's those Rastas at it again, someone laughs. It looks like they're playing music.

We look out at the group of people in the rain on the square. About twenty of them, singing, dancing, banging drums, I can't make out exactly how many, the rain is so thick, the figures appear and disappear like ghost-figures, the way figures look in pictures of rock paintings I have seen, half erased, lost in the surface of the rock.

Mum says, it looks like some kind of rain dance.

They're wearing no clothes, giggles Amy.

The Rastas form a single file. The rain lightens up briefly and I can see more clearly. No, they're wearing cloths round their hips, I say.

I watch them, sticklike in the distance, fathers, mothers, children, dancing in single file. They bang drums and sing. I can hear the music through the drumming of the rain, distant, but also clear between bursts of raindrops. The rain streams down across their semi-nakedness. They form a circle and dance and sing in the circle. The rain forms a watery curtain between them and us. Their voices grow fainter as the rain progresses, into the rumbling of thunder as a full storm breaks loose, darkening the whole square, creating a periodic stroboscopic effect as lightning flecks down, through which we see the Rastas still dancing. Then the wind changes direction and the rain pursues us onlookers back from the balcony as it drenches us in seconds.

You can go back to the courtroom now, someone says.

We move with the crowd towards the doorway leading off the balcony. I look back out at the pouring rain and I wonder what it must be like to dance naked on the grass, with the rain pouring down on young and old alike, on bodies, on drums, drumming with the rain, rain drumming on heads, on dreads, on hair and feet, feet stamping in the wet sodden grass, mud stamping between toes. As we leave the balcony, I hear the drums and the chanting through the hammering of raindrops and the beat of thunder, the swishing of the trees in the wind, and I feel the drumming inside me, and I want to run out there, and be free too.

I am still feeling the warm raindrops on my face as we are ushered back into the dry safe mustiness of the inner corridors and courtrooms. As the rain gradually dies down, outside I hear the drumming die down as well, the chanting like a hum in my heart.

Mrs Chanderpaul has turned up during the rain, puffing and panting in her sari, long curling hair around her florid made-up face.

Don't worry, dears, she says to us. Everything happens late here. It's just a preliminary. She squeezes into a seat on the bench in front of us, and every now and then turns round and smiles at us with her big red-lipsticked smile as if to say, don't worry, everything is going just fine.

When we get to our court case it all happens very quickly. Dad's lawyer stands up and says something, and Mum's lawyer stands up and says very little, then the judge bangs his hammer on the table and says a date.

That's for the proper court case, says Mum.

Next case, says the judge.

Mr Sawyers and Mr Thomassen nod to each other and get up and leave swiftly through the courtroom door.

Is that all?

It's just the way it's done, says Mrs Chanderpaul. Come on. She huffs and puffs her way out of the courtroom with us. She seems pleased. You two girls are very sweet, she says. I have two little children of my own. Don't worry, she says to Mum. It will all be fine.

Mrs Rey's daughter Petal who is seventeen and staying in Miami comes to visit us while Mrs Rey is away.

Mrs Rey's daughter Petal is not fragile like a flower. Flowers are pretty and soft, but Petal is strong, like a boy. Petal is fun and loud, not that tall. She's dark, like charcoal, so the sun gleams off her, and she has dark curly hair. I'm black, and proud of it, says Petal. She says it to her girlfriend, and laughs.

Petal's girlfriend is Amber. We think it's a bit strange a woman going out with a woman, and we ask Mum, why's that? and Mum says, they're lesbians, and we say, what is that? and Mum says, it means they sleep together in the same bed at night, like a man and wife, some people are just different that way. I think of them sleeping in the same bed and I guess it's not much different from when a man and woman sleep together at night, I suppose some women just prefer women. I don't really understand it all. I think of Kuzi and I think, well if I were grown up I'd probably prefer to sleep with Kuzi, although I'm still not sure what happens after fade-out.

Amber has got a name like a jewel, but she's even less like a jewel than Petal is like a flower. Petal is small and bouncy and black, but Amber is square and large and blonde and white. Mum says she's butch. What's that? we say. Like a man, Mum says.

Amber even has a deep voice like a man's and I reckon, well, if she's more like a man than a woman anyway, that's probably why Petal likes her, it's not that different. The only thing like amber about Amber is the orange-red colour that comes onto her cheeks sometimes when she gets worked up talking. She stands like a man and she says to Petal in her deep voice, come on, we must get going, and Petal winks at us and says, okay, time to go.

Mum says Amber seems more like a man, but she's the softer one really. Petal and Amber are nice, and they say they will both come to visit to see how things are while Mrs Rey is away.

Amber and Petal both really like Amy. Petal says Amy is very pretty and she's going to be beautiful one day. Maybe we have a boyfriend for you, Amy, and she winks again, because she's going to bring Patrick round, her cousin who's twelve, the same age as Amy. Petal likes to tease.

Then Petal looks at me and then she looks at Amber and Amber looks at Petal and then she looks at me again and their eyes seem to say something to each other and Petal says, and Mai will be pretty too when she gets older and loses some of her round chubby cheeks and gets nice cheekbones, and Amber looks at me and nods and says, yes, like I'm some sort of a sculpture they're working on or something, but I know they're just being polite because I have a moon face, everyone says so, round like the moon, and slanted eyes, and people think that's funny.

So Petal brings Patrick round and says, here's your boyfriend, Amy, and she winks again, so of course we're rude to him at first. But then we can't help talking, he's quite fun after all and he would talk to anyone, in fact he doesn't stop. He has curly hair and biggish lips.

You must call us Auntie Petal and Auntie Amber, says Petal, and that is cousin Patrick. Okay, we say. And he does feel like a cousin.

Petal and Amber take us out with Patrick for a visit to the beach and we have fun, playing in the sand and the waves.

It's a pity, says Amber to Petal. It can't be nice, two young girls stuck in all day like that on weekends and weekdays. Maybe Patrick and Amy will grow up and get married one day, says Petal, they get on very well, don't they? And she winks again.

Amy and Patrick like to race around outside together.

Mum keeps asking me to ask for my pay from Mrs Chanderpaul, it's much more than one month already, she says. I asked once, but nothing happened. Ask again, says Mum, it's already coming up to two months and she's paid you nothing yet. So I keep asking.

One day I finish my work at Mrs Chanderpaul's and she gives me a sealed envelope. You must give your mother this, she says, smiling. This is the pay for your work at the office. For everything you have done so far and to the end of this month.

Thank you, I say.

I come up the hill past the Rastas and to the house with the envelope Mrs Chanderpaul gave me, guarding it carefully. This is my pay, Mum, I say. Mrs Chanderpaul said so. At last, says Mum.

Mum opens the envelope and takes out the money. But her face changes when she takes it out. Only two hundred dollars? Is this all? Is that all she gave you? There must be some mistake. Is this for the whole time you worked? I don't say anything except, yes, Mum, that's it. It's for everything I've done. And to the end of the month.

Two hundred dollars seems like a lot to me, because I never get money like that, but Mum is saying, I don't believe it, she's had you there all that time, these last two months, and that's all she's paid you, it's slave labour, it's exploitation, it's absolutely nothing. It barely pays your taxi fare there and back these last two months. We'll never be able to survive off this. It's just a few

379

days' food, it won't last us until the end of next week. How are we going to eat? You must stop working for her, it's pointless. You're not going back.

And Mum looks so disappointed, I feel like I've been working for nothing, all those trips up and down the hill every day, all the time thinking I was helping. I know I didn't do that much there, photocopying and filing, but now I wonder if it was worth anything at all.

Mum says things are really difficult, because she tried to get a statement from Rashid's old psychiatrist, Mr Eadie, about Rashid's stay in the mental hospital and the child abuse, but Mr Eadie says it's confidential and he won't release any information. Mum's upset. She says she's trying to contact the social worker to provide a statement, but she's moved and it will take time to find out where.

It's really hard to contact people in England from Joulou. I can't get hold of people, says Mum. I can't get hold of any proof.

I wish Rashid had been prosecuted for child molestation, says Mum, at least he'd have a criminal record. I shouldn't have agreed he could go for private treatment. I was a fool. Now I can't prove anything.

Mum says she is changing her lawyer. Mrs Chanderpaul keeps making promises, but she doesn't live up to them, Mum says. She came and said her husband said she must stop representing us, says Mum, because, although before it was certain she would win the court case, Rashid is being too clever and he has crooked lawyers and he might be bribing people, and it's not going as smoothly as the Chanderpauls thought it would. So there's a risk I'll lose and that means I would have to pay them, and I can't. So now I'm going on legal aid, says Mum.

Mum goes to town with me to visit the legal-aid lawyer. He is quite young, with a beard, and seems very nice. Mum sits and talks with him while he takes notes and I wait outside the office. I think he'll be much better, says Mum.

When Mum gets home she sits down and says, we're running very short of money. When I wrote to Granddad I asked him for some money, says Mum, so we can survive, but I have no idea when the letter will get to him, or when he will get back to me. All my time has been going towards the court case. I've hardly got any money left.

I'll put an ad in the paper, says Mum. And I say, what for? and she says, I'll work as a maid, a house cleaner. Maybe we can all live in if I'm a live-in maid, because Mrs Rey will be back soon and she will need the cottage. People will think it's strange having an English maid in this country but maybe they'll see it as prestigious or something to have an English maid, so it might be easy to get work.

So Mum sits, writing out an advertisement.

I'll send it to the paper tomorrow, she says. It should come out in a few days. Mum puts the ad in the paper to be a cleaning lady. At least we'll have some money, she says.

Mum, eat more food, I say. You're not eating enough. You're getting very thin.

You think so? says Mum. Do you think I've got thinner?

Much thinner, I say.

Mum looks worried. We have to be careful with the food, she says.

Well, you should eat more. You should keep strong.

I do eat, she says. But I am worried too. Maybe I'm eating less because I'm worried.

Then you should eat more, Mum.

I'll try, she says.

22

Silence

It's Amy's birthday in a few days' time. Mum was due to go visit Matti and Babs at our old house last Wednesday afternoon, because she has visiting rights. Last time Mum was meant to visit, it was a public holiday. The police who were meant to escort her let her down. We are understaffed, they told her. Mum has rearranged to visit Matti and Babs this Friday.

Mum puts the phone down. She's just been talking to Matti and Babs. It's very strange, says Mum. I spoke to Matti and Babs on the telephone. They said Rashid took them to the mosque to pray last Wednesday morning. He's up to something, she says. I know he's up to something. He took them to the mosque to pray on the morning of the day I was due to visit, last Wednesday, before I got let down by the police. Why would he go to the mosque? He never goes to the mosque. He isn't even a proper Muslim. He even drinks alcohol. He hasn't gone in all the years I've known him. Something is up. Something's happened, or he has planned something very serious. I don't know what. Maybe he's done something to Babs. I can't figure it out. He has to have done something, or be up to something. He must be really guilty about something. Why would he go to the mosque? And he took them to the mosque with him. He's never, ever done that before. I'm worried, says Mum. I'm really worried. I must go and see them, to check if they're okay. The police have rearranged to escort me on Friday, so I'll go on Friday instead.

It's Friday morning, three days before Amy's birthday. It is very early. Amber and Petal arrive in the morning to spend the day with us. We're going out, they say, and will be back this evening, and Patrick is going to spend the day with you. See, Amy, we brought your boyfriend for you again. And they wink at us, and head off again in their car, leaving Patrick grinning at us.

It is still early. We hear Mum arguing on the phone with the police. She is angry with them. I have a meeting this morning. You promised an escort today, because you didn't come last time. Now you tell me no one is free again. There's a court order that I have to see them, and it's your duty to carry it out, I'm supposed to have police protection. A child is at risk. How can not one person be available? Next week Wednesday? No, it's not okay. I have to see if my children are okay. I'll go on my own then if you won't help. Okay, I am going on my own. Mum slams the phone down and she looks at us. I set up a meeting with Rashid today like they agreed, and now the police say there's nobody free to go with me. Again. They just can't be bothered to go, even though there's a court order. But I'll go anyway.

No, Mum, you can't go, Amy and I say. You have to get a police escort.

I have to go this morning, says Mum. Just to check on Babs and Matti. I'm worried about them, especially Babs. If the police won't come, I'll go on my own. It's fine, Rashid won't dare do anything. He's got a court case coming and he knows it will count against him if he tries anything with me and he'll lose the court case. I'm really worried about them. Why would Rashid go to pray at the mosque? It's not normal for him, he has never been religious at all. What could he have done that he has to pray to

God about it? He must have done something really bad. I spoke with Babs early this morning on the phone, says Mum, and I think Rashid has her sleeping in his bed at night, and I'm really worried. Babs started telling me something about it on the phone, and I think he must have left the room and come back in, because then she clammed up suddenly and wouldn't say anything more. God knows what he's been doing to her.

I feel something really bad has happened, says Mum. I know it. I think he's done something terrible or he's planning something. Maybe he's going to flee the country with them again. I have to see if they're okay. I'm very worried about Matti and Babs. I'm worried he'll do something to Babs, or he's done it already. I thought he wasn't going to touch Babs, he'd be too scared with the court case. I have to find out what's happened.

Mum has a distant look in her eyes as she speaks.

Mum, you shouldn't go without the police, Amy and I say.

What else can I do? says Mum. I arranged a meeting with the kids and I don't want to let them down. I'm just going to check everything is okay. He's expecting me. I'll catch a local taxi there. Don't worry, I'll be back soon. I'll be fine.

Don't go, Mum, says Amy. Wait for the police to come. Don't trust him. I'm warning you.

It will be fine, says Mum. I'll be back this afternoon, by three. He won't dare do anything to lose the case. I have to see them. I have to see if they are okay, she says.

Mum walks down the garden path to catch a taxi.

It is twelve midday. Everyone is tense.

Amy and Patrick have a big fight. I don't even know what it is about. Amy wants to hit Patrick. Patrick has locked himself in the bathroom and Amy is crying and pounding on the door. Be quiet, I say. Amy is screaming with rage. It is their worst fight ever.

I can't stand it.

Patrick comes out of the bathroom and makes friends. We are still all tense. We stay tense all afternoon.

It is three thirty p.m. Mum is a bit late.

Something's happened to Mum, says Amy. She said she'd be back at three.

No, I say, of course not, she got delayed, that's all.

It's not like her to be late, says Amy.

It is now five o'clock. Mum is still not back, and Amy is crying.

Something's happened, Amy cries, something's happened. I know it.

Maybe she had trouble getting transport back, I say. I'm sure there's a reason.

I try to put away the nervousness inside me. But as it gets later and the sun sets I look at the oncoming dark. I hope the transport was okay and the taxi didn't break down, or something didn't happen, like Dad trying one of his nasty tricks – maybe he's beating her up for information, or maybe he fled with the children to Morocco and Mum's trying to sort it out.

We continue to wait. We all watch the sky turn darker and darker and wait for Mum to come back but she doesn't. It is very, very late. It is very, very late and dark. We are all worried now. Patrick tries to joke around, but he can't cheer us up. Amy starts crying again, and doesn't stop. I know something's happened to Mum, Amy says. Something terrible's happened. She starts crying louder and louder. We keep listening for Mum's footsteps coming down the garden path, but we don't hear them. Every noise feels like the beginning of a footstep, but it isn't. Outside we hear only the night noises, cars passing, crickets chirping.

We'll have to wait for Amber and Petal to come back, I say. They'll know what to do. They shouldn't be long.

But Amber and Petal are also very late. Amy and Patrick and I wait and wait, Amy crying more and more, but soon we are all very quiet.

After eleven, Amber and Petal arrive. They are both smiling and laughing, and they are surprised to see us all waiting there quietly and Amy with tears in her eyes.

What's up? asks Amber. Where's your mother?

Mum went to see our little brother and sister at Dad's place, we say. And she hasn't come back.

I'm sure there's a reason, says Petal. Perhaps she got delayed. Did she say she was going anywhere else?

No, we say.

Perhaps she got delayed with the transport or maybe she went to see a friend, says Amber. She's probably just out having a good time. She winks at Petal, and Petal laughs.

Maybe she ended up at a party, says Petal.

She would call, I say. She would tell us if she went somewhere else.

Maybe she didn't have time.

Our Mum doesn't do that, says Amy.

She always calls, I say.

Amber and Petal look at my face, and Amy's. They can see how sure we are.

She always calls. She never lets us down, says Amy. Something bad has happened. I know something's happened. We have to find her. Something's happened to Mum. Something terrible. I know it has. Amy starts to cry again.

Now, says Petal, hugging Amy, it probably isn't that bad. Who took her to see Matti and Babs?

She got a taxi because the police wouldn't escort her like they said they would, I say. Maybe the taxi broke down and she got stuck somewhere and couldn't get back.

Do you think we should check your old house where your Dad is staying? asks Petal.

I don't know, I say, pausing. We don't like to go near Dad. Maybe, I add. She definitely went there.

Okay, we'll go check there first, says Amber, looking at our faces. Eat something first, and I'll drive you there.

I want to find Mum first, says Amy, through her tears.

It's okay, I say. We don't want to eat. We just want to see if she's okay.

It's a warm night. Amber and Petal drive the car along the familiar main road where we used to live. There's noises. The usual noises. The kind of sounds that the heat soaks up, muffles, then accentuates so they become discernible, yet are all part of the heat. The sound of crickets, cars, sometimes a voice speaking from one of the houses as we pass, trees rustling, I don't know what, it all gets mingled and blends together, so in a way it seems quiet. Only the car engine makes a noise, a phut phut, and Amber and Petal's voices, and Patrick is in the car too, and he's saying things like, I wonder what could have happened, maybe she couldn't get a taxi or something. Someone, a girl, walks past, the white headlights illuminating her like a brown-white statue; unhurried, she stops and looks at the car. The night is dark, almost moonless, so dark we can hardly see the trees. We pass along houses, lights in windows. This part of town is not congested and it's quiet now because it's a quarter to midnight, I can see on my watch. There's land and garden, and shanty houses and big houses all together, and the shanty houses are made of corrugated iron but have TV aerials sticking out of them, and you can hear snatches of TV programmes coming out of them.

Something's happened, says Amy over and over again. I know something's happened.

The night swallows us in silence.

Amber and Petal turn on the radio, joke a lot.

She probably just got held up, says Amber.

It's not like Mum, says Amy. She said she'd be back at three but she wasn't. That's not like her. She wouldn't do it.

I'm sure there's an explanation, says Amber. Don't worry, we'll be there in a few minutes and we'll find out.

The radio is playing music. I think she went partying, says Patrick. Maybe she went to a party and got too drunk to come home.

That's not funny, says Amy. My mum doesn't do that.

That's enough, Patrick, says Petal.

Are you sure it's not like her to not come back? says Amber.

She's never done it before, we say.

Can't you think of any reason she could be late? Was there anyone else she had to see?

No, I say. She'd have rung, anyway.

Yes, she always calls, says Amy.

Well, we're there now, says Amber, as she turns the car left, onto the final stretch of road before we turn into our street. Amber switches off the radio. It's quiet in this area. Trees, a stream, further down, the bridge we cross to the corner shop. We swerve gently around the corner. I feel my hopes lift as we turn, knowing we'll see her soon, find out why she's so late. It's beautifully quiet. I can hear the chirps of the grasshoppers, the rustling of tree branches, and the call of bell birds.

Oh my God, says Amber. What's this?

Towards the end of the road there are police cars. They are stretched along the road outside our driveway, in a straight line along the long low wooden fence that runs from the neighbour's garden to ours. They have bright lights. One police car is parked inside the driveway of our house. They don't have their sirens on, but their lights flash through the warm evening haziness. Red, white and blue lights, flash, flash.

Something's happened. Something's happened, says Amy. I told you something terrible has happened.

Amber drives down the road towards our driveway. We drive past the police cars, one … two … three parked down our street. Two policemen stand in our garden close to the police car in our driveway, one on the front porch, another by the police car. A third policeman stands in the hallway behind the open front door, and light pours out from inside. The police lights flicker like glow-flies, on and off.

We reach the front of the house and Amber pulls into our driveway and stops behind the police car. The two policemen walk towards us.

Something's happened to Mum, says Amy. Nobody would believe me, I told you something's happened.

We'll find out, says Amber.

I'm looking at the police cars. It's like a dream, all these lights around our house. Why are they parked in our driveway? Maybe Mum has fled the country, I think. Run away. And he's complained, trying to get the police onto her. Or maybe he ran away with Babs and Matti and she called the police.

Amber switches off the engine, and gets out as the two police-men approach. Petal gets out as well. I get out too. Stay in the back of the car, says Petal to Amy and Patrick. Just stay inside, we'll find out what's wrong.

Amber and Petal are in front of me. I hear Amber say to the policemen, what's happened? We've come to see why the girls' mother, Elizabeth, hasn't come home. We expected her back at three p.m. today.

Who are they? says one of the policemen, indicating me, and Amy and Patrick at the back of the car, with his head.

We have her two girls with us. They've been waiting for her all day. We know she came to visit her other two children, her little boy and girl who are currently with her husband, and she hasn't returned home, so we said we'd drive up and find out what is happening. Then the policeman looks at me and says, is she one of them? and they say yes. Then the policeman looks away, and steps right up really close to Amber and Petal and says something to them in a low voice right next to their ears so I can't hear. And then Amber says, oh my God, and they both just stand there, and then they talk quietly with the policeman.

What's wrong? Amy is shouting from the back of the car. You have to tell me what's happened. She's my mum. You have to tell me. She's my mum, I have to know. You have to tell me.

Then Petal walks to the car and opens the back door and puts her head in there and says something to Amy in the back of the car, and then Amy is screaming and kicking and saying, no, no, it's not true, you're lying, and she's kicking Petal, and Petal is trying to hold her still and Amy is just screaming and crying at the top of her voice, and I can see her legs and arms kicking and flying in and out of the car door. Mum's been injured, I think. He must have beaten her up really badly and now she's in hospital, really hurt, she's really badly injured and she's in a wheelchair and can't walk any more. Maybe she's brain damaged. I walk up to Amber.

What's wrong? I ask.

Amber looks at me, like she's trying to pause and think but she can't, and she speaks like the words are just taking hold of her and coming out anyway.

Your mum's dead, love. Your stepfather killed her. Today, when she came to visit.

I stare at her. Are those really Amber's words?

How?

He stabbed her to death, with a kitchen knife.

I think of the kitchen knife with the thick strong steel blade that Mum bought. I think of her saying, look at my new kitchen knife, it's a proper butcher's knife, it is really strong and sharp, and has a large orange plastic handle shaped so you can hold it properly. All I can see is the knife with the big orange handle. I know he used it.

The police are standing still looking at me and Amber. They don't know what to say. And we're just standing there, and I'm thinking, how do I know it's true? How do I know she's just not so badly injured they can't tell us and it's easier to say she's dead, because she's brain damaged or something? I'd rather know the truth even if she is brain damaged. I can hear Amy still scream-ing – it's not true, it's not true – in the back of the car, and see Petal trying to hold and comfort her, and I think, no, we have to know if it's true.

Is she inside? I ask.

Yes, says the policeman.

Can we see her? I ask.

Then they mutter together, the policemen and Amber. And they say, are you sure you want to, it might not be very nice. And I say, yes, I have to know if it's true. Then Amber says something I can't hear to the policeman. I hear the policeman say, it doesn't look too bad, she's face down, although I don't think I'm meant to hear that. Then they say, okay, they can see her. They go to Amy and ask her and she says yes, too, and she gets out of the car.

You stay here, says Petal to Patrick in the back of the car, we'll be back soon.

Then we walk up the three steps to our own front door.

They let me and Amy go in first, me at the front behind the first policeman, Amy with Petal's arm around her, still comforting her, then Amber and the second policeman behind us. We walk

392

into our hallway, then left into the wooden corridor, then left across the floorboards to the entrance of Amy's and my bedroom, and we walk into our old bedroom.

It's bare. Just the beds, the floorboards, and two policemen in the room, and everyone stops still and stops talking, even the two policemen already in the room. There's a strange quietness. And we all freeze like statues, because there she is, Mum, lying on my old bed, in the corner of the room. She's face down, dressed in her brown corduroy dress, the one she made herself. Normally you can sense people breathing – I mean, surely, hair and skin and things quiver. We take it for granted that people breathe, all the time they're moving, even when people are still, it's all moving inside them, heart, liver, cells, circulation, everything is moving, you sense it – even hairs pricking a little on the skin, tiny musculature twitches, minutiae of movement, the blink of a lid, a lip quivering slightly.

But Mum is lying so still, she's not like Mum, she's got nothing real about her. A dead person doesn't move anywhere, inside or outside; a dead person just lies really still, so still, we know even from the beginning that Mum hasn't got anything living about her, she might as well be part of a bed, or a chair. I think of all the descriptions of dead people I have read or heard about. But I never thought it would be quite like this – so still, so much like a piece of furniture, that's what Mum is, I'm thinking, she's like the bed she's lying on, my bed, the one I used to sleep in, in our house. They look the same to me. I can't see Mum's face. She's lying on her tummy, with her arms straight beside her. Even the blood dried on the back of her head looks the same as the bed: inert and motionless. It's the stillest I've ever seen her. And there's more blood. And it's still too, because it's dried in a big splash on the back of her leg. It has really matted the back of her hair, dried it a dark brown-red, hard, I imagine, tied in a ponytail at the base of her neck. I can see Mum's watch strap still on her wrist. I can't see the watch face but I guess that's still ticking, still moving. Or maybe that stopped too with all the fighting for her life. I didn't expect Mum to be so still, I expected her to be angry or something.

Everyone else seems like they're trying to be dead too, because it's like they're scarcely breathing. They pay respect to her by trying to be as deadly quiet and still as she is. The policemen in the room have taken their caps off and are holding them still and tight in their hands in front of them, like statues. There are two by the bed, guarding her, and another standing at the far end of the room, and the two policemen with us, and of course there's Amber and Petal and Amy. A fat policeman with a bulging tummy in his khaki shirt coughs and I look at him. He looks down and shuffles uneasily on his feet.

We don't mean much to the policemen, I think. That's why they're embarrassed, they don't know what to do. They're not looking directly at us, and the one who coughs looks away when I look at him. It's like the police and Petal and Amber are looking at us only when we're not looking at them.

I wonder if death is catching, if it fills the room, and makes people still and quiet, and murmur and whisper in quiet voices, as if she'll get up if they speak too loud, as if they want to keep her dead. It's like I can feel the whole room thinking, the poor children, as if their thoughts are all funnelling down onto my dead mum, who isn't moving. They're all funnelling in on her, and I'm thinking, it's like a radio switched off, that still shape, but it's not Mum, because I feel her energy still with me, not in that still body on the bed. I'm thinking, well, it's finally happened. And now I know I have to make it work on my own, for the rest of us. I'm sure Amy must be thinking the same, but I can't see her because she's behind me. Amy's gone all quiet now and she's not hysterical or hitting anyone or kicking anyone any more.

It's happened, I think. It's finally happened. It's like the end of a book.

Do you want to go now? someone asks, and I say, yes, I've seen everything now. I'm very calm, and Amy's very calm. We're both calm because Mum is somewhere with us, calming us, I know Mum wants us to get through this, to be calm for her. Anyway, what can we do about it, it's not like I haven't lived through this in my mind over and over, as if I haven't been through the pain or fear already. It's done now, I think, what I must do now is accept it, and I know Mum is somehow with me giving me strength and calm to survive.

Well, at least we know for real, I think, because imagine you only heard she died, you didn't see it with your own eyes. You'd think, no, it was a clever trick, Mum faked it because there was no other way to get out, she pretended she died so she could run away, and she couldn't let her children think she'd run away from them too, so they had to say she was dead, because it would be worse if we knew Mum had abandoned us.

The policemen say, this way, and start to lead us out the doorway. And I think, yeah, you're going to go home tonight and tell the story that you saw the dead body of this woman and that her children were there and it was really terrible and you'll probably steal her watch and gold wedding ring, because we'll never see it. And the only reason she's dead is because none of you offered to give her any police protection when she was supposed to visit her children, you never took her seriously enough. And I think how Mum says, or said, because she's dead now, how most police in this place are corrupt and they take bribes, just like the lawyers.

It feels strange that, thinking *said*. Sort of surreal, detached. Like the whole world just drifted away and only the word said is left. The present has somehow metamorphosed from the present to the irrevocable past in the simple acknowledgement of one single word. Irrevocable means you can't go back. I learnt it at school. Now I understand what it means. I think how all the emotional upheaval and chaotic events leading up to Mum's death are now all summarised in the word said. I feel cheated. It shouldn't be that easy, not just the word said. I realise, from now on, it will always have to be past tense.

What time did she die? I ask, when we get back outside.

I probably seem calm to them. Inside, thoughts are racing, tumbling over each other. But it is also clear. Final. Definite. And yet not.

Around twelve midday, says Amber. That's what the police say.

I think of the huge fight Amy and Patrick had at midday. So much anger in the air. Did we know somehow, did we feel it? I don't know. Maybe I am confused. It could have been earlier, or later. But I remember how we were at that time.

Mr and Mrs Kincaid, the neighbours, come around. Mr Kincaid is looking very excited and is talking very fast. I haven't seen him look so thin or tall before, and he looks quite pale, but it's like he's in a cops and robbers movie, talking like it's a story or something.

Where are Matti and Babs? I ask.

Your stepfather brought them to the Shahizes, says Mr Kincaid, and left them on the porch with two packed suitcases and a note for the Shahizes. The Shahizes had gone out for the evening and came home late to find the two little ones standing outside in the dark on their porch with their suitcases. The note said he didn't have a choice, they must look after them, it was the only way to sort everything out and keep his children. The Shahizes came over to the house straight away and they found your mother dead, and him drinking a bottle of wine, drowsy, and taking sleeping pills, saying he was going to kill himself.

Did he kill himself? I ask.

No, says Mr Kincaid, they took him to the hospital for a check-up but he was fine and now he's at the police station.

Of course he wasn't going to kill himself, I say. He only swallowed a few tablets, there was no way he was going to kill himself. I'm sure he just took enough to make it look like he intended it. He didn't even have to stay in the hospital. It was all fake, just to cover up, just to try to get himself out of blame. He must have planned it. Why else take Matti and Babs to the mosque on the Wednesday morning when Mum was originally meant to come over to see them?

You mustn't tell anyone, says Mr Kincaid, but I opened the suitcases and they were full of traveller's cheques for thousands of pounds that he'd saved up. It looked like he was planning to leave the country. And there were his diaries there but they're all in Arabic so I can't read them. You know, says Mr Kincaid leaning forwards in excitement, and seeming even thinner and scrawnier and wetting his lips and pausing to add suspense, what is really sinister, is that I looked in his diaries and although I couldn't read them, there is a razor blade in the diary as a bookmark for today, the day he killed her. But I couldn't read what was written in the diaries.

The diaries must explain what has been going on, they're full of his writing, says Mr Kincaid. So I took them out as evidence, along with all the traveller's cheques, and I put them in my safe at home. But you mustn't tell anyone I took them, as it's not strictly legal. You must promise, he says. Amy and I both promise.

There were lots of photographs of all of you, on outings and things, so I took them out too, and you girls can have them. Do you want them?

Yes please, says Amy.

Mr Kincaid gives Amy a plastic bag with a packet of photographs.

Corinne's parents, Mr and Mrs Maharaj, have offered to look after you and Amy for now, says Petal. It's very kind of them.

What about Matti and Babs? I ask.

Mr and Mrs Kincaid are going to look after them for now. Mr and Mrs Maharaj can't manage the four of you.

And what about our stepfather?

He's being held by the police. In a secure cell. He won't be able to get out. They will be charging him with murder. First-degree murder, and you get hanged here, says Mr Kincaid.

Did he admit to it?

He's claiming self-defence. He says your mother attacked him first.

What, Mum? She's only five foot two and he's six foot. What did she attack him with?

He says a stick, says Mr Kincaid.

So he killed her to protect himself? I say.

Don't worry, no one will believe him, says Mr Kincaid. I assure you, he won't get away with it. It won't hold. He'll get life, you'll be sure.

We'll wait and see, I say. He's very clever.

I'm not so sure. Rashid always wins. He even found us when we ran away in England and changed our names and hid in a battered wives' home with the police hiding us.

It's hard to feel. What's the point of getting angry or hurt – what good will that do, what good will anything do? I am just floating, drifting now, thinking, it's up to me now, it's up to me. Because, in life, you either sink or swim, and I've got to swim. It's up to me to keep us all together. I am so used to not feeling, not fighting, just swimming.

I don't know how we get back to the car. I don't remember what happens next, it's all a blank, really, all of it. We go here, and there, we see more people, we see the Kincaids again.

We go back to Mrs Rey's for the weekend, before we gather our things to bring to Mr and Mrs Maharaj's on Monday, and Petal and Amber stay in the cottage with us for the weekend, after dropping Patrick home.

The next morning the phone rings.

Hello, I say, picking it up.

A woman's voice. I'm calling about the advert. In the paper.

What advert? I say.

The one about the maid. Is Mrs Akbar there?

Oh, I say, remembering.

Yes, Mrs Akbar, is she there?

No, I say.

Who am I talking to?

Her daughter, I say.

Can you leave a message for when she gets back please?

Sorry, she won't be back, I say.

What, not at all?

No, I say.

Has she got another job already?

No, I say.

Oh, is she on holiday then?

No, I say.

Well, then why won't she be available?

I don't know what else to say.

She's dead, I say.

Sorry? The voice is shocked, like it thinks it heard wrong.

She's dead.

When did she die?

Yesterday.

Oh. Silence.

How?

She was killed, I say.

There is a pause.

I'm sorry. I'm really sorry to have bothered you, says the woman. She rings off. Klut. The receiver goes down.

Who was that? asks Amy.

Someone ringing about the advert Mum put in for being a maid.

Oh, says Amy.

What am I supposed to do? It seems strange, saying these things. And I think of how Mum was so unhappy with the money from Mrs Chanderpaul and how she sat writing the ad for the paper, and now it all seems so useless, there's this ad in the paper, like Mum's last hope for money, and now comes this phone call and she's not even here to get it, and none of this means anything any more.

On Monday it is Amy's thirteenth birthday and we are leaving the cottage to go to the Maharajs. Mrs Mac comes around. She has only just heard the news, and is crying, tears streaming down her face. In her hand she holds a card, a birthday card for Amy that she bought. Mrs Mac can't read and the card says 'Happy Birthday One Year Old', and Amy says, thank you, looking at the pink teddy bear and clumsy signature inside.

Mrs Mac is the only person I've seen cry about Mum. Everyone else is just excited, and busy. No one even says Happy Birthday to Amy. All these people say they care, but Mrs Mac's the only person who remembered my birthday, says Amy, as we walk down the path carrying the few belongings we have.

23

Recovery

One by one, they are gone. My teeth are falling out. I am trying to stop them, but they are crumbling. One by one, they are gone. The harder I try, the more I clench my teeth, the more they fall out. I am in despair, panicking. One by one, they crumble and crash to the floor. However much I try, I can't stop grinding them and they are all still falling.

I open my eyes. It is early morning. Amy is still fast asleep in her bed on the opposite side of the room. The sunlight pours in through the window, but I can smell it has been raining earlier, the beginning of the rainy season again. The sun has that rained-on look, as if it has been washed. I think of Mum washing the clothes outside in the sink at home, with washing powder on her hands. They have a washing machine here.

The walls of the room are bare, wood-panelled. They seem to soak in the sun and the rain, and send it out again. I look at the window, and through it see the early blue sky. I check my teeth with my tongue. They are all there.

For the last three mornings I have woken up in this room at the Maharajs, wondering if it has all been a dream. I look at the sun shining off the walls of the room. Then the horror comes back. No, it's not a dream, it's true. *One by one, they are gone.* I bury my head under the covers. I want to go back to the dream where my teeth are falling out.

Sometimes the rain smells like the clean metal edge of a knife after it has been washed.

I can hear noises from downstairs, the clanking of pans and cutlery. It's Mrs Maharaj, Corinne and Corinne's brother Jonathan, up before us, preparing breakfast. I have noticed that Mrs Maharaj wakes them before us, deliberately leaving us to sleep in. Perhaps they think it will be easier for us.

Mrs Maharaj cooks really good food. She makes curries and Italian casseroles, and the nicest, hottest, spiciest corn bread. She makes gingerbread and chocolate cake and big flat fluffy rotis she tosses up and down in her hands to make the lightest, crumbliest, crispiest, flaky rotis we've tasted.

Mr Maharaj eats lots of pepper. A Joulou man needs his pepper, he says.

Every day I have been waking up and the morning seems like a stranger. I don't understand the sun, or the rain falling outside. It is fresh and clean, as if everything is washed away. But it is so empty. No anything. Just a blank nothingness. The sun shines off the wood-panelled wall, and, although I know it is warm, and I can smell the fresh-washed brown earth outside, I can't find the warmth in any of it. Everything seems unreal, as if it shouldn't be happening.

We are walking down the street and we pass a newspaper stand and there is a billboard with big letters – MOTHER PREDICTS OWN DEATH. And on the front of the newspaper is a small old photograph from an instant photo booth, one that Amy and I took a while ago with Mum, but Mrs Maharaj tells us to move on quickly before we can look at it properly.

How did they get the photo? we ask.

I don't know, says Mrs Maharaj.

Petal and Amber must have let the reporters in on the weekend, says Amy.

Amy is angry. They stole our photo, she says. It was in Mrs Rey's cottage where we were staying. How could they steal our photo of Mum? she says.

Outside in the Maharajs' garden, the hummingbirds dash from flower to flower, poking their beaks into the centre of the large hibiscus petals, vanishing into the centre; the wind ripples the grass, and the leaves on the trees. But now all this seems cold, as if it doesn't belong here, as if Amy and I and the Maharajs' house don't belong here. I have never known days so cold and empty. I would rather be back hiding in my dreams as my teeth crumble and fall into dust, one by one, until there is nothing left in my mouth at all.

I think Mum would want to be buried in a churchyard in England, I say when the Maharajs ask me, but later everyone says it will cost far too much money to take her body back. What do you want written on the gravestone? they say.

But Mum is buried without a gravestone. I'm sorry, we couldn't afford a gravestone in the end, say Mr and Mrs Maharaj. Your mother died without any money. She only had two hundred dollars in the bank when she died and that went towards the funeral. We had a collection, but it was just too expensive – after the funeral expenses there wasn't enough money left so everyone decided to put what was left towards your schooling. We could only afford a five-year plot.

What happens after five years? I ask.

I think they reuse the grave, says Mrs Maharaj. It's too crowd-ed in the cemetery, because Joulou's such a small island. Mrs Maharaj looks apologetic. I say nothing. Just nod. These days, I have nothing to say. Why are they telling me? Why bother? As if I even had a say.

Dust to dust. Ashes to ashes, said the priest. I've only heard those words in films before. When I hear them in films people look solemn and bow their heads. I am in a film. The priest is waving a smoking bowl before him. Someone found out your mother was brought up Roman Catholic, says someone. So we gave her a Roman Catholic funeral.

At Mum's funeral I want to wear white, something pure, that symbolises what I feel for her, and celebrates what she means to me, not the darkness of blood on her hair. So I find the nearest to white I can, my cream top, and my cream skirt Mrs Kincaid bought as a present for me when she found out Amy and I had hardly any clothes. Amy and I stand at the front, in the first row of wooden benches. In the chapel on the bench behind us are all the staff of Mrs Chanderpaul's. Mrs Chanderpaul is in a large black sari, sniffling into a handkerchief, Mr Chanderpaul standing beside her. Mr Shahiz and his wife are also there, the neighbours the Naidoos, and of course Corinne's family, accompanying us. At the opposite side are Matti and Babs with the Kincaids. Mr and Mrs Mac are also there. Everyone seems to be looking at us out of the corners of their eyes. I wonder if they are staring at me because I am wearing white.

Poor children, I hear one of the secretaries whisper, I wonder what will happen to them now?

It's a small gathering. I think of all the people Mum met, and how few people seem to be here. I think how few helped her when she really needed it. I don't want to look at any of these people. They could have done something, taken Mum seriously, gone with her to see Matti and Babs.

I'm so sorry, one of the secretaries from Mrs Chanderpaul's office says I as walk down to the front bench. She came to the office a few times and she was a really nice lady. None of us really know what to say. I look at her, accepting her words. None of them seem to be really there.

I don't cry. I sit in the front row, beside Amy. At the front is a coffin, wooden, brown, plain. A priest starts saying things, waving things around, a metal shiny thing with smoke coming out of it. I concentrate on the coffin. On the closed lid.

When I first walked in, the coffin lid was open. People were going up to look inside, in a long queue. One of the secretaries from Mrs Chanderpaul's walked up and looked over, then took out a handkerchief and started dabbing her eyes. Then she let out a sob and walked back, still dabbing her eyes. I hear voices.

The poor children, without a mother …

She died so young.

How old was she?

Only thirty-nine …

How old are the girls?

Thirteen and fourteen.

It's terrible, what are they going to do now?

And the little ones?

Eight and six years old.

Why don't you go and look at your mother? asks Mrs Kincaid. They've made her look very nice. She looks really pretty.

I shake my head. I don't want to, I say. It's not real, I think. I don't want to remember her like that. It seems false.

Didn't she look lovely? I hear one of the secretaries whisper behind me. So tragic …

Amy says she wants to go see. Mrs Maharaj takes her to the front, and she comes back crying.

I want to remember my mother, face down, blood on her head and legs, and all my love for her concentrated in that moment. I'm scared she won't seem real, made pretty in a box. The real her was in that room, like an energy in the air. She won't seem real, made pretty in a box, like a plastic doll they have done up, pretending they didn't know, pretending they couldn't see what was happening, pretending they couldn't help her. I want to remember her as she was. I want to remember what he did to her.

Mum disappears into the ground, into an anonymous space of dry yellow earth. But it is not her in the ground. It is her in my mind and my limbs. It's her in the strange new energy I carry within me. I can live for Mum too. I can live for the both of us.

Nothing seems real any more.

They are going to bring Matti and Babs to spend an afternoon with us. Please speak to Matti, says Mrs Kincaid. To say what he saw. The children were the only witnesses. He has to testify as a witness at the trial. Can you ask him to tell you what happened? Then can you ask him if he will tell the courtroom the same thing and not be afraid? We'll help him all we can. All we can, we promise. We thought it best you speak with him first, as his eldest sister.

Are we going to stay together? I ask.

Yes, of course, say the Kincaids. The little ones are just staying with us for now because it's too much for the Maharajs to take all four of you at once. But you will all go back to the UK together.

But how can an eight-year-old be a witness? I say.

Apparently he can. He and Babs were the only ones who were there. Babs is too little but Matti is old enough to tell the truth from lies. That's what the court says.

Will Rashid be there in the courtroom when he tells them?

He will, but you must tell Matti not to be afraid. Just to tell the truth. That he mustn't worry.

So Matti and Babs come to visit. We play in the garden with them.

Then I take Matti to the side to talk with him. Matti and I stand together in the garden.

Matti, I have to ask you some things, I say. They are very important.

Yes, Mai, he says.

Can you remember what happened on the day Mummy died?

You mean when she came to visit? says Matti.

Yes. Can you think back and tell me everything? I need to know the truth because you're going to have to tell other people. You will need to be very brave. They have to know the truth too.

Yes, Mai.

So what happened when Mummy came to visit?

Well, Mummy came and she said hello to both of us, and she played and talked with us for a while. She asked if we were all right. Then she went in the other room.

The bedroom?

Yes, Mummy's and Daddy's bedroom.

And where were you?

Daddy told us to stay in the room next door.

You mean my and Amy's bedroom?

Yes, we use it since you're gone.

And then what happened?

We heard them talking. We heard Daddy's voice, loud.

Did you hear what he said?

No. He sounded angry. Then we heard banging sounds, like fighting.

What happened next?

We ran to the bedroom to see what was happening but Daddy told us to go back in the other room, that we mustn't come out again.

Did you see Mummy when you ran in the room?

Yes. She had a stick in her hand and Daddy had a stick in his hand. But Daddy said we had to go back and said we had to stay inside the room.

What do you mean, a stick?

I don't know. They had sticks.

So did you stay next door?

We heard more banging and then there was shouting and Daddy sounded angry. Then we heard Daddy go to the kitchen so I thought it was safe to run out and see how Mummy was.

And was she all right?

She was washing her hand in the bathroom. There was blood on it, but she said, don't worry, it's okay, don't be scared, everything will be all right, just go back, you'll be fine, everything's all right now.

Then we heard Daddy coming back so I ran in the room again and Daddy came in and he said we had to stay there and we mustn't go out or we will be in trouble and he shut the bedroom door. Then it went quiet and he went back again in the bedroom and we heard nothing. Then we heard Mummy shouting.

Shouting?

Yes, she was shouting and shouting for me and Babs to get help, to run outside and get help.

And what did you do?

We stayed there because Daddy said don't go out of the room. We were too scared. We didn't know what to do.

What was she shouting?

Matti and Babs get help, get help. She kept shouting get help. But Daddy said we mustn't move.

So then what happened?

Mummy kept shouting and shouting and she shouted and shouted for a long time and we didn't know what to do. Then it went quiet. Then I heard Daddy go outside and I went out of the room to see what was happening.

And what did you see?

Mummy was in the bathroom. She was lying down and she

was moving her head side to side and talking but I didn't understand what she was saying. And I kept saying, Mummy, are you all right? but she couldn't see me. She just kept talking to herself and moving her head side to side. Why couldn't Mummy see me, Mai?

I look at Matti. What can I say to him?

I think she was hurt, I say. What happened after that?

Then Mummy stopped moving.

She stopped moving?

Yes, she didn't move any more. Then I heard Daddy coming back and I ran back in the bedroom before he saw me.

What happened next?

Then Daddy came into the bedroom and said come out on the balcony and he had two big suitcases there. He said get in the car and he took us to Mr and Mrs Shahiz. They were out and he told us to wait for Mr and Mrs Shahiz on the porch.

And then?

He drove away and left us there, so we waited and then it got dark and we waited more and then Mr and Mrs Shahiz came home.

How long did you wait?

I don't know. A long time. It got dark and we were scared.

Is there anything else you remember?

No.

Matti, do you think if you had to say this to lots of people in a big room, you would tell them the truth?

Yes.

You see, you must tell them the truth, because it's very important. Everyone has to know what happened to Mummy. Everyone must know the truth about what Daddy did. Will you do it?

Yes.

Mai, says Matti. When will we be together again, Mai?

I don't know yet, I say. Don't worry, everyone says we'll stay together and I'll look after you now that Mummy's not here. I don't know when but we will be back together. If you tell the courtroom the truth, things should work out, and I promise you we can be together.

Where are we going to go? asks Matti.

We'll be going back to England together, I say. Babs and you are just staying with the Kincaids for now because we can't all stay with the Maharajs. When we get to England, we'll probably stay in a children's home.

You won't leave us? asks Matti.

Of course not. We're still a family. I hug him. I love you very much and you've been very brave. You must stay very brave, I say to him. Just tell the truth about what you saw. And don't worry. Then we can stay together.

Before Matti and Babs leave I hug them both. Don't worry, I promise you we'll stay together, I say to both of them. I'm your big sister and I love you both and I'll look after both of you.

He'll get convicted for murder, Mr and Mrs Kincaid say when they hear Matti's story. There is so much evidence. He'll get life, just wait and see.

We're not sure. Rashid always gets his way, say Amy and I. He always wins.

Don't be silly, of course he won't get away with it. Mr Kincaid has his diaries as evidence. All in Arabic. He confessed.

He said it was self-defence, I say.

He did. But no one will believe him. There's far too much against him, says Mr Kincaid.

We are watching the television in the TV room with Corinne and Jonathan. We are all chatting when the six o'clock news comes on and a man says the trial of Rashid Akbar concerning the murder of his wife, Elizabeth Akbar, has commenced and there is a photograph of Rashid. The man keeps talking but we stop talking. Everyone is silent. Corinne gets up and changes the channel.

See, you're famous now, says Jonathan. You're both national celebrities. You made the six o'clock news. You should be happy, and he laughs.

Amy starts crying and Jonathan is quiet.

Shut up, says Amy. Shut up.

You're stupid, Jonathan, says Corinne.

I was just trying to make them feel better, says Jonathan. I'm sorry. I thought if I joked about it, it would seem less serious.

That's my mother you're joking about, says Amy. How would you feel if it happened to your mother?

We don't see any more news after that. I think Corinne and Jonathan are told to keep the news away from us. And nobody talks to us about our mother either. Nobody really talks about anything.

Jonathan and Corinne are arguing about who will lay the table. Amy and I are in the kitchen with them. Jonathan lifts a knife and points it at Corinne, and I step back, frozen inside.

I'll kill you, heh heh, he jokes, and he waves the knife at her.

She stops and looks. Amy looks too, but Jonathan doesn't realise, he's only thirteen, but Amy, who is thirteen too, does.

Stop it, Jonathan, says Corinne. Put it away.

Put the knives away. Put the knives away, knives shining in kitchens, the sharp edges cutting through meat, through bread, through large ripe tomatoes. Put the knives away.

I remember tomatoes, peeling them from the hot water, helping Mrs Smith put them in the freezer. Slice, slice. They slice, and things fall apart. They fall apart, and the cut is so clean, you can't put the edges back again.

At dinner, people wave pieces of cutlery at you while talking, bright, shiny and sparkling, like the tip of an icicle ready to pierce.

I have never seen so many knives at once: spilling out of kitchen drawers, decoratively arranged on dinner tables, wielded in films on TV. Don't people realise they are holding murder weapons?

Sounds of Joulou music. Over the hills. Drifting up from the bottom of the road. They are rehearsing for the next carnival. The smell of rain sinking into the ground. The cry of parrots in trees. How much is real, how much not? The people, dark shapes wandering. The leaves bending under raindrops. Raindrops slide off onto the tip of my finger and I remember ladybirds.

At night, I don't like the idea of my mum under the ground. The outside world is a mass of warm leaves, dying insects – even glowflies die. I try to hide under the bedspread, pull it up over my head. It's as if the dark is trying to get in there, take over. But being under the bedclothes reminds me too much of being buried. So I poke my head out. But the dark is out here instead. Round and round in circles. Things merging, converging. I don't want to cry, Mum. I don't want to cry. And I resolve to never cry again, never. Head tucked under blankets. Hiding, hiding, from all of it. Even the night sounds outside aren't friendly any more. I keep thinking, what is happening to Mum, I can't think of her decaying, slowly going away, dissolving. I try to keep her spirit with me. What am I to think of? I didn't want to look in the coffin, I didn't want to see her made pretty, false. I wanted to see the truth, her body lying on the bed face down, blood on the back of her head and legs, so I never forget what he did to her. If we had been with her, would we be dead too? Can a world empty out like that; just empty out; become nothing? Is that what happens to the world when it empties? Do we float around, in big empty spaces, with the dark a bigger empty space? I think how I would have been waiting for her to come back, I wouldn't have believed them, if I hadn't seen her, the strange still body lying face down on the bed. And yet seeing her wasn't being with her.

I hold her within me, as much as I can, but, really, I'm here alone. And I'm supposed to make sense of it. What kind of sense is this?

I am sleepy, sleepy. Falling asleep might mean I don't wake up, but if I stay awake it's also scary. I'm scared of bad dreams too. I tell myself not to dream nightmares. I lie in bed, and hide my head under the blanket, thinking of Mum. I'm frightened to let even the tiniest bit of night in, because it's so safe under there, but also I'm frightened because it must be what it's like to be inside a coffin and that's where Mum is, so I lift the blanket back again, gasping for air. Then the world seems to be threatening again and I put my head back under the blanket for safety. I haven't known such emptiness, such coldness. It doesn't matter where I go. Even under my blankets I'm not safe from my own mind.

But I never cry. No, I could never do that, because I know I have to stay as strong as steel and never give in; if you give up swimming you sink under, and if you sink under maybe you never come up for air. So I lie under my blankets, pulling them completely over me, then off again, over and over, feeling the loneliness in the world.

Mr and Mrs Kincaid come back from the trial. Your little brother gave an amazing testimony, says Mrs Kincaid. He looked his father straight in the eye, and said everything as it was.

I think of our conversation in the garden, me and Matti. We'll be together soon, I said.

Yes, he looked his father straight in the eye and didn't look scared at all, says Mrs Kincaid. Rashid's plea changed though. He changed his plea from self-defence to not guilty due to diminished responsibility, says Mr Kincaid. He got himself a defence lawyer. A barrister. The best in the Caribbean. Paid a lot of money for him. The best. He's quite famous because he got done for contempt of court last time but he still won his case.

Oh, I say.

But he still won't get away with it, says Mr Kincaid. He hasn't got a leg to stand on. He'll get life, or hang. First-degree murder and you get hanged.

And the diaries? I ask. Will they use them as evidence?

Of course, says Mr Kincaid. But the police say they must translate them first, nobody speaks Arabic here, they might run out of time.

We'll wait and see, I say. Rashid has always got his way before.

Will we be back together with Matti and Babs soon? I ask.

Of course. No one will split you up, say Mr and Mrs Kincaid.

Are you sure? I say.

We promise you, they say. You'll be together.

24

Losing

Sorry, say Mr and Mrs Kincaid. We didn't know.

But you said we could stay together, I say. You said we could be together, even if we were all in a children's home. You said we wouldn't get split up.

I'm really sorry, Mrs Kincaid says. We really thought you could, but you can't. By law, Matti and Babs are still his children. He has the rights to them. We tried, but the law says that, even though your stepfather killed your mother, they are still his, even though they are being split from their two sisters. He has first say. We can't do anything. We know it's crazy.

But he's a murderer. He killed their own mother. How can he get them?

I know, says Mr Kincaid. But it's the law. There is nothing we can legally do about it.

Rashid's brother has come from Morocco to collect Matti and Babs and will take them back to Rabat in a few days' time, says Mrs Kincaid.

I promised them we would stay together, I say.

Sorry, there's nothing we can do, say Mr and Mrs Kincaid. You can visit them before they go.

So Rashid got them after all, I say. He got what he wanted. He killed Mum and it was the way to get what he wanted.

Inside me, I feel a well of hate. Why promise these things if they're not true? Don't they know I've already told Matti and Babs that we will stay together and now I've lied to them? And I feel I've let them both down, and Amy. I promised I'd look after them, and now everything I asked Matti to do, and promised, was for nothing, and they are my little brother and sister and there's nothing I can do at all.

They take us to see Matti and Babs at the Kincaids for an afternoon before they go away. Rashid's brother will be there, the Maharajs say. He wants to talk to you. What about? we ask. He rang beforehand and says you have personal things belonging to Rashid and it's illegal to keep them. So Rashid's brother is going to collect them from you when we go to visit Matti and Babs. Do you have any idea what he means?

I think it's the photos Mr and Mrs Kincaid took from the suitcases, Amy says. But they're all the pictures we have of Matti and Babs and Mum.

Why not keep the negatives? the Maharajs say. Just give the photos.

Okay, says Amy.

We play in the Kincaids' garden with Matti and Babs.

Then Rashid's brother comes into the garden. He looks so similar to Rashid, clean, well dressed, with rounder cheeks. We don't trust him. I don't want to talk to him but we have to. He says, Rashid wants his personal things back. We don't want to give them to him, but we're scared. So we hand over the photographs. There's not many. Little pieces of us in black and white and some colour. Like the pictures of Mum that Granddad had when we were small, sitting on the lions in Trafalgar Square.

Take them, I think. You've taken everything else anyway.

Rashid's brother takes the photographs. Thank you, he says.

416

Then he looks at them and seems surprised. Then he says, there are other things you took too. What about the other things?

Amy and I say, that's all we have, just these.

No, Rashid's brother says, Rashid says you have more of his belongings from the suitcases, personal things. It feels as if it wasn't really the photos he wanted, but something else.

No we don't, we say.

Didn't you take anything else that was in the suitcases? he asks.

No, Amy and I say again.

Are you sure?

Yes. We're puzzled.

Really, I say. We don't have anything else.

Other belongings are missing from the suitcases, says Rashid's brother. Who has them? Do you know?

I don't tell him Mr Kincaid took the diaries and traveller's cheques because Mr Kincaid said I mustn't say anything, and I promised. No, I say.

Then Rashid's brother tries to give us money, peeling several hundred-dollar notes from a wedge of them that he takes from his pocket, holding them out towards my hand.

Take, please, he says. I am sorry about everything.

No, I say, we don't want it. We're fine.

Why is he trying to give them to us? It's like he's trying to give us money to replace our mum and brother and sister. To pretend that everything's okay.

Keep it, I say.

Rashid's brother puts the money back and goes back inside the house.

I kept the negatives like the Kincaids said, says Amy. Do you think he meant those? I'm not losing the only pictures of Mum and Matti and Babs we have.

No, I say, I think it must be the diaries Mr Kincaid took. Or maybe the traveller's cheques.

It was like he was trying to bribe us, Amy says. It didn't feel nice.

I know, I say.

I watch Matti and Babs playing in the garden and I think, there's nothing I can do, that's just how it is, I promised them we'd stay together, but I let them down. I want to explain how it's not my fault. But I just hug them and smile at them. I can't find it in me to say I let them down, they don't understand I made promises and there's nothing I can do to keep them. They seem like strangers already, they've been living apart from us for months now. I can't bear to tell them I let them down.

It's not my fault, I want to say. It's not my fault. I promised we could stay together but nobody lets me have a say in anything, even though I'm your big sister. They're taking you away, and I can't do anything. I told them a lie and I can't even face seeing Matti and Babs any more.

Amber and Petal tell us a few days later that Matti and Babs are leaving on the plane next Wednesday for Rabat. We can take you to the airport to say goodbye in the morning before they go, Petal says.

Amy wants to go.

I don't.

I don't want to say goodbye to them. Everyone's tearing themselves apart from me, and it's tearing me apart from them.

You must come, Mai, says Amy. You don't know if you'll ever see them again.

No, I say.

Why not?

I don't want to go, I say. I said goodbye when I saw them last time. I don't need to do it again.

Amy looks disappointed and puzzled. Amy doesn't realise they are going away but I promised we'd stay together.

Amber and Petal look shocked. How can you not want to say goodbye to your own little brother and sister? say Amber and Petal. Amy wants to.

You are selfish, says Amy. You don't care. How can you be so cold as to not say goodbye to your little brother and sister?

I am cold.

I am so cold from it all, because I promised Matti and Babs we'd stay together. How can I face them to say goodbye? What will they think of me? I think of promising Matti that if he told the truth in court we'd stay together. They'll be so hurt I've let them down, that they have to leave. I don't want to say goodbye. I can't. I won't.

You will stay together, the Kincaids had said. They promised, but see how people are, they come back again and shake their heads. Sorry, they say, we know you wanted a gravestone for your mother, but there just wasn't enough money. Gravestones are just too expensive. Sure, I think. I'm used to people's promises. Somehow, it doesn't surprise me any more. Like Matti and Babs.

We would have loved to keep them, say the Kincaids. They're such wonderful children. If we could have, we would have.

Sure, I think. Why did you ever promise in the first place? Why do you make promises you can't keep? I won't make promises any more. And I don't listen to them. Nobody means anything they say. I'll just get back to England with Amy and somehow we'll survive.

Why don't you go see your brother and sister off? ask the Maharajs.

I don't want to, I say.

419

So I stay behind in the garden on my own while Amy and the Maharajs go off with Amber and Petal to the airport to see Matti and Babs off. Instead, I stand in the Maharajs' garden, watch the wind blow on the bushes and the leaves move, and look at the hills and the sky that is taking my little brother and sister away from me. But, inside me, I am saying goodbye, goodbye to everything.

And the next day they are gone, travelling the world.

25

Fading

The rows spread out and out. It is early afternoon. It is hot, the sun beaming down.

The walls are concrete. All around, lots of straight concrete lines next to each other.

Amber and Petal walk down the rows. Amy and I do too, carrying the two small green plants. We walk past all the rows.

Amber and Petal are looking at a piece of paper.

They keep walking, then they turn and walk down between two of the rows, still looking at the piece of paper. Then they stop.

Here we are, says Amber. This is where your mother is.

Amber points to a rectangular piece of yellow earth with nothing on it, just one or two weeds and bits of grass sticking up, and a concrete border marking the edges of the rectangle.

Amber and I stare down at the ground. Just a rectangular piece of earth.

Are you sure? I ask.

Yes, says Amber. I've got the number.

What if it's the wrong one?

No, it's not, says Amber. I'm certain this is it.

It's a big open space in the centre of the town, but it's very crowded, Amber and Petal say, because there are very few graveyards in Joulou, so there's not much room to go around. The graves go on and on, all squashed up, lots of rectangles, row after row, in double lines, one grave backed onto another. There's no grass, like I imagined graveyards to be. It's so crowded, one body next to another. Mrs Maharaj said they only got a five-year rent, because it's so crowded, and afterwards they put another body in, because they need the space. But I think, maybe no one wanted to pay the rent for another five years.

Before the funeral, Mr and Mrs Maharaj said she could have been cremated.

What does that mean? I ask.

They pause, before Mrs Maharaj replies. She says, well, she's burnt in a fire.

Oh, I say, no, I think she wanted to be buried. She once said she wanted to be buried in a churchyard.

I don't remember her going in the ground. Just the coffin rolling off behind some curtains, that's all, and the Roman Catholic priest waving a bowl on some metal chains around. They decided Mum was Roman Catholic, but I'm not so sure, I don't think so, she never even went to church.

But Mum, it would have been better if you had gone up in a ball of flame, in smoke, in a ball of angry flame so high we could all see it; better to be in smoke and fire and anger; better to blaze strong, better than us standing here by your grave tugging at little weeds and bits of earth and trying to make it look nice, because Amber and Petal say it's All Souls' Day, the day you respect the dead, you must tidy up your mother's grave, and there isn't even a gravestone because there was no money left to pay for it.

It's so easy to destroy. One push. One shove. One plunge of anger; an instant in a flash; it's too easy. So quick – destroying comes fast. I think of it, but my mind won't let me. My mind is hiding from the thoughts. And I think of the coffin crumbling, my mother's body crumbling underground, but ugh, it's too horrible to think about.

I say, but why do we need to do this, she knows we love her. So her soul can be at rest, says Petal. Amber just looks a bit surprised and says, go on, tidy it up, she'll appreciate it, God bless her soul.

So Mum, this ground is all dry and we can't grow anything in it, it's like sand and all crumbly and just a rectangular space. Amber knows where the grave is because it has a number or something, but I can't tell it was here. Amber just stopped and said, here it is, here's where your mother is buried.

And now we're digging at this earth and it's hot and there's no shade, and we're trying to make it look nice like Amber and Petal say, but really I'd rather not be here at all. And that first push of the spade is tough; it won't go in, and we need to whack it in, and it feels like it is going into her body and it makes me think what it must have been like when he killed her. I don't think we could ever make this piece of ground look nice, it's just horrible, and I don't care if Mum is under here or not, I don't think she would want us here, trying to remember her at this empty grave without a gravestone. I would rather look at the clouds and sky and all the trees and think of her, or a big bunch of flowers, or the hummingbirds, because they are more like my mum than this piece of earth we can't even get our spades in.

Amber says, good, you've turned the earth over, now we can put the plants in.

I know Amber and Petal have gone to so much effort to do this but I don't think Amy and I want to do it, we're not saying anything or talking to each other. We put in the first small plant, and Amber says, that's good, now pull out all the weeds. Then we put the other plant in but it looks very lonely on that piece of bare ground, next to the other tiny plant; it looked better with all the weeds in. But Amy really wants the plants to look nice, she pats the earth carefully around them and makes them straight. And all the time we're trying not to look at each other and around at other people at different graves because they've got gravestones and we haven't, and all we have are two little plants. And all the other people are making their graves look beautiful, with lots of flowers and decoration, and when they look sideways at us, we pretend to ignore them.

Then we hear a voice. Then two voices, out of the sky. They're laughing.

We look up from the earth and the plants.

It's two guys opposite us, they've just arrived. There's one guy sitting on a gravestone in the row behind us. The second one is beside him, leaning back on his spade. They're not so old, perhaps in their twenties, and the first one is saying, heh heh, look whitey got no gravestone, look how whitey too stingy to pay a gravestone for his own kind. What kin' a culture is that, can't even get a gravestone on his grave? Look how tight whitey is, heh heh – and the other guy beside him is laughing, leaning back on his spade.

Who die then? says the first guy. Who die you hate so much you won't pay one gravestone for his grave?

We freeze in our movements. It is so still even the earth seems to be moving more than us. I don't think I even breathe. My eyes look down at the earth, the plant just patted down by Amy's spade. We both look at the two guys, dark skin, the one who spoke with his legs spread to each side of the gravestone he is sitting on.

The world has gone still and quiet.

I think they can read the quietness in our faces, maybe in our eyes, maybe in mine, I don't know.

So, whitey, who die you won't pay one gravestone? Your family too tight to pay, or this person so unpopular? But he doesn't sound so sure now. His friend starts to look uncomfortable.

I am so frozen, I can't even blink my eyes. Amber and Petal are frozen too.

Come on, says the guy's friend to him. Stop now.

Amy looks up from where she has finished patting down the second little plant. Her face twists up like I've never seen it before.

Then Amy explodes. She picks up the big garden spade with the long wooden handle and she's waving the pointed metal end at them and threatening them with it, and she's in tears, screaming, shut up, shut up, go away, no one's going to talk about her like that, don't talk about her like that, you're not going to talk about her like that, shut up! That's my mum you're talking about! Go away, don't you dare talk about her like that. Amy is crying and her face is all twisted up and the tears are running down her face.

Then Amy takes the spade in the air above her head. It's so heavy she can barely lift it. She lifts the spade up as high as she can towards the man and aims it down at the guy's knees, staggering with the weight of it. She brings it down *whack*, and the man ducks and moves his legs out of the way just in time as it lands on the ground in front of him.

He looks shocked. Both men are very quiet.

I think you'd better leave it, Dennis, says the guy next to him.

If you want to know, says Amber, it's the girls' mother. She was killed, and she was all the family they have and now they're orphans. And they don't have any money to pay for the gravestone and nor does anyone else. So why don't you go away and stop bothering us?

The two men stare in silence.

Petal has her arm round Amy's shoulders, who's crying and crying. See what you've done now? Petal says. You're supposed to be respecting the dead, not insulting them. You'd better just go away. Why don't you look after your own family's grave? Isn't that what you're here for?

Come on, Dennis, says the other guy.

I thought *she* was their mother, mutters the man, looking at Amber.

The two go back to their gravestone on the other side of the row.

Petal still hugs Amy. I'm still frozen. Amy's so brave, lifting the spade at the guy. And so angry. It's like a big explosion. I couldn't do that. I learnt not to be brave years ago, because you don't know if that guy is going to grab your spade and beat you up so much he'll kill you.

I am still rooted to the ground, and suddenly our little rectangle of land looks even worse now, and the two plants look even more lonely and the ground even drier.

Sorry, Mum, I think. Sorry you don't have a gravestone.

I feel ashamed to be here. Mum wouldn't want us to be here either. She wanted a nice quiet corner of an English churchyard with green grass and roses, not dry yellow earth and people fighting over her grave.

The two guys come back.

Look, I'm sorry, says the guy called Dennis. I didn't think it was the girls' mother. I thought it was their grandmother or something, I mean, someone more distant. I didn't realise. I thought you were their mother, he says, looking at Amber. I'm sorry, he says, to Amy and me.

Amy and I say nothing. Amy is still wiping the tears from her eyes.

I think you've caused enough harm already, says Amber. Don't you see they don't want to talk to you?

I was just trying, says the guy. I'm just trying to say sorry. I didn't mean it that way. The two guys go away again and start digging on the other side.

I think about the word Amber used. Orphans. Is that what we are now? Is that what orphans are, like those people in books I read, all the little children in storybooks, like Pollyanna and Anne of Green Gables? I look at Amy, only just thirteen and look-

426

ing smaller than thirteen because she's always been thin and small, and she hates it when I call her thin and small, and I think of her holding the spade in the air high above her head and screaming at the man Dennis and I think, is that what orphan means? This is so strange, it's like it's not real, suddenly we're orphans digging over our mother's grave, and I look up and around the graveyard and it's full of other people digging at the graves throughout the huge graveyard and cleaning the gravestones and decorating them and putting in plants, and ours is the only one without a grave-stone. And suddenly I feel worse than I've ever felt before, and I don't care about anything, not this grave, or Amber and Petal who brought us here, I'll never feel anything any more, it's like the whole world closes off, and this is all just a picture, because if you feel anything people hurt each other, and I hate anger and I hate violence and I hate fear.

Mr and Mrs Kincaid come back again from the last day of the trial. They are shocked.

He got off, they say. He won his plea of diminished responsi-bility.

I'm sorry, Mrs Kincaid says. He had a really good lawyer and he got him off.

So he's not going to prison?

No. He's going to the local mental hospital.

How long for?

Five years. Less for good behaviour. He has his own room there, and comforts, and he can have visitors.

Is that all? I thought he was going to get life.

His lawyer was very clever. Mr Kincaid looks apologetic. Ap-parently it's hard to convict a foreigner of murder here – because they have to hang a murderer and if they hang a foreigner it

427

could be politically embarrassing. He had the best lawyer in the Caribbean.

And the diaries? I ask. I thought they were going to translate them and use them as evidence?

Mr Kincaid looks embarrassed. I don't know what happened to them. I gave them to the police. We didn't hear anything about them after that. I don't think they managed to translate them in time.

Nothing is a surprise any more.

I told you, I say. Rashid always gets his way.

Always gets his own way, I think. Nobody cares about anything. They think they did their best. But no one listened when Mum warned them. They thought she was exaggerating. If they'd believed her, and she had had some protection, she wouldn't be dead.

I'm fourteen and I don't have a say in the whole wide world, and Rashid has got off, and now there's only me and Amy left.

One by one, they crumble and fall …

26

Fluttering

I am tasting channa doubles in Joulou, two small flat fried-dough pancakes sandwiching a little curried dal in the centre, wrapped in greaseproof paper. I get the doubles from the lady who has a stall by the school gate; it is a free lunch the school provides for me and Amy now, two channa doubles, and I share it with my friends at the Spot. By the school gates are guavas that grow along the fence. We break one off and open it and there are white maggots inside. A chenette tree grows above the fence and we break off bunches of the green lychee-like fruit, break through the thin green shells with our teeth and eat the flesh to the centre, a large pip surrounded by a sweet white layer of flesh.

There is chattering around me. The hummingbirds dip in and out of the hibiscus, like darts at dartboards, hovering with wings that are merely a blur; hummingbirds don't sip as they say in books and poems, they jab ferociously at the long stamens and into the nectar-filled trumpets. The flowers swallow them up like temporary coffins, then release them, bobbing back as if to say thank you, as the hummingbirds, bright blue velvets and greens, sharp pointed beaks, dip in and out, then retreat.

The grease from the channa doubles soaks through the grease-proof paper to my fingers. I wonder why they call it greaseproof. I bite into the channa and feel the pastry rubbery between my teeth, the spicy pepper sauce biting my tongue, the yellow-green curry and soft channa dal, chickpea curry, dissolving like powder on my tongue.

We wear the school uniform, red-purple tartan and long white socks to below our knees; a pleated skirt not above knee length; a white blouse under the pinafore top – inappropriate clothes for a tropical island, but the legacy of colonialism, says Corinne's father. He believes that, as is happening now in Joulou, books must be written in local dialect, and so must the O level literature exams, which are set in Cambridge, and West Indian literature must be studied. All the history books in school have been rewritten, he says, which is why you learnt the stories of the decimation of the Amerindians by the Conquistadores, of slavery and negritude. How can you expect a West Indian schoolchild to understand a book excerpt that describes a snow scene, when they have never seen snow? Corinne's dad asks.

Sometimes there is too much pepper in the channa curry in the doubles and I feel the sweat break out around the bridge of my nose as the pepper bites. It's hot, eh? the other schoolgirls say, and my friends giggle.

I want more chilli, says Corinne, it's not hot enough.

Don't speak with your mouth full, says Patsy-Anne.

These days the sky feels bigger than ever, and emptier. The clouds above us seem far apart with huge spaces in between. The grey concrete playground and huge green grass sports field with running track seem surreal – super real and solid, unlike my and Amy's lives, which feel fragile, transparent and impermanent. I feel the channa dal chilli bite hard on my tongue and the roof of my mouth, and it is the only thing that feels real.

Now it hot enough, says Corinne, who has swamped her doubles in hot yellow habanero pepper sauce from the woman in the doubles stall. Now it hot, eh? Like chow, boy, it hot like my father mango chow. She smacks her lips and licks her fingers. Now it hot. Now it good.

Music plays. They're rehearsing in the yard at the bottom of the hill, drumming from the days of slavery tinkling out across the landscape.

When we went back to school no one said anything to us. They must have heard, I think. It was all over the news. But no one said anything. They seemed a bit quiet, but everyone seemed normal. No one ever asks how we feel. Nobody at school asks about Mum. They act like nothing happened. Nobody says anything. Maybe they think we'll forget. Or maybe they just don't know what to say.

The only person who said anything was Patsy-Anne. I'm really sorry to hear about your mother, she said, I spoke with her a few times and she seemed really kind. Thanks, I say to Patsy-Anne. Then I ask, how come no one is asking me anything about her? Don't they know? They do, says Patsy-Anne, we all heard it on the news, and the headmistress announced it over the intercom when we got back to school, and said no one is to say anything about it, not to each other or to you, and to behave like normal towards you. But I just wanted to say I'm sorry, because I really liked her. Thanks, I say.

Patsy-Anne's sorry speaks for everyone. Now I know why they are so quiet.

It was very kind of all the parents, says Mrs Maharaj, to contribute towards your education. All the parents in the school committee clubbed together to fund Amy's and your education. Without them, you would have had to leave school. It was either that or a headstone for your mother's grave. It was very kind of them, she says. You are very lucky.

Mai's always daydreaming, says Mrs Maharaj. Always lost in her own head.

I know why I'm lost in my own head. This is all there in front of me, but I can't be part of it, not the bookshelves, not the meals, not the games. I can't just race around like Amy, climbing trees and laughing all the time, I can't pretend the world is going on just like it should. When I see Amy get angry, or laugh a lot, or cry, I'm jealous, because I can't do that. I've got to be strong, to think for both of us. Because the world might look beautiful but there are other things going on at the same time.

I wander around Mr and Mrs Maharaj's garden, look at the mango tree, the hills rich with vegetation, the avocado plant Mr Maharaj said he planted that gave him his first avocado he was so proud of.

Everything seems like nothing. It is all bland. Cold. Distant. I watch Jonathan and Amy climbing trees and they say, come up, come up, you cowardy custard, and I say, no, I don't want to. I don't want to climb up the tree and look down on the world. I want to stay right here, feet planted on the ground, connected to the earth.

That way, I'm more connected to her.

In the early morning every day now, you hear the sound of the music bands warming up down the bottom of the hill, the notes trickling and tinkling through the early mist for hours and hours. I hear the notes, thin, delicate, then getting stronger and stronger as time goes on. You hear them in the afternoon and evening, after work, the tinkle as the sun sets. People are talking about the singing competition, who's going to win this year. The bands are practising hard for carnival, says Mrs Maharaj. It's very close.

But the traditional music isn't what it used to be, says Mr Maharaj. It's all this new electronic stuff now.

I realise we have been here in Joulou for almost two years.

We're looking forward to carnival. I remember the big-bellied Chinese man falling over and the sea coming rolling down the street around me.

Your Uncle Gregory has sent tickets for you to go home to England, says Mrs Maharaj. He says he will look after you and Amy. He lives in a big house in the countryside with his wife and two children. They'll give you a family. They are going to be your guardians.

I'm not so sure. Not from what Mum used to say about Uncle Gregory. I remember when Uncle Gregory gave his son a ten-pound note for Christmas, saying, I'm sorry it's late, and his son looking surprised and saying, wow, I hadn't expected that, Dad – are you feeling okay?

Can't we wait for carnival? I say.

The tickets are booked already, says Mrs Maharaj. I'm sorry, you'll have to leave before. I'm sorry, it's very short notice.

I'm used to sorry now.

I don't want to go to Uncle Gregory, says Amy when I tell her. I want to go to a children's home. Mum always said he was very selfish. Maybe he's got better over the years, I say. Mrs Maharaj says he's settled now and he runs his own business and says he will look after us very well. I don't like him, says Amy. He isn't nice. We'll manage anyway, I say to Amy. We have to, for Mum's sake. You don't think she went through all that for us not to carry on?

Can't we stay here? says Amy. I like it with the Maharajs.

If they really wanted us here then they would have asked us, I say.

When we came here Amy got on with everyone right away. Everyone says she's so open and lovable, she's tiny and cute, and the smallest in her class. I know they like her more than me, because I'm not the same, I'm closed off from people, I know it, but wherever I look I'm trying to make sense of things. I can't lose my temper and fight like Amy and Jonathan do, or Corinne, because I'm scared of anger, because when I sense anger I see Rashid's fists beating my mother, and the knife going down and down into her, it's when people lose control that people get hurt, and I want to take all the anger and feeling out of the world so people don't hurt each other.

I don't want to be a burden to anyone where I'm not wanted, I just want to be me, and all I know is I'm there to look after and protect Amy.

So I keep myself away from everything, because I know we have to leave, so I mustn't get to like the Maharajs too much. Inside my head is another person who doesn't come out and would like to run and play in the trees and garden like Amy. But I have to stay as cold and strong as steel, because that's what the world makes you do, if you want to make sure you're okay and you need to make your future work for you.

27

Circling

We are on the plane to England.

I sit next to Amy and we are by the window. Amy sits to the right of me. We can see out of the window into the airport. We have said goodbye to the Maharajs and now we are on our own.

The air hostess comes to check if we're okay. She gives us sweets to chew when we go up. We have special stickers that say *Unaccompanied Children.*

We are leaving sun and trees and mangoes and bananas and the sounds of schoolchildren and the sounds of taxis and hawkers and the sounds of a machete slicing into green coconut. We are leaving the music and singing and the records going round and round in the Maharajs' living room. It feels like leaving ourselves, our small selves down there on that small island. Us, like birds flying in the sky, but the centre of us down there, buried in the ground, among the earth, the plants, the animals, the insects.

The engine starts. Amy starts crying. I don't want to go away, she is saying. The air hostess rushes by but she is too busy to notice my sister is crying. I put my arm across her shoulder. Don't cry, Amy, I say. Don't worry, everything will be fine.

The sweets the air hostess gave us taste alien, sugary and sterile in our mouths. Eat them to stop your ears popping, she says. We chew the sweets, Amy beside me, tears rolling down her cheeks.

The aeroplane cabin feels stale, lifeless. The white bodies that fill the cabin seem cold and robotic. Everyone looks bleached. The people here smell like milk and machines and pieces of old material and cold air. They smell of lavatories and schools and pavements and oil and feet slipping on dog dirt. They smell of chimneys and cold wind and rain and air. They smell of children and shaven beards and expensive and not-expensive perfumes sprayed liberally over pale bodies. Perhaps I'm not English any more, I think.

As the plane rises in the air, Joulou shrinks below us. We rise through the conical puffed clouds that seem to reach up forever, over the blue sea. It feels like we are in a bubble in the sky – drifting, reflecting the clouds and sun and light around us, moving with the breeze and air and cold, lifeless wind – and if you pricked it, it would burst and there would be nothing.

I can see Joulou's coastline beneath us as the plane turns slowly on its flight path. I see the deep green rugged hills, the sea pulsing below on the curved beaches, the water shining and catching the light in brief flashes like a huge mirror. I think of Mattie and Babs, far away now in Morocco, how they must have felt when they left.

Your brother gave a wonderful testimony, said Mrs Kincaid. He looked his father straight in the eye, not scared at all, and told everything. I think of Matti standing in the witness box, a small eight-year-old, and his father facing him in the courtroom. He really was very brave, said Mrs Kincaid. I remember her voice and I remember the feeling I had when I found out I would never see my brother and sister again. You can write to them, she said. But it will be too hard. They are staying with Rashid's brother. Rashid has too much power. Rashid always gets his own way, I think.

I look at Amy beside me, still crying. Don't worry, Amy. I'm sure everything will be fine when we arrive. I'd rather go to a children's home than Uncle Gregory's, she says. I keep my arm around her shoulder as I look out of the window. Joulou's green patches grow smaller and smaller as we begin to move away across huge stretches of ocean.

I don't cry. I never cry. Well, I used to cry, but I don't cry any more, I have to stay strong. I have to stay strong and never cry, because if you cry all the shutters fall down and the building collapses around you and they can see you're weak inside and then you can't be strong. I can't cry because Amy will see me and she won't see there's still a future, a bright light ahead of us, because we are still going forwards. I mustn't cry because Mum said if it can't get any worse it has to get better and then she would laugh and we would laugh with her and, although it didn't work for her, it has to work for us.

It has to get better because there's no other way. Unless we give up altogether, and that's not what strong people do. And Mum would never want us to give up. She'd pat us on the back and say, don't worry, you've still got two legs and arms and you can still smile and there are still birds in the trees and the sun still shines, and some people don't even have that, so what are you being miserable about, you've got a lot of living to do on my behalf, you know. So I've got to smile and I've got to make sure I know the sun still shines and I can see the birds in the trees and that I can still laugh. If I don't laugh, then I would cry, and what would be the point of anything at all?

Don't cry, Amy, I say. A huge tear wells up in my left eye and starts to spill over. I turn my head away and wipe the tear from my eye with my finger. Then I wipe the tear starting in my right eye too. Amy mustn't see.

Don't you cry now too, Mai, I say to myself. You're the one who's strong.

I see the last green patches of Joulou and its rugged shore turning into sea, and I feel the wrench in my own body, away from the past, and away from Mum, whose body lies there, part of the island and the sea sparkling like a jewel in the sun, as we start our long journey across huge stretches of ocean. I still don't know what freedom is. Is it the moment when the jet engines force the aeroplane away from the ground, and the huge silver body carries us up, into the clouds, Joulou falling away beneath us like a green gem? Is it when the ground shrinks away, smaller and smaller behind us, and we're still there, staring out of the window, down at the world?

I am flying away like a silver bird. I ask myself, am I free? Is Mum free? Is all this over, the past behind us, this lifting of the huge metal engines a last farewell to prison, where now I can read books, brush my teeth any way I like? Free, from everything, even my family – my mother, brother Matti and sister Babs – only Amy and me left? From all these things that have been so central, so surrounding to myself – is this freedom?

In my heart, I say a last goodbye to Joulou, our past struggles, my mother who I carry inside me, and everything I have ever known. As the tears dry up on Amy's face, I tell myself all will be different in our new future.

Joulou disappears in a wash of mist. We keep circling, circling, up above the clouds, and the sun is shining and all the world is golden and beautiful and the sea is sparkling like a jewel underneath. And suddenly I realise it's not fairy tales now because there isn't always a happy ending and people don't always live happily ever after, there's only me, and all I can do is try to make the world as beautiful a place as possible and live freedom for my mum as much as I can, because now the story starts with me and where I am going.

Your life wasn't wasted, Mum, I tell myself. I am flying, I think, I am flying, and the world is spinning away and now this is the start of a new journey, and all I want to do is live, live, live, to give meaning to Mum's life. And I think again of Mum's words – if it can't get any worse, it can only get better – and in some strange way, it gives me comfort.

I remember the ladybirds. In my mind's eye I am pulling them from the hedgerows and releasing them, one by one, like jewels into the sky, shimmering, into sunlight. Where do stories end and where do they begin? I end with the ending. Or is it only the beginning? When my mother spoke of Mexico, her eyes lit up with the mists of memory. Mexico was beautiful, she said, the sights, the sounds, the sea. I see my father. I see my mother. It is hot. It is sunset. It is Mexico and their bodies are bathed in the scent of oranges and his eyes slant like the wings of gulls flying in the sky. He kisses her and she is so happy there are tears in her eyes and those tears are the tears of the world. Forever, they say. Outside glowflies circle, writing stories in their secret calligraphy of light. And if I don't catch this story and write it down, it too, like the lights of glowflies, will burn brightly, then fade away and be lost into darkness forever.

One day, I'll tell Mum's story, I tell myself, and maybe someone will hear. The aeroplane wings flash with light, on and off, on and off, and we climb up over the clouds, heading towards freedom, towards uncertainty.

ACKNOWLEDGEMENTS

No book comes into being without a world of supporters, fellow creators and visionaries, as well as places and people. In particular, I am indebted to two main people – Anne Schuster, author and writing-workshop facilitator, and author Máire Fisher, without whose enthusiasm, input and support in the early stages this book may never have reached publication. I am also indebted to the sharp eye of author Tracey Farren and to all the people in Anne Schuster's writing classes that I took part in over the years – you know who you are. I am particularly thankful to readers and commentators in South Africa and abroad who responded to novel drafts and excerpts along the way – Malika Ndlovu, Lawrence Scott, Jenny Green, Miki Flockemann, Louise Lakier, Marian Palaia, Anna Musin, Kristie McLean, Debu Majumdar, Christine Coates, Erica Coetzee, Nella Freund, Dan Fisher, Megan Black, Geraldine Do Machin, Wanjiku Mwagiru, Eduard Burle and Jacques Coetzee. I am also grateful to previous writing groups and writers in London – the late John Petherbridge's writing group at the City Lit Institute, and The Original Writers Group, then in Battersea.

For publishing advice and encouragement, thank you to Kenneth Ramchand, Tracy Gilpin, Keith Gottschalk, Sahra Ryklief, Rahla Xenopoulos and Lynn Woolfrey. I also appreciate the support of the Wits City Institute, University of the Witwatersrand. For those who championed lessening the gap between academic and creative worlds, some not even realising the inspiration they gave by example, I have to thank academic creatives Ari Sitas, Jane Taylor, Noeleen Murray, Brenda Dixon-Gottschild, Jill Flanders Crosby, Susanne Keuchler, Harry Garuba, Gordon Pirie and Patricia Repar, as well as Joanne Corrigall and Millicent Johnnie, and many others I do not have the space to list here. I also must thank my fellow writer colleagues and friends in the Cape Town Writers' Circle, all unbelievably talented, who provided laughter and inspiration during the final stages.

I am also indebted to the gentle intuitiveness yet complete clarity in the leadership of publisher Fourie Botha, the insightfulness and advice of Beth Lindop, the vision of cover designer Jacques Kaiser, and the exactness and astute editing skills of my editor Jenefer Shute.

Last, but not least, I thank my new family – Neville, Sonia, Mij, Rowan, Monette, Alex, Julian and Bailey – for being there for me in tough moments. I thank my past family, those I know, and those I don't. I thank glowflies and sunsets and mountains and sea, because without them, neither I nor this book would exist. Finally, I thank my original mother. This book is her memorial. Whenever I see the world, I see her in it. If even one woman looks at her children and is compelled to get out of a situation where her life is at risk, as a result of someone reading *Glowfly Dance*, then it will have done its work.